BLOODLINES

TRANSCENDENCE

MICHAEL MANOSCA

Edited by
REGENA SLATER
Edited by
ANSELMO G. MANOSCA

Visit the author's website at www.michaelmanosca.com

Edited by: Regena Slater & Anselmo G. Manosca

ISBN:

979-8-9927666-7-7 (paperback)

979-8-9927666-6-0 (electronic)

979-8-9927666-8-4 (hardcover)

Library of Congress Control Number: 2025912844

First Edition.

Los Angeles, California, United State of America

At a night market in Hong Kong, 2001, an elderly Cantonese fortune teller's eyes blazed with recognition as she bowed to the imperial scribe she claimed I had been 986 years before.

Her reverence for this Song Dynasty official embarrassed my friend and unsettled me, but her words planted the seed for this story about lineage, memory, and the mysterious ways souls find each other across the centuries.

The double helix is a spiral staircase that connects all life across time—each rung a choice, each turn a generation, each strand a story that began long before us and will continue long after.

Time is not a river running in one direction. It is an ocean, and we are all swimming in different depths of the same water.

CONTENTS

PREFACE

When I began writing *Bloodlines: Transcendence* I thought I was venturing into uncharted territory—fantasy fiction, a genre I'd never attempted before. What I discovered instead was that my compass had been pointing toward the same true north all along: the magnetic pull of chosen family, that gravitational force that seems to guide every story I tell, whether I set out for that destination or not.

This is not a vampire story in any traditional sense. There are no fangs gleaming in moonlight, no dramatic transformations, no mystical powers defying the laws of physics. Instead, I found myself playing evolutionary biologist alongside romance author and psychologist, crafting two distinct branches of human evolution—the Elders and the Regulars—that diverged during a specific climatic event in Earth's distant past. What emerged was a biological explanation for traits we've long attributed to supernatural forces: enhanced longevity, heightened senses, metabolic differences that require alternative nutrition sources.

The vampirism in these pages is simply evolution taking an unexpected path, no more magical than the way some humans developed lactose tolerance while others retained childhood's inability to process dairy. It's Charles Darwin wearing a cape instead of Bram Stoker wielding a pen.

At its heart, this remains what it was always going to be: a simple love story about loss and second chances. Two sets of individuals, separated by time and circumstances, discover they are interconnected like the helical strands of DNA itself—twisting around each other, supporting each other's structure, creating something stronger than either could achieve alone. Academic research becomes the thread that weaves through generations, continents, and cultures, revealing how family extends far beyond the boundaries of genetics or geography.

The academic framework was irresistible to me: multiple branches of a family tree spanning countless generations, research methodology driving narrative discovery, the way knowledge accumulates and connects across time. How could a story *not* emerge from such rich material? But the scholarship serves the heart of the matter, which is really about time—how we spend it, how we waste it, how we discover that love makes even immortality meaningful.

This is also a story about coming out in all its forms. Coming out of isolation. Coming out of shame about who and what you are. Coming out of the closet, yes, but also coming out of hiding from family, coming out of academic theories into lived experience, coming out of survival mode and into the vulnerable territory of building a life with people who choose to stay.

I've spent years writing around the edges of chosen family without quite naming it, but *Bloodlines: Transcendence* forced me to examine what happens when people actively decide to become each other's permanence. Not because biology demands it, not because social convention expects it, but because they recognize something in each other that feels like home.

No magic. No mystery. No movie tricks. Just biology, heart, and acceptance.

That, it turns out, was the fantasy I'd been trying to write all along.

Michael Manosca
October 2025

PROLOGUE

NORTHERN LAPLAND, ~2465 BCE

1989 years.

That is how old I was when I first saw the woman who would change everything I thought I knew about love.

At nearly two millennia old, I thought I understood the weight of endless time. I had learned to maintain careful distance from the brief lives of what we called mortals—primarily *Homo sapiens,* whose lifespans seemed impossibly short compared to ours, though the term applied to any of the human species who lacked our longevity modifications. I had perfected the art of solitary existence through necessity. I had loved before—*Homo sapiens,* unmodified Denisovans—had watched partners age and die while I remained unchanged, carrying the weight of their loss across centuries of memory. Each time, I had sworn it would be the last. The pain of watching mortality claim those I cared for had taught me that solitude was safer than attachment.

Her name was Astrid.

She was twenty years old, a Denisovan like the ancestors of my people, though she lacked the modifications that had allowed my kind to transcend normal lifespans. When I found her in the forests of northern Lapland, she was the sole survivor of a massacre that had claimed her entire village just weeks earlier. Yet she carried herself with a dignity that impressed even someone of my experience.

I belonged to the **Aldizōz**—Elders, in the common tongue—descendants of *Homo denisova* populations who had undergone remarkable evolutionary adaptations during the brutal ice ages that gripped this region over 220,000 years earlier. Long before *Homo sapiens* began their great migration out of

Africa, our isolated ancestors had faced evolutionary pressures that triggered changes beyond normal mammalian adaptation.

The process had begun at the cellular level. Traditional mitochondrial function proved inadequate for the extreme caloric restrictions imposed by our glacial environment. Over countless generations, natural selection favored those whose cellular metabolism could extract maximum efficiency from minimal resources. Our mitochondria evolved into hyperefficient organelles capable of sustaining normal function with dramatically reduced fuel requirements while processing cellular waste products that would prove toxic to unmodified physiology.

The benefits were extraordinary. Enhanced cellular regeneration. Dramatically slowed aging. Physical capabilities that far exceeded baseline parameters. But perhaps most significantly, we developed the ability to enter extended periods of metabolic stasis, allowing us to survive environmental pressures that eliminated our unmodified cousins.

The **Blōdawīsōz**—literally 'blood-bound'—who had destroyed Astrid's village represented an entirely different evolutionary path. Around 30,000 years earlier, during another ice age in eastern Europe, an isolated community of Elders had faced extinction. In their desperation, they turned to cannibalistic practices, consuming the blood and tissue of their own dead.

For most, this brought only madness and death. But for a handful of survivors, constant exposure to concentrated Elder blood triggered a secondary evolutionary adaptation. Their remaining mitochondria essentially ceased to function, replaced by a parasitic dependency on external blood products. As their kind spread across the globe over millennia, they came to be known as "Regulars"—a practical shorthand acknowledging their more frequent need to feed compared to us ancient **Aldizōz**.

The **Blōdawīsōz** called us "Elders" with good reason—where they might live a single millennium if fortunate, we measured our existence in tens of millennia. The difference between a thousand years and ten thousand years was the difference between a brief candle and the slow burning of stars.

Homo sapiens, with their decades-long lifespans, could hardly comprehend such scales. To them, tens of thousands of years seemed unimaginable, infinite. And it was lengthy, even to us. But each Elder learned to be adjusted by it, shaped by time in ways that changed not just our bodies, but our very nature.

In my youth—those first few centuries of existence—I had been like any young being, full of questions and uncertainty. I spoke constantly, argued passionately, needed to hear my own voice to validate my thoughts and fears. The need to prove rightness or wrongness, to work through understanding by voicing every doubt—these were the concerns of the young, whether Elder, Regular, or mortal.

Even the **Blōdawīsōz**, with their thousand-year lifespans, rarely achieved the comfortable silence that came naturally to ancient Elders. You could always identify a younger Regular by their constant chatter, their need to fill silence with words, their anxious justification of every thought. But an older Regular, one who had lived perhaps eight or nine centuries, began to resemble a younger Elder—more measured in speech, more confident in silence, understanding that words were tools to be used sparingly rather than crutches for uncertain minds.

But as millennia passed for us Elders, those needs faded entirely. Speech became unnecessary for most thoughts. We learned more, understood more, and found little purpose in hearing ourselves debate what we already knew. The constant chatter of youth gave way to comfortable silence. Words became precious, reserved for true necessity rather than the anxious validation that plagued all shorter-lived beings.

What truly frightened unmodified humans—whether *Homo sapiens* or Denisovans—was our relationship with blood. The very mention of it would send them fleeing, conjuring images of monsters from their worst nightmares. Yet the reality, as with most things, was far more complex than their terror suggested.

We Elders could survive quite comfortably on the same foods as our mortal cousins—grains, fruits, vegetables, the flesh of animals. Our enhanced metabolism processed these efficiently enough to sustain us indefinitely. But mammalian blood? Blood was an exquisite delicacy, the most nourishment-packed energy source imaginable. The taste, the immediate vitality it provided —a single feeding could sustain an Elder for weeks, even months, without need for other sustenance. It was like comparing simple bread to the finest feast.

We partook rarely, but when we did, it was transcendent. Much as mortals might savor fine wine or rare delicacies, we appreciated blood for what it was—pure, concentrated life force.

For the **Blōdawīsōz**, however, blood was not luxury but necessity. Their altered cellular composition and physiology demanded it for survival itself. Most Regulars I had encountered over the centuries maintained what could only be described as civilized practices—raising small mammals much as mortals raised chickens or cattle, consuming blood in formal, even ritualistic ways that bore no resemblance to the savage feeding of horror stories.

Some preferred to hunt, like any human hunter seeking game, preferring what they called "organic" sustenance to the blander taste of farm-raised sources. As cities expanded and wild lands disappeared, these hunters were forced into urban environments, working at night through neighborhoods where they could command the least attention.

Most Regulars understood their reputation and wished to avoid confrontation. They knew the legends mortals told about them, knew the fear their very existence inspired. Hunting humans was avoided not just from practical necessity, but from a desire to coexist without detection.

Yet there were exceptions, as there always are among any population. Some, resentful of feeling "lesser" in the eyes of both mortals and Elders, actively sought human prey—particularly those who were most vocal in their hatred of difference. Others maintained a twisted sense of justice, hunting only those they deemed to have forfeited their right to life: murderers, thieves, those who preyed upon the innocent.

And then there were the rare few who hunted humans for sport alone. These were the ones who created the legends, who wanted mortals to fear them. They left traces deliberately, reveled in the terror they inspired, turned feeding into theater designed to horrify. They were aberrations among their own kind, but their actions tainted the reputation of all **Blōdawīsōz** for millennia to come.

The irony was that these monstrous few represented perhaps one in ten thousand of their population, yet they became the face of their entire species in mortal imagination.

The relationship between our peoples was... complicated. I considered many **Blōdawīsōz** to be friends, certainly. We shared common origins, after all, and faced similar challenges in remaining hidden among mortal populations. Yet I would be dishonest if I claimed we viewed them as equals.

There was an unspoken hierarchy among our kinds, as natural and immutable as the order of the seasons. Elders occupied the highest position—our longevity, our enhanced capabilities, our accumulated wisdom placing us above all others. The **Blōdawīsōz**, despite their own modifications, remained... lesser. They looked up to us with a mixture of respect and envy that they rarely bothered to conceal. Not unlike how a merchant might regard nobility—useful in their own way, but ultimately aware of their station.

Both our peoples, I must admit, viewed unmodified humans with the benevolent condescension typically reserved for the working classes. *Homo sapiens*, Denisovans like my beloved Astrid—they served their purpose in the world, but they were fundamentally limited by their brief lifespans and unenhanced physiology.

If confrontation ever arose between Elder and Regular—and there had been a few skirmishes over the millennia, mostly in the ancient past, now remembered only in folklore—there was never any question of outcome. Elders would prevail. Always. It was not arrogance but simple biological fact. Our cellular modifications provided advantages in strength, speed, endurance, and healing that the **Blōdawīsōz** could never match. Everyone understood this hierarchy. Few were foolish enough to test it.

Which made my love for Astrid all the more remarkable, perhaps even scandalous to some of my kind. Here I was, an Elder of nearly two millennia, completely captivated by a young Denisovan woman who represented everything we typically considered beneath our notice.

Astrid was, as it happened, among the last of her pure lineage. Even by our time together, Denisovan populations were dwindling, gradually absorbed into the rapidly expanding *Homo sapiens* communities or simply outcompeted for resources. Their genetic legacy would persist—I knew that traces of Denisovan DNA would survive in eastern populations, down to the northern islands of what mortals would one day call the Philippines—but as a distinct people, they were fading.

I had witnessed this pattern countless times over my long existence. Species rose, flourished, then yielded to others better adapted to changing conditions. It was the natural order of things, as inevitable as the turning of seasons. Even we Elders, for all our enhancements, understood that our time too would eventually pass. Nothing in this world was truly eternal, no matter how permanent it might seem in the moment.

But watching it happen to Astrid's people, knowing that she might be among the very last to carry their pure heritage, added a poignancy to our relationship that transcended mere romantic attachment. In loving her, I was loving a piece of history that would soon be lost forever.

She should have meant nothing to me. In my nearly two thousand years, I had perfected emotional distance from mortal lives—those brief, bright existences of unmodified humans, regardless of their specific lineage. By my time, *Homo sapiens* were spreading rapidly and becoming the dominant human species, though Denisovan populations like Astrid's still thrived in many regions. All carried the spark of consciousness, culture, love, loss. All deserved respect, even if their time was limited compared to ours.

But something in Astrid's determined survival, her refusal to succumb to despair even after losing everything, stirred feelings I thought permanently buried. Our initial encounter—my offer of assistance, her proud acceptance—extended into weeks of conversation that revealed intelligence and resilience transcending her limited expected lifespan.

That Astrid could draw conversation from me after centuries of comfortable silence should have been my first warning that she was different. I found myself speaking again, not from youthful uncertainty, but from genuine desire to share thoughts with someone whose perspective might add to my own understanding. It had been thousands of years since another being's mind had seemed worthy of such effort.

"You're different," she observed during one evening talk, studying my face with uncomfortable accuracy. "Much older than you appear. There's something ancient in your expression, like you've seen things that happened long before anyone alive was born."

"And you," I replied carefully, "ask more questions than might be wise."

What followed was a courtship spanning decades—mere blinks of time for me, but nearly half her expected natural lifespan. Despite my vast experience, I found myself caught between growing certainty of love and the biological impossibility of our union. Elder reproductive physiology was incompatible with unmodified genetics. Even if we could overcome cellular incompatibilities, I would watch her age and die while I remained unchanged.

My parents, whose own romance had played out over tens of thousands of years, counseled patience. Astrid would die. I would grieve. In centuries, the pain would become distant memory. This was natural order.

But natural order hadn't accounted for legends older than recorded history.

The stories spoke of ancient relics—transformation compounds created by the first Elder communities—that could somehow bridge the gap between our kinds. It was barely more than whispered folklore, dismissed by most as impossible fantasy. The legends claimed these substances could extend a mortal's lifespan, perhaps even grant them something approaching our longevity. We had never discussed what such a transformation might entail, what side effects might accompany such a change, or even whether the stories held any truth at all. We simply hoped—desperately, irrationally—that somewhere in these myths lay the possibility of more time together.

The search consumed nearly two decades—a frantic quest across northern Europe for traces of original Elder bloodlines, mythical families said to possess these relics from the first great transformation. Most leads proved false, but my desperation drove me to pursue every possibility. My age and experience, once advantages, now felt like burdens. I had dismissed these legends as folklore for centuries. But love made me willing to believe in impossibilities, to chase shadows if it meant Astrid and I might have centuries rather than decades.

We found her by accident around 2430 BCE.

The ancient woman lived alone in a cottage that seemed to grow from the forest itself. She was old even by Elder standards—her life spanning hundreds of centuries, predating not just agriculture and organized civilization, but having witnessed the last of the Neanderthals, the great migrations that spread *Homo sapiens* across continents, the flourishing of diverse Denisovan communities. To her, the distinctions between human species were merely academic—consciousness and love transcended genetics.

When I met her gaze, I felt something I hadn't experienced in my nearly two millennia: the humbling recognition of someone far older and wiser than myself.

For months, we visited regularly, sharing meals and stories. I continued pursuing legends, but privately had begun accepting they were just stories. The ancient gifts, if they'd ever existed, were lost. I would love Astrid as long as possible, then carry grief for the rest of my existence. It was a familiar pattern.

Then Astrid fell ill.

What seemed like simple fatigue after our evening meal escalated into something serious. Fever, delirium, her body convulsing as if fighting invisible toxin. Despite my vast experience with mortal frailty, I was beside myself with panic.

"Be patient," the old woman said quietly, pulling me aside. "This wasn't meant to happen so soon. I had hoped to prepare you both..."

"Explain what?" I demanded, my composure cracking. "What's happening to her?"

She retrieved a wooden box that looked older than anything in my extensive memory. "The legend is real, child. The transformation compounds exist. And your beloved has just received one."

For a moment, I could only stare at her. In nearly two millennia of existence, I had never been rendered speechless. The revelation hit like a physical blow—

not just that these mythical substances actually existed, but that Astrid was dying because one was coursing through her system at this very moment.

"You're telling me the stories are true?" I said, my voice barely recognizable. "That you actually possess—" I stopped, looking toward where Astrid lay convulsing with fever. "Without her consent? Without even telling us what you were doing?"

The old woman simply watched as everything I had built over centuries of careful control began to crumble. The composure that marked my kind, the measured wisdom that came with extreme age—all of it shattered as raw panic took hold.

"She could die!" I shouted, the sound foreign to my own ears. I hadn't raised my voice in anger for over a thousand years. "She could die, and you gave her something she never asked for, never agreed to! How could you—why would you—"

I found myself pacing like a caged animal, gesturing wildly, my thoughts tumbling over each other in a way that would have horrified any Elder who witnessed it. This was not how my kind behaved. This was not the careful, measured response of someone who had lived nearly two millennia. This was the desperate fear of someone who had everything to lose.

"She will die anyway," the old woman said quietly, letting my outburst run its course. "In decades rather than millennia. At least this way, love has a chance."

"But she didn't choose it!" I continued, the words pouring out of me. "She doesn't even know what's happening to her! What if she doesn't want this? What if the transformation fails? What if—"

"Then you will have lost her attempting to save her, rather than simply watching time claim her," the ancient woman interrupted, her voice carrying the weight of eons. "The next six weeks will determine everything. But know this—the compounds exist, they work, and your beloved now carries within her the possibility of standing beside you through centuries rather than decades."

For forty-two days, I watched helplessly as Astrid's body underwent incomprehensible changes. Despite millennia of knowledge, I was reduced to the same vigil any mortal lover would keep. Some days brought recovery signs. Others, renewed fever that made me certain I was losing her. The ancient woman guided me through the process—how to help her body accept cellular changes, what signs to watch for.

When Astrid finally opened her eyes with clarity after weeks, I wept with relief I hadn't allowed myself in centuries.

"What happened to me?" she asked weakly, studying my tear-streaked face. "Gunnar, I remember falling ill, but everything after that..."

I explained what had been done, what she had become, what our future held. As understanding dawned—shock, wonder, awareness of the magnitude of her unwilling gift—we held each other in silence, processing impossible reality.

We were together now, truly together, with centuries stretching ahead instead of decades. But joy was tempered by how close we'd come to losing everything, by complex emotions surrounding this gift given.

The wooden box contained six remaining samples of original transformation compounds—the only means by which rigid boundaries between hominin and Elder could be crossed. The ancient woman's final words echoed as her own long life approached conclusion: "Guard them carefully. Love like yours deserves to endure. But remember—immortality isn't always the gift it appears. Time changes everything, including love itself. Be certain of what you're offering before you offer it." Ironic, it felt, given she'd not lived her words.

For over twenty-three centuries, Astrid and I lived as true partners, sharing experiences spanning empires' rise and fall, languages' birth, humanity's slow progress across continents. We witnessed *Homo sapiens* emergence as the dominant species, agriculture's development in the fertile crescents of Mesopotamia, the first cities rising along great rivers, the invention of writing itself in Sumerian cuneiform.

We watched the construction of the great pyramids in Egypt, observed as bronze gave way to iron across the Mediterranean world. We saw the rise of classical civilizations—Greek city-states flowering with philosophy and art, the Roman Republic expanding across continents we had known when they were populated only by scattered tribes.

When Astrid conceived around 165 BCE, Rome was asserting dominance over the Mediterranean, and in distant China, the Han Dynasty was consolidating power under Emperor Wu. The world was changing rapidly, empires claiming territories that had remained unchanged for millennia. It seemed fitting that new life should begin during such a time of transformation.

For nearly eight decades, she carried our child—a gestation period that spanned the fall of the Roman Republic, the rise of Augustus, and the establishment of the Pax Romana. When our son finally drew his first breath under the midnight sun of a Scandinavian winter in 85 BCE, Julius Caesar was still a young man dreaming of conquest, and the Christ child would not be born for another eight decades.

"Aleksander," Astrid whispered, cradling our newborn son. "Aleksander Henrik Johan Nordh." She looked up at me with exhausted joy. "He has your eyes, Gunnar. Ancient eyes, even now."

We named him for carrying forward family tradition and hope of new beginnings. He represented not just our love made manifest, but continuation of ancient bloodlines stretching back to humanity's first evolutionary leap.

As our son grew through his first centuries, we watched empires that had seemed eternal crumble into dust. Rome fell to barbarian invasions while Aleksander still appeared to be a child. The Western Roman Empire collapsed when he had the appearance of perhaps a twelve-year-old boy, though he carried within him already the wisdom of five centuries. By the time he appeared to reach physical maturity, Charlemagne had risen and fallen, the

Vikings had discovered new continents, and the great library of Alexandria—which I had seen in its glory—was nothing but memory.

We didn't know that Aleksander, when he finally fell in love after more than two millennia of solitary existence—having witnessed the rise and fall of the Byzantine Empire, the spread of Christianity and Islam, the Renaissance, the age of exploration, the industrial revolution, two world wars, and humanity's first steps into space—would face exactly the same impossible choice we had confronted in northern Lapland's forests over four and a half thousand years earlier.

Like his father before him, he would learn the weight of silence that comes with true age. Like me, he would discover that love could break through even the most carefully constructed emotional defenses. And like both his parents, he would find himself torn between the wisdom of solitude and the desperate hope that love might transcend the barriers of biology and time.

1

LOST AND FOUND

FLAT 3B, 47 MARCHMONT STREET, BLOOMSBURY, LONDON WC1N 1AP

Soren Jensen

The Saturday morning London air carried the crisp promise of October as I set out from my flat in Bloomsbury, my leather messenger bag weighted with notebooks and the careful optimism that comes with new beginnings. Three weeks into my life as a graduate student at King's College, I'd finally worked up the courage to navigate to the British Library on my own—no tube map, no careful directions written on scraps of paper, just memory and what I hoped was a decent sense of direction.

I'd studied the route obsessively the night before, tracing the path from my shared flat to the imposing red-brick facade of the library that housed more genealogical treasures than I could explore in a lifetime. Russell Square to Euston Road, past the gothic spires of St. Pancras, then north toward the modern glass and steel that promised answers to questions I'd been carrying since childhood. Simple enough, in theory.

The tree-lined streets of Bloomsbury felt familiar now, their Georgian terraces and garden squares reminding me of the carefully planned neighborhoods back home in Minneapolis. But as I walked, counting streets and checking building numbers against my mental map, London's medieval logic began to assert itself. Streets that should have run parallel curved unexpectedly. Roads I remembered as straight developed mysterious bends that led me past buildings I'd never seen before.

Twenty minutes into what should have been a fifteen-minute walk, I found myself standing at the intersection of two streets whose names meant nothing to me, staring at a row of Victorian houses that belonged in a completely different neighborhood from the one I'd intended to visit.

I pulled out the small notebook where I'd sketched my route, comparing my careful drawings to the reality of London's stubborn refusal to conform to logical city planning. The problem, I realized, was that I'd been thinking like an American—assuming that streets would maintain their names and directions for more than a few blocks, that "north" would remain consistently north rather than veering through the organic curves that centuries of development had carved into the landscape.

This was exactly the kind of methodical problem-solving that had gotten me through four years of undergraduate research. I reoriented myself using the sun's position, identified a major thoroughfare that should lead me back toward familiar territory, and set off with renewed confidence.

Fifteen minutes later, I was more lost than before.

The neighborhood I'd wandered into was clearly residential, lined with the kind of elegant Victorian houses that spoke of old money and established families. Children's voices drifted from a nearby playground, mixing with the sounds of weekend life—lawn mowers, music from open windows, the casual conversations of people who belonged somewhere and knew exactly where that somewhere was.

I paused at the edge of a small park, watching a group of students who looked about my age spilling out of a pub across the street. They moved with the easy camaraderie of people who'd known each other for years, their laughter carrying the kind of genuine warmth that comes from shared history and inside jokes. One of them—a girl with short auburn hair—was doing an elaborate impression of someone, gesturing wildly while the others doubled over with amusement.

Further down the street, a group of runners jogged past in coordinated athletic gear, calling out encouragement to each other as they navigated the weekend foot traffic. They looked like they were training for something specific, maybe a charity marathon, their shared purpose evident in the way they moved as a unit.

I found myself gravitating toward an empty bench that faced the small playground, settling down with the weight of my bag and the heavier weight of questions I'd been avoiding since arriving in London. The bench was positioned under an old oak tree whose canopy provided dappled shade and a perfect vantage point for observing the life I seemed to be watching rather than participating in.

What was I doing here?

The question had been building for weeks, underlying every interaction with my polite but distant flatmates, every solitary meal in the college dining hall, every evening spent alone in my room while other students socialized in ways that seemed as foreign to me as the accent I was slowly learning to understand.

I'd come to London with such clear purpose: pursue my graduate degree in Cultural History, specializing in Scandinavian migration patterns. Use my own family's story as the foundation for research that might advance my academic career while finally answering the questions that had nagged at me since childhood. Who were the Jensens before they became Swedish-Americans? What stories had been lost in the transition from old world to new? What traditions had my great-great-great-grandfather carried with him across the Atlantic, and which ones had he left behind in the necessity of assimilation?

But sitting here in this unfamiliar neighborhood, watching people who seemed to navigate both geography and friendship with effortless ease, the whole endeavor felt suddenly foolish. Back home in Minneapolis, surrounded by the comfortable certainty of family and familiar places, my genealogical obsession had felt important, even noble. I was preserving family history, honoring the sacrifices of previous generations, contributing to academic understanding of immigration patterns.

Here, three thousand miles from everyone who knew my name or cared about my research, it felt like elaborate procrastination. An excuse to avoid the more immediate challenge of figuring out how to exist in the present rather than constantly excavating the past.

The truth was, I'd been lonely for years before coming to London. Not just alone—I'd chosen solitude often enough, preferring the company of books and archival documents to the complicated social dynamics that seemed to exhaust me. But lonely in the deeper sense, feeling fundamentally disconnected from my peers, my community, sometimes even my own family.

I was twenty-four years old and had never been in love. Not really. I'd had relationships before—both intelligent, attractive women who deserved better than someone going through the motions. I'd told myself the hollow feeling was normal, that passion was overrated, that compatibility mattered more than chemistry.

But the truth I'd been avoiding was simpler: I'd never felt what I was supposed to feel. The connections other people described—that spark, that magnetic pull, that sense of rightness—had remained frustratingly theoretical to me. I could intellectually understand romantic attraction, could observe it in others, could even approximate it for short periods. But I'd never actually experienced it.

Those failed relationships had left me feeling more isolated than before, convinced that something fundamental was missing from my emotional makeup. I'd never experienced the kind of deep friendship I observed in others, never felt that sense of belonging that seemed to come so naturally to everyone else. I'd told myself it was because I was focused on my studies, because I was more mature than my classmates, because I had important work to do that required sacrifice and dedication.

But maybe the truth was simpler and more disturbing: maybe I just didn't know how to connect with people. Maybe all my research into family history was really just an elaborate way of avoiding the fact that I couldn't seem to create meaningful relationships in the present.

The runners passed by again, completing their circuit through the neighborhood, their easy conversation and shared rhythm a reminder of all the types of connection I'd never experienced. The students from the pub had moved on, probably to someone's flat for the kind of impromptu gathering that filled Saturday afternoons with friendship and possibility.

And here I was, lost in a neighborhood I couldn't name, pursuing ancestors who might not have any answers to give me, wondering if I'd made a terrible mistake in thinking that London—or graduate school, or genealogical research—could solve whatever was missing from my life.

"Excuse me, are you quite alright?"

The voice came from my left, carrying a slight accent that wasn't quite English but suggested European education and careful pronunciation. I looked up to see a young man standing beside the bench, his expression holding the kind of genuine concern that seemed increasingly rare in urban settings.

He appeared to be roughly my age, perhaps slightly younger, though something in his bearing suggested a maturity that went beyond years. His dark hair was perfectly styled without looking artificial, and his clothes—casual weekend wear that nonetheless managed to look expensive—suggested someone comfortable with quality and attention to detail. There was something almost regal about his posture, the way he held himself with unconscious authority while maintaining an approachable warmth.

I felt immediately self-conscious, aware that I probably looked exactly like what I was: a confused American tourist who'd gotten himself thoroughly lost while trying to navigate a city he didn't understand.

"I was... I'm new in London," I said, feeling heat rise to my cheeks. "I was trying to find my way to the British Library and I've gotten myself turned around somehow."

His smile was immediate and genuine, transforming his features from merely handsome to something approaching radiant. "Ah, you have indeed gotten turned around," he said with gentle amusement. "But all is not lost. After all, how do you get found if you never allow yourself to get lost?"

The philosophical observation, delivered with such natural warmth, made me smile despite my embarrassment. There was something both wise and playful about the comment, as if he genuinely believed that disorientation might be a necessary part of discovery.

"The British Library is actually quite far from here," he continued, his tone becoming more practical. "You're in Hampstead now, which is lovely for wandering but rather inconvenient if you were hoping to reach Euston Road before closing time."

Hampstead. I'd somehow managed to walk miles in the wrong direction, ending up in one of London's most expensive neighborhoods while aiming for the research district. The mistake was so thoroughly American—the assumption that urban geography would follow logical patterns rather than the organic evolution of centuries.

"However," he said, clearly noting my expression of dismay, "the Heath is quite beautiful this time of year, and there are several excellent cafés nearby if you need to regroup before attempting the journey back. Sometimes the detour provides better discoveries than the intended destination."

He gave me careful directions back to familiar territory, his explanations clear and detailed without being condescending. As he spoke, I found myself studying his face—the sharp cheekbones that spoke of good genetics, the eyes that seemed to hold more knowledge than his apparent age should allow, the way he gestured with elegant precision when describing landmarks.

"Thank you," I said when he finished, meaning it more than the simple courtesy suggested. "You've been incredibly kind to a lost American."

"My pleasure entirely," he replied with another smile that seemed to linger a moment longer than mere politeness required. "I hope you find what you're looking for at the British Library."

He began to move away with the same fluid grace that had characterized his approach, but after a few steps, he turned back to look at me once more. The expression on his face held something I couldn't quite identify—curiosity, perhaps, or recognition of some possibility neither of us had quite articulated.

Then he was gone, disappearing around the corner with the kind of elegant efficiency that left me wondering if the entire encounter had been real or imagined.

I sat on the bench for several more minutes, no longer thinking about my research or my loneliness or the complicated questions that had driven me to London. Instead, I found myself replaying the conversation, the warmth in his voice, the way he'd looked at me as if I were someone worth helping rather than just another confused tourist cluttering up his Saturday afternoon.

When I finally rose to begin the long journey back toward familiar territory, I carried with me the strange certainty that something significant had just occurred. Not just the practical assistance of getting directions, but something more fundamental—a reminder that London might hold possibilities I hadn't yet imagined, connections I hadn't thought to seek.

The walk back to Bloomsbury passed more quickly than expected, my feet finding their way along routes that suddenly seemed less foreign, less intimidating. By the time I reached my flat, the morning's frustration had transformed into something approaching gratitude.

I'd set out to find the British Library and had gotten thoroughly lost instead. But maybe that stranger in Hampstead had been right about the value of disorientation.

Maybe getting lost was exactly what I'd needed to do.

2
FIRST MEETINGS

FLAT 7, 28 CADOGAN SQUARE, CHELSEA, LONDON SW1X 0JP

Aleksander (Henry) Nordh

It had been only four days since our encounter in Hampstead, but I had thought of little else. The young man I had helped with directions—lost, endearingly flustered, carrying himself with that particular combination of academic intensity and gentle courtesy that had reminded me so powerfully of Mikael. When I had first seen him, the resemblance had been striking enough, but it was the scent that had truly undone me. That achingly familiar fragrance of bergamot and warmth and something essentially Mikael that had haunted me for 131 years. In that moment in Hampstead, watching him struggle with his map, I had felt Mikael's presence so strongly it had taken my breath away.

I should have introduced myself properly then. It would have been the polite thing to do, especially to someone as handsome as this young man. But his look, his scent, the little connections, his blood pulsing through his veins... I had felt Mikael so strongly, so overwhelmingly, that I had needed to retreat. To give myself room to regain composure, to be certain of what I was sensing. I had thought about returning, circling back with some excuse to continue our conversation, but he had already set about on his journey. Besides, that would have seemed off-putting. Ungentlemanly, even.

But now, here he was at King's College... as if Mikael had guided him again, whispering down through the years that yes, indeed, he is mine. I had given him directions to the British Library, but here he was in the King's College library instead.

The autumn semester had settled into its familiar rhythm—seminars on British poetry where I carefully modulated my responses to appear appropriately graduate-level, research groups where I pretended to struggle with concepts I had witnessed firsthand, the endless pantomime of being twenty-two in an era where I had already lived through more than two millennia. It was a comfortable enough existence, this latest incarnation of student life, though I sometimes wondered if I was becoming too fond of universities. The fourth time in fifty years at the same institution risked drawing attention, even with careful identity management.

But that Tuesday afternoon in the Gothic Revival library, as I sat reviewing Tennyson's letters for a seminar I could have taught myself, the recognition came flooding back with renewed intensity.

There he was.

The recognition hit me anew—not just sight this time, but that same overwhelming memory that had nearly undone me in Hampstead. That achingly familiar warmth and something essentially Mikael suddenly filled my senses as clearly as if Mikael himself were standing beside me. Now, in the controlled environment of the library, I could truly appreciate what I was experiencing. For one impossible moment, my carefully maintained composure cracked entirely. My hands gripped the edge of the wooden table, and I had to remind myself to breathe normally, to keep my enhanced hearing from focusing too intently on every heartbeat in the room.

It was him. It was really him—Mikael's descendant, here as if destiny had intervened.

I turned slowly, following the trail that my Elder senses tracked as easily as following a map. The world may refer to my kind as vampires—a detestable and vulgar term coined by Victorian sensationalists—but we are far more refined than any of those narrow-minded humans ever considered. We are Elders, an ancient and noble species, not the monsters of their fevered imaginings.

Across the reading room, perhaps thirty feet away, sat the young man from Hampstead with his head bent over a collection of immigration records. The afternoon light streaming through the tall windows caught the lighter strands in his dark blonde hair—hair that fell across his forehead in exactly the same way Mikael's had when he was concentrating.

The physical resemblance was striking enough that any human might have noted it, but for me it went far deeper than mere appearance. Every sense I possessed confirmed what my eyes suggested: this was Mikael's blood, Mikael's line, carried forward through generations I had never dared to trace.

His descendant. A descendant I never knew existed.

The young man looked up from his documents, perhaps aware he was being observed, and our eyes met across the reading room. Blue-grey eyes with those distinctive flecks near the pupils—Jensen eyes, I realized with a start. Recognition flickered across his features—brief but unmistakable—as he placed me as the helpful stranger from Hampstead. When he offered a polite, slightly apologetic smile for the prolonged stare, I saw Mikael's mouth, Mikael's gesture of gentle courtesy to strangers. Then, with that particular brand of friendly openness that marked him unmistakably American, he raised his hand in a small wave.

The gesture was so unexpected, so charmingly informal in the hushed formality of the library, that I found myself returning it before conscious thought could intervene. My own hand lifted in response—an uncharacteristic breach of the careful reserve I maintained in public spaces. Our smiles lingered a moment longer than mere politeness required, a shared recognition that stretched across the reading room like an invisible thread connecting us.

Then, as if by mutual agreement, we broke eye contact and returned to our respective tasks. But I found myself acutely aware of his presence in my peripheral vision, the way he occasionally glanced up from his documents to look in my direction. Each stolen glance sent another wave of recognition through me, confirmation that this impossible coincidence was becoming something more deliberate.

How was this possible? I had been so careful never to investigate Mikael's American life, never to intrude upon the family he had built. Yet here was clear evidence that his line had continued, had produced this young man who carried not just his physical features but something deeper—that unmistakable genetic signature that sang to every enhanced sense I possessed.

The young man tended to his research, but I found concentration impossible. For the remainder of the afternoon, I remained acutely aware of his presence—the sound of pages turning, the occasional soft sigh when he encountered frustrating gaps in records, the way he absently tapped his pen against his lips when thinking. All achingly familiar gestures, inherited across generations like eye color or the shape of a smile.

When he finally gathered his materials and left the library, I waited precisely ten minutes before following. Not to intrude or make contact—I had no plan, no justification for approaching him. But I needed to know more. Needed to understand how fate or coincidence had brought Mikael's descendant to the same London university where I was living yet another borrowed life.

CAREFUL INVESTIGATIONS

Over the following week, I learned everything the university's systems could tell me about Soren Mikael Jensen. Graduate student in Cultural History, specializing in Scandinavian diaspora studies. From Minneapolis, Minnesota—exactly where Mikael had settled after leaving Copenhagen. Age twenty-four, unmarried, focused on research that traced Swedish-American communities across multiple generations.

Mikael's great-great-great-grandson, researching the very family history I had helped to shape.

The irony was almost unbearable. Here was a young man dedicating his academic career to understanding the cultural preservation and identity formation of immigrants like his ancestor—the ancestor I had loved and lost over a century ago. Every day I watched him in the library, surrounded by documents and photographs that chronicled the American branch of the Jensen family, while I sat twenty feet away with memories of the European chapter he was trying to piece together.

I knew I should leave him alone. My species had survived for millennia by avoiding exactly this kind of personal entanglement with humans. The wise course would be to change universities, disappear back into the anonymity that had protected me for centuries. Soren Jensen was living his own life, pursuing his own goals, and had no need for an Elder's complicated history intruding upon his research.

But I found I couldn't stay away.

It started innocuously enough—positioning myself where I might overhear his conversations with librarians about specific archives, noting which collections he requested, observing the gaps in his research that I could so easily fill. He was methodical and thorough, but working without knowledge of the most crucial period of Mikael's life. His family tree stopped abruptly at Mikael's arrival in America, with only speculation about what had prompted the emigration from Stockholm.

He has no idea about Copenhagen. No idea about me.

The temptation to help, to share what I knew, grew stronger each day. I had letters from Mikael, photographs from our time together, documentation of exactly why he had chosen America over remaining in Denmark. Information that would transform Soren's understanding of his ancestor from speculation into living history.

But sharing such materials would require explanations I wasn't prepared to give. How does one explain possessing 131-year-old correspondence without revealing the impossible truth about one's own longevity? How could I justify knowing intimate details of Mikael's emotional life without exposing the nature of our relationship?

The opportunity came to me on a Thursday morning as I watched the familiar figure struggle with a particularly recalcitrant microfilm machine. It was definitely him—the lost American from Hampstead, now successfully navigating London's academic resources with more success than his first day suggested.

From across the library, the visual resemblance was unmistakable. The bone structure, the way he held his shoulders, even the color of his hair catching the afternoon light streaming through the tall windows. It was as if Mikael had been reborn into this century, given another chance at the life that had been cut short.

But resemblance alone, I had learned over the centuries, could be deceiving. Genetics created patterns, but they did not recreate souls.

The young man—Soren, I had learned from discreet inquiries—was growing increasingly frustrated with the temperamental machine. I watched him try the same sequence of operations three times, each attempt growing more forceful. When the fourth attempt failed, he stepped back from the machine with obvious exasperation.

Then it happened.

Soren reached up with his right hand, fingers threading through his hair to push it back from his forehead—but instead of simply smoothing it down, he paused mid-gesture, hand still buried in the sandy strands, and looked up and slightly to the right. His eyes focused on some invisible point in the middle distance, as if he were consulting some internal compass or waiting for guidance from an unseen advisor.

The movement was so achingly familiar, so precisely identical to a gesture I had seen countless times 131 years ago, that I gripped the edge of my reading table hard enough to leave finger impressions in the wood.

Copenhagen, 1882. The docks. Mikael removing his hat after the long ship journey from Stockholm, brushing the travel from his hair, then that same pause—hand arrested mid-motion, eyes seeking something beyond the physical world, that moment of internal consultation that I had found so endearing, so distinctly his.

This wasn't learned behavior. This wasn't coincidence. This was genetic inheritance expressing itself across five generations, a family mannerism as distinctive as eye color or the shape of a smile.

When the young man finally gave up on the machine and walked away in search of assistance, I saw my chance. I moved quickly to the troublesome microfilm reader, coaxing it into proper functioning through the kind of mechanical sympathy that came with decades of experience with temperamental equipment.

By the time he returned with a librarian, I was standing beside the now-cooperative machine, positioning myself precisely where I needed to be.

"We meet again," I said as they approached, offering a smile of recognition. "Though you seem to have found your way to a library successfully this time—just not quite the one you were originally seeking. I think I may have solved your machine problem while trying to fix my own."

"Oh, thank goodness," Soren replied, and his voice—deeper than Mikael's had been, but with the same careful pronunciation—sent another wave of recognition through me. "I was beginning to think it was designed by someone who actively hated researchers. And what are the odds of running into my Hampstead rescuer again?"

As he moved closer to examine the machine, to see what I had done to restore it to working order, I positioned myself to help guide him through the loading process. The proximity was necessary, I told myself, purely practical for showing him the proper technique.

That was when his scent reached me.

Every Elder possessed enhanced olfactory capabilities, but I had learned over the millennia to keep such senses carefully controlled in human environments.

The modern world was full of artificial fragrances and chemical pollution that could overwhelm supernatural awareness. But this close to Soren, with my guard momentarily down due to shock of recognition, his natural scent hit me with the force of a physical blow.

It wasn't just human. It wasn't just male. It wasn't even just the general genetic signature that marked family lineages to those with the senses to detect them.

This was Mikael's bloodline. Not similar to it, not reminiscent of it, but *identical* to it at the molecular level. The same genetic markers, the same hereditary pheromone signature, the same fundamental biological identity that I had memorized during four years of intimate partnership.

I had to grip the edge of the machine to steady myself as the implications crashed over me. This wasn't coincidence. This wasn't even extraordinary luck. This was Mikael's direct descendant, carrying his blood, his genes, his family's distinctive biological signature.

"Are you alright?" Soren asked, noticing my sudden stillness. "You look like you've seen a ghost."

If only he knew, I thought, struggling to regain my composure. In a sense, I had. But not a ghost—something far more miraculous. A continuation of a bloodline I had thought lost to me forever.

"I'm fine," I managed, my voice hopefully steadier than I felt. "Just... déjà vu, I suppose. Sometimes these old buildings hold more memories than expected."

I laughed, and the sound felt strange after so many careful, measured interactions with fellow students. "I've had the same thought about the machine. Though I suspect it's more likely designed by engineers who never actually used microfilm themselves. As for the coincidence—London's academic community is smaller than you'd expect."

But even as I spoke, even as I helped him load the film with hands that I hoped appeared steady, my mind was reeling with the impossibility of what I had discovered.

Mikael's great-great-great-grandson. Here. Now. Researching the very family history I had helped to shape.

The universe, it seemed, had a sense of irony that spanned centuries.

The librarian, satisfied that the crisis was resolved, disappeared back into the stacks. Soren began loading his film with the focused attention I had observed from across the room, but now I was close enough to see what he was researching. Scandinavian immigration records, ship manifests, parish records from Swedish churches in Minnesota.

"Research project?" I asked, though I already knew the answer.

"Dissertation, actually. Cultural preservation in immigrant communities." He glanced up with that same polite smile that had first stopped my heart. "Looking at how Swedish families maintained traditions while adapting to American life. It's more complex than you'd expect—lots of negotiation between old world identity and new world opportunities."

If only you knew how complex.

"That sounds fascinating," I said, meaning it completely. "Are you focusing on a particular time period?"

"Late nineteenth, early twentieth century primarily. The period when immigration patterns shifted from individual adventurers to entire family units." He threaded the film through the machine with practiced efficiency. "Though I'm hitting some frustrating gaps in the records. Family stories don't always align with official documentation."

"Have you ever considered going to Sweden to research the archives directly?" I asked. "Sometimes the European records contain details that never made it into American documentation."

"I'd love to, but graduate student budgets don't exactly allow for international research trips," he said with a rueful smile. "Maybe someday, if I can secure funding."

An opening. A perfectly natural opportunity to offer assistance without seeming intrusive.

"I might be able to help with that," I said carefully. "My own family has some connections to that period and region. My family history is Scandinavian—I'm originally from there myself, actually. English isn't my native language." I paused, then added, "Nothing directly related to your research, I'm sure, but sometimes the peripheral sources fill in interesting details."

Soren looked up with genuine interest. "Your English is excellent, though. If not for you mentioning it, I would never have guessed. There's perhaps a slight... regal quality to your accent, but nothing that suggests it's not your first language."

I felt heat rise to my cheeks—an involuntary response I hadn't experienced in 131 years, not since Mikael had complimented my careful pronunciation during our language lessons in Copenhagen. The unexpected blush caught me completely off guard.

Regal. Mikael had used almost the same word when describing how I spoke English, teasing me about sounding like nobility trying to blend in with commoners.

"What kind of connections?" he continued.

"Letters, mostly. Some photographs. My family has always been somewhat obsessive about preserving documentation." True enough, though the family in question was Mikael's rather than my own fictional background. "If you'd like, I could take a look at what you're missing and see if anything in our collection might be useful."

For a moment, he seemed to consider the offer carefully—a researcher's natural caution about accepting help from strangers warring with academic curiosity. Finally, curiosity won.

"That would be incredibly generous," he said. "I should properly introduce myself—I'm Soren, by the way. Soren Jensen. And thank you again for the directions the other day—I did eventually make it to the British Library, though clearly I'm finding King's collection useful as well."

Jensen. Hearing him speak Mikael's surname aloud nearly undid me completely.

"Henry," I replied, offering the name I had used consistently at King's College. "Henry Nordh. I'm glad the directions proved helpful, even if they led you on something of a scenic route through London."

As we shook hands—his grip firm and warm, so achingly familiar—I wondered if I was making the wisest decision of my long life or the most catastrophically foolish. The coincidence of meeting again seemed to please him as much as it did me, though for vastly different reasons.

But looking into those blue-grey eyes, seeing Mikael's curiosity and kindness reflected in his descendant's face, I found I didn't care about wisdom.

For the first time in 131 years, I was no longer entirely alone with my memories.

THE WEIGHT OF KNOWLEDGE

Our first real conversation lasted three hours.

I had suggested meeting at a quiet café near the university, somewhere we could spread out documents without the library's restrictions on food and drink. Soren arrived precisely on time—another inherited trait, I noted—carrying a leather portfolio that spoke of someone who took his research seriously.

"I brought copies of what I have so far," he said as we settled at a corner table. "Fair warning: it's a bit obsessive. My friends think I take the family history thing too seriously."

If only he knew how seriously I had once taken his family's history.

He opened the portfolio to reveal meticulously organized documents—photocopied ship manifests, immigration records, translated letters, carefully constructed family trees that traced the Jensen line from Sweden through Copenhagen to Minnesota. It was thorough, impressive work that demonstrated both academic rigor and genuine personal investment.

But there were gaps. Significant gaps that I could fill with a few casual revelations.

"This is excellent work," I said, meaning it. "You've traced the line back to... Mikael Johan Jensen, born 1860 near Stockholm."

"Right. He's the furthest back I can get with any certainty." Soren pointed to the entry on his family tree. "I know he emigrated to America in 1882, settled in Minnesota, married a Swedish-American woman. But there's this mysterious period before that—apparently he spent several years in Copenhagen first, but I can't find any record of what he was doing there or why he chose to stay before continuing to America."

Because he was falling in love with someone who couldn't follow him to his new life.

"Copenhagen was a common stopping point," I said carefully. "Many Scandinavian emigrants used it as a staging ground—earning money for passage, learning languages, sometimes reconsidering their plans entirely."

"That's what I assumed, but..." Soren hesitated, then pulled out a letter from his collection. "This is from his son, written many years later. There's a reference to his father having 'left something precious behind in Denmark' but no details about what that might have been."

I recognized the handwriting immediately—John Mikael Jensen, Mikael's eldest son. The boy who had been playing in the farmyard when I glimpsed Mikael's American life from the tree line. Now a grown man, writing about a father's hidden sadness.

Something precious behind in Denmark. Yes, Mikael had left something precious. Someone precious. But how could I explain that to his great-great-grandson without revealing truths that would shatter his understanding of the world?

"Family stories often preserve emotional truths even when they lose factual details," I said. "It's possible your ancestor formed meaningful connections during his time in Copenhagen—friendships, perhaps even romantic attachments—that made leaving difficult."

Soren nodded thoughtfully. "That's what I've wondered. The timing suggests he was there during his late teens and early twenties, exactly when someone would be forming significant relationships." He paused, studying the letter again. "Though given the era and his eventual marriage, I'm not sure how much detail would have been preserved about any romantic connections."

More detail than you could imagine, if only I dared to share it.

"What kind of documentation are you hoping to find?" I asked.

"Anything, really. Letters, diary entries, official records of residence or employment. Even photographs would help." His enthusiasm was infectious, exactly the kind of passionate scholarly curiosity that made him so achingly reminiscent of Mikael. "I'm particularly interested in how cultural identity evolved during that transitional period. Did he maintain Swedish traditions while in Copenhagen? Did he adopt Danish customs? How did those experiences influence the choices he made in America?"

Every question he asked, I could answer. I had witnessed Mikael's cultural adaptation firsthand, had been part of the process as he navigated between Swedish heritage, Danish integration, and American ambitions. I had watched him struggle with questions of identity and belonging that his descendant was now trying to understand through historical analysis.

"I might actually have some materials that could help," I said, hoping my voice remained casual. "Nothing directly related to your Mikael, but correspondence from the same period and location. Letters that describe the social world he would have inhabited, the kinds of choices and pressures young Scandinavian men faced in Copenhagen during the 1870s and 1880s."

Soren's eyes lit up. "That would be incredibly valuable for context, even if it's not family-specific."

It is family-specific. More specific than you could possibly understand.

"I'll need to go through the collection carefully," I said. "Some of the materials are quite personal—my family has always been protective of certain private correspondences. But I'm sure I can find things that would be appropriate for academic research."

"I completely understand about family privacy," Soren assured me. "I've run into the same issues with some of my own relatives. People are often reluctant to share materials that might reveal unflattering details about ancestors."

If only unflattering details were all I had to worry about.

We spent the remainder of the afternoon going through his research, with me offering suggestions about additional archives to explore, alternative approaches to genealogical dead ends, and general encouragement for what was clearly a labor of love as much as academic necessity. With each hour that passed, I found myself more drawn to his combination of scholarly rigor and personal investment, his way of treating historical figures as real people rather than abstract data points.

He was so much like Mikael in that regard—possessing an instinctive understanding that behind every document was a human story worth preserving and honoring.

When we finally parted company, I had committed to reviewing my family's papers and meeting again the following week. As I watched him walk away, portfolio clutched against his chest like something precious, I realized I had crossed a line I had maintained for over a century.

I was no longer simply observing Mikael's descendant from a safe distance. I was actively participating in his research, contributing to his understanding of the family history I had helped to shape. And despite every rational argument against such involvement, I found myself looking forward to our next meeting with an anticipation I hadn't felt in decades.

What am I doing? I wondered as I made my way back to my flat. What possible good can come from entangling myself in his life?

But even as I asked the questions, I knew the answers wouldn't matter. For the first time since that painful encounter in the Minnesota general store, I had found a connection to Mikael that didn't require hiding in shadows or watching from afar.

Whatever the consequences, I wasn't ready to give that up.

DANGEROUS TERRITORY

By our third meeting, I had become reckless.

Not in any way that Soren would recognize—I remained scrupulously careful about maintaining my fictional background, about explaining my knowledge in ways that seemed plausible for a fellow graduate student with unusually good family records. But internally, I was taking risks that would have horrified my younger self.

I had given him letters. Actual letters from Mikael, though I claimed they were from a family friend who had known him in Copenhagen. Photographs from our time together, presented as part of a collection documenting social life among Scandinavian expatriates. Details about Mikael's personality, his interests, his daily routines during those four crucial years—all offered as educated speculation based on the social context of the period.

Soren absorbed every piece of information with the hunger of someone who had been starving for exactly this kind of detail. His research had been thorough but necessarily limited to official records and family stories passed down through generations. What I was providing filled in the human dimension that made historical figures come alive.

"This is extraordinary," he said, examining a photograph of Mikael taken during our second year together. I had claimed it came from a collection documenting life in Copenhagen's international community. "You can see so much personality in his expression. He looks... thoughtful but optimistic. Like someone who's found his place in the world but still has plans for something better."

He had found his place, for a time. With me.

"The photographer captured something authentic," I agreed, though what the image actually showed was Mikael on a Sunday morning in my flat, laughing at something I had said just before the shutter clicked. One of dozens of photographs I had taken during our time together, preserved in perfect detail by my obsessive need to document every moment of our brief happiness.

"And these letters," Soren continued, handling the documents with appropriate reverence. "They provide such insight into the social world. The way he writes about balancing Swedish identity with Danish integration, about trying to decide whether America represents opportunity or abandonment of heritage... it's exactly the kind of cultural tension I'm trying to document."

The letters were among Mikael's most personal correspondences with me, though I had carefully selected passages that dealt with identity and belonging rather than our relationship. Still, they revealed aspects of his character that no official record could capture—his thoughtfulness, his genuine care for the people around him, his way of approaching difficult decisions with both emotional intelligence and practical consideration.

"Your family friend must have been quite close to him," Soren observed. "These letters suggest a deep level of trust and intimacy."

Deeper than you could possibly imagine.

"They seem to have been very good friends," I said carefully. "The correspondence suggests your ancestor was someone who inspired strong loyalty in the people who knew him."

It was true, though it understated the case considerably. Mikael had inspired not just loyalty but love—devoted, transformative love that had lasted 131 years beyond his death. Love that I was now sharing, in carefully disguised form, with his descendant.

"I'm starting to understand why he might have been reluctant to leave Copenhagen," Soren said, studying the photograph again. "If he had formed meaningful friendships, found a community where he felt understood... the decision to emigrate would have required giving up significant emotional connections."

It required giving up everything that mattered to him, except his sense of duty to his family's expectations.

"What do you think ultimately motivated his decision to leave?" I asked, though I knew the answer in painful detail.

Soren considered the question seriously. "Based on what I'm learning about his time in Copenhagen, I think he was torn between personal happiness and social obligation. The letters suggest he was genuinely content there, but he would have felt pressure to establish himself economically, to marry and start a family according to Swedish traditions. America represented the possibility of achieving those expectations while building something entirely his own."

And Copenhagen represented the impossibility of achieving them while remaining true to his heart.

"You think he saw emigration as a way to resolve competing loyalties?"

"I think he saw it as the only way to become the man his family needed him to be," Soren said quietly. "Even if it meant sacrificing the man he might have preferred to be."

The insight was so accurate, so perfectly aligned with Mikael's actual struggle, that I had to look away to compose myself. Here was his descendant, working from partial information and historical context, yet arriving at a understanding of Mikael's choice that captured its essential tragedy.

"That must have been an incredibly difficult decision," I managed.

"It explains why his family always said he carried a certain sadness," Soren replied. "Not regret, exactly, but awareness of what he had given up. The price of choosing duty over personal desire."

The price of choosing a life I couldn't be part of over a love that couldn't survive in his world.

We spent the rest of the afternoon integrating the new materials into his research, watching his family tree grow more detailed and his understanding of Mikael's experience become more nuanced. With each revelation, I saw Soren's connection to his ancestor deepen—not just as a subject of academic study, but as a person whose choices and sacrifices had shaped the trajectory that led to Soren's own existence.

"I feel like I'm finally beginning to know him," Soren said as we prepared to leave. "Not just the facts of his life, but something about who he was as a person.

That's incredibly rare in genealogical research—usually you get dates and locations but very little sense of personality or motivation."

You're knowing him through my memories, though you don't realize it.

"Your ancestor seems to have been someone worth knowing," I said.

"I think so too." Soren hesitated, then looked at me directly. "Henry, can I ask you something that might seem strange?"

My enhanced senses immediately picked up subtle changes in his heartbeat and body language that suggested nervousness or uncertainty. Whatever he was about to ask, it was something he had been considering carefully.

"Of course."

"How is it that your family has such detailed documentation from this period? I don't mean to be suspicious, but the level of detail is unusual for personal correspondence that's over a century old. Most families I've researched have bits and pieces, but nothing this comprehensive or well-preserved."

The question I had been dreading and expecting in equal measure. Soren was too good a researcher not to notice the improbability of what I was sharing. Too intelligent not to question sources that seemed almost too perfect for his needs.

"Family obsession," I said, hoping my voice remained steady. "My ancestors were somewhat compulsive about documentation. They treated personal correspondence like historical artifacts worth preserving for future generations. It's unusual, I admit, but not unheard of in families with academic inclinations."

Soren nodded slowly, but I could see him processing the explanation with the same analytical approach he brought to all his research. Not rejecting it, but not fully accepting it either.

"The preservation quality is remarkable," he said. "These letters look almost as clear as if they were written yesterday."

Because I've taken extraordinary care of them for 131 years.

"Modern archival techniques," I replied. "My family invested heavily in proper storage and preservation methods."

It was a plausible explanation, and Soren seemed to accept it. But I could tell he was filing away his observations, adding them to some mental catalog of things that didn't quite align with normal expectations. He was too careful a researcher to dismiss anomalies, even when working with helpful sources.

As we parted that afternoon, I realized I was walking an increasingly narrow line between revelation and exposure. Each meeting brought us closer together, but also brought me closer to questions I couldn't answer honestly without destroying the careful fiction of my identity.

Still, watching Soren walk away with his portfolio now full of materials that would transform his understanding of his family history, I felt a satisfaction I hadn't experienced in decades. For the first time since losing Mikael, I was contributing something positive to his legacy rather than simply mourning what had been lost.

But how long can I maintain this deception? And what happens when he starts asking questions I can't answer?

The rational response would be to begin distancing myself, to find reasons why my family's collection had been exhausted or why my academic schedule no longer permitted our meetings. To fade back into the anonymity that had protected me for centuries.

Instead, I found myself already planning what materials I might share next, what aspects of Mikael's story I could reveal without compromising my own secret. I was in dangerous territory, but I was no longer certain I wanted to find my way back to safety.

For better or worse, I was becoming part of Soren's research. And he, whether he knew it or not, was becoming part of my carefully guarded heart.

3
GROWING CLOSENESS

THE LAMB & FLAG 33 ROSE STREET, BLOOMSBURY, LONDON WC1E 7LS

Soren Jensen

Three weeks into our collaboration, my dissertation had become something entirely different from what I'd originally proposed. What had started as a modest study of Swedish cultural preservation in Minnesota communities was evolving into a comprehensive examination of individual identity formation during the immigration experience. Henry had provided materials that transformed abstract academic concepts into lived human experience.

"I found something else you might find interesting," Henry said during our fourth meeting, producing yet another carefully preserved document. "A letter from the Copenhagen parish where your ancestor attended services. It mentions him specifically—apparently he helped translate for other Swedish immigrants during mass."

I examined the letter with the same reverence I'd learned to show all of Henry's materials. The parish priest's description of Mikael painted a picture of someone who served as a bridge between cultures, comfortable enough with Danish to help his countrymen while maintaining his Swedish identity.

"This is incredible," I murmured, already thinking about how this evidence supported my developing thesis about adaptive cultural mediation. "How did you even know to look for this?"

Henry's response came a fraction too quickly. "Family stories mentioned religious involvement. I thought church records might yield something."

It was plausible, but I was beginning to notice these moments—slight hesitations followed by explanations that felt rehearsed. Henry always had logical reasons for his discoveries, but the consistency of his success was beginning to feel improbable.

Still, I found myself caring less about the source of the materials and more about spending time with Henry himself. Our research sessions had stretched longer each week, often extending past library closing into nearby cafés where we'd continue discussing cultural theory over coffee that grew cold while we talked.

"You know," I said during one such conversation, "my advisor is going to think I've completely changed topics when I submit my revised proposal."

"Is that a problem?" Henry asked, and something in his voice suggested genuine concern for my academic standing.

"Actually, no. It's better than my original idea. More personal, more... human." I hesitated, then added, "I couldn't have done this without your help."

Henry's smile in response was different from his usual polite expressions—warmer, more genuine. "I'm glad I could contribute something useful."

The way he said it made me wonder, not for the first time, what he was getting out of our collaboration. He seemed as invested in my research as I was, sometimes bringing materials I hadn't even requested, staying late to help me organize and cross-reference documents. It felt like more than casual academic assistance.

FUMBLING TOWARD SOMETHING

By our sixth meeting, I had worked up the courage to suggest we grab dinner after our library session.

"There's a pub near my flat that does excellent fish and chips," I said, trying to sound casual while my heart hammered against my ribs. "If you're not busy tonight, I mean. We could continue discussing the cultural assimilation patterns over food."

The words tumbled out awkwardly, academic justification mixed with something that felt dangerously close to asking for a date. I immediately regretted the suggestion, certain I'd misread whatever dynamic was developing between us.

But Henry's face lit up with what looked like genuine pleasure. "I'd like that very much."

Dinner was a revelation. Away from documents and research materials, our conversation ranged across literature, travel, music, and dozens of other topics that had nothing to do with genealogy. Henry had opinions about everything—nuanced, thoughtful perspectives that suggested extensive reading and experience. His knowledge seemed remarkably broad for someone his age, but I found myself too caught up in the pleasure of conversation to analyze the inconsistency.

"You know," I said as we walked back toward the university, "I don't think I've ever talked to anyone who gets so enthusiastic about 19th-century Danish social policy."

Henry laughed—a sound I was becoming fond of hearing. "I find historical social systems fascinating. The way cultures adapt to change, develop new institutions to meet evolving needs."

"Most people my age would rather discuss football scores or weekend plans."

"Most people your age haven't spent years researching their family history," Henry replied. "Your perspective is... refreshing."

There was something in the way he said it that made me glance at him sideways. His expression was thoughtful, almost wistful, as if he were remembering something from long ago rather than commenting on present company.

"Henry," I said impulsively, "can I ask you something personal?"

His step faltered almost imperceptibly. "Of course."

"Do you ever feel like you don't quite fit with people your own age? Like you're somehow out of step with what everyone else finds important?"

The question hung between us for several moments before Henry answered quietly, "Every day."

The honesty in his voice made something in my chest tighten. I'd spent so many years feeling isolated by my interests, my maturity, my general sense of being displaced in time. Finding someone who understood that feeling was both relief and revelation.

"It's nice," I said, barely above a whisper, "not feeling alone in that."

Henry stopped walking entirely and turned to face me. In the lamplight, his expression was intense in a way that made my breath catch.

"You're not alone, Soren," he said, and the way he spoke my name sent warmth spreading through my chest. "Not in that, and not in... other things."

I wasn't sure what he meant by "other things," but the weight of his gaze suggested layers of meaning I wasn't quite ready to examine. We stood there for a moment, close enough that I could see the unusual flecks of gold in his eyes, before Henry stepped back and resumed walking.

The rest of our walk passed in comfortable silence, but something had shifted between us. The careful boundaries we'd maintained around our growing friendship had become more porous, allowing glimpses of something deeper and more complex.

CONFUSION AND REVELATION

That night, lying in bed, I found myself replaying every moment of the evening. The way Henry had looked at me when I'd confessed to feeling out of step with my peers. The warmth in his voice when he'd said I wasn't alone. The moment of tension when we'd stood too close under the streetlight.

I'd never given much serious thought to romantic relationships. Through school, I'd been too focused on academic achievement and family research to pay attention to the social dynamics that seemed to consume my classmates. I'd assumed I'd figure out such things eventually, when I had time to focus on them.

But Henry was making me reconsider what I might want, what I might be capable of feeling. The comfortable ease of our conversations, the way I found myself looking forward to our meetings with an intensity that went beyond academic interest, the growing desire to know more about him as a person rather than just a research collaborator.

Was this attraction? The thought both thrilled and terrified me. I'd never been attracted to anyone before—male or female—and I wasn't sure how to interpret the warm, nervous energy that filled my chest whenever Henry smiled at me.

More concerning was the possibility that these feelings weren't reciprocal. Henry was unfailingly kind and helpful, but that didn't necessarily mean anything beyond friendship. What if I was misreading his politeness as something more? What if suggesting dinner had already pushed the boundaries of our professional relationship?

The uncertainty kept me awake until nearly dawn, running through scenarios both hopeful and mortifying.

SMALL GESTURES

Our next meeting felt different from the moment I walked into the library. Henry looked up from his notes with a smile that seemed warmer than usual, and when I settled into the chair beside him, he'd already ordered coffee the way I liked it.

"I did some additional research," he said, producing a folder of documents. "I thought you might find these interesting for your section on community formation."

The materials were, as always, exactly what I needed—parish records showing how Swedish immigrants had gradually integrated into Danish religious communities while maintaining distinct cultural practices. But what struck me more than the documents themselves was the care Henry had obviously taken in their presentation. Everything was clearly labeled, cross-referenced, and organized according to the thematic structure I'd been developing.

"Henry, this is..." I began, then stopped, overwhelmed by the thoughtfulness of the gesture. "This must have taken hours."

He shrugged as if it were nothing, but I caught a hint of pleased embarrassment in his expression. "I wanted to make sure you had everything you needed for your chapter on religious adaptation."

Throughout our session, I found myself noticing small things—the way Henry anticipated which documents I'd want to examine next, how he unconsciously mirrored my posture as we worked, the careful attention he paid to my theories and observations. It felt like being studied, but in the most flattering possible way.

When I mentioned being hungry, Henry immediately suggested a nearby café he'd "heard was good." When I struggled with a particularly faded section of handwriting, he leaned close enough to help decipher it that I could feel the warmth radiating from his body. When I got excited about a connection I'd discovered between two seemingly unrelated documents, Henry's face lit up as if my academic breakthrough was personally meaningful to him.

"You know," I said as we packed up our materials, "I keep feeling like I should be paying you for research assistance. You're doing as much work on this project as I am."

"I'm enjoying it," Henry replied, and something in his tone suggested that was an understatement. "It's... meaningful to see these family stories preserved and honored."

Again, that slightly odd phrasing that made it sound like he had personal investment in Mikael's story. But before I could think too much about it, Henry was suggesting we walk rather than take the tube back toward our respective flats.

"It's a lovely evening," he said. "And I thought you might enjoy seeing the Thames from Tower Bridge at sunset."

THE MOMENT OF TRUTH

The walk along the Thames was everything Henry had promised—the evening light turning the water golden, the historic buildings casting long shadows, the tourist crowds thinning as office workers hurried home. We walked slowly, our conversation meandering between observations about London's architecture and continued discussion of cultural adaptation theories.

"I still can't get over how much material you've been able to provide," I said as we approached the Tower of London. "It's like your family maintained a complete archive of Danish immigrant social life."

"My family has always been... thorough about documentation," Henry replied, but something in his voice sounded almost apologetic.

I was about to ask what he meant when Henry suddenly went very still beside me. His head tilted slightly, as if he were listening to something I couldn't hear.

"Soren, move—"

Before I could ask what he was talking about, Henry's hands were on my shoulders, pulling me sideways with surprising strength and speed. I stumbled toward the river embankment, momentarily disoriented, as a cyclist whooshed past exactly where I'd been standing.

"Sorry!" the cyclist called over his shoulder, not slowing down. "Didn't see you there!"

I found myself pressed against the stone barrier overlooking the Thames, Henry's body partially shielding me from the pathway, his hands still gripping my shoulders. We were close enough that I could see the concern in his eyes, could feel his breath against my face.

"Are you alright?" he asked quietly.

I nodded, though my heart was racing—from the near-accident, from Henry's proximity, from the growing awareness that something about what had just happened didn't quite make sense.

"How did you..." I began, then stopped. How did you know to move us before I even heard the bicycle? How did you react so quickly in the dark? How are you strong enough to move both of us so easily when you're smaller than I am?

But standing there with Henry still holding me, his face inches from mine, those questions seemed less important than the sudden, overwhelming certainty that I was falling in love with someone I knew almost nothing about.

"Henry," I whispered, not sure what I was going to say next.

His expression shifted, becoming almost pained. "Soren..."

For a moment, I thought he might kiss me. The way he was looking at me suggested he wanted to, was perhaps fighting against the impulse. But then he stepped back, releasing my shoulders, and the moment fractured.

"We should probably head back," he said, his voice carefully neutral. "It's getting late."

As we walked toward Tower Bridge, the questions I'd pushed aside began reasserting themselves. The superhuman reflexes. The impossible strength. The way Henry had known danger was approaching before I'd had any awareness of it.

None of it made sense. But then again, nothing about Henry had made complete sense from the beginning—his extensive knowledge, his perfectly preserved historical materials, his formal way of speaking that sometimes seemed to belong to another era entirely.

By the time we parted ways at the tube station, I had made a decision. I needed answers, even if asking for them risked destroying whatever was developing between us.

Tomorrow, I was going to find the courage to ask Henry who he really was.

4
THE WEIGHT OF CENTURIES

BREDGADE 23, 1260 KØBENHAVN K

Aleksander (Henry) Nordh

I stood at my window overlooking the quiet London street, watching the last of the evening commuters make their way home while my mind wandered through corridors of memory I'd kept carefully locked for decades. It was past midnight, but sleep felt impossible. Soren had left hours ago, portfolio clutched against his chest like something precious, his eyes bright with the excitement of discovery.

But it was the moment just before he'd left that haunted me now—the way he'd looked at those photographs of Mikael I'd shared with him. Something in his expression had shifted, a flicker of curiosity that went beyond academic interest. He'd seen something, recognized something, though he couldn't possibly understand what.

I pressed my forehead against the cool glass and allowed myself to remember.

The memory rose unbidden, as vivid as if it were happening now rather than 131 years ago.

COPENHAGEN, SEPTEMBER 1882

Mikael sat at my writing desk, laboriously forming letters with the careful concentration I'd come to adore. His tongue poked out slightly between his lips when he was thinking—a habit that never failed to make my chest tight with affection. The afternoon light caught the gold in his hair, and I found myself memorizing the curve of his neck, the way his shoulders moved as he wrote.

"Henrik," he said without looking up, "may I ask you something?"

"Always."

"Sometimes you speak as if you've seen things... experienced things that would be impossible for someone your age." He set down the pen and turned to face me. "And you have books, artifacts, knowledge that suggests..." He trailed off, searching for words.

My heart hammered against my ribs. This was the moment I'd both dreaded and hoped for—the moment when his natural curiosity led him to questions I couldn't answer without revealing everything.

"What are you asking, Mikael?"

"I'm asking who you really are." His blue-grey eyes—so like Soren's—held mine steadily. "Because I don't think you're simply the second son of a Danish merchant family, as you've told me."

The truth sat on my tongue like a stone. *I am over sixteen hundred years old. I have watched empires rise and fall. I am not human in the way you understand humanity.* The words were right there, begging to be spoken, demanding the honesty that love deserved.

But what came out instead was: "Sometimes I think you have too active an imagination."

Mikael's face fell almost imperceptibly. "Perhaps you're right."

He returned to his writing, but something had changed in the room. A distance had opened between us that I'd created with my cowardice, and I didn't know how to bridge it without revealing truths that might destroy us both.

BACK TO THE PRESENT

I turned away from the window, unable to bear the memory any longer. That moment had been the beginning of the end, though neither of us had understood it at the time. My inability to trust him with the truth had created a crack in our foundation that had only widened over the months that followed.

How many times had Mikael given me openings? How many opportunities had I squandered because I was too afraid of rejection, too terrified of seeing fear replace love in his eyes?

And when the letters from his family became more insistent, when the pressure to return to Sweden and fulfill his obligations grew too strong to ignore, I had chosen the coward's path. Instead of fighting for us, instead of trusting him with the truth and letting him make an informed choice, I had encouraged his departure.

"You have a duty to your family," I had said, each word like glass in my throat. "America offers opportunities you'll never have here. You could build something magnificent there."

What I hadn't said: *I am too afraid to tell you what I am. I am too selfish to burden you with loving a monster. I am too weak to watch you choose duty over love when you know the full truth.*

So I had made the choice for both of us.

OTHER GHOSTS

Mikael hadn't been my first heartbreak, though he had been my deepest. There had been others across the centuries—mortal lovers who had glimpsed edges of my true nature and fled, or whom I had left before they could discover the impossibility of what I was.

There was teenage Brother Augustin in 8th-century Francia, in the monastery that would one day become the heart of Paris. A learned monk whose curiosity about ancient texts had drawn us together over long winter nights in the scriptorium. His gentle hands copying illuminated manuscripts, his questions about sources I claimed to have read that predated any collection the monastery possessed. But it was my apparent youth that made everything impossible—despite being over a millennium old, I appeared no more than a boy of perhaps ten. The scandal such a relationship would have caused, the danger it would have placed us both in, made honesty unthinkable. When his scholarly mind began connecting the impossibilities in my knowledge, when he started asking why I never seemed to age despite the seasons we'd spent in study together, I had simply vanished one dawn, leaving only a note claiming pilgrimage called me elsewhere.

The centuries that followed were marked by similar impossibilities. Until nearly the industrial revolution, I could never pass as an adult, despite carrying the wisdom and emotional complexity of ages. Every connection I formed was tainted by the appearance of impropriety, by the knowledge that society would see corruption where there was only love between ancient minds in mismatched forms.

There was Marcus in Renaissance Florence, when I finally appeared old enough to move through the world as a young man rather than a boy. A young artist whose curiosity about my knowledge of "ancient" techniques had grown too keen. I had disappeared one night, leaving only a note claiming family obligations called me away.

There was James in early Victorian London, a writer whose sharp mind had started connecting inconsistencies in my carefully constructed background. I had simply vanished, as I had so many times before. It is from there that I arrived again in Copenhagen.

But Mikael... Mikael had been different. With him, I had come closest to revelation, closest to trust. And my failure of courage with him had cost us both more than all the others combined.

THE PATTERN

I moved to the bookshelf where I kept my most precious possessions, retrieving a small wooden box I rarely opened. Inside, wrapped in silk, were tokens from each love I'd lost to my own fear: a small painting from Marcus, a pressed flower from James, a manuscript page from Augustin, and most precious of all, a letter from Mikael written from America.

My dear Henrik,

I think of Copenhagen often, and of you most of all. I pray that you have found happiness in whatever path your life has taken. I would write more, but there are things we could never say aloud that feel even more dangerous on paper.

Know that you have my fondest thoughts always.

I had never responded. How could I? What could I say that wouldn't risk exposing both of us to censure or worse?

But now, holding that letter in the lamplight of my London flat, I wondered if my silence had been another act of cowardice disguised as protection.

THE DECISION

Soren's face rose in my mind—earnest, intelligent, carrying so much of Mikael in his features but possessing his own unique warmth. In the weeks we'd been meeting, I'd watched him grow more confident, more comfortable in his own skin. There was something about his acceptance of complexity, his scholar's hunger for truth regardless of how challenging it might be, that made me wonder...

What if I was approaching this wrong? What if the pattern I'd established across centuries—hide, deflect, disappear—was the problem rather than the solution?

What if honesty, however terrifying, was the only path to something real?

I thought about the way Soren had looked at that photograph of Mikael, the questions I'd seen forming in his eyes. His research mind was already working, already noticing inconsistencies. Soon he would start asking the same kinds of questions Mikael had asked. And when that moment came, I would have a choice to make.

I could deflect again, create distance, perhaps even disappear as I had so many times before. It would be safe. It would be lonely. It would be exactly what I'd done for over two millennia.

Or I could choose courage. I could trust in the connection I felt growing between us, trust in his intelligence and his capacity for acceptance, trust that perhaps this time, honesty might be rewarded rather than punished.

The thought terrified me more than any physical danger I'd faced across the centuries. But it also filled me with something I'd almost forgotten how to feel: hope.

As dawn began to lighten the London sky, I made a decision that would have been unthinkable just months ago. When Soren inevitably came asking questions—and he would, his scholar's mind wouldn't let him ignore the inconsistencies forever—I would tell him the truth.

All of it.

Whatever the consequences might be.

5
QUESTIONS IN THE DARK

FLAT 3B, 47 MARCHMONT STREET, BLOOMSBURY, LONDON WC1N 1AP

Soren Jensen

I lay in my narrow bed, staring at the ceiling while my mind raced through everything that had happened with Henry over the past few weeks. Outside my window, London settled into its late-night rhythms, but sleep felt impossible. Every time I closed my eyes, I saw that photograph of Mikael—and more importantly, I saw Henry's face when he'd looked at it.

The materials Henry had shared were extraordinary, yes. They would transform my research, add depth and humanity to what had been mere names and dates. But it was Henry himself who kept my thoughts spinning in circles I couldn't quite navigate.

I rolled onto my side, reaching for the bedside lamp. If I wasn't going to sleep, I might as well organize my thoughts properly. I grabbed a notebook and pen, opening to a fresh page. At the top, I wrote: "Questions about Henry."

Then I stared at the blank page, unsure how to begin.

ACADEMIC CURIOSITIES

The inconsistencies had been building for weeks, small things that individually meant little but collectively painted a picture I couldn't quite decipher.

His knowledge of historical context was remarkable for someone our age.

When we discussed 19th-century Danish society, he spoke with the kind of detailed understanding that usually came from years of specialized study. But his official field was British literature, not Scandinavian history.

His language skills were extraordinary. I'd heard him speak what sounded like fluent Danish with a librarian, switch to French with a café owner, and reference German texts with ease. That level of multilingual ability typically took decades to develop.

The preservation quality of his family documents was almost impossible. Letters that should have shown their age, photographs that looked as clear as if they'd been taken yesterday, paper that showed no signs of the deterioration that affected every other 19th-century document I'd encountered.

And then there was his manner of speaking. Formal, precise, occasionally using turns of phrase that seemed to belong to an earlier era. Sometimes he sounded like someone who'd learned English as a second language, but other times he seemed to possess an understanding of linguistic nuance that suggested extensive education.

None of it made sense for a twenty-two-year-old graduate student.

PERSONAL RECOGNITION

But the academic inconsistencies weren't what kept me awake. It was the growing awareness that my interest in Henry had moved far beyond professional collaboration.

I'd had relationships before—Sarah during my junior year, Emma for three months senior year. Both intelligent, attractive women who deserved better than someone going through the motions. I'd told myself the hollow feeling in those relationships was normal, that passion was overrated, that compatibility mattered more than chemistry.

But I'd been lying to myself. My attraction to women had always felt performative, like following a script rather than expressing genuine desire. Even during physical intimacy, part of me had felt detached, present but not truly engaged.

It wasn't that I hadn't noticed attractive men over the years. I had—lingering glances I'd rationalized as aesthetic appreciation, certain actors or athletes who captured my attention in ways that felt different from casual interest.

With Henry, those rationalizations were crumbling.

I found myself looking forward to our meetings with an anticipation that had nothing to do with research. When we sat close together examining documents, I was acutely aware of his presence—the way his fingers moved across aged paper, the subtle scent of his cologne, the rare moments when his formal demeanor gave way to genuine laughter.

And there had been moments—brief instances when I'd caught him looking at me with an intensity that seemed to go beyond professional courtesy.

Moments when our hands had brushed reaching for the same document, and neither of us had pulled away immediately.

I wasn't naive. I was twenty-four years old, had lived in dormitories and shared flats, had friends who were openly gay. I understood attraction when I felt it.

The realization wasn't "What is this feeling?" It was "So this is what I've been avoiding."

THE WEIGHT OF UNDERSTANDING

What terrified me wasn't the recognition of my attraction to Henry. It was the understanding that this attraction felt fundamentally different from anything I'd experienced before.

With my previous relationships, physical intimacy had felt like following a script—pleasant enough, but somehow disconnected from any deeper emotional need. With Henry, even our most innocent interactions carried an undercurrent of tension that made my pulse quicken.

I wanted to know what his skin felt like. I wanted to see him first thing in the morning, rumpled and unguarded. I wanted to kiss him until neither of us could think about anything else.

The intensity of these desires was both thrilling and overwhelming. This wasn't the polite interest I'd felt for Sarah or Emma. This was the kind of want that could reshape a life.

As dawn began to lighten the London sky, I made a decision that would have been unthinkable just months ago. Whatever Henry's secrets were, whatever inconsistencies I'd noticed in his background, I was going to pursue this. I was going to find out if what I thought I saw in his eyes was real.

For the first time in my life, I was going to stop performing and start living.

THE PHOTOGRAPH

I thought again about Henry's reaction to that photograph of Mikael. The intensity in his expression, the way his breathing had changed, the careful reverence with which he'd handled the image.

He'd looked at my ancestor like someone looking at a lost love.

The thought should have been ridiculous. Henry was twenty-two years old. Mikael had died decades before Henry was born. There was no logical connection between them beyond the historical materials Henry's family had preserved.

But logic seemed inadequate to explain what I'd witnessed. There had been something profoundly personal in Henry's response, something that went beyond academic interest or even family connection.

What if Henry's family had some deeper relationship to mine than he'd revealed? What if there were secrets buried in our shared history that he wasn't ready to discuss?

Or what if—and this thought felt simultaneously impossible and inevitable—there was something about Henry himself that I didn't understand? Something that would explain the inconsistencies, the anachronistic knowledge, the way he sometimes seemed to carry more weight than someone his age should bear?

GROWING FEELINGS

Despite all my questions and uncertainties, one thing had become crystal clear: I cared about Henry in ways that had nothing to do with research.

I wanted to know what made him laugh, what worried him, what he dreamed about when he let his guard down. I wanted to understand the sadness I sometimes glimpsed behind his careful politeness. I wanted to be the person he turned to when the world felt too heavy to carry alone.

The intensity of these feelings frightened me. I'd never experienced anything remotely similar, had no framework for understanding what it meant to care this deeply about another person's happiness and well-being.

But beneath the fear was something else: a sense of rightness, of pieces falling into place that I hadn't even realized were scattered.

Whatever questions I had about Henry's background, whatever mysteries surrounded his knowledge and his materials, whatever implications my feelings might have for my understanding of myself—none of it changed the fundamental truth that had been building for weeks.

I was falling for him. Had fallen for him, perhaps, somewhere between that first conversation about Danish immigration patterns and tonight's revelation about Mikael's personal letters.

TOMORROW'S COURAGE

As the first hints of dawn began to lighten my window, I closed the notebook and set it aside. I hadn't answered any of my questions, hadn't resolved any of the mysteries that surrounded Henry or my own identity.

But I'd acknowledged something that felt like the beginning of truth: I wanted more than research collaboration. I wanted friendship, companionship, and possibly something deeper than I'd ever allowed myself to imagine.

The next time I saw Henry, I would find the courage to ask some of my questions. Not all of them—some truths had to be approached gradually. But I would start the conversation that might lead us both toward honesty.

Whatever that honesty might reveal.

As I finally drifted toward sleep, I carried with me the image of Henry's face when he'd looked at that photograph—vulnerable, longing, touched by a sadness that seemed to span years rather than moments.

Tomorrow, I would begin trying to understand why.

6
THE CHOICE TO TRUST

FLAT 7, 28 CADOGAN SQUARE, CHELSEA, LONDON SW1X 0JP

Aleksander (Henry) Nordh

Three days had passed since I'd given Soren those materials about Mikael, and I could feel the questions building in him like pressure behind a dam. He was too good a researcher, too intelligent, too naturally curious to let the inconsistencies slide much longer. During our meeting at the library yesterday, I'd caught him studying me when he thought I wasn't looking, his expression thoughtful in a way that made my centuries-old instincts scream warnings.

He was going to ask. Soon.

And for the first time in over two millennia, I was going to answer honestly.

The decision had been building since that sleepless night when I'd allowed myself to remember all the times I'd chosen safety over truth. But it crystallized this morning when I'd received an email from Soren suggesting we meet at my flat to examine some additional materials I'd mentioned.

"If you're comfortable having me in your space," he'd written, *"I'd love to see more of your family's collection. And perhaps we could talk more about some questions I've been having."*

Questions. The word carried weight that had nothing to do with academic inquiry.

I'd stared at that email for twenty minutes before responding with a simple: *"Of course. Six o'clock?"*

Now, as evening approached, I found myself preparing for a conversation that would either destroy the most meaningful connection I'd formed in over a century, or transform it into something deeper than I'd ever dared hope for.

PREPARING THE GROUND

I moved through my flat, seeing it as Soren would see it—looking for the telltale signs of a life that had lasted far longer than any human existence should allow. The books dating back centuries, carefully preserved but obviously aged. The artwork that should have been in museums. The small artifacts that spoke of travels across time as well as geography.

For decades, I'd been careful to display only items that could be explained away as family heirlooms or good reproductions. But tonight, I found myself leaving everything as it was. If I was going to trust Soren with the truth, I might as well trust him with all of it.

I paused before the glass case containing the Erikskrönikan, the medieval Swedish chronicle that had been one of my most prized possessions for over six centuries. No twenty-two-year-old graduate student could reasonably own such a thing. When Soren saw it—and he would, his scholar's eye caught everything—he would know that something fundamental about my story didn't add up.

Good. Let him ask. Let him push until I had no choice but to answer.

MEMORIES OF COURAGE FAILED

My reflection in the window showed the same face that had disappointed Mikael all those years ago. Young, careful, carrying secrets I'd been too afraid to share. How many times had he given me openings? How many opportunities had I squandered because I couldn't bring myself to trust in his love?

"Henrik, sometimes I feel like I know you completely, and other times like you're a stranger," he'd said one autumn evening as we walked along the Copenhagen harbor. *"As if there are parts of yourself you keep locked away where I can't reach them."*

I should have told him then. Should have found the words to explain what I was, what loving me would mean, what challenges we would face. Instead, I'd deflected with a joke about Danish reserve and changed the subject to his latest letter from his parents.

The memory of his disappointed expression still had the power to cut through me like a blade.

With Mikael, I'd convinced myself that honesty was cruelty—that burdening him with the truth of my nature would only make his inevitable departure more painful. I'd told myself I was protecting him by keeping my secrets, that he was better off loving an illusion than facing the impossible reality.

But the truth was simpler and more selfish: I'd been protecting myself. I'd been too afraid of seeing love turn to fear, too terrified of being rejected for what I truly was, too cowardly to give him the choice that was rightfully his.

I wouldn't make that mistake again.

SOREN'S ARRIVAL

The knock on my door came precisely at six o'clock, because Soren was nothing if not punctual. I opened it to find him standing in the hallway with that familiar combination of academic excitement and nervous energy that had become so dear to me.

"Good evening," I said, stepping aside to let him enter. "How was your day?"

"Productive," he replied, but there was something different in his manner. More focused, more purposeful. "I've been thinking about our conversation the other day, about the materials you've shared. I have some questions."

"I thought you might." I closed the door and turned to face him. "Would you like tea first, or shall we dive directly into whatever's on your mind?"

Soren set down his bag and looked around my flat with obvious curiosity. I watched his scholar's eye take in the details—the quality of the furnishings, the age of some of the books, the subtle signs of a life that didn't match the modest circumstances of a typical graduate student.

His gaze stopped on the medieval manuscript in its display case, and I saw the exact moment when academic recognition hit him.

"Soren," I said quietly, before he could ask the question I could see forming. "Before you examine anything else, before you ask any questions, I need you to know something important."

He turned to face me, and I could see both curiosity and concern in his expression.

"I'm going to tell you the truth," I continued. "All of it. But once I begin, once you hear what I have to say, everything between us will change. I need you to be certain you're ready for that."

THE MOMENT OF TRUTH

Soren studied my face with that direct, analytical gaze that had first drawn me to him. "Henry, what are you saying? You're scaring me a little."

"I'm saying that some truths are difficult to believe, and even more difficult to accept." I moved to the window, needing the slight distance to find my courage. "I'm saying that if you want to continue our research collaboration exactly as it has been, if you want to maintain the comfortable boundaries we've established, then perhaps you should leave now."

"Is this about your family? About how you came to have these materials?"

I turned back to him, seeing the genuine concern in his eyes, the willingness to listen despite his obvious confusion. This beautiful, brave young man who had stumbled into my carefully ordered existence and made me want things I'd given up hoping for.

"It's about everything," I said. "My family, yes. The materials, yes. But more than that. It's about who I am, what I am, and why I've been too afraid to trust you with the truth until now."

Soren sat down on my sofa, his expression serious but not frightened. "Whatever it is, Henry, you can tell me. I'm not going anywhere."

The simple faith in those words nearly undid me. Here was everything I'd wished for with Mikael but had been too cowardly to reach for. Here was trust offered freely, before it had even been earned.

I took a deep breath and made the choice that would change both our lives forever.

"My name is Aleksander Henrik Johan Nordh," I began. "And I'm not twenty-two years old. I'm not a graduate student. I'm not even remotely human in the way you understand humanity."

I watched his face carefully, ready to see confusion turn to disbelief, ready for the questions and challenges that would inevitably follow.

"I am what your world would call a vampire, though we prefer the term Elder. I was born over two thousand years ago. And everything I've told you about knowing your ancestor's story? It's all true. Because I was there. I knew Mikael personally."

The silence that followed felt like holding my breath underwater, waiting to see if I would surface or drown.

COURAGE AT LAST

"I loved him," I continued, the words coming easier now that I'd begun. "For four years in Copenhagen, we were together. Until I convinced him to leave for America, because I thought it was what was best for him. Because I was too afraid to tell him what I am, too cowardly to trust him with the truth I'm trusting you with now."

Soren sat perfectly still, his expression unreadable. I couldn't tell if he was processing my words or preparing to flee, but I'd come too far to stop now.

"I've spent 131 years regretting that choice," I said. "Regretting that I let fear make my decisions, that I chose safety over trust, that I never gave him the chance to make an informed choice about what loving me would mean."

I moved closer to the sofa, close enough to see the flecks of color in his eyes, close enough to memorize his face in case this was the last time I would see it.

"I won't make that mistake again, Soren. I won't insult your intelligence or your courage by hiding from you. Whatever this is between us, whatever it might become, it will be built on honesty. Complete honesty."

The words hung in the air between us, irreversible and terrifying and somehow liberating. After more than two millennia of careful secrets, I had finally chosen truth.

Now all that remained was to discover whether trust would be rewarded or if I had just destroyed the most precious thing to enter my life in over a century.

The next move was Soren's.

7
THE WEIGHT OF IMPOSSIBLE TRUTHS

FLAT 7, 28 CADOGAN SQUARE, CHELSEA, LONDON SW1X 0JP

Soren Jensen

I sat in Henry's—Aleksander's—flat, my mind reeling as I tried to process what he'd just told me. Vampire. Elder. Over two thousand years old. Loved my ancestor personally, intimately, in 1880s Copenhagen.

It should have been impossible. Everything I knew about reality, about the natural world, about the limitations of human existence, screamed that this was fantasy, delusion, some kind of elaborate joke.

But looking at his face—vulnerable, terrified, absolutely sincere—I knew he believed every word he was saying. The question was whether I could believe it too.

"Prove it," I said quietly, the words coming out before I could stop them.

"What?"

"If you're really what you say you are, prove it. Show me something that couldn't be explained any other way." I stood up abruptly, pacing to the window and back. "Because this is insane, Aleksander. People don't live for two thousand years. Vampires—Elders—whatever you want to call them, they don't exist. This has to be some kind of... of elaborate fantasy, or joke, or..."

I trailed off, seeing something flicker across his expression—not offense or anger, but understanding. He reached for his wallet with deliberate slowness, as if giving me time to stop him if I wanted to.

"Those things could be explained away, couldn't they?" he said, easily explaining enhanced abilities or historical knowledge. "Exceptional genetics, photographic memory, extensive study."

He pulled out a worn piece of paper and held it out to me. "This can't be."

THE PHOTOGRAPH

I took the paper with hands that had begun to tremble slightly. It was an old photograph, obviously aged but carefully preserved, the kind of formal portrait that was common in the late 19th century.

As I looked closer, my breath caught.

There was Mikael—unmistakably my great-great-great-grandfather, though younger than in any photograph I'd seen before. He was genuinely happy in this image, laughing with an openness and joy that transformed his entire face. But it wasn't just seeing Mikael that made my heart race.

Standing beside him, as close as lovers, was Aleksander.

Not someone who looked like Aleksander. Not a relative or ancestor who bore a family resemblance. It was unmistakably him—the same face that sat across from me now, unchanged by time. The same dark hair, the same sharp cheekbones, the same gold-flecked eyes that were looking at me with nervous anticipation.

In the photograph, he was smiling with a joy so radiant it took my breath away, as if he'd allowed himself to be completely vulnerable and happy for just that moment.

"I don't understand," I whispered, staring at the image. "This is impossible."

"I love you," Aleksander said softly.

I jolted, looking up from the photograph. "What?"

"That's what I said just before the photographer snapped the shutter," he explained, his voice gentle and full of memory. "It made Mikael startle, as I knew it would. He always laughed when he was surprised—it was a trait he had."

Something clicked in my mind. When someone startled me, I didn't yelp or scream like most people. I laughed. It was such a small, specific detail, but...

"I wanted something to remember him by before he left," Aleksander continued, his voice growing tender. "Something to prove to myself that we'd been happy, even if it couldn't last."

THE WEIGHT OF TRUTH

I stared at the photograph, then back at Aleksander, my entire worldview crumbling and rebuilding itself around this impossible evidence. The level of detail in the image, the authentic aging of the paper, the expression on Mikael's face—this wasn't something that could be faked or staged.

This was real.

Which meant everything Aleksander had told me was real.

"My God," I breathed. "You're actually telling the truth."

"Yes."

The simple confirmation hit me like a physical blow. Not painful, but overwhelming in its finality. There was no going back from this moment, no returning to the comfortable certainty of a world where vampires were fiction and the supernatural was safely contained in books and movies.

I need..." I started, then stopped, my voice catching. The photograph trembled in my hands as the magnitude of what I was holding—what I was learning—crashed over me. "I need some air. I need to walk. I need to think."

Something flickered across Aleksander's face—fear, disappointment, the look of someone who'd gambled everything and wasn't sure if they'd won or lost.

"Of course," he said carefully. "I understand if this is too much. If you need time to—"

"No," I interrupted, standing abruptly but still clutching the photograph. "I mean, yes, I need time. But not... I'm not running away. I'm not abandoning this. I just need to process what you've told me, and I can't do that sitting here looking at you."

The relief in his expression was palpable, though worry still creased his features.

"How long do you need?"

"I don't know. A few hours? Maybe overnight?" I looked down at the photograph again—at Mikael's joyful surprise, at Aleksander's unguarded love—and felt something fundamental shift inside me. "Can I... will you be here tomorrow? Can we talk more tomorrow?"

"I'll be wherever you need me to be," he said simply.

I started to hand the photograph back to him, but Aleksander gently closed my fingers around it.

"Keep it," he said softly. "I want you to have it while you think. Just…" he paused, his eyes glazed looking as if he was surrounding the very lifeblood of his existence.

I stared at him, understanding the magnitude of what he was entrusting to me. This wasn't just a photograph—it was his most precious possession, a piece of his heart preserved across more than a century.

"Are you sure?" I whispered.

"I'm sure. I… I trust you with it, Soren. I trust you with all of it."

I carefully slipped the photograph into my wallet, feeling its weight like a sacred responsibility.

"Thank you," I said quietly. "For trusting me with this. For trusting me with the truth."

"Thank you for listening," he replied. "For not running immediately."

WALKING THE NIGHT

London at midnight was a different city—quieter, more intimate, filled with shadows that seemed to hold secrets of their own. I walked without destination, letting my feet carry me through neighborhoods I barely recognized while my mind wrestled with revelations that challenged everything I thought I knew about the world.

Aleksander was an Elder. A vampire, though apparently that was considered a derogatory term. He'd been alive for over two millennia, had witnessed the rise and fall of empires, had loved my great-great-great-grandfather in Copenhagen over 130 years ago.

The photograph had been the final piece of evidence, the proof that made denial impossible. I'd seen Mikael's face in enough family pictures to recognize him instantly, but I'd never seen him look so radiantly happy. And I'd never seen any evidence that he'd had a relationship like the one that photograph captured —intimate, joyful, deeply loving.

But it wasn't just the historical impossibility that had my mind reeling. It was the personal implications, the growing awareness that my confused feelings about Henry—about Aleksander—were becoming something I could no longer ignore or rationalize away.

I was attracted to him. Had been attracted to him for weeks, though I'd barely been able to admit it to myself. And learning the truth about what he was hadn't changed that—if anything, it had intensified my fascination.

Which raised questions about myself that I wasn't sure I was ready to confront.

IDENTITY IN CONTEXT

I found myself on a bench in Russell Square, surrounded by the sleeping city, trying to sort through layers of revelation that went far beyond the supernatural.

All through university, while my classmates discussed relationships and dating, I'd remained on the periphery. I'd told myself it was because I was more serious, more focused on my goals. But sitting here in the dark, I had to confront the possibility that I'd been avoiding something fundamental about myself.

I'd never been genuinely attracted to women. Not really. With Sarah and Emma, I'd gone through the motions because it seemed like what I was supposed to do—I could recognize they were beautiful, could appreciate attractiveness in an aesthetic sense, but I'd never felt the pull my male friends described when they talked about desire. I'd never experienced that magnetic draw, that physical yearning, that sense of needing to be close to someone.

I'd told myself it was because I was more cerebral, more focused on intellectual connection than physical attraction. But the truth was simpler: I'd been following a script for a relationship I didn't actually want, trying to feel something that was never going to develop.

With Aleksander, I felt all the things I'd never experienced before. The nervous excitement when we made plans to meet. The way my heart rate increased when he smiled at me. The moments when conversation flowed so easily that hours passed without notice. The growing desire to know more about him as a person, not just as a research collaborator.

And now, learning that he was something beyond human experience, that he'd loved my ancestor over a century ago, that he'd trusted me with secrets he'd kept for millennia—it only made him more fascinating, not less.

THE WEIGHT OF TRUST

As the hours passed and my initial shock began to settle, what struck me most was not what Aleksander was, but what he'd chosen to do.

He'd trusted me. After over two thousand years of keeping secrets, after losing Mikael to his own fear of revelation, he'd chosen to be honest with me. He'd gambled his safety, his carefully constructed identity, his emotional well-being on the belief that I could handle the truth.

That trust felt heavier than any supernatural revelation. It was a gift I wasn't sure I deserved but one I was determined to prove worthy of.

I thought about my own struggles with identity, my confusion about attraction and relationships, my sense of being somehow displaced among my peers. Those challenges seemed small now compared to the isolation Aleksander must have experienced across centuries of human connections that could never be fully honest.

The photograph had shown me something precious—evidence of love that had been real and deep and joyful, even if it couldn't last. If Aleksander could find that kind of connection once, perhaps he could find it again.

Perhaps we could find it together.

DAWN REALIZATIONS

As sunrise would soon begin to lighten the London sky, I made my way back toward Aleksander's flat with a clarity I hadn't possessed when I'd fled into the night.

He was right that everything between us would change. But not in the way he feared.

I'd spent my adult life feeling like I was watching other people live while I remained safely on the sidelines, too cautious or too confused to fully engage with my own emotions. Meeting Aleksander had begun to change that—had made me want things I'd never allowed myself to want, feel things I'd never experienced.

Learning the truth about what he was only intensified those feelings. Here was someone who'd chosen to trust me with his deepest secrets, who'd risked everything for the possibility of honest connection, who'd seen something in me worth that extraordinary gamble.

I might be young and inexperienced and still figuring out basic things about my own identity. But I knew what it felt like to care about someone's happiness more than my own comfort. I knew what it meant to want to be the person someone could trust with their vulnerabilities.

And I knew, with surprising certainty, that whatever challenges lay ahead for us, I wanted to face them together, no matter how crazy that sounded. I wasn't even sure it was a good idea, myself, but my heart tugged me along as I walked the steps in the night air.

RETURNING

I stood outside Aleksander's building as the city would soon awaken around me, gathering courage for a conversation that would define the rest of both our lives. Whatever fears or uncertainties I carried, whatever questions still needed answers, one truth had emerged from my night of walking and thinking.

I was falling in love with him. Had been falling in love with him for weeks, perhaps since that first conversation about Danish immigration patterns. Learning about his supernatural nature didn't change that—if anything, it explained the depth of connection I'd felt, the sense that he understood something about isolation and longing that matched my own experience.

The practical challenges were enormous. The gap in our experience was vast. The implications for any future we might build together were complex beyond anything I'd ever imagined.

But for the first time in my life, I was ready to choose courage over safety, truth over comfort, love over fear.

I climbed the stairs to his flat and knocked softly on the door, ready to begin the next chapter of whatever impossible story we were writing together.

Ready to prove that his trust in me hadn't been misplaced.

Ready to discover what love looked like when it was built on complete honesty from the very beginning.

The door opened, and Aleksander's face—ancient, beautiful, filled with nervous hope—reminded me that some things were worth any risk.

"I have questions," I said, stepping inside. "So many questions. But first, I need you to know that I'm here. I'm staying. And I want to understand everything."

But…" I paused to catch my breath.

"Yes?"

"I'm terrified."

8
THE MIRRORS TRUTH

FLAT 7, 28 CADOGAN SQUARE, CHELSEA, LONDON SW1X 0JP

Aleksander (Henry) Nordh

I stood before the ornate mirror above my fireplace mantle, studying my reflection with the kind of critical assessment I hadn't indulged in for decades. The glass showed exactly what any human would see—a young man of twenty-two with pale skin, dark hair, and eyes that carried perhaps more weight than his apparent years would suggest. No mysterious absence, no supernatural void. Just another ridiculous myth perpetuated by gothic novels and penny dreadfuls.

But the face looking back at me was the same one that had gazed out from this mirror for over two millennia, unchanged by time, unmarked by the centuries that should have aged me into dust. Tonight, however, something was different. There was a vulnerability in my expression that I hadn't seen since...

Since Copenhagen. Since Mikael.

What have you done?

The question echoed in my mind as I turned away from my reflection, unable to bear the weight of what I'd just risked. For the first time in over two thousand years, I had told another living soul the complete truth about what I was. I had handed Soren that photograph—my most precious possession—and watched his world crumble and rebuild itself around impossible revelations.

And then he had left to think.

. . .

THE WEIGHT OF TRUTH

I moved to the window overlooking the London street below, my hands gripping the sill as I tried to steady myself. The evening was quiet, most of my neighbors settling in for the night, unaware that one of their number was wrestling with questions that spanned millennia.

Had I made the right choice? For weeks, I had agonized over whether to trust Soren with the truth, weighing my growing feelings for him against centuries of careful self-preservation. The decision to reveal myself had felt inevitable, necessary, the only path forward that honored what was building between us.

But watching him walk away after seeing the photograph clutched in his hands, seeing the overwhelm in his eyes despite his promise to return, I wondered if I had just repeated my greatest mistake in a different form.

THE COPENHAGEN PARALLEL

I had been so careful for centuries before Mikael. So disciplined in my interactions with humans, treating them as temporary companions in an existence that stretched far beyond their brief lives. I had learned early that attachment led only to pain—watching those you cared for age and die while you remained unchanged was a torment I had endured too many times in my youth.

But then came Copenhagen, and the sixteen-year-old Swedish boy who had looked lost and determined in equal measure as he searched for lodging in the international quarter. I had told myself I was simply being helpful, offering guidance to a fellow Scandinavian in a foreign city. Nothing more than common courtesy.

The lie had unraveled within weeks.

Mikael had possessed something I hadn't encountered in centuries of human interaction—a combination of earnest curiosity and genuine kindness that drew me in despite every instinct screaming warnings. His questions about Danish culture weren't mere politeness; he genuinely wanted to understand, to adapt, to become part of something larger than himself. His gratitude for small gestures wasn't calculated; he truly appreciated help when offered.

And when he smiled—that rare, unguarded expression that transformed his entire face—I felt something I had thought lost forever. Hope. Connection.

. . .

DANGEROUS TERRITORY

With Soren, I was walking that same dangerous territory. Worse, perhaps, because this time I knew exactly what I was risking. The pain of losing Mikael had nearly destroyed me. The decades following his death had been an exercise in careful numbness, in never allowing myself to care too deeply about any mortal soul.

Yet here I was, having just revealed everything to his descendant, a twenty-four-year-old graduate student whose intelligence and quiet strength reminded me why I had fallen for his ancestor in the first place.

The photograph I had given him wasn't just evidence of past love—it was my most treasured possession, the only tangible proof I possessed that love had once been real, honest, and mutual. Letting it leave my flat, watching Soren carry it away like a talisman, felt like handing over my heart on a silver platter.

But perhaps that was exactly what I had done.

THE GIFT AND THE CURSE

I returned to the mirror, studying my face once more. The vulnerability was still there, more pronounced now in the aftermath of complete honesty. For over two millennia, I had been careful never to show this much of myself to anyone.

The symbolic weight of that gesture hadn't been lost on me even as I'd revealed my true identity without saying a word. I was giving away my past to make room for a potential future.

But had I been wise to do so? Or had I just handed over the most precious thing I possessed to someone who might decide he wanted no part of the impossible story it represented?

The image was burned into my memory regardless—Mikael's delighted surprise, my own unguarded joy, the moment when love had been declared and captured forever. But having Soren hold that physical proof, seeing him understand what it meant, had felt like a bridge between past and present that might finally allow me to stop living in memory and start building new experiences worth treasuring.

If he came back.

WAITING

The hours stretched ahead like a chasm I couldn't cross. Soren had said he needed time to think, that he would return tomorrow for more conversation. But promises made in moments of shock and overwhelm weren't always kept when the full weight of reality settled in.

I had lived through enough human lifetimes to know how easily good intentions could crumble under the pressure of impossible circumstances.

Still, something about Soren's response gave me hope. He hadn't fled in terror or disgust. He hadn't demanded proof I couldn't provide or dismissed my revelations as fantasy. He had asked for time to process, which suggested he was taking everything seriously enough to consider rather than simply reject.

And he had handled that photograph with such reverence, such understanding of what it represented, that I couldn't help but believe he grasped the magnitude of what I was sharing with him.

THE MIRROR'S REFLECTION

I returned to the mirror, studying my face once more in the lamplight. The vulnerability was still there, more pronounced now in the aftermath of complete honesty. For over two millennia, I had been careful never to show this much of myself to anyone.

But perhaps that was exactly what had been wrong with my approach all along. Perhaps the careful distance I'd maintained, the protective barriers I'd constructed, had been less about safety and more about fear. Fear of rejection, fear of loss, fear of the kind of pain that came from allowing someone else to matter too much.

With Soren, I had chosen courage over caution. Whatever happened next, at least I would know I had tried. At least I would know I had given love—real, honest, complete love—a chance to flourish without the poison of deception.

DAWN APPROACHING

As the first hints of dawn began to lighten the London sky, I realized I had been standing vigil all night, wrestling with fears and hopes in equal measure. Whatever Soren decided, whatever choice he made about the impossible future I had offered him, I would face it with the same honesty I had finally found the courage to give him.

The mirror showed me the same face that had gazed back for centuries, but something fundamental had changed. I was no longer hiding. I was no longer performing a careful dance of partial truths and managed revelations.

For the first time in over two thousand years, I was simply myself, vulnerable and exposed and waiting for love to decide whether I was worth the risk.

9
QUESTIONS IN THE FIRELIGHT

FLAT 7, 28 CADOGAN SQUARE, CHELSEA, LONDON SW1X 0JP

Soren Jensen

I returned to Aleksander's flat as dawn broke over London, my night of walking through the city's quiet streets having clarified something essential: learning about his supernatural nature hadn't changed how I felt about him. If anything, it explained the magnetic pull I'd been fighting for weeks, the sense of recognition that had struck me from our first conversation. But I admit I should have been quaking in my boots, afraid of what this meant.

When he opened the door, the relief in his eyes was unmistakable. Whatever fears he'd wrestled with during our separation, my presence answered at least one of them.

"I wasn't sure you'd come back," he said quietly, stepping aside to let me in.

"I told you I would," I replied, meeting his gaze directly. "I may be new to this, but I keep my promises."

The flat felt different now—no longer the carefully curated space of someone performing humanity, but a genuine sanctuary where he could simply be himself. I moved toward the fireplace where flames cast dancing shadows across walls lined with books, feeling the weight of everything that had changed between us since his revelation.

ACCEPTING THE IMPOSSIBLE

"How are you feeling?" Aleksander asked, settling onto the settee beside me.

Not too close, not too distant—giving me space to process while making his presence available.

"Overwhelmed," I admitted, wrapping my hands around the warm teacup he'd given me. "But not in the way you might expect. It's more like... everything finally makes sense."

His eyebrows rose slightly. "Makes sense how?"

"The way you sometimes seemed to know exactly what I was thinking. How you'd reference historical events with the kind of detail that felt like personal memory. The way you looked at me sometimes, like you were seeing someone else entirely." I paused, considering. "And the way being around you felt like coming home to something I didn't know I'd been missing."

THE MANUSCRIPT DISCOVERY

My eyes drifted around the room as I organized my thoughts, and that's when I saw it properly for the first time. Displayed in a glass case near the window, illuminated by subtle lighting that suggested its importance, was what I now knew to be a genuine medieval manuscript. The calligraphy was exquisite, the illuminated letters still vibrant after what must have been centuries.

But it was the title page that made my breath catch with new understanding.

The Erikskrönikan.

I knew that name. Every student of Scandinavian history knew that name. The Chronicle of Erik—one of the most important medieval Swedish texts, chronicling the reign of King Erik Menved in the early 14th century. Before yesterday, I would have assumed this was an impossible reproduction. Now...

"The manuscript," I said, nodding toward the display case. "The Erikskrönikan. You actually own an original."

Aleksander followed my gaze, and something shifted in his expression—no longer the careful surprise of someone caught with an impossible possession, but the quiet pride of a collector showing his treasures.

"I do," he said simply. "I acquired it in 1387, directly from the scriptorium where it was created. The monk who illuminated those letters... Brother Matthias... he was quite proud of his work."

The casual way he spoke about acquiring it over six centuries ago, about knowing the actual illuminator, sent electricity through me. This wasn't just academic knowledge—this was personal history.

"You were there," I said, still trying to wrap my mind around what that meant. "You witnessed the events it chronicles."

"Some of them. Erik Menved was... a complex ruler. History has been kinder to him than his contemporaries were." Aleksander's expression grew distant with memory. "I spent several years at his court. The political intrigues were fascinating, though exhausting."

. . .

PERSONAL QUESTIONS

"Tell me about your childhood," I said, settling back with my tea. "I mean, if you age so slowly, how did that work? Did you have playmates? Go to school?"

Aleksander's smile was both warm and wistful. "My early years were quite different from human childhood. I was born in a small Elder community in what you'd now call northern Lapland. We lived separately from human settlements, so my 'playmates' were other Elder children who aged at similar rates."

"How slowly do you age exactly?"

"In my first century, I aged perhaps one year for every ten that passed. So when I appeared to be ten years old, I was actually approaching my hundredth birthday. The rate slows even further as we mature—now I might age one year for every hundred."

I tried to wrap my mind around that. "So when did you first live among humans?"

"When I appeared to be around fourteen or fifteen, though I was already over two centuries old. That's when I began learning to navigate human society." His expression grew more serious. "It was... challenging. Especially in ancient times, when life was more communal and strangers were viewed with suspicion."

"How did you manage it?"

"Carefully constructed stories about being an orphan, or the ward of distant relatives. I became quite skilled at appearing older than I looked, at mimicking the mannerisms of maturity. And when questions became too persistent, I would simply disappear and reinvent myself elsewhere."

REVEALING ANCIENT LOVE

"Alek," I said, settling back against the cushions with my wine, "can I ask you something personal?"

"Everything we discuss is personal now," he replied with a slight smile.

"When you mentioned loving someone before Mikael... what was that like? I mean, what was love like centuries ago?"

His expression grew distant, and suddenly I could see the weight of millennia in his eyes—not the careful performance of someone playing at being older, but the genuine depth of someone who had lived through ages I could barely comprehend.

"Augustin," he said softly, and the way he spoke the name—with tender reverence, as if it were something precious he'd kept locked away—made me understand that this wasn't just memory, but cherished experience preserved across centuries.

"He was... luminous," Aleksander continued, his voice taking on a quality I'd never heard before—wistful, almost dreamy. "We met in the monastery scriptorium during the winter of 782. I was posing as an orphan ward, though I was already over a millennium old. He was barely seventeen, a novice monk with the most incredible hands."

The detail was staggering. Not the broad strokes someone might remember about a past relationship, but the tiny, intimate observations that only came from being completely, helplessly in love.

"His fingers," Aleksander said, unconsciously tracing patterns in the air as he spoke, "were long and elegant, stained permanently with ink from his work copying manuscripts. When he was concentrating on particularly difficult passages, he would bite his lower lip just slightly, and this tiny crease would appear between his eyebrows."

I felt my throat tighten. This wasn't someone remembering an old boyfriend. This was someone reliving a love so profound that twelve centuries hadn't dimmed the clarity of his memory.

"He had this habit of humming while he worked," Aleksander continued, lost in recollection. "Not hymns, but these little melodies he'd make up—different tunes for different manuscripts, as if each text deserved its own music. On cold mornings, when the scriptorium was nearly freezing, I would position myself close enough to hear him humming and feel the warmth from his body."

THE WEIGHT OF TIME

I watched, fascinated but, I admit with something like jealousy, as Aleksander's entire demeanor transformed. The careful control he usually maintained melted away, replaced by the expression of someone allowing himself to remember perfect happiness.

"We would work side by side for hours," he said, his voice growing softer. "I was supposedly helping with simpler copying tasks, but really I was just finding excuses to be near him. He would explain the meaning behind illuminated letters, describe the significance of different pigments, share stories about the texts we were preserving."

The love in his voice was unmistakable—not the fond remembrance of something long past, but the kind of aching tenderness that suggested the feelings themselves were as fresh as if they'd happened yesterday.

"What did he look like?" I asked, though I wasn't sure I wanted to know.

"Beautiful," Aleksander said immediately. "Not in an obvious way—he was quite plain, actually, by conventional standards. But when he smiled, his entire face transformed. He had these green eyes that seemed to hold all the warmth missing from those cold stone walls, and when he laughed..." Aleksander paused, smiling at something I couldn't see. "When he laughed, it was like church bells, bright and clear and absolutely joyous."

THE IMPOSSIBLE SITUATION

The matter-of-fact way he described these details—the kind of minute observations that only lovers noticed—hit me with unexpected force. This wasn't ancient history to him. This was vivid, living memory of someone who had meant everything.

"How long were you together?" I managed to ask.

"Three seasons," he said. "From that first winter until the autumn of 784. Not long by my standards, but it was... everything, while it lasted."

"What happened?"

Aleksander's expression darkened. "The same thing that always happened. I appeared to be perhaps ten years old, despite being over a millennium. Augustin was seventeen, and what we felt for each other—what we were to each other—would have been seen as..." He trailed off, the pain still evident after all these centuries.

"You had to leave," I said quietly.

"I had to leave," he confirmed. "But worse than that, I had to let him believe he was somehow... corrupted. That what he felt was wrong. I couldn't tell him the truth about what I was, couldn't explain that the boy he loved actually carried the mind and heart of someone ancient enough to understand exactly what we meant to each other."

LIVING MEMORIES

I stared at him, overwhelmed by the realization of what I was witnessing. This wasn't someone telling stories about their past—this was someone whose every romantic experience was preserved in perfect detail, carried forward across centuries like treasures too precious to let fade.

"You remember everything," I said, and it wasn't a question.

"Everything," he confirmed. "The way he smelled like honey and parchment when he kissed my cheek in the empty scriptorium after Compline prayers. The sound he made when I touched him. The way he whispered my name—the name I was using then—like it was a sonnet he wasn't supposed to know."

The intimacy of these details, preserved across twelve centuries with crystalline clarity, made me understand something fundamental about what loving Aleksander meant. Every touch, every word, every moment of tenderness would become part of an eternal collection. Nothing would be forgotten. Nothing would fade.

"How do you bear it?" I asked, the question coming out smaller than I intended.

He looked at me directly then, and I saw not just the pain of loss but the terrible weight of perfect memory.

"You learn that love is worth the pain of losing it," he said quietly. "And you hope—perhaps foolishly—that someday you'll find someone who understands that the weight of that memory is also its gift."

. . .

UNDERSTANDING

The silence stretched between us, heavy with newfound understanding. I was beginning to grasp the true scope of what Aleksander carried—not just years of experience, but centuries of love preserved in perfect detail. Every relationship he'd ever had was still vivid, still present, still part of who he was.

"That's..." I struggled for words. "That's incredible. And terrifying."

"Which part?"

"All of it. The depth of what you're capable of feeling. The way you preserve every detail. The fact that nothing ever really ends for you—it all just becomes part of this vast collection of memory."

Aleksander nodded slowly. "It can be overwhelming, even for me sometimes. But it's also what makes each connection precious. When you know you'll remember everything forever, you pay attention differently."

I looked at him—really looked at him—and saw not just the man I was growing to care about, but the repository of centuries of human experience, love, and loss. The scope of it was almost incomprehensible.

"I'm starting to understand," I said finally, "what it means to be with someone who has lived as long as you have."

"And does that understanding change anything for you?"

I considered the question seriously. Did it change things? Knowing that every moment between us would be preserved with crystalline clarity for centuries to come? Knowing that I was entering into something with someone whose capacity for memory—and therefore for love—was so vast?

"Yes," I said honestly. "But not in the way you might think."

"How then?"

"It makes me want to be worthy of remembering."

Aleksander's smile was gentle, approving. "That," he said, "is exactly the right thing to want."

Aleksander Nordh

GROWING ATTRACTION

As the evening progressed, I found myself watching the way firelight played across Soren's features, highlighting the strong line of his jaw, the intelligence in his eyes. He had shed his nervous energy from the previous day, replaced by a quiet confidence that I found increasingly attractive.

"Aleksander," he said, and the way he used my real name sent warmth through me. "Can I ask you something… else?"

I acknowledged with a slight smile.

"When you told me about Mikael yesterday, you mentioned that you loved him. But you also said you'd been hiding parts of yourself even then." He paused, considering his words. "What would it be like to love someone without hiding anything?"

The question hung in the air between us, loaded with implications neither of us was quite ready to voice directly.

"I don't know," I admitted. "I've never had the opportunity to find out."

SOREN'S REVELATION

"I think I want to find out," Soren said quietly, his eyes meeting mine across the small space between us. "With you."

The directness of his statement caught me off guard. This wasn't the uncertain graduate student I'd been carefully guiding through revelations. This was a man who had considered his options and made a choice.

"Soren..."

"I know what you're thinking," he continued. "I'm young compared to you. I'm inexperienced. I'm probably in over my head." He leaned forward slightly. "But I'm also twenty-four years old, not sixteen. I've made mistakes before, and I've learned from them. I know what it feels like to want someone I can't have."

THE CONFESSION

"You've been in relationships before," I observed, noting the certainty in his voice.

"A few. With women." He didn't look embarrassed by the admission. "I thought something was wrong with me for the longest time. I could go through all the motions, could care about them as people, but there was always something missing. A spark, a connection, something that made it feel... real."

I nodded, understanding more than he probably realized.

"It wasn't until I met you that I understood what I'd been missing," he continued. "And it wasn't until yesterday that I understood why I'd never felt that spark with anyone else."

His honesty deserved mine in return. "What do you want from me, Soren?"

"I want to know you," he said simply. "The real you, not the careful version you show the world. I want to understand what two thousand years of experiences have taught you. I want to learn what it means to love someone without reservation."

He paused, his eyes steady on mine. "And I want you to know me. Not as Mikael's descendant, not as some echo of your past, but as myself."

THE SHIFT

Something fundamental shifted between us in that moment. The careful distance we'd been maintaining dissolved, replaced by recognition of mutual attraction and intent. When I reached across the space between us to touch his face, he didn't pull away. Instead, he leaned into the contact, his eyes closing briefly.

"Are you certain?" I asked. "Because once we cross this line, there's no going back to careful friendship."

"I've never been more certain of anything in my life," he replied, his hand coming up to cover mine where it rested against his cheek.

THE KISS

When our lips met, it was with none of the tentative exploration of first love. This was the kiss of two adults who had considered the implications and chosen connection over safety. Soren's mouth was warm and confident, his hands sure as they pulled me closer.

When we broke apart, both breathing harder, the last barriers between us had crumbled.

"I should probably mention," Soren said, his voice slightly rough, "that I'm a very quick learner."

I laughed, the sound rich with anticipation and desire. "I was counting on that."

MUTUAL RECOGNITION

As we settled back into comfortable proximity—his body warm against mine, my arm around his shoulders—I marveled at how natural this felt. Not the careful choreography of seduction, but the easy intimacy of two people who had found something worth keeping.

"Aleksander?" Soren said, his voice soft in the firelight.

"Yes?"

"Thank you for trusting me with the truth. All of it."

"Thank you," I replied, pressing a kiss to the top of his head, "for making it worth the risk."

Outside, London settled into another night, but inside my flat, something new was beginning. Something built on honesty, mutual desire, and the kind of love that could bridge any gap—even the one between mortal and immortal hearts.

For the first time in 131 years, I was no longer alone with my memories. And for the first time ever, I was building new memories worth preserving alongside the old.

10
THE FIRST MEMORY

FLAT 7, 28 CADOGAN SQUARE, CHELSEA, LONDON SW1X 0JP

Soren Jensen

I woke slowly, consciousness returning in gentle waves that brought with them the gradual awareness that everything in my world had changed overnight. The bed was unfamiliar—larger and more comfortable than my narrow single in Bloomsbury—and there was warmth pressed against my back, an arm draped over my waist with casual intimacy that should have felt strange but somehow felt perfectly right.

Aleksander.

The events of the previous evening came flooding back: his revelation about what he truly was, my night of walking and processing, our marathon conversation that had stretched until dawn, and finally—most importantly—the moment when we'd stopped talking and started discovering what it felt like to be completely honest with each other.

I was still wearing yesterday's clothes—wrinkled now from sleep, but I'd been too emotionally exhausted to care about changing when we'd finally collapsed into bed together. My wallet lay on the bedside table where I'd carefully placed it before sleep, and through the leather I could feel the outline of the photograph Aleksander had entrusted to me.

Carefully, so as not to wake him, I reached for my wallet and withdrew the precious image. In the soft morning light filtering through his curtains, I studied it with new eyes—this proof of love that had sustained him through 131 years of loneliness, now passed to me as a bridge between past and present.

. . .

Aleksander Nordh

I had been awake for nearly an hour, content to lie still and listen to the steady rhythm of Soren's breathing while my mind marveled at the impossibility of this moment. For the first time in 131 years, I was sharing a bed with someone who knew exactly what I was. No careful disguises, no elaborate backstories, no constant vigilance about what I might accidentally reveal. Just honesty, acceptance, and the overwhelming relief of being truly known.

When Soren stirred and reached for something in his wallet, I remained motionless, giving him the privacy to process whatever thoughts were occupying his mind. Through my enhanced senses, I could detect the subtle changes in his heartbeat and breathing that suggested deep contemplation rather than distress.

"Good morning," I said softly when I felt him settle back against me.

"Morning," he replied, his voice still thick with sleep. "How long have you been awake?"

"A while. I don't require as much sleep as humans, but I didn't want to disturb you." I pressed a gentle kiss to the back of his neck. "You were thinking quite intently about something."

PROCESSING IN DAYLIGHT

I turned in his arms so I could see his face, struck again by how young he appeared despite carrying over two millennia of experience. In the morning light, the impossibility of what he'd told me seemed both more and less believable—more because I could see the weight of centuries in his eyes, less because he looked so perfectly normal lying beside me.

"I was looking at the photograph," I admitted, showing him the image. "Trying to understand how it all connects—Mikael, you, me, this moment right now."

"And what conclusions did you reach?"

I studied the picture again—Mikael's delighted surprise, Aleksander's radiant joy, the moment when love had been declared and captured forever. "I think I understand why you kept it all these years. It's not just evidence of what happened, it's proof that love like this is possible."

Aleksander Nordh

The maturity of his observation took my breath away. Here was someone who could look at impossible circumstances and find meaning rather than just impossibility.

"And do you believe it's possible?" I asked carefully. "For us, I mean?"

Soren was quiet for a moment, his fingers tracing the edge of the photograph. "Yesterday I would have said I didn't know what love felt like, that I'd never experienced anything that might qualify. But looking at this picture, seeing the way you looked at him, the way he looked at you..." He met my eyes. "I think I'm beginning to understand."

"What are you beginning to understand?"

"That what I've been feeling for you—the way my heart races when you smile, the way I've been thinking about you constantly, the way being near you feels like coming home to a place I've never been before—that might actually be love."

FIRST MORNING INTIMACIES

The confession hung between us like a bridge I'd finally found the courage to cross. Aleksander's expression shifted, becoming softer and more vulnerable than I'd ever seen it.

"It might be," he agreed quietly. "Though I should warn you—I'm not exactly an expert at recognizing it when it's happening to me rather than just being remembered from the past."

I laughed, feeling some of the tension ease. "Well, that makes two of us, then. Though I have to ask—is it always this overwhelming? Because I feel like my entire understanding of myself has shifted in the past twenty-four hours."

"The good news," Aleksander said, his hand finding mine beneath the covers, "is that we have time to figure it out. No pressure, no urgency, just... discovery."

"Time," I repeated, testing the word. "You really do have all the time in the world, don't you?"

"We do," he corrected gently. "For as long as you want to be part of this story."

PRACTICAL MORNING CONCERNS

The reminder of practical reality began to intrude on our intimate bubble. "I should probably head back to my flat at some point," I said reluctantly. "I have classes this afternoon, and my flatmates will start to worry if I disappear without explanation."

"Of course," Aleksander agreed, though I could see his own reluctance to end this perfect morning. "Though perhaps we could have breakfast first? I make excellent coffee, and I'd like to hear more about these classes of yours."

The casual domesticity of the suggestion—sharing breakfast, discussing my daily routine—felt both thrilling and terrifying. This was what normal couples did, wasn't it? Woke up together, shared meals, integrated their lives in small, meaningful ways.

Except nothing about our situation was normal.

Aleksander Nordh

I could see Soren wrestling with the implications of what we were becoming, trying to navigate the gap between the extraordinary circumstances of our relationship and his desire for something that felt genuine and sustainable.

"Soren," I said gently, "we don't have to figure everything out this morning. We can take this as slowly as you need, let it develop naturally."

"I know," he replied. "It's just... I've never done this before. Any of this. Waking up with someone, feeling this way about another person, trying to balance a relationship with everything else in my life."

"Neither have I," I admitted. "Not like this. Not with complete honesty from the beginning."

NEW BEGINNINGS

Something about his admission—that this was new territory for him too, despite his vast experience—made me feel less alone in my uncertainty. We were both learning, both making it up as we went along.

"So what do we do now?" I asked. "I mean, practically speaking. Do we tell people we're dating? Do we keep meeting for research? Do we pretend to be something we're not when we're around others?"

Aleksander considered this seriously. "What would you like to do?"

"I'd like to be honest," I said, surprising myself with the certainty in my voice. "Not about what you are—that's your secret to share or not share. But about us. About the fact that you're not just my research collaborator anymore."

"You're certain? It would mean acknowledging that you're gay, if you haven't done that publicly before."

The word hung in the air between us, and I realized that somewhere in the past twenty-four hours, I'd stopped questioning that part of my identity. Looking at Aleksander, feeling what I felt for him, the label seemed less important than the reality.

"I'm certain," I said. "Whatever I am, whoever I am, it includes loving you. And I don't want to hide that."

. . .

COFFEE AND CONVERSATION

Aleksander Nordh

Twenty minutes later, we were sitting at my small kitchen table, sharing coffee and the kind of comfortable morning conversation that felt remarkably normal despite the extraordinary circumstances. Soren had borrowed one of my shirts—slightly too small for his tall frame but somehow perfect nonetheless—and was telling me about his upcoming seminars with an enthusiasm that reminded me why I'd fallen for his academic passion in the first place.

"Professor Williams wants us to present our preliminary research findings next week," he was saying. "I'm thinking about focusing on the materials you've shared—though obviously I'll need to be creative about citing my sources."

"How creative?"

"'Private family collection' should suffice," he said with a grin. "Unless you'd prefer 'ancient supernatural boyfriend with impossible memory and extensive archives.'"

The casual way he said 'boyfriend' made something warm bloom in my chest. "The first option is probably more academically acceptable."

Soren Jensen

"I should go," I said finally, though every part of me wanted to stay. "I need to get back to my flat, shower, change clothes before my afternoon classes. But could we... would you like to have dinner tonight? Somewhere public, like a proper date?"

Aleksander's smile was radiant. "I'd like that very much."

As I gathered my things—wallet, keys, the few items I'd brought—I caught sight of myself in his hallway mirror. I looked rumpled and slightly disheveled, but somehow more settled, more certain of myself despite my wrinkled clothes and sleep-mussed hair. The confused graduate student who'd walked into this flat yesterday evening was gone, replaced by someone who knew what he wanted and was brave enough to reach for it.

I carefully tucked my wallet into my jacket pocket, acutely aware of the photograph resting safely inside. "I'll take very good care of it," I said, knowing Aleksander would understand what I meant.

"I know you will," he replied, reaching up to smooth down my disheveled hair with tender affection. "And Soren? You might want to think of a story for your flatmates about where you spent the night."

I felt heat rise to my cheeks as the practical implications hit me. "Right. I hadn't thought of that."

"The truth usually works best," he said with gentle amusement. "Just perhaps not the complete truth."

DEPARTURE AND PROMISE

I walked Soren to the door, reluctant to let him go but understanding the need to maintain some normalcy in our drastically changed world.

"Thank you," he said, pausing on the threshold.

"For what?"

"For trusting me with the truth. For being patient with all my questions. For showing me what it feels like to be completely accepted by someone who matters."

I reached up to touch his cheek, marveling at how natural the gesture felt. "Thank you for staying. For choosing this, choosing us, despite all the impossibilities."

As he walked down the hallway toward the stairs, I called after him softly.

"Soren?"

He turned back, eyebrows raised in question.

"Tonight when we have dinner—it won't be our first date."

"No?"

"Yesterday evening, sitting by the fire, sharing everything we shared—that was our first date. Tonight will be our second."

His smile could have powered the entire city. "I'll see you tonight, Aleksander."

Soren Jensen

As I made my way home through the London morning, the photograph safely tucked in my wallet and the memory of Aleksander's kiss still warm on my lips, I realized that everything I'd thought I knew about myself had been transformed in the space of a single night.

I was gay. I was in love. I was dating someone supernatural who'd lived for over two millennia and loved my ancestor over a century ago.

By any reasonable standard, it should have been overwhelming. Instead, it felt like the first morning of the rest of my life.

The photograph in my wallet wasn't just evidence of past love anymore—it was a promise of what love could become when built on honesty, trust, and the courage to embrace the impossible.

As I climbed the stairs to my flat, I was already counting the hours until our dinner, already planning what I wanted to tell him, already looking forward to the next chapter of whatever extraordinary story we were writing together.

For the first time in my life, I knew exactly who I was and what I wanted.

And what I wanted was waiting for me at seven o'clock, probably already planning the perfect restaurant for our second first date.

11
LEARNING TO BE CLOSE

FLAT 7, 28 CADOGAN SQUARE, CHELSEA, LONDON SW1X 0JP

Soren Jensen

An hour had passed, maybe more. I'd lost track of time entirely, which was unlike me. I was always conscious of schedules, deadlines, the ticking of clocks. But lying here against Aleksander's chest, feeling the steady rhythm of his breathing, listening to the soft crackle of the fire, time seemed irrelevant.

We'd shifted gradually from sitting side by side to this more intimate position—my head resting on his shoulder, his arm around me, both of us learning what it felt like to simply be close to another person. For me, it was entirely new. For him, it had been 131 years since he'd experienced this kind of gentle intimacy.

"Henry," I said softly, then caught myself. "Sorry—Aleksander. I keep doing that."

He chuckled, a sound that rumbled through his chest. "Actually, you might want to keep calling me Henry, at least around other students. They know me as Henry Nordh. It would raise questions if you suddenly started using a different name."

"Right, that makes sense." I paused, then looked up at him. "But when it's just us?"

"When it's just us, I'm Aleksander. Or Alek, if you prefer."

Aleksander Nordh

The way Soren said my name—my real name—sent warmth through me that had nothing to do with the fire. He was so careful with it, as if it were something precious. And perhaps it was. I hadn't been called Aleksander by someone who mattered to me since...

Since Mikael.

But this felt different. With Mikael, I had always been performing, always hiding essential parts of myself. With Soren, for the first time in over two millennia, I was simply being myself. The relief of it was almost overwhelming.

"I have so many questions," Soren said, settling more comfortably against me. "I hope you don't mind."

"Ask me anything," I replied, meaning it completely. "I've spent centuries keeping secrets. It's... liberating to have someone I can be honest with."

THE CURIOUS MIND

Soren Jensen

The questions tumbled out of me faster than Aleksander could answer them. Each response only sparked three new inquiries. It was like being given access to a living encyclopedia of history, biology, and experiences I could never have imagined.

"Do you have family? Parents? Are they still... around?" I asked, then immediately worried I'd been insensitive. "I'm sorry, I don't know how any of this works. I don't want to ask the wrong questions."

"You can't ask the wrong questions," Aleksander assured me. "And yes, my parents are still alive. They're in their middle years now—around 4,500 years old. They moved to Australia in the 18th century and seem quite content there."

"You have a relationship with them?"

"We correspond regularly, visit occasionally. It's... different from human family dynamics. When you have millennia together, you don't feel the same urgency about constant contact."

Aleksander Nordh

His curiosity was infectious. I found myself sharing stories I hadn't told anyone in centuries—about my childhood in ancient Lapland, about the gradual changes I'd witnessed in human civilization, about the other Elders I'd known over the years.

"So there are others? Many of you?" Soren asked.

"Globally, perhaps twenty to twenty-five thousand of us. We're careful about reproducing—our long lifespans mean overpopulation would be catastrophic. Most of us live integrated lives among humans, though we maintain networks for communication and mutual support."

"Is there like... a government? A council?"

I smiled at the idea. "Nothing so formal. More like loose associations based on geography and common interests. We're quite independent by nature."

"And the Regular vampires? Do you interact with them?"

"Some do. I've had limited contact myself. There's..." I hesitated, not wanting to sound prejudiced. "There are cultural differences. They face challenges we don't—the sun sensitivity, the feeding restrictions. It creates different perspectives on how to live among humans."

"A hierarchy?" Soren's academic mind was clearly working.

"Unfortunately, yes. Many Elders consider Regulars... lesser. I find that attitude distasteful, but it exists."

FAMILY STORIES

Aleksander Nordh

"Tell me about your family," I said, genuinely curious. I'd spent so much time sharing my own impossible history that I wanted to ground myself in his very human, very normal world.

"They're lovely," Soren said with obvious affection. "My parents are both academics—Dad teaches Scandinavian Studies, Mom's in library sciences. Very supportive, maybe a bit bemused by how seriously I take genealogy research."

"Any other family? Siblings? Cousins?"

"Just a younger brother and sister. He's going to college and she's a typical high school student. Both think I'm a bookworm. Some cousins scattered around Minnesota and Wisconsin. There's one family story that..." He paused, looking slightly embarrassed. "Actually, it might interest you, given everything we've talked about tonight."

"Oh?"

Soren Jensen

I felt myself blushing again, but plowed ahead. "There was this great-uncle, Peter, who took over one of the family farms after World War II. He lived with this farmhand, Thomas, who came to help during the war and just... never left. They were together for like forty years until Peter died."

Aleksander was listening intently, a soft smile on his face.

"Family always called them 'special friends,'" I continued. "Very accepting for the time, but nobody talked about it directly. Looking back, it's pretty clear they were... well, like us, I guess."

"Like us," Aleksander repeated quietly.

"I used to wonder how difficult it must have been for them back then. Having to be so careful, so secretive about something that was just... love."

Aleksander Nordh

His empathy for relatives he'd never met, his instinctive understanding of the weight of hidden love—it was so quintessentially Soren. And it explained so much about why he'd accepted my revelation with such grace.

"That understanding," I said carefully, "that acceptance of love in different forms—it's part of why I fell for Mikael. And part of why I'm falling for you."

He looked up at me with those earnest blue-grey eyes. "It must have been even worse for Mikael. At least Peter and Thomas had each other and their farm. Mikael had to choose between love and everything else his family expected."

"It was," I admitted. "And it's part of why I was so afraid. Why I pushed him away instead of fighting for what we had."

"Wait a minute. You're… falling for me?"

"I will always be honest with you, Soren. Does it bother you?"

"I… I guess not," he replied, a torrent of red flushing his face. "I'm just… this is still so new to me."

Aleksander cuddled my hand with his. "We've plenty of time, Soren, but you're remarkably easy to fall for."

THE QUESTION

Soren Jensen

We'd been talking for what felt like hours, covering everything from Elder biology to historical events Aleksander had witnessed (most of which, he assured me, were far less exciting than history books made them seem). But there was one question that had been building in my mind all evening.

I shifted so I could see his face properly. Aleksander was lying back against the sofa cushions, completely relaxed in a way I suspected was rare for him. His hand was gently stroking mine, an absent gesture that sent little sparks through me every time.

"Alek," I said softly. "What do you think Mikael would feel about us?"

Aleksander Nordh

The question hit me like a physical blow, though not an unpleasant one. I'd been wondering the same thing since the moment I'd first seen Soren in the library, but I'd been afraid to examine it too closely.

I was quiet for a long moment, considering how to answer honestly. Soren waited patiently, his fingers intertwined with mine, his weight warm and solid against my chest.

"I think," I said finally, "he would be happy that I found someone who makes me feel alive again. Mikael always worried about my loneliness, even when he didn't fully understand what I was."

I paused, remembering conversations by the Copenhagen harbor, Mikael's concerned questions about my family, my apparent lack of close connections.

"He used to say I seemed like someone carrying an enormous burden alone. He'd tell me I deserved to share that weight with someone who cared about me."

Soren was quiet, absorbing this.

"I think he'd be pleased that it's you," I continued. "His own blood, someone who inherited his curiosity and kindness and capacity for accepting impossible things. It feels like..." I struggled for the right words. "Like he's still helping me find my way to love, even after all these years."

His answer made my throat tight with emotion. The idea that somehow, across time and death, Mikael's influence had led us to each other was both beautiful and overwhelming.

"Do you think he'd approve of you finally telling the truth?" I asked. "Being honest instead of hiding?"

Aleksander smiled, the expression transforming his entire face. "I think he'd say it was about time. Mikael always believed in honesty, even when it was difficult. Especially when it was difficult."

He lifted our joined hands, pressing a gentle kiss to my knuckles. "I think he'd tell me I was an idiot for waiting 131 years to learn the lesson he tried to teach me in Copenhagen."

"What lesson?"

"That love is worth the risk. Always."

12

LETTERS FROM ABROAD

Minnesota, October 1883

My dear Henrik,

I take pen to paper tonight as I have so many times before, though my hand is shakier now from the cold of Minnesota autumn than it ever was in your warm study. The candle flickers as I write, reminding me of those evenings when you sat beside me, your patience endless as I struggled with letters that seemed to fight my very fingers.

Today I held my son for the first time. John Aleksander Jensen—I hope you understand why I gave him your name. Linnea asked no questions when I suggested it, only nodded as if she too felt the rightness of it. When the pastor spoke the name at his baptism, my heart swelled with such strange mixture of joy and longing that I nearly wept before the congregation.

I know you told me not to look back across the Atlantic with regret, but Henrik, how can I not? You were right that I needed to come here, needed to build something of my own. The farm prospers, my wife is good and kind, and I have a son who may grow to be better than his father. I am grateful for all of it. But gratitude is not the same as contentment, and I find myself thinking of Copenhagen more often than a married man should.

The love I have for Linnea is real—warm and steady like the hearth that keeps our home comfortable. She deserves a husband who honors her, and I do. She deserves children who will make her proud, and God willing, young Aleksander is the first of many. But the love I had—have—for you burns differently. It burns like the forge when the bellows breathe life into iron, making something precious from something common.

I know you are different, Henrik. Not just in the ways that make us careful in public, but in ways I could never quite name. The stories you tell span centuries, though you speak as if you lived them yourself. The languages that come to you as easily as breathing. The way you sometimes look at me as if memorizing my face for a farewell longer than any ship's voyage. I never asked because I feared the answer might be stranger than I could accept, but I want you to know—I would have accepted it. Whatever you are, wherever you come from, it does not change what I feel.

You taught me to write so I could put what was in my heart on paper for you to see. Here it is, plain as I can make it: I love you still. Distance has not dimmed it, marriage has not erased it, fatherhood has not replaced it. It exists alongside these other loves, different but no less true.

I know you will never come to Minnesota. I know you have reasons—perhaps the same ones that made you encourage my leaving. But if you ever change your mind, if you ever tire of wandering or simply wish to see what became of the boy who learned his letters in your study, you would be welcome here. There is always a place at my table, always warmth by my fire. Linnea would welcome any friend of mine, and little Aleksander should know the man whose name he carries.

My door is open, Henrik. More importantly, my heart remains so.

I hope your life in Copenhagen brings you contentment. I hope you find someone worthy of the patience and kindness you showed me. I hope you remember, on cold nights when the harbor wind blows sharp, that somewhere in America a man thinks of you with unchanged affection and speaks your name each time he calls his son.

Give my regards to the old places we walked together. When spring comes, walk once more along the harbor at sunset and *know that I am watching the sun set here, thinking of you watching it rise there.*

With all my love and hope that this letter finds you well,

Mikael

P.S. - I still practice my letters sometimes, late at night when the house is quiet. Your voice echoes in my memory, reminding me to steady my hand, to breathe between words. Some lessons, it seems, are written too deep in the heart to fade.

13

THE FIRST NIGHT

FLAT 7, 28 CADOGAN SQUARE, CHELSEA, LONDON SW1X 0JP

Soren Jensen

The evening had stretched on beautifully—hours of conversation, shared meals, and the kind of easy intimacy that felt like we'd been doing this for months rather than days. But as the night deepened and the fire burned lower, I found myself acutely aware of the question hanging unspoken between us.

I wasn't naive about what I wanted. The attraction that had been building for weeks had crystallized into something much more definite. Every glance, every casual touch, every moment of comfortable silence had been leading to this decision point.

"Alek," I said, settling my teacup aside and turning to face him fully. "I should probably head back to my flat soon."

He nodded, though I caught the slight reluctance in his expression. "Of course. It's getting quite late."

But neither of us moved to end the evening.

"Unless," I continued, meeting his eyes directly, "you'd prefer I didn't."

ALEKSANDER'S RESPONSE

The directness of my statement seemed to surprise him. Not the careful, tentative suggestion of someone unsure of their welcome, but the clear communication of someone who knew what they wanted.

"What are you asking, Soren?" he said softly.

"I'm asking if you want me to stay tonight." I paused, holding his gaze. "Not as a houseguest who needs somewhere to sleep. As someone who wants to be here, with you."

His eyes searched my face, looking for uncertainty or hesitation he wouldn't find.

"Are you certain? There's no pressure—"

"Aleksander." I reached for his hand, twining our fingers together. "I'm twenty-four years old. I've been thinking about this for weeks, not minutes. I know what I'm asking for."

THE DECISION

Something shifted in his expression then—recognition, perhaps, that this wasn't the fumbling inexperience he'd been carefully managing, but adult desire clearly expressed.

"I've wanted you to stay," he admitted quietly. "I've wanted it every night since our first dinner together. But I didn't want to assume, didn't want to push—"

"You're not pushing," I interrupted. "I'm asking. There's a difference."

He stood, extending his hand to help me up from the settee. When I rose to meet him, we were standing close enough that I could feel the warmth radiating from his body, could see the way his eyes had darkened with something that had nothing to do with the dimmed lighting.

"Soren," he said, my name soft on his lips.

"Yes?"

"I need you to understand what you're choosing. Not just tonight, but... this. Us. It's not simple."

I stepped closer, eliminating the careful distance we'd been maintaining. "I'm not looking for simple. I'm looking for real."

MUTUAL DESIRE

When he kissed me this time, it was with none of the careful restraint of our earlier encounters. His hands found my face, my hair, pulling me closer with a hunger that matched my own. I responded with equal intensity, my body pressing against his, my hands exploring the solid warmth of his chest through his shirt.

"Are you certain?" he asked against my lips, though his hands hadn't stopped their exploration.

Instead of answering with words, I began unbuttoning his shirt, my movements deliberate and sure. His breathing hitched as my fingers brushed his skin, and I felt a thrill of power at the response I could draw from someone with millennia of experience.

"Very certain," I said, letting my lips follow the path my hands had traced.

. . .

Aleksander Nordh

This was not the careful seduction I had been preparing myself for. This was mutual desire, adult attraction, two people who had considered their options and chosen each other with full awareness of what they were doing.

Soren's hands were confident as they explored my body, his mouth sure as it moved against mine. When he began unbuttoning his own shirt, there was no hesitation, no pause for permission—just the natural progression of two adults moving toward intimacy.

"You're beautiful," I murmured, taking in the sight of him in the firelight. Tall, lean, with the kind of quiet confidence that had drawn me to him from the beginning.

"So are you," he replied, his eyes traveling over me with obvious appreciation. "I've been wondering what you looked like without all those careful layers."

MOVING TO THE BEDROOM

The transition to my bedroom felt natural, inevitable. No awkward negotiation about boundaries or expectations—just the shared understanding that this was what we both wanted.

"I should mention," Soren said as we paused beside my bed, "that I'm not completely inexperienced. Just... new to this. New to wanting someone this much."

His honesty deserved honesty in return. "I haven't been with anyone since Mikael," I admitted. "131 years is a long time to be alone."

"Then we're both exactly where we need to be," he said simply, reaching for me again.

THE NIGHT

What followed was a revelation in intimacy—not the careful, instructional encounter I had been bracing myself for, but genuine passion between two adults who had found something worth keeping. Soren was curious, responsive, unashamed of his desire or his pleasure.

When he laughed softly at his own enthusiasm, when he whispered my name like a prayer, when he fell asleep afterward with his head on my chest and his arm thrown possessively across my waist, I realized something fundamental had shifted.

This wasn't nostalgia for my past with Mikael. This wasn't me trying to recapture something lost. This was entirely new, entirely ours, entirely present.

Soren Jensen

As I drifted toward sleep wrapped in Aleksander's arms, I marveled at how right this felt. No regrets, no second-guessing, no embarrassment. Just satisfaction, contentment, and the deep certainty that this was exactly where I belonged.

I had been honest when I told him I wasn't completely inexperienced—my relationships with women had taught me about physical intimacy, even if they'd never felt emotionally authentic. But this was different. This was connection that went beyond the physical, beyond the momentary pleasure of attraction satisfied.

This was love, I realized with startling clarity. Not the confused fumbling of first attraction, but mature love between two people who had chosen each other with full knowledge of the risks and complications involved.

MORNING RECOGNITION

When I woke hours later to find myself still wrapped in his embrace, still naked and unashamed in his luxurious bed, I knew that everything had changed between us. Not because of what we'd done—though that had been revelation enough—but because of the choice we'd made to be completely honest with each other.

No careful boundaries, no tentative exploration, no apologetic requests for permission. Just two adults who had recognized what they wanted and reached for it with both hands.

As I watched the early morning light filter through his bedroom curtains, I smiled to myself. Whatever complications lay ahead, whatever challenges our unusual circumstances might bring, I was exactly where I wanted to be.

And from the way Aleksander's arms tightened around me even in sleep, I suspected he felt the same way. Discovering the truth about what he was, I felt no uncertainty about my choice. I wasn't Mikael's confused young descendant stumbling through circumstances beyond his understanding. I was Soren Jensen, graduate student, researcher, and now lover of an extraordinary man who had waited 131 years to trust someone with his whole self.

The morning would bring new conversations, new questions, new discoveries about what our relationship might become. But tonight had answered the most important question of all: we wanted this enough to reach for it, complications and all.

And that was more than enough to build a future on.

14
THE MORNING AFTER

FLAT 7, 28 CADOGAN SQUARE, CHELSEA, LONDON SW1X 0JP

Soren Jensen

I woke slowly, consciousness returning in gentle waves accompanied by the unfamiliar luxury of silk sheets and the warmth of another body pressed against my back. For a moment, I let myself simply exist in the sensation—Aleksander's arm draped over my waist, his breath warm against my shoulder, the complete rightness of waking up beside him.

The myths about vampires being cold, lifeless creatures seemed laughable now. Aleksander was wonderfully warm, almost radiating heat. I could feel his heartbeat against my back, faster than human normal but steady and strong. Everything about him was vibrantly, undeniably alive.

Memory flooded back—not just the revelation about his supernatural nature, but everything that had followed. Our honest conversations, the mutual decision to stop holding back, the night we'd spent discovering each other without reservation or apology.

I shifted slightly, noting the pleasant soreness that came with new intimacy, and smiled to myself. No regrets, no embarrassment, no second-guessing. Just satisfaction and the deep certainty that I'd made exactly the right choice.

AWAKENING

"Good morning," came Aleksander's voice, soft and slightly rough with sleep.

"Good morning," I replied, turning in his arms to face him. His hair was mussed, his eyes still heavy with sleep, and he looked more human and approachable than I'd ever seen him.

"Sleep well?" he asked, a hint of amusement in his voice that suggested he was perfectly aware of how well we'd both slept.

"Better than I have in years," I admitted, stretching languidly in his arms. The movement caused the sheet to slip lower, and I noticed Aleksander's eyes following the line of my chest and shoulders with obvious appreciation.

"You're not shy about your body," he observed, sounding both surprised and pleased.

I raised an eyebrow. "Should I be? I take care of myself. And after last night..." I let the implication hang in the air with a slight smile. "I think we're past the point of false modesty."

MORNING INTIMACY

His expression shifted to something warmer, more appreciative. "You continue to surprise me."

"Good surprise or concerning surprise?" I asked, settling more comfortably against him, our bodies fitting together with the kind of easy intimacy that usually took months to develop.

"The very best kind," he replied, pressing a kiss to my forehead. "I was prepared for awkwardness, uncertainty, perhaps some regret in the harsh light of day. Instead, you seem..."

"Satisfied?" I suggested. "Content? Ready to do it again when the opportunity presents itself?"

His laugh was rich and genuine. "All of the above, I hope."

ADULT CONVERSATIONS

"Can I ask you something?" I said, propping myself up on one elbow to look at him properly.

"Of course."

"How does this work, exactly? The physical compatibility between Elders and humans?" I wasn't blushing or stammering—this was practical information I wanted to understand. "Are there things I should know about? Differences beyond the obvious?"

Aleksander seemed taken aback by the directness of the question, but pleased by my matter-of-fact approach.

"Enhanced senses mean I experience everything more intensely," he said thoughtfully. "Physical pleasure, emotional connection, even simple touch. What might feel pleasant to you could be overwhelming for me, and vice versa."

"Is that why you were so responsive last night?" I asked with a slight grin. "I was rather proud of myself for the reactions I got out of someone with millennia of experience."

"You should be proud," he replied, his own smile widening. "And yes, partly. But mostly it was because I haven't felt this connected to someone in over a century. Your touch, your attention, your obvious pleasure in what we were doing—it was intoxicating."

Aleksander Nordh

As Soren settled back against the pillows, clearly comfortable with both his nakedness and our newfound intimacy, I felt something shift inside my chest—a dangerous warmth that I recognized with growing alarm.

Love.

The realization hit me like a physical blow. Not attraction, not affection, not even the deep caring I'd felt growing between us. This was love, complete and consuming and absolutely terrifying in its implications.

I thought of my father's words, spoken centuries ago when I was still young enough to believe I might avoid the trap that had claimed so many of our kind: *"Be careful with mortals, Aleksander. They burn so bright and so briefly. Every connection you make will end in loss. Guard your heart accordingly."*

For over two millennia, I had heeded that advice. I had loved, yes, but always with careful reservations, always holding back some essential part of myself as protection against the inevitable. Even with Mikael, even in the depths of passion and connection, I had maintained barriers that I told myself were necessary.

But lying here beside Soren, watching him move with unconscious confidence through his first morning as my lover, I realized those barriers had already crumbled without my permission.

THE WEIGHT OF MEMORY

I thought of Brother Augustin, dead now for twelve centuries but still vivid in my memory. I thought of Marcus, of James, of all the others who had flickered through my existence like candles—beautiful while they burned, devastating when they were extinguished.

And Mikael. God, Mikael, whose loss had nearly destroyed me despite all my careful emotional distance. If I had loved him this completely, this unreservedly, his death would have been unbearable.

Yet here I was, feeling that same depth of connection with his descendant. Worse than that—I was feeling it more intensely, because this time there were no barriers, no careful reservations, no part of myself held in protective reserve.

Soren would age. Soren would die. In seventy years, perhaps eighty if he was fortunate, I would watch the light fade from his eyes while I remained unchanged. I would carry his memory for centuries, just as I carried all the others, but the pain of losing him would be magnified by how completely I had allowed myself to love him.

My father had been right. Love between Elder and mortal was a recipe for heartbreak on a scale that most beings could never comprehend.

THE CHOICE

But as I watched Soren stretch again, as I saw the contentment in his expression and the trust in his eyes, I realized something that my father's ancient wisdom had never accounted for.

The love was already there. Complete, consuming, undeniable. The choice wasn't whether to feel it—that decision had been made without my conscious participation. The choice was whether to acknowledge it, to give it voice, to allow it to exist openly between us.

I could remain silent, continue pretending that what I felt was manageable attraction rather than devastating love. I could protect myself by never voicing the depth of my feelings, never making myself that vulnerable.

But wouldn't that be another form of hiding? Another way of keeping barriers between us, of loving only partially, only safely?

"So my concern isn't about basic compatibility," Soren was saying, and I realized I had been lost in thought long enough for the conversation to continue without me.

"What is your concern?" I asked, though my mind was still wrestling with the weight of what I had realized.

"Sustainability. Whether the intensity of what we shared last night is something we can build on, or whether it was a beautiful anomaly that won't translate to a real relationship."

His words hit me with unexpected force. Here he was, thinking practically about our future, while I was spiraling into ancient fears about inevitable loss. He was choosing hope; I was choosing worry.

DECLARATIONS

Soren," I said, my voice coming out rougher than I intended.

He looked at me with immediate attention, clearly hearing something in my tone that made him focus completely on my face.

"There's something I need to tell you," I continued, my heart hammering against my ribs in a way that had nothing to do with my enhanced metabolism.

"What is it?"

I took a breath, thinking of my father's warnings, of centuries of careful emotional distance, of all the loves I had lost and the pain I had carried. Then I looked at Soren's face—open, trusting, beautiful in the morning light—and made my choice.

"I love you," I said simply.

The words hung in the air between us, heavy with implication and vulnerability. I had just handed him the power to destroy me, just acknowledged feelings that made his inevitable loss infinitely more painful to contemplate.

"I know it's too soon," I continued, the words tumbling out now that the dam had broken. "I know we've barely begun to understand what this is between us. I know that my... nature... makes everything complicated. But I needed you to know. I needed to stop hiding behind careful distance and tell you the truth."

Soren Jensen

The simple declaration hit me like lightning—not because it was unexpected, but because of the weight of vulnerability I could hear in his voice. This wasn't casual affection or post-intimacy emotion. This was someone who had lived for over two millennia, who had loved and lost across centuries, choosing to make himself completely vulnerable.

"Alek," I said softly, reaching up to touch his face. I could see something like fear in his eyes, as if he was bracing himself for rejection or withdrawal.

"You're not too soon," I said, my own heart racing as I realized what I was about to admit. "You're exactly on time."

I leaned up and kissed him, soft and sure and full of everything I was feeling but hadn't yet found the courage to voice.

"I love you too," I whispered against his lips. "I've been falling in love with you for weeks, probably since that first dinner. Learning about what you are didn't change that—it just made me understand why the connection felt so intense from the beginning."

Aleksander Nordh

The relief that flooded through me at his words was almost overwhelming. Not just because he had reciprocated, but because I could see in his eyes that he understood the weight of what we had just exchanged.

"My father warned me about this," I admitted, pulling him closer. "About loving mortals. About the inevitable pain of loss."

"And?" Soren asked, seemingly untroubled by the reference to his own mortality.

"And I've decided he was wrong. Not about the pain—that's real, that's inevitable. But about whether it's worth it." I looked into his eyes, marveling at the courage it took to choose temporary happiness over permanent safety. "You're worth it. This is worth it."

"Good," Soren said, settling back into my arms with the confidence of someone who had just heard everything he needed to hear. "Because I intend to make the most of whatever time we have."

MORNING RECOGNITION

As we lay together in comfortable silence, I realized that something fundamental had shifted between us. Not just the physical intimacy we had shared, not just the emotional declarations we had made, but the choice we had both made to love completely despite the complications and inevitable challenges ahead.

For the first time in over two millennia, I had chosen courage over caution, vulnerability over protection, temporary joy over permanent safety. And lying there with Soren warm and content in my arms, I knew I had made exactly the right choice.

Whatever pain lay ahead—and there would be pain, my father had been right about that—it would be worth every moment of this happiness.

"I should probably mention," Soren said, his voice slightly muffled against my chest, "that I'm a very quick learner when it comes to things I care about."

I laughed, the sound rich with contentment and possibility. "I was counting on that."

Soren Jensen

I sat up fully, letting the sheet fall away without self-consciousness, and stretched again. Aleksander's eyes followed the movement appreciatively, and I felt a thrill of power at the response I could draw from him.

"So," I said with obvious satisfaction, "boyfriends who are in love. That has a nice ring to it."

Aleksander raised an eyebrow, a slight smile playing at the corners of his mouth. "Boyfriends?"

"What's wrong with boyfriends?" I asked, suddenly uncertain. "Too casual? Too... teenage?"

"It's not wrong," he said carefully. "It's just... I'm over two thousand years old, Soren. 'Boyfriend' feels a bit..."

"Inadequate?" I suggested.

"Precisely." He reached up to touch my face gently. "What we just shared, what we just admitted to each other—it feels like it deserves terminology with more weight."

I considered this. "Partners?"

"Better, but still feels somewhat... clinical."

"Lovers?"

"True, but incomplete." His eyes held mine steadily. "What about simply... the person you're in love with?"

I laughed, the sound rich with contentment. "That's a mouthful for introductions. 'Hi, I'd like you to meet Aleksander, the person I'm in love with.'"

"I think I could live with that," he said, pulling me back down beside him.

"All right," I conceded, settling into his arms. "But for practical purposes, when we're not being philosophical about it, I reserve the right to call you my boyfriend."

"And I reserve the right to call you something more meaningful when the mood strikes me."

"Deal."

IDENTITIES

"Alek," I said, settling more comfortably against him, "can I ask you something else?"

"Haven't we established that you can ask me anything?"

"Did you always know? About being... attracted to men, I mean?"

He was quiet for a moment, considering. "The word 'gay' is relatively recent, you know. When I was young—truly young, not just appearing young—there wasn't the same framework for categorizing attraction that exists now."

"What do you mean?"

"In ancient times, in many cultures, love was simply love. The Romans, the Greeks—they had different concepts of sexuality than what developed later. It wasn't about identity categories so much as about individual connections." He traced patterns on my chest as he spoke. "Of course, depending on where you lived, your social class, the specific time period... it could still be dangerous to be too open about certain relationships."

"But you knew you preferred men?"

"I knew I was drawn to intelligence, to beauty, to strength—and those qualities seemed to manifest more often in men, at least for me. My first real attraction was to another young Elder when I was young. Bjorn." He smiled at the memory. "He was everything I thought I wanted—strong, confident, older than me in actual years though we appeared the same age."

"What happened with him?"

"Nothing, unfortunately. He was interested in someone else." Aleksander's expression grew more serious. "But it clarified something for me about what I was looking for."

"Do your parents know?"

"Of course." His answer was immediate and matter-of-fact. "My father's advice about being careful with mortals? That came after I told him about Marcus in Florence. He wasn't concerned about Marcus being male—he was concerned about Marcus being human."

"And your mother?"

Aleksander's smile was warm with memory. "She said she'd always known. Apparently, the way I looked at certain people gave me away from a young age. Mothers tend to notice these things."

TURNING THE TABLE

"What about you?" Aleksander asked, turning slightly to look at me directly. "I know you mentioned dating women, but I'm your first man, right?"

I felt heat rise to my cheeks, though I wasn't sure why. "Yes. You're my first... everything, really. First man, first time feeling this way about anyone."

"How are you processing that? It's not a small realization."

"Honestly? It feels like relief more than anything else. Like I finally understand why nothing felt right before." I paused, considering. "All those years of thinking something was wrong with me, that I was just a late bloomer or too focused on academics..."

"And now?"

"Now I know I was just waiting for the right person to show me what I actually wanted."

Aleksander's expression grew tender. "That's a lovely way to put it."

"Though I'll admit, I never imagined the right person would be a two-thousand-year-old supernatural being," I added with a laugh.

"Life has a sense of irony," he agreed. "Speaking of which—do you think you'll tell your family? About us, I mean?"

The question made my stomach tighten slightly. I'd been so focused on processing my own feelings that I hadn't really thought about the practical implications.

"I... yes, I think so. Eventually. My parents are academics, they're relatively progressive. The bigger challenge might be explaining that my boyfriend appears to be barely older than me but has somehow accumulated decades worth of historical knowledge."

"We'll figure out a story that works," Aleksander said easily. "I've had centuries of practice creating believable backgrounds."

"What about the gay part specifically?" I asked. "I mean, I've never brought anyone home before. Anyone at all. They're going to have questions."

"Are you worried about their reaction?"

I considered this honestly. "Not about disapproval, exactly. More about... I don't know, feeling like I should have figured this out sooner? Like they'll wonder how I got to twenty-four without understanding something so fundamental about myself."

"Some people know from childhood," Aleksander said gently. "Others take time to understand themselves. Neither path is wrong."

"Did you worry about that? When you were figuring things out?"

"I was fortunate to grow up in a community that didn't pathologize different types of love. But I understand the concern." He pressed a kiss to the top of my head. "For what it's worth, I think your parents will be happy that you've found someone who makes you this content."

"Even if that someone is technically older than several civilizations?"

"Especially then. Think of all the interesting dinner conversations."

"You seem remarkably composed for someone whose entire worldview changed in the span of a few days," he observed.

I considered this. "I suppose I am. But that's because this feels right in a way nothing else in my life ever has. Learning about your true nature didn't change how I felt about you—it explained why I felt it so strongly from the beginning."

PRACTICAL MATTERS

"So where does that leave us?" Aleksander asked, his expression growing more serious. "What do you want this to be?"

"I want to explore it," I said simply. "I want to learn what kind of relationship is possible between us. I want to understand how your unique circumstances affect the way we connect, and I want to find out whether what we have can grow into something lasting."

I leaned down to kiss him, slow and thorough. "And I want to do all of that while enjoying the considerable physical chemistry we've discovered."

His smile was radiant. "I'd like that very much."

MOVING FORWARD

"Good," I said, climbing out of bed with easy confidence. "Because I'm starving, and I believe you promised me breakfast."

As I moved around the room gathering my clothes, I was aware of Aleksander watching me with something approaching wonder. Not the careful assessment of someone trying to manage a delicate situation, but the frank appreciation of someone who liked very much what he was seeing.

"You're remarkable, you know that?" he said.

"I'm practical," I corrected, pulling on my shirt. "And I'm honest about what I want. Both of which are going to serve us well as we figure this out."

I paused in buttoning my shirt to look at him directly. "This isn't going to be simple, Alek. The supernatural element adds complications I can't even begin to anticipate yet. But it's real, and it's worth whatever effort it takes to make it work."

Aleksander Nordh

Watching Soren move around my bedroom with such easy confidence, seeing him approach our new relationship with mature pragmatism rather than starry-eyed romance or anxious uncertainty, I realized how completely I had underestimated him.

This wasn't Mikael's descendant fumbling through circumstances beyond his understanding. This was Soren Jensen—intelligent, self-aware, sexually confident, and apparently determined to build something lasting with me despite the considerable complications involved.

"You're right," I said, climbing out of bed myself. "It won't be simple. But then, the best things rarely are."

As we prepared to leave my flat together—boyfriends, lovers, partners in whatever this was becoming—I realized I was embarking on something I hadn't dared hope for in over a century: a relationship built on complete honesty, mutual desire, and the possibility of a shared future that honored both our natures.

15
MORNING DISCOVERIES

PATTERSON'S CAFÉ 15 FLASK WALK, HAMPSTEAD, LONDON NW3 1HE

Soren Jensen

The tube journey took us further north than I'd ever ventured in London, past familiar stops and into areas I didn't recognize. Aleksander sat beside me, our shoulders touching as the carriage swayed, and I found myself hyperaware of every point of contact between us. The morning light streaming through the windows caught the gold flecks in his eyes, and I had to resist the urge to stare.

"Where exactly are we going?" I asked as we emerged from the station into a neighborhood that felt more like a village than part of London. Tree-lined streets stretched ahead, with Victorian houses tucked behind gardens that actually had space to breathe.

"Hampstead Heath," Aleksander replied, taking my hand as naturally as breathing. "There's a little place I know. Very quiet, very private. I thought you might enjoy it."

The casualness of his touch sent warmth up my arm. We were holding hands. In public. I'd never held anyone's hand before, let alone another man's, but somehow it felt like the most natural thing in the world.

A MOMENT OF REALITY

We had walked perhaps fifty meters from the station when I heard the squeal of brakes and the angry honking of a car horn. I looked up just in time to see a black taxi careening around the corner at what had to be twice the legal speed limit, tires smoking as the driver swerved to avoid an elderly woman who'd stepped into the crosswalk with the light.

The cab missed us by inches—close enough that I could feel the wind displacement ruffle my hair and catch the smell of exhaust and burning rubber.

"Jesus fucking Christ!" I shouted after the disappearing vehicle, my heart hammering against my ribs. "Are you completely bloody insane?!"

Aleksander stopped walking and stared at me with obvious surprise. I realized I'd just unleashed a string of profanity that would have horrified my parents and impressed my university flatmates.

"Sorry," I muttered, feeling heat rise to my cheeks as the adrenaline began to fade. "I just... that was too close. Bloody idiot could have killed someone."

"Don't apologize," Aleksander said, and I was startled to see amusement rather than disapproval in his expression. "I was beginning to think you were too well-mannered to be entirely human."

"What's that supposed to mean?"

"It means," he said, taking my arm to steer us safely down the sidewalk, "that I'm relieved to discover you have a normal emotional range. Anger, frustration, the occasional 'fuck' when nearly flattened by a taxi—it's all quite endearing, actually."

I looked at him sideways. "You find my cursing endearing?"

"I find your humanity endearing. All of it. Even the parts that would make your mother blush."

Aleksander Nordh (Henrik Lindqvist)

Watching Soren's flash of genuine anger—the way his carefully maintained politeness had completely evaporated in the face of real danger—was oddly reassuring. For weeks, I'd been getting to know someone who seemed almost too composed, too thoughtful, too consistently pleasant to be entirely authentic.

This glimpse of his unfiltered reaction, complete with creative profanity and righteous indignation, felt like seeing past another carefully maintained facade to the real person underneath.

"Besides," I added, "your concern was entirely justified. London taxi drivers can be... aggressive."

"Aggressive?" Soren shook his head, still clearly rattled. "That wasn't aggressive, that was homicidal. And that poor woman—she had the right of way!"

The protective anger on behalf of a stranger, the genuine outrage at injustice —it reminded me why I'd been drawn to him from the beginning. Beneath his academic composure was someone who cared deeply about fairness and human decency.

"Come," I said gently. "Let's get you some coffee and proper food. You'll feel better once the adrenaline wears off."

I watched Soren take in the surroundings with that same careful attention he brought to historical documents. Everything was new to him—the quiet streets, the way the morning light filtered through ancient oak trees, the sensation of walking hand in hand with someone he cared about. Two millennia of experience hadn't prepared me for how precious it would feel to see the world through his eyes again.

The café I'd chosen was tucked away on a side street, the kind of place locals discovered by accident and tourists never found. I'd been coming here for decades, under different identities, always appreciating its unchanging character and the way the elderly proprietress minded her own business.

"Good morning, Henrik," Mrs. Patterson called from behind the counter as we entered. She'd known me as Henrik Lindqvist for the past fifteen years—a Swedish graduate student who came by occasionally for their excellent coffee and the quiet corner table by the window.

"Good morning, Mrs. Patterson. This is my friend Soren," I replied, guiding him toward the table I'd claimed as my own over the years.

SETTLING IN

Soren Jensen

The café was everything Aleksander had promised—cozy, intimate, with mismatched furniture that somehow worked perfectly together. Bookshelves lined the walls, and the smell of fresh coffee mixed with something that might have been cinnamon bread. Only a handful of other customers occupied the scattered tables, each absorbed in their newspapers or quiet conversations.

"This is lovely," I said, settling into a chair that faced both Aleksander and the window overlooking the tree-lined street. "How did you find this place?"

"I have a talent for discovering hidden corners," Aleksander replied with a slight smile. "London has thousands of places like this, tucked away from the main thoroughfares. You just have to know how to look."

Mrs. Patterson approached with menus and a knowing smile. "The usual for you, Henrik? And what can I get for your young man?"

I felt heat rise to my cheeks at her assumption, but Aleksander didn't correct her. Instead, he looked at me with an expression of gentle amusement.

"I'll have the full English breakfast," I said, suddenly ravenous. "And coffee, please. Very strong coffee."

"Two coffees it is," she said, bustling away with a warmth that suggested she genuinely enjoyed her customers.

. . .

Aleksander Nordh (Henrik Lindqvist)

Watching Soren navigate this simple interaction—being referred to as "my young man," making his first breakfast decision as part of a couple—filled me with an unexpected tenderness. Everything was a first for him, and I was privileged to witness these small moments of discovery.

"You seem comfortable here," Soren observed once we were alone. "Do you come often?"

"When I need to think," I admitted. "It's one of the few places in London where I can simply exist without performance or pretense."

"Like you do with me?"

The question was so direct, so hopeful, that it took my breath away. "Exactly like I do with you."

MORNING REVELATIONS

Soren Jensen

Our food arrived quickly—my full English breakfast and Aleksander's more modest selection of toast, fruit, and what appeared to be some kind of small steak. I noticed he ate with the precise manners of someone who'd had centuries to perfect etiquette, but there was nothing affected about it.

"Can I ask you something?" I said between bites of perfectly prepared eggs. "About your... dietary needs?"

"Of course." Aleksander cut a piece of his steak with surgical precision. "What would you like to know?"

"Last night you mentioned needing certain nutrients from blood plasma. But you're eating normal food now..."

"I am. As I said, we're not limited to blood alone like Regulars. I require about five times the caloric intake of an average human due to my accelerated metabolism, and I need to supplement with blood plasma roughly twice a month." He paused, studying my face. "Does that disturb you?"

I considered this seriously. "No, actually. It's fascinating from a biological perspective. How do you... I mean, do you..."

"Hunt?" Aleksander's expression became more serious. "I should clarify something important, Soren. I don't hunt at all. As an Elder, I don't need to. I have other ways to obtain the nutrients I require—quite easily, actually—and they don't involve *Homo sapiens* plasma."

He paused, cutting another piece of his steak with deliberate precision. "Ethical feeding, or harvesting as some call it, isn't something Elders practice. We don't need to. But Regulars... that's a different matter entirely."

"Do you approve of such practices?" I asked, unable to keep the concern from my voice.

Aleksander was quiet for a long moment, considering his words carefully. "It's complicated. While I don't care for the idea of hunting or killing, I also understand it's akin to hunting animals for food. Yet we're speaking of humans, and that presents... problems. Given the differences in our species, it gets messy philosophically."

He set down his knife and looked at me directly. "I've spent centuries studying arguments and writings about this—the ethics of survival, the nature of existence, practically everything. In the end, it's not something that affects me personally as an Elder since we don't need to hunt. But it does present issues for me given the fear surrounding 'my kind,' especially when the Victorians began calling all of us by that crude term and accusing all of us of horrible things, regardless of our actual practices."

Soren Jensen

I hadn't thought of it that way—how the actions of one species could taint the reputation of another, how Aleksander and other Elders might be judged for things they didn't even do. It was complicated, as he said.

There was one last thought among many that I was ashamed to ask, but something in Aleksander's expression suggested he sensed my unspoken concern.

Aleksander Nordh (Henrik Lindqvist)

I could see there was still something weighing on Soren's mind, something he was too polite or perhaps too frightened to voice. Reaching across the table, I took his hand gently.

"Soren," I said softly, "I don't lust after your blood. There are no hunger cravings for you in that way. It doesn't work like that." I squeezed his hand reassuringly. "Once or twice a month, the most I have to do is simply drink the equivalent of a protein shake. It's far more mundane than anything you might be imagining."

I watched Soren process this information with the same analytical approach he brought to his research. No horror, no revulsion—just genuine curiosity about the practical realities of my existence. It was one of the things that made him so remarkable.

"You have more questions," I observed.

"About a thousand," he admitted with a smile. "But there's one that's been nagging at me since last night."

"Only one?"

"Well, one that feels most important right now." He set down his fork and looked at me directly. "Do you have friends? Other people like you that you keep in contact with?"

The question caught me off guard, perhaps because it touched on something I'd been thinking about myself. "Some. We're not particularly social as a species, and trust doesn't come easily when you've lived as long as we have."

"But there are others? In London?"

"A few Elders, yes. And some Regulars as well." I paused, considering how much to share. "Actually, there's someone I've been... mentoring, I suppose you'd call it. A Regular who's had a particularly difficult time adjusting."

Soren Jensen

Something in Aleksander's tone made me lean forward. "Difficult how?"

"He was transformed against his will by someone I once knew. The transformation process for Regulars is... traumatic under the best of circumstances. When it's forced, when there's no preparation or guidance..." Aleksander's expression darkened. "Let's just say he's struggled to find his place in the world."

"How long ago?"

"About eleven years now. He came to London several years after his transformation, and a mutual acquaintance asked if I might help him. I've been trying to gain his trust ever since."

I felt a surge of sympathy for this unknown person. "That's incredibly kind of you."

"Perhaps. Or perhaps it's selfish—helping others helps me feel less isolated myself." Aleksander met my eyes. "His name is Rafael. And lately, I've been sensing something familiar about him, though I can't quite place what."

"Familiar how?"

"It's difficult to explain. Sometimes, when I'm near him, I get the strangest feeling... as if Mikael is somehow present." Aleksander shook his head. "It sounds absurd, I know."

Aleksander Nordh (Henrik Lindqvist)

Soren was quiet for a long moment, absorbing this information. I could see his academic mind working, making connections, filing away details for future consideration.

"Would you like to meet him?" I asked impulsively. "Rafael, I mean. He's still very shy, very guarded, but I think... I think he might benefit from meeting someone outside our world. Someone human who knows the truth but isn't threatened by it."

"I'd like that very much," Soren said without hesitation. "When someone's been through trauma, sometimes the best thing is simply knowing they're not alone."

His immediate compassion for a stranger, his instinctive understanding of what Rafael might need—it was so quintessentially Soren that my chest tightened with affection.

"There's something else," I said quietly. "Something I haven't told Rafael yet, though I suspect he may have guessed."

"What?"

"I believe his transformation may not have been as random as it appeared. The man who turned him, Professor Nazari, was ancient even by our standards. He'd lived for over two millennia, and in his final years, he became... selective about whom he chose for transformation."

Soren's eyes widened. "You think he chose Rafael specifically?"

"I think Nazari recognized something in Rafael that even Rafael doesn't understand about himself yet." I reached across the table and took Soren's hand. "Something that might explain why being near him feels like being near Mikael."

Soren Jensen

The implications of what Aleksander was suggesting began to dawn on me. "You think Rafael might be... related to my family somehow?"

"It's possible. The timing would be right—if John Mikael Jensen had descendants through other branches we haven't discovered yet..." Aleksander trailed off, leaving the possibility hanging between us.

"The Philippines," I whispered. "John was stationed in the Philippines."

"Exactly." Aleksander squeezed my hand. "It's only a theory, but if Rafael is carrying Mikael's bloodline..."

"Then he's family." The thought sent a strange thrill through me. "He's family, and he doesn't even know it."

Aleksander Nordh (Henrik Lindqvist)

Watching the pieces come together in Soren's mind, seeing the excitement and compassion in his eyes, I felt something I hadn't experienced in over a century: the possibility of family. Not just the romantic love I'd found with Soren, but something larger—a sense of belonging that extended beyond the two of us.

"When can we meet him?" Soren asked, his breakfast forgotten in his enthusiasm.

"Soon," I promised. "Though we'll need to go slowly. Rafael has been hurt badly, and trust doesn't come easily to him anymore."

"Of course. We'll take as much time as he needs." Soren paused, then smiled with an expression of wonder. "Aleksander, do you realize what this means?"

"Tell me."

"If Rafael is family, if he's carrying the same bloodline that brought you to me..." Soren's voice caught slightly. "Then maybe Mikael didn't just find his way to America. Maybe part of him found his way to you after all."

The truth of those words hit me like a physical blow, beautiful and devastating at once. Perhaps I hadn't lost Mikael as completely as I'd thought. Perhaps love, like bloodlines, had a way of finding its way home across impossible distances and unbearable spans of time.

"Yes," I whispered, lifting our joined hands to my lips. "Maybe he did."

16
THE WEIGHT OF MEMORY

WHITESTONE POND, HAMPSTEAD HEATH, LONDON NW3 6ST

Soren Jensen

The walk from the café took us deeper into Hampstead Heath, following paths that wound between ancient trees and rolling meadows that seemed impossible in the heart of London. Aleksander moved with the easy familiarity of someone who'd walked these routes countless times, guiding us toward a secluded bench that overlooked one of the ponds where families fed ducks and couples walked hand in hand.

The morning had grown warmer, though autumn's chill still lingered in the shadows. I found myself studying Aleksander's profile as we settled onto the weathered wooden bench, noting the way the dappled sunlight through the leaves caught the gold flecks in his eyes—the same eyes that had looked upon my ancestor over a century ago.

"Can I ask you something else?" I said, my voice quieter now that we were away from the café's gentle bustle. "Something more personal?"

Aleksander turned to face me fully, his expression open and patient. "Of course. Ask me anything."

Aleksander Nordh

The change in Soren's tone told me we were moving into more delicate territory. Over our weeks together, I'd learned to read the subtle variations in his voice—when he was academically curious versus when he was seeking emotional understanding. This was the latter, and I felt both anticipation and apprehension at what he might want to know.

"What would you like to understand?" I asked gently.

Soren Jensen

I took a breath, gathering courage for questions I'd been carrying since our first conversations about Mikael. "You loved him for four years in Copenhagen. You've missed him for 131 years since he left. But in all that time... did you ever consider going to see him? To Minnesota, I mean. You could have, couldn't you?"

The question hung between us like a bridge I wasn't sure either of us was ready to cross. But I needed to understand the choices that had shaped both their lives—and, by extension, the path that had led to my own existence.

Aleksander Nordh

The question struck at the heart of a guilt I'd carried for over a century. How many times had I stood at the edge of decision, passport in hand, train tickets purchased, only to retreat at the last moment? How many sleepless nights had I spent imagining what it would be like to see Mikael again, to know if he was happy, if he ever thought of our time together?

"I considered it," I said finally, my voice careful and measured. "Many times, especially in the early years after he left. I would make plans, research travel routes, even purchase passage sometimes."

"But you never went."

"No. I never went."

Soren Jensen

The pain in his voice was unmistakable, and I felt a rush of sympathy for this ancient being who had loved my ancestor and lost him to duty and expectation. But I also needed to understand the reasoning that had kept them apart.

"Why not?" I asked softly. "What stopped you?"

Aleksander Nordh

How could I explain the complex calculations that had governed those decisions? The fear that my presence would disrupt the life Mikael had built, that seeing me would reopen wounds he needed to heal? The terror that he might have forgotten me entirely, or worse—that he might remember but wish he could forget?

"Because I had encouraged him to leave," I said slowly. "I had told him that America was his future, that duty to his family was more important than... than what we had together. How could I then appear in his new life, disrupting the very path I had insisted he take?"

I paused, watching a family of ducks glide across the pond's surface, their movements creating gentle ripples that spread outward in ever-widening circles.

"And because I was afraid," I continued. "Afraid that seeing him with his wife, with his children, living the life I had convinced him to choose... afraid it would break something in me that was already barely holding together."

Soren Jensen

The honesty in his admission made my chest tight with emotion. Here was someone who had lived for millennia, who possessed supernatural abilities and ancient wisdom, revealing himself to be as vulnerable to love and loss as any human.

"Do you regret it?" I asked. "Pushing him away, I mean. Not going to see him when you could have?"

Aleksander Nordh

The question I had asked myself ten thousand times, especially in the darkest hours of the deepest nights. Did I regret the choice that had defined both our lives? Did I regret choosing what I believed was his happiness over my own desperate need?

"I regret the pain it caused him," I said carefully. "I regret that our parting was fraught with duty and obligation rather than love and understanding. I regret that he carried sadness about our separation into his new life."

I turned to meet Soren's eyes directly. "But I don't regret encouraging him to leave Copenhagen. He built a beautiful life in America—married a woman who loved him, raised children who adored him, contributed to a community that valued him. That life led, through generations of love and growth, to you. How could I regret choices that ultimately brought you into existence?"

Soren Jensen

His words sent warmth through me, but they also raised another question that I wasn't sure I had the right to ask. Still, if we were going to build something real together, it had to be based on complete honesty.

"What about his wife?" I said quietly. "Linnea. Knowing that he loved you, that part of his heart would always belong to what you'd shared... were you ever jealous of her?"

Aleksander Nordh

The question caught me off guard, though perhaps it shouldn't have. Of course Soren would wonder about the woman who had claimed the life I couldn't share, who had been able to give Mikael the family and social acceptance that our love had made impossible.

I was quiet for a long moment, sifting through memories and emotions I'd kept carefully compartmentalized for over a century.

"I was," I admitted finally. "In the beginning, when I first learned of his marriage, I felt such jealousy it nearly consumed me. This woman who had never known him as I knew him, who couldn't understand the depth of his character or the complexity of his dreams, was sharing his bed, his daily life, his future. It felt profoundly unfair."

The questions had been building for weeks.

First, it was the dockworkers asking pointed questions about where Mikael lodged, why he never brought his "landlord" around for drinks, what sort of arrangement allowed a working man to live in such comfortable quarters. Then came the letters from home—his mother's increasingly direct inquiries about "this gentleman you mention so often," his sister's blunt questions about when he planned to marry and settle down.

But tonight, over what should have been another peaceful dinner in the warmth of our shared lodging, everything came to a head.

I had been steering the conversation carefully toward America, toward the opportunities I'd been hearing about from other Scandinavian immigrants. Land ownership, business ventures, the chance to build something substantial. It hurt to speak of it, but I told myself it was necessary. Mikael deserved a full life—marriage, children, prosperity—not the half-existence he would have loving someone who could never give him those things.

"You've been talking about America quite a lot lately," Mikael said, his voice careful in a way that made my chest tighten with foreboding.

"The opportunities seem genuine," I replied, focusing on cutting my meat with unnecessary precision. "Johan Lindström just wrote to his brother about purchasing forty acres in Minnesota. Rich farmland, he says. Room to build something lasting."

"Something lasting," Mikael repeated, and there was an edge to his voice I'd never heard before. "For me, you mean. Not for us."

I looked up to find him studying me with an expression I couldn't quite read. "Mikael—"

"No, I want to understand this," he interrupted, setting down his fork with deliberate care. "For weeks now, you've been suggesting I look into opportunities elsewhere. America, specifically. You've mentioned Minnesota three times this week alone. Are you trying to get rid of me?"

The accusation hit me like a physical blow. "Of course not. I only want—"

"What you want is for me to leave," he said, his voice rising. "Politely, civilly, because that's how civilized people handle these things. But you want me gone."

"That's not—"

"Is there someone else?" The question came out harsh, desperate. "Another boy? A mistress, perhaps? Someone more suited to your... elevated circumstances?"

I stared at him, shocked into momentary silence. "How can you even suggest—"

"Or maybe it's the money," he continued, the words tumbling out now like water through a broken dam. "Am I too costly to support? Am I draining your family's reserves? Because I work, Aleksander. I earn wages. I'm not some kept boy living off your charity."

"You know that's not what this is about," I said, but he wasn't finished.

"Or perhaps," and his voice went quiet now, dangerously so, "perhaps I'm simply not good enough for you. Not refined enough for all this splendor, this comfortable life you've made for yourself while us working folk use our hands to survive."

The words hung between us like a blade, cutting deeper than he could possibly know. That he could think I saw him as beneath me, that he could believe I cared about class or money or social position when all I wanted was to protect him from the truth of what I was—

"How dare you," I said, my voice barely controlled. "How dare you suggest that I—that what we have means so little to me that I would—"

"Then explain it!" Mikael shouted, standing so abruptly his chair scraped against the floor. "Explain why you keep pushing me toward America! Explain why you won't talk about our future! Explain why you seem so eager to be rid of me!"

"Because I love you!" The words tore out of me with a force that surprised us both. "Because I love you more than you could possibly understand, and that love is going to destroy us both if I don't do something to stop it!"

The silence that followed was deafening. Mikael stared at me, his face cycling through confusion, hurt, anger.

"That makes no sense," he said finally. "If you love me—"

"If you only knew," I whispered, sinking back into my chair as centuries of careful control finally crumbled. "If you only knew what loving me means. What it would cost you. What it would do to both of us."

"Then tell me," Mikael said, and his voice was quiet now, intense. "Tell me what's so terrible about loving you that it requires sending me across an ocean."

I looked up at him—this beautiful, mortal man who had somehow become everything to me—and felt the weight of impossible truth pressing against my chest. How could I explain that loving me meant watching me remain unchanged while he aged and died? How could I tell him that every day we spent together was borrowed time, that the future he dreamed of was biologically impossible?

"I can't," I said, the words breaking on the way out.

Something shifted in Mikael's expression then, hurt hardening into something closer to betrayal.

"I see," he said, his voice flat. "So I'm good enough to share your bed, but not your secrets. Good enough for your company, but not your trust."

"Mikael, please—"

But he was already moving, grabbing his coat from the hook by the door. On the table, the steamship ticket I had purchased—second-class passage to New York, leaving in three days—lay among the remains of our dinner like an accusation.

He picked it up, stared at it for a long moment, then tore it in half.

"Keep your charity," he said, the pieces fluttering to the floor. "And keep your secrets. I hope they serve you better than I have."

The door slammed behind him with such force that the windows rattled.

I sat alone in the sudden silence, staring at the torn ticket, my father's words echoing in my memory with cruel clarity: *To love a mortal is to place yourself into a ticking clock, counting down the painful years to the inevitable.*

I had tried to stop the clock. Instead, I had shattered it completely.

~

Soren Jensen

I could hear the old pain in his voice, though it seemed tempered by time and perspective. "But that changed?"

Aleksander Nordh

"It changed," I confirmed, "because of a letter I received. Completely unexpected, some years after Mikael's departure from Copenhagen. Just before he died."

I reached into my jacket pocket, withdrawing a carefully preserved envelope that I had carried with me for 110 years. The paper was cream-colored with age, the handwriting feminine and careful.

"She wrote to me," I said, offering the letter to Soren. "Linnea Jensen, writing to someone she had never met, whose name she had found among her husband's most precious possessions."

Soren Jensen

I took the letter with reverent care, noting how the paper had been preserved in perfect condition despite its age. The envelope was addressed to "Mr. A. Nordh" at a Copenhagen address, with careful script that spoke of careful determination and refinement.

"She knew about you?"

"Not explicitly. But she knew that someone in Copenhagen had mattered deeply to her husband. And she was wise enough to understand that love takes many forms."

I carefully unfolded the letter, revealing pages of thoughtful handwriting. As I began to read, I felt tears prick at my eyes.

Aleksander Nordh

I watched Soren read Linnea's words—words I had memorized decades ago but still found profoundly moving. She had written about Mikael's initial sadness upon arriving in Minnesota, about the careful way he spoke of Copenhagen, about his obvious love for someone he couldn't name but couldn't forget.

But more than that, she had written about her own understanding that love was not diminished by being shared, that the capacity for deep feeling was something to be honored rather than feared.

Soren Jensen

"'I want you to know,'" I read aloud, my voice thick with emotion, "'that I have never resented this love you shared with my husband. How could I, when it shaped him into the man who became my sanctuary? Whatever you gave him in those Copenhagen years, it made him capable of the love he has shown me and our children.'"

I looked up at Aleksander, seeing tears in his eyes that matched my own.

"She goes on to say that she hopes you found happiness, that she knows Mikael carries good memories of your friendship, and that..." I paused, overwhelmed by the generosity of spirit the letter revealed. "'I hope someday we might meet, so I can thank you properly for helping to make him the loving, thoughtful man who has become my husband.'"

Aleksander Nordh

"She signed it 'With deep gratitude and affection, Linnea Kristina Jensen,'" I said softly. "A woman I had never met, writing to someone she viewed not as a threat but as a blessing in her husband's life."

I took the letter back from Soren, refolding it with the same careful attention I had given it for over a century.

"That letter changed everything for me," I continued. "It made me understand that Anna wasn't my rival—she was Mikael's partner in building the life he had chosen. She loved him not despite his capacity for deep feeling, but because of it. She honored what we had shared rather than resenting it."

Soren Jensen

"Did you ever write back to her?"

Aleksander Nordh

"I did. A brief response, thanking her for her kindness and assuring her that Mikael was fortunate to have found someone who understood his heart so completely." I managed a slight smile. "I told her that her letter had given me peace about his choice to leave Copenhagen, that knowing he was loved and understood made my own loss bearable."

"And the jealousy?"

"Transformed into gratitude. Linnea had given Mikael what I couldn't—a life that satisfied both his heart and his sense of duty. She had loved him completely while honoring his past. How could I resent someone who had made the man I loved happy?"

Soren Jensen

We sat in comfortable silence for several minutes, watching the ducks glide across the pond while I processed everything Aleksander had shared. The weight of his choices, the complexity of his feelings, the way love had persisted across impossible circumstances—all of it painted a picture of devotion that was both heartbreaking and beautiful.

"I think," I said finally, "that you made the right choices. All of them. Letting him go, staying away, finding peace with his happiness instead of wallowing in your own loss."

Aleksander Nordh

Soren's words offered absolution I hadn't realized I still needed. For 131 years, I had second-guessed every decision, wondering if different choices might have led to different outcomes. But looking at this remarkable young man who carried Mikael's blood and his own unique gifts, I found myself finally able to accept that perhaps my choices had been right after all.

"And now?" Soren asked softly.

"Now I have you," I replied, reaching for his hand. "Mikael's descendant, carrying his kindness and curiosity and capacity for love. The bloodline found its way back to me, bringing gifts I never could have imagined."

Soren Jensen

"I'm not him," I said, needing to establish that boundary even as I treasured the connection.

"No," Aleksander agreed, bringing our joined hands to his lips. "You're not him. You're you—brilliant and thoughtful and brave enough to love someone like me despite all the complications it entails. You're the man who makes me grateful for every choice that led us to this moment."

As we sat together in the dappled sunlight of Hampstead Heath, I realized that Aleksander's story with Mikael wasn't a tragedy that had ended in loss. It was a love story that had endured across time, evolving and transforming until it had become the foundation for something new and equally precious.

The helix had indeed crossed itself, another circle intertwined, carrying love across impossible spans of time and distance, proving that some connections transcend every boundary we think defines the limits of human experience.

Aleksander Nordh

"Shall we head back?" I asked as the afternoon light began to shift toward evening.

"In a moment," Soren replied, settling closer against my side. "I'm not quite ready to leave this conversation behind. It feels too precious to rush."

So we remained on the bench, surrounded by the ancient peace of the Heath, two people separated by millennia but united by a budding love that was finding a home.

17
A RELEASE

Minnesota, September 1905

Dear Henrik,

I hope you will forgive the liberty of addressing you by the name my husband spoke in his dreams, though he never told me of you directly. I am Linnea Jensen, Mikael's wife these past twenty-three years, and I write to you now as he lies sleeping in the room beside me, his breathing grown shallow with the fever that may soon take him from us.

I found his letter to you quite by accident while searching for his will among his papers. I did not read it by design—a wife should not pry into her husband's private thoughts—but once I saw your name and understood what it contained, I could not stop myself. Please do not think poorly of me for this.

I have always known there was someone before me, someone who taught my Mikael the gentleness he shows our children and the quiet strength that has sustained our family through difficult times. I knew by the way he sometimes looked toward the horizon, as if searching for something he had lost. I knew by the careful way he taught our sons to write, with a patience that spoke of having been taught by someone who cherished the very act of learning. I knew by the way he named our firstborn John Aleksander, and how his voice grew soft whenever he spoke that middle name.

Henrik, I want you to know that I have never resented this love you shared with my husband. How could I, when it shaped him into the man who became my sanctuary? Whatever you gave him in those Copenhagen years, it made him capable of the love he has shown me and our children. A lesser man might have been diminished by such a loss. Mikael was made stronger, more gentle, more present in each moment shared.

I am not learned as you must be, but I understand enough to know that men like my husband—men like you—must often wear masks in this world. I have seen how carefully Mikael chooses his words, how he teaches our sons to be strong yet kind, how he shows them there are many ways to be a man. I believe this wisdom came from you, and from the courage it must have taken for both of you to love truly, even when the world would not understand.

I wish I could have met you, Henrik. From what I glimpse in my husband's unguarded moments, you must be someone of rare intelligence and compassion. I would have welcomed you at our table, as Mikael promised in his letter. Any man who could inspire such devotion in my husband would find a place in our home and in my heart.

But more than that, I wish to offer you my gratitude. You helped make Mikael the man who has been my partner in building this life, who has given me children who carry the best parts of both of us. You gave him something I could never give—the knowledge that he was worthy of a love that asked nothing but his happiness. That gift made him able to love me fully, without reservation, without always looking back.

I know you encouraged him to come to America, to build a life here. I know you put his welfare above your own heart. This is the deepest kind of love, Henrik, and I am humbled by it. I want you to know that your sacrifice bore fruit. Mikael has been happy here. Not complete, perhaps—I am not foolish enough to believe any of us can be complete—but happy in the way that comes from living an honest life, surrounded by people who love him.

Our eldest, John Aleksander, is now twenty-two, the same age Mikael was when he left Copenhagen. He has his father's gentle strength and his careful way with words. Our second son Erik is twenty and shows promise as a farmer and businessman. Both boys know they are loved, know they are valued for who they are, not who the world expects them to be. This too is your gift to them, passed down through their father's heart.

If this letter ever finds you, please know that Mikael Johan Jensen lived a good life. He was respected in our community, cherished by his family, and never forgot the man who taught him he was worthy of love. He spoke your name every time he called our son. He carried your memory in the patient way he taught our boys their letters. He honored what you gave him by becoming the kind of man who made others feel valued and understood.

I do not know where you are now, or even if you still walk this earth. But if you do, and if these words ever reach you, please carry with you the knowledge that your love —however brief, however difficult—created ripples of goodness that have spread far beyond what you could have imagined. You helped raise fine sons, Henrik, even though you never held them. You helped create a family built on the foundation of the love you taught their father was possible. I hope someday we might meet, so I can thank you properly for helping to make him the loving, thoughtful man who has become my husband.

I have posted this letter to the address I discovered along Mikael's, hoping that someday, somehow, it might find its way to you. Until then, please know that somewhere in Minnesota, a woman who never met you thinks of you as part of her family, and wishes you peace.

With deep gratitude and affection,

Linnea Kristina Jensen

P.S. - I have enclosed a photograph of our family taken this past summer. I thought you might like to see the man Mikael became, and the children who carry forward the love you helped him learn to give.

18
RESEARCH AND INVITATION

THE BRITISH LIBRARY 96 EUSTON ROAD, LONDON NW1 2DB

Soren Jensen

The British Library had become our second home. Over the past three weeks, Aleksander and I had claimed the same corner table each afternoon, spreading out military records, immigration documents, and ship manifests like archaeologists piecing together fragments of an ancient civilization. What had started as my individual research project had transformed into something far more personal—and far more complex.

"Look at this," I said, sliding a photocopied document across the table to Aleksander. "Battalion deployment records from the 13th Minnesota. John's unit was stationed specifically in the San Miguel district of Manila from March 1903 through February 1904."

Aleksander studied the document with the careful attention he brought to everything. "That's remarkably specific. Most military records from that period are frustratingly vague about exact locations."

"Which means we can narrow down where he would have been living, where he would have interacted with the local population." I pulled out a hand-drawn map I'd been working on. "I've been plotting all the locations mentioned in his correspondence with locations where we know prominent Filipino families lived."

Over the weeks, our research had revealed a clearer picture of John Mikael Jensen's time in the Philippines. The social registry documents Aleksander had found proved John attended multiple events where the Mercado family was present. More importantly, we'd discovered that Professor Antonio Mercado had served as an unofficial liaison between the American administration and Filipino intellectuals—exactly the kind of person a thoughtful soldier like John would have encountered regularly.

Aleksander Nordh

Watching Soren work was like watching a master craftsman. His methodical approach to genealogical research, combined with his genuine passion for understanding his family's story, reminded me constantly of why I'd fallen for Mikael—and why I was falling deeper for Soren with each passing day.

But there was something else driving my interest in this research, something I hadn't yet shared with Soren. Each piece of evidence we uncovered about John's time in Manila felt like confirmation of a theory that had been growing in my mind for months. The timing, the location, the social connections—everything aligned with what I knew about Rafael's family background.

"Soren," I said, setting down a shipping manifest we'd been examining. "I think it's time I arranged that meeting with Rafael."

He looked up from his notes, excitement immediate in his expression. "Really? You think he's ready?"

"I think we need to find out. The research has given us enough circumstantial evidence to suggest a connection, but if Rafael truly is related to your family..." I paused, choosing my words carefully. "He deserves to know. And more importantly, he deserves to have family, even if he doesn't understand that's what it is yet."

~

THE APPROACH

I found Rafael where I usually did—in the rare books section of Senate House Library, seated at a table far from the windows, surrounded by art history texts and auction catalogs. Even after years of acquaintance, our interactions remained carefully formal. Rafael had built walls around himself that I respected but had never quite managed to breach.

"Good evening, Rafael," I said quietly, settling into the chair across from him.

He looked up, offering that polite smile that never quite reached his eyes. "Aleksander. I didn't expect to see you tonight."

"I was hoping we might be able to meet for dinner sometime this week," I said, keeping my tone casual. "There's a lovely little place in Clerkenwell I thought you might enjoy. Very quiet, very discreet."

As always, Rafael's response was gracious but distant. "That's very kind, but I'm rather busy with research at the moment. Perhaps another time?"

I had expected this—Rafael always found polite ways to decline social invitations. But tonight, I pressed on.

"Actually, I was hoping you might allow me to bring someone along. My boyfriend, Soren. I'd very much like you to meet him."

Rafael Mercado

The word stopped me cold. Boyfriend. In all our years of careful acquaintance, Aleksander had never mentioned anyone significant in his life. I'd simply assumed—perhaps wrongly—that Elder vampires maintained their solitary existence across centuries. The idea that Aleksander had found someone, that he was willing to share that connection with me, was both surprising and oddly touching.

"I... I didn't know you were..." I began, then stopped, embarrassed by my assumption.

"Gay?" Aleksander's expression was gentle, amused. "Yes, well, it's not something we've discussed. We've kept our conversations rather... professional."

That was true. Despite his kindness over the years, despite his occasional attempts to help me navigate vampire society, we'd never moved beyond the surface level of mentor and reluctant student. I'd been too guarded, too damaged by my transformation to allow a real connection.

But something about his willingness to share this personal detail, to trust me with something precious to him, cracked something in my carefully maintained defenses.

"He's human?" I asked quietly.

"He is. He knows about us—about what we are—and he's... remarkable." There was something in Aleksander's voice I'd never heard before. Warmth. Genuine happiness. "I think you'd like him."

The offer terrified me. I hadn't had a social interaction beyond these careful meetings with Aleksander in... years. The thought of meeting someone new, someone human who knew about their kind, someone important to Aleksander —it felt like standing at the edge of a cliff.

But beneath the fear was something else. Loneliness. Curiosity. A desperate hunger for connection that I'd been denying for so long I'd almost forgotten it existed.

"I..." I started, then stopped. Aleksander waited patiently while I struggled with myself. "Would Tuesday evening work? Somewhere... not too crowded?"

"Perfect. There's a restaurant in Clerkenwell, very quiet after ten o'clock. The owner is... understanding about unusual dining hours."

"Ten o'clock," I repeated, already wondering if I was making a terrible mistake. "And his name is Soren?"

"Soren Jensen. He's a graduate student, researching cultural history. Very thoughtful, very kind." Aleksander paused. "You don't need to worry about impressing him, Rafael. Just be yourself."

Just be yourself. If only it were that simple. I hadn't been myself in so long I wasn't sure I remembered who that was.

~

PREPARATION

Soren Jensen

"He said yes?" I couldn't hide my excitement as Aleksander related the conversation. "He actually agreed to meet?"

"He did, though I suspect he's already regretting it." Aleksander settled beside me on his sofa, pulling me close in the way that had become natural over these past weeks. "Rafael doesn't do well with social situations. His transformation was... traumatic. He's been essentially isolated for over a decade."

I tried to imagine it—being cut off from family, from friends, from any meaningful human connection for eleven years. The loneliness must have been crushing.

"What should I know about him? How can I make this easier?"

Aleksander was quiet for a moment, considering. "He's brilliant, cultured, passionate about art and beauty. But he's also deeply ashamed of what he is, convinced he's somehow monstrous despite appearing completely human. He'll be analyzing every word you say, every expression, looking for signs of fear or disgust."

"And he has no idea he might be related to my family?"

"None. As far as Rafael knows, his family history ends with his parents in Manila, who believe he died by suicide eleven years ago."

The tragedy of it hit me fresh. Here was someone who might be my cousin, alone in the world, convinced his family was better off thinking him dead. Someone who'd lost everything to a transformation he never chose.

"Aleksander," I said quietly, "we have to help him. Whatever it takes."

Aleksander Nordh

Soren's immediate compassion for someone he'd never met, his instinctive understanding of Rafael's pain—it was so perfectly him that my chest tightened with affection. Over these weeks of research and growing intimacy, I'd watched Soren evolve from a shy graduate student into someone confident in his own skin, secure in our relationship, ready to extend that security to others.

"The dinner location—I chose it carefully," I said. "A small place in Clerkenwell, tucked away from main streets. The owner, Marcus, is someone I've known for years. He understands the need for discretion."

"Will Rafael be safe? I mean, meeting at night, in a quiet area..."

"Regulars are actually quite resilient. Stronger and faster than humans, enhanced senses. It's daylight that's their weakness, not darkness." I paused. "Though Rafael's greatest vulnerabilities aren't physical."

We spent the evening discussing how to approach the meeting—keeping conversation light, avoiding questions about Rafael's transformation, letting him guide the interaction. But ultimately, we decided Aleksander's earlier advice was best: just be ourselves.

TUESDAY EVENING

Rafael Mercado

I stood in my warehouse flat, staring at my reflection in the floor-length mirror I'd positioned specifically to check my appearance before any public outing. The face looking back at me appeared human enough—pale but not unnaturally so, features sharp but not otherworldly. To any casual observer, I would simply seem like a young man dressed with perhaps more care than the occasion warranted.

But I knew the truth beneath the surface. The accelerated metabolism that required careful feeding schedules. The sensitivity to UV radiation that kept me largely nocturnal. The enhanced strength that I had to constantly monitor and control. The biological markers that would scream "other" to anyone who looked closely enough.

The restaurant was a fifteen-minute walk through quiet Clerkenwell streets. I'd scouted the route twice over the past week, identifying exit strategies and ensuring I could reach the location without passing through areas with heavy foot traffic. Paranoid, perhaps, but eleven years of careful existence had taught me the value of preparation.

Ten o'clock arrived. Then ten-fifteen. Ten-thirty.

I remained in my flat, fully dressed, ready to leave, paralyzed by a fear I couldn't name or overcome.

Soren Jensen

The restaurant was exactly as Aleksander had described—intimate, dimly lit, with only a handful of occupied tables despite the Tuesday evening hour. Marcus, the owner, had greeted Aleksander with the familiarity of long acquaintance and shown us to a corner table with clear sightlines to both entrances.

"He'll come," I said, more to convince myself than Aleksander. "He's probably just nervous."

"Probably," Aleksander agreed, but I could see the concern in his expression.

Ten-fifteen came and went. Then ten-thirty. By ten forty-five, it was clear that Rafael wasn't coming.

"I pushed too hard," Aleksander said quietly, his disappointment evident. "I should have waited longer, built more trust before suggesting this."

I reached across the table and took his hand. "You couldn't have known. Maybe he just needs more time."

But even as I said it, I felt the weight of missed opportunity. Somewhere across London, there was someone who might be family, who was sitting alone rather than taking the risk of connection. Someone who'd been isolated for so long that even the possibility of friendship felt too dangerous to attempt.

Aleksander Nordh

As we walked home through the quiet London streets, I found myself thinking about patterns—how fear and isolation reinforced each other, how trauma could trap someone in an endless cycle of loneliness. I saw it in other Regulars who'd struggled with their transformation, but Rafael's case felt different. More profound. More heartbreaking.

"We'll try again," Soren said as we reached my flat. "However long it takes."

"Yes," I agreed, though I wondered if Rafael would ever trust me enough to accept another invitation after failing to appear tonight. "However long it takes."

But in my heart, I feared that some wounds ran too deep for even time and patience to heal. And somewhere in London, Rafael was learning once again that it was safer to remain alone than to risk the possibility of connection—and loss.

~

ACROSS TOWN

Rafael Mercado

I sat in my warehouse flat until well past midnight, still dressed for a dinner I couldn't bring myself to attend. The carefully chosen outfit—black wool trousers, dark blue cashmere sweater, the vintage watch I'd inherited from my grandfather—felt like costume pieces for a role I'd forgotten how to play.

The rational part of my mind catalogued all the reasons I should have gone: Aleksander's kindness over the years, my desperate need for connection, the simple courtesy of not standing someone up without explanation. But rationality had no power over the paralyzing certainty that I would somehow contaminate whatever happiness Aleksander had found with his human boyfriend.

Better to be thought rude than to be seen for what I truly was.

As I finally changed into sleeping clothes, I caught sight of my reflection again. Same pale skin, same sharp features, same illusion of humanity. But now I could see what lay beneath—the monster who fed on blood, who had abandoned his family to their grief, who was too damaged to accept even the simplest gesture of friendship.

Tomorrow, I would return to my carefully constructed solitude. And Aleksander would learn, once and for all, that some people were meant to remain alone.

19
STOCKHOLM DISCOVERIES

34,000 FEET NORTH SEA, INTERNATIONAL WATERS

Soren Jensen

The flight to Stockholm felt surreal. While I'd flown internationally before—from Minnesota to London for graduate school—this was my first time traveling on such short notice, and my first time visiting anywhere with such deeply personal significance. Aleksander sat beside me, apparently comfortable with the casual luxury of business class seats—another reminder of the vast differences in our circumstances. But what struck me more was how relaxed he seemed, a contrast to the controlled tension I'd grown used to seeing in him.

"You're different when you travel," I observed as we leveled off over the North Sea.

"How so?"

"More... yourself, I think. Less carefully managed." I watched him sip his coffee without the usual precise movements. "Like you don't have to perform as much."

Aleksander considered this, looking out the window at the clouds below. "Perhaps because I'm between identities right now. Henrik Nordh stays in London. Aleksander gets to visit Sweden. For a few days, I don't have to maintain a character."

The honesty in his voice made my chest tight. How exhausting it must be, I thought, to always be performing some version of yourself for public consumption.

"What was Mikael like when you two went places together?" I asked. "When you traveled?"

"We didn't travel far—Copenhagen to nearby Danish towns, occasionally across to southern Sweden by ferry," Aleksander said, his expression softening with memory. "Nothing like this—no comfortable flights or luxury hotels. We'd take the train to Helsingør, or ride the ferry to Malmö for a weekend. Once we went as far as Gothenburg, which felt like an enormous adventure at the time."

He paused, looking out at the clouds below us. "But Mikael was curious about everything, wherever we went. He'd strike up conversations with fellow passengers, ask questions about local customs, insist on trying every regional dish. He made me see familiar places through fresh eyes."

Aleksander's smile was wistful. "He would have been absolutely enchanted by this—the ease of flight, the speed of travel, the luxury of it all. But mostly, he would have loved the purpose of the journey. Mikael was always excited about discovery, about understanding where things came from."

Aleksander Nordh

Describing Mikael to Soren felt strange—not painful, as I'd expected, but almost healing. For so long, my memories of him had been private, protected, sacred. Sharing them felt like letting sunlight into a room that had been shuttered for decades.

"He would have loved this," I said, watching Soren study the flight map with the same careful attention he brought to historical documents. "Planning the research, anticipating what we might find. Mikael was always excited about discovery."

"Like me?"

"Very much like you." I reached for his hand, intertwining our fingers. "Though you're more methodical than he was. Mikael was all intuition and enthusiasm. You balance those with actual planning."

As we began our descent into Stockholm, I felt something I hadn't anticipated: peace. For the first time in 131 years, I was returning to Mikael's homeland not to mourn what I'd lost, but to share what I'd found.

STOCKHOLM ARCHIVES

Soren Jensen

The Swedish National Archives occupied a modern building that seemed designed to intimidate researchers into respectful silence. But Aleksander moved through the registration process with the confidence of someone who'd navigated countless bureaucracies across centuries. Within an hour, we were seated at a research table with boxes of 19th-century parish records and municipal documents.

"Parish records from Rättviks kommun," the archivist had explained, "covering the area north of Lake Siljan where your ancestor would have been born. And here are some municipal records from Stockholm for the 1870s, when he would have been working there before emigrating."

I opened the first record book with trembling hands. The pages were filled with careful Swedish script documenting births, deaths, marriages, and confirmations dating back to the 1840s. Each entry told a story—families growing, children being born, lives being lived in a small farming community that felt impossibly distant from modern Stockholm.

"Here," Aleksander said quietly, pointing to an entry dated October 15, 1860. "Mikael Johan Jensen, son of Johan Erik Jensen and Astrid Kristina Larsson."

Aleksander Nordh

Seeing Mikael's birth recorded in the parish registry hit me harder than I'd expected. Here was official documentation of the beginning of a life that had shaped mine in ways the parish clerk could never have imagined. The careful script noted not just his birth, but his baptism three weeks later, his parents' occupations (farmer and seamstress), and their address in the village.

"His parents," Soren said, studying the record. "Johan Erik and Astrid Kristina. And look—he had siblings." He traced other entries with his finger. "An older sister, Margareta, born in 1858. A younger brother, Gustaf, born in 1862."

Family members I'd never known about. People who had shaped Mikael's childhood, influenced his character, perhaps even contributed to the gentle strength that had drawn me to him. For the first time, I understood that the man I'd loved had come from somewhere specific, had been part of a web of relationships that preceded our meeting.

"There's more," Soren continued, turning pages carefully. "Confirmation records from 1875, when Mikael would have been fifteen. And here..." He paused, studying an entry. "A note about the family moving to Stockholm in

1876. 'Johan Erik Jensen and family relocated to Stockholm for employment opportunities.'"

Soren Jensen

The records painted a picture of a family adapting to changing times. Sweden in the 1870s was undergoing rapid industrialization, and families like the Jensens were leaving rural communities for opportunities in the cities. Mikael's move to Copenhagen, I realized, was part of a larger pattern of young Scandinavians seeking their fortunes beyond their birthplaces.

"But why Copenhagen instead of staying in Stockholm?" I wondered aloud.

"Independence," Aleksander replied immediately. "Mikael mentioned once that he wanted to be his own man before returning to family expectations. Stockholm would have meant living under his father's watchful eye."

We spent the morning tracing the Jensen family through various records—employment documents showing Johan Erik working as a carpenter in Stockholm, marriage records for Margareta in 1878, military service papers for Gustaf showing his service in Sweden. Each document added another piece to the puzzle of Mikael's background.

"This is fascinating," I said, making notes as we worked through the documents. "You can really see how families adapted to the changing economy. Johan Erik moving from farming to carpentry, Mikael seeking opportunities beyond Sweden..."

"And Gustaf remained," Aleksander added, studying the records. "He served in the Swedish military, stayed close to home. The cautious one in the family, perhaps."

As the afternoon progressed, we continued our methodical search through immigration and military records, but found ourselves hitting the same wall that had frustrated us in London. The connections we were seeking remained elusive.

CONTINUING THE SEARCH

Soren Jensen

We'd moved on to immigration records, hoping to find documentation of Mikael's departure for Copenhagen, and perhaps other family movements. The archivist brought us passenger manifests from Swedish ports during the late

1870s and early 1880s. I was methodically working through lists, but after hours of searching, we found little more than we already knew.

"We're still missing something," I said, leaning back in my chair with frustration. "All these records show us Mikael's family, his background, his context, but they don't bring us any closer to understanding the connection to Rafael."

Aleksander nodded thoughtfully. "Perhaps the connection isn't through Mikael's immediate family. Perhaps it's something more distant, or through different branches we haven't considered yet."

Aleksander Nordh

I could see the disappointment in Soren's face, and I understood it completely. We'd come so far, uncovered so much about Mikael's early life, yet we were still no closer to proving the connection that might help Rafael.

"Wait," Soren said suddenly, pulling one of the record books back toward him. "There's something odd about Gustaf's records."

I leaned over as he traced through the documents we'd found. "What do you mean?"

"He never married. Look—no marriage record, no children listed anywhere. But he inherited property, and when he died, everything went to his nephews." Soren frowned, studying the papers. "That's unusual for the era. Most men his age would have married, especially if they had property to pass down."

"Perhaps he was simply devoted to remaining a bachelor," I suggested, though something about the pattern felt familiar in a way I couldn't quite place.

"And here's something else," Soren continued, pulling out a shipping manifest we'd almost overlooked. "This entry is dated 1883, just after Mikael left for America. 'Gustaf Jensen, age 21, Stockholm to Copenhagen. Purpose: Employment.'"

I felt a chill of recognition. "He followed Mikael to Copenhagen."

"But there's no record of him ever returning to Sweden. And look at this—" Soren opened another document, this one clearly a will. "His final testament. Written in Danish, not Swedish."

The document was old and faded, the ink barely legible in places. I used my enhanced vision to make out the formal legal language, but even with my abilities, some sections were nearly impossible to decipher.

"Most of the estate goes to his nephew, as we saw," I said, reading carefully. "But there's something else here... a smaller bequest." I squinted at the faded script. "To one 'R. Jørgensen'—a collection of books, it appears."

"R. Jørgensen?" Soren repeated. "Who would that be? And why would Gustaf be making bequests to someone with a Danish surname if he'd remained in Sweden? Maybe he didn't go back after all?"

The pieces were forming a picture I wasn't sure I wanted to see. Gustaf following Mikael to Copenhagen. A life that apparently remained unmarried. A will written in Danish, suggesting he'd made Denmark his permanent home. And a mysterious "R. Jørgensen" who had meant enough to Gustaf to inherit his books.

"Alek," Soren said quietly, "do you think Gustaf might have been..."

"Like Mikael?" I finished, understanding immediately what he was suggesting. "Living a life in Copenhagen that he couldn't live in Sweden?"

The possibility hung between us, unspoken but understood. If Gustaf had followed his brother to Copenhagen, if he too had found love and acceptance in that more cosmopolitan city, it would explain so much about the scattered records and the life that seemed to exist in the margins of official documentation.

EVENING REFLECTIONS

Soren Jensen

We returned to our hotel as the sun set over Stockholm's harbor, our heads spinning with discoveries. The small, elegant room Aleksander had booked overlooked the old town, and I stood at the window watching lights come on in medieval buildings while processing everything we'd learned.

"Gustaf Jensen," I said, reflecting on what we'd learned. "Mikael's brother who followed him to Copenhagen."

"A different path than we initially thought," Aleksander confirmed. He was sitting on the bed, having shed his jacket and tie, looking more contemplative than I'd ever seen him. "Gustaf apparently never married, never had children. His property went to nephews back in Sweden, but he himself seems to have made Copenhagen his home."

"And this R. Jørgensen," I mused, still puzzling over the mysterious name in Gustaf's will. "Important enough to inherit Gustaf's books, but we have no idea who they were."

"Books are often the most personal possessions," Aleksander said softly. "You don't leave your library to casual acquaintances. That bequest suggests real affection, real connection."

I looked at him, understanding the implication. "You think Gustaf found what Mikael found in Copenhagen? Someone to love?"

"It's possible. Two brothers, both leaving Sweden for the freedom Copenhagen offered, both perhaps finding acceptance there that they couldn't find at home." Aleksander's expression was thoughtful. "It would explain why

Gustaf never returned, why his will was written in Danish, why he remained unmarried by conventional standards."

Aleksander Nordh

As Soren joined me on the bed, curling against my side in the way that had become natural between us, I found myself thinking about the patterns we'd uncovered. Two Jensen brothers, both drawn to Copenhagen, both apparently finding lives there that differed from conventional expectations.

"It makes me wonder," I said, stroking Soren's hair as he settled against my chest, "about the kinds of secrets families keep, the stories that don't make it into official records."

"You mean like yours and Mikael's relationship?" Soren asked quietly.

"Exactly. If someone were researching Mikael's life a century from now, they'd find records of his marriage, his children, his respectable American life. They'd never know about our four years together, about what meant most to him during that time."

"So Gustaf and this R. Jørgensen..."

"Might represent another love story that history tried to erase," I finished. "Another connection that mattered deeply to the people involved, even if it couldn't be officially acknowledged."

"Tomorrow we visit the village," I said after a moment. "We'll see the church where Mikael was baptized, maybe find the farm where he grew up."

"Are you ready for that?"

I considered the question seriously. A week ago, the prospect would have terrified me. But now, having spent the day uncovering evidence of love persisting in unexpected places, having shared those discoveries with Soren, the idea of visiting Mikael's birthplace felt less like confronting loss and more like honoring a legacy of courage.

"Yes," I said, surprised by how much I meant it. "I think I finally am."

As we prepared for sleep, I realized that while we hadn't found the concrete evidence about Rafael's connection to our families, we had discovered something perhaps more important—that love finds a way to persist across generations, even when the official records try to deny its existence. Sometimes, that was its own kind of proof.

~

SATURDAY MORNING: THE VILLAGE

Soren Jensen

The train journey north from Stockholm took us through landscapes that seemed frozen in time—dense forests, red wooden houses, lakes that reflected the autumn sky like mirrors. As we traveled deeper into the countryside, I could see Aleksander growing quieter, more contemplative.

"Nervous?" I asked as we pulled into the small station that served Rättvik and the surrounding farming communities.

"Anticipatory," he corrected, but I could see the tension in his shoulders.

The village itself was smaller than I'd expected—a collection of traditional wooden buildings clustered around a white stone church that had clearly stood for centuries. The autumn air was crisp and clean, carrying the scent of woodsmoke and fallen leaves.

"The church first?" Aleksander suggested, though his voice was carefully controlled.

As we walked up the path to the entrance, I realized we were retracing steps Mikael had taken countless times as a child. The worn stones beneath our feet, the heavy wooden door, the peaceful cemetery surrounding the building—all of it had been part of his daily world.

"Aleksander," I said, taking his hand as we paused before the church door. "We can do this together."

His smile was grateful and genuine. "Together," he agreed, and pushed open the door.

The interior was simple but beautiful—white-painted walls, wooden pews worn smooth by generations of worshippers, afternoon light streaming through tall windows. At the front, an ornate pulpit bore the inscription "Herren är min herde" in flowing script.

"The Lord is my shepherd," Aleksander translated softly. "Mikael would have heard those words every Sunday."

We found the baptismal font near the entrance—an ancient stone basin that had welcomed countless children into the faith over the centuries. I tried to imagine a three-week-old Mikael being held over this same font, his parents and siblings gathered around, his whole life stretching ahead of him.

"He stood here for his confirmation," Aleksander said, approaching the altar area. "Fifteen years old, promising to live as a faithful Christian. He told me once that he took those vows seriously, even when his life took unexpected turns."

The weight of history in that simple statement nearly overwhelmed me. Here was the foundation of the man who had shaped both our lives—his faith, his values, his sense of right and wrong all formed in this quiet place.

. . .

Aleksander Nordh

Standing in Mikael's childhood church felt like touching something sacred. Not just the religious sanctity of the space, but the deeper holiness of understanding where someone you loved had learned to be the person you fell in love with.

"Thank you," I whispered, though I wasn't sure if I was addressing Mikael, his memory, or something larger. "Thank you for leading me here. For leading me to Soren. For making this possible."

As we prepared to leave, the elderly pastor approached us with curiosity and kindness. "Visitors?" he asked in accented English, having heard us speaking.

"My boyfriend's ancestor was baptized here," Soren explained. "Mikael Johan Jensen, in 1860."

The pastor's face lit up with interest. "Jensen! Yes, there are many Jensen graves in our cemetery. And the old farm is still standing, you know. Just north of the village, perhaps a kilometer walk. The family who owns it now might be willing to show you around, if you're interested."

Soren looked at me with barely contained excitement. "Would you like to see where he grew up?"

For the first time in 131 years, the answer was an unqualified yes.

"Very much," I said, meaning it completely. "Let's go home."

20
FINDING FAMILY

JENSEN FAMILY FARM (HISTORICAL) SILJANSNÄS 47, 795 91 RÄTTVIK, SWEDEN

Soren Jensen

The walk to the farm took us through countryside that seemed untouched by time. Rolling fields stretched toward distant forests, interrupted by traditional red wooden buildings and stone walls that had probably stood for centuries. The autumn air carried the scent of woodsmoke and dying leaves, and I found myself trying to imagine a young Mikael walking these same paths.

"There," Aleksander said quietly, pointing ahead to a cluster of buildings nestled in a valley. "That must be it."

The farmhouse was larger than I'd expected—a two-story wooden structure painted the traditional Swedish red, with white trim around windows that gleamed in the afternoon sunlight. Outbuildings surrounded it: a massive barn, several smaller storage structures, and what looked like a workshop. Smoke curled from the chimney, and I could see figures moving around the yard.

As we approached, an older woman emerged from the house, wiping her hands on an apron. She had the same general build as the people in the old photographs we'd seen—sturdy, practical, with sharp blue eyes that seemed to take in everything at once. When those eyes fixed on me, she went very still.

"Marta Eriksson," she said in accented English, extending a work-roughened hand. "You are looking for Jensen family, yes?"

"Yes," I replied, suddenly nervous. "I'm Soren Jensen, from America. We were hoping—"

"Jensen eyes," she interrupted, studying my face with intensity that made me uncomfortable. "You have Jensen eyes. And the jaw." She tilted her head, considering. "Soren, you said? Mikael's line?"

Aleksander Nordh

Watching this recognition unfold felt like witnessing something magical. Here was a woman who could see Mikael in Soren's features, who knew the family history well enough to place him immediately. The ease with which she accepted his presence, the way her entire demeanor warmed once she'd made the connection—it was everything I'd hoped for but hadn't dared expect.

"Come," Marta said, already turning toward the house. "Lars! Lars, come meet the boy. Mikael's boy, from America!"

A man appeared from the barn—tall, weathered, with the same sharp eyes as his wife. Lars Eriksson moved with the careful economy of someone who'd spent his life doing physical labor, but his face lit up when he saw us.

"Mikael's line?" he asked in English that was better than his wife's. "Truly?"

"My great-great-great grandfather," Soren confirmed, and I watched as both Erikssons broke into delighted smiles.

"Come inside," Marta insisted. "Coffee. Food. You must tell us everything."

AFTERNOON DISCOVERIES

Soren Jensen

The farmhouse interior was exactly what I'd imagined from stories about Swedish country homes—low ceilings, whitewashed walls, and furniture that had been carefully maintained for generations. But what struck me most were the photographs covering every available surface. Dozens of them, spanning what looked like over a century of family history.

"Margareta was my great-grandmother," Marta explained, pointing to a formal portrait of a stern-looking woman in Victorian dress. "Mikael's older sister. She married into the Eriksson family, and when Gustaf inherited the farm, it stayed with us."

"So you're direct descendants of Mikael's sister," I said, feeling excitement build in my chest. "We're actually cousins."

"Distant cousins," Lars corrected with a smile. "But family is family, ja?"

"So you're studying Swedish family history?" Lars asked, settling back in his chair with interest. "That's good work, important work. But why come all the way to London for that? We have excellent universities here in Sweden - Uppsala, Stockholm University, ja? Wouldn't it make more sense to study Swedish heritage where it actually comes from?"

Soren exchanged a glance with Aleksander before answering. "That's actually a really good question, and one my advisor asked too. My research focuses specifically on Swedish-American migration patterns - how Swedish culture adapted and changed after immigration to America. King's College has one of the best Cultural History departments for studying transatlantic migration, and their archives include extensive records of Scandinavian diaspora communities. Plus, London's position as a historical hub means they have colonial and migration records that you can't find anywhere else—"

I felt Aleksander's gentle touch on my arm and caught sight of Lars and Marta's slightly glazed expressions. Heat crept up my neck as I realized I'd slipped into full academic mode.

"Sorry," I said, clearing my throat. "What I mean is... I'm studying what happened to Swedish families after they left Sweden, not Swedish families who stayed. And the British kept really good records of everyone who passed through London on their way somewhere else."

"Ah," Marta said, her expression brightening with understanding. "So you need British filing cabinets, not Swedish ones."

Lars chuckled, and I noticed his eyes flick briefly to where Aleksander's hand still rested on my arm. "Much clearer, young man. Though next time, maybe lead with the simple version, ja?"

Aleksander squeezed my arm gently before letting go, and I caught the smallest hint of amusement in his voice when he said, "Soren sometimes forgets not everyone has spent years in graduate seminars."

"It's an occupational hazard," I admitted sheepishly.

As the afternoon progressed, I found myself taking charge of the conversation in a way that surprised me. Usually, Aleksander was the one who guided social interactions, but something about being surrounded by Jensen family history made me more confident, more naturally social. I asked questions about family traditions, shared stories about our Swedish-American heritage, and marveled at the photographs and documents they brought out.

Aleksander Nordh

Watching Soren come alive in this environment was beautiful and heartbreaking in equal measure. This was his element—surrounded by family, sharing stories, building connections across generations and continents. He moved through the farmhouse with increasing confidence, asking all the right questions, showing genuine interest in every photograph and anecdote.

But for me, every corner of this place held echoes of Mikael. The way afternoon light slanted through the kitchen windows, the creak of floorboards that he would have known by heart, the view from the bedroom where he'd probably slept as a child—all of it overwhelmed me with a mixture of joy and profound loss.

"You are quiet," Marta observed, refilling my coffee cup. "Is difficult, yes? To see where he grew up?"

I nodded, not trusting my voice.

"He was special boy," she continued. "My great-grandmother, she told stories. Always curious, always asking questions. Always dreaming of places beyond here."

"Yes," I managed. "He was."

UNEXPECTED COMPANY

Soren Jensen

We'd been there for several hours when Lars suggested we stay for dinner. Marta was already bustling around the kitchen, despite our protests that we didn't want to impose.

"Family is not imposition," she declared. "Besides, Erik comes for dinner soon. Our grandson. He should meet American cousins."

As if summoned by her words, the front door opened and a teenager slouched in, pulling earbuds from his ears and stuffing his phone into the pocket of an oversized hoodie. He looked like any fifteen-year-old—slightly sullen, more interested in his device than his surroundings, dark hair falling across his eyes.

"Erik," Marta called. "Come meet family. From America."

The boy—Erik—glanced up briefly, offered a halfhearted wave, and headed for the kitchen.

"Family is sometimes..." Marta searched for the word, speaking to us in a lower voice. "Mixed up? Erik's parents, they have troubles. He lives with us now."

I felt a pang of sympathy for this kid, clearly dealing with family disruption while trying to navigate being a teenager. When we all sat down to dinner, Erik picked at his food and stared at his phone, largely ignoring the adults' conversation about genealogy and old photographs.

But after Marta and Lars had cleared the dishes and retreated to the kitchen, Erik looked up from his phone and fixed us with an unexpectedly direct gaze.

"So how long have you guys been boyfriends?" he asked casually.

Aleksander Nordh

The question caught me completely off guard, though I tried not to show it. Soren went slightly red around the ears—a sure sign of embarrassment.

"How could you tell?" Soren asked. "We thought we were being discreet."

Erik snorted. "Please. It's obvious. The way you look at each other, the way you sit. I mean, it's not like you're holding hands or anything, but come on." He shrugged. "I'm cool with it. I mean, I'm gay too. Who cares?"

I found myself laughing despite my surprise. "Direct, aren't you?"

"My grandparents think I don't pay attention to anything except my phone," Erik said with a slight smile. "But I notice stuff."

"Do you know who we are?" I asked, curious about his perspective. "Beyond being distant relatives?"

"Should I?"

"We're related," Soren explained.

"Yeah?"

"Yeah."

"How?"

I studied the boy for a moment, thinking about kids his age. Sometimes they appreciated directness over polite circumlocution. "Because I was his lover," I said simply, nodding toward the photographs of Mikael that still covered the coffee table. "Your great-great-great uncle Mikael. In Copenhagen, over 130 years ago."

Erik Eriksson

For a second, I just stared at him. Like, what? This guy was claiming he'd been alive over 130 years ago? That was... that was impossible. I looked at Soren, expecting him to laugh or roll his eyes or something, but he just sat there looking completely normal. Like Aleksander had just said he'd met Mikael at the grocery store last week.

At first I thought maybe they were messing with me. Adults did that sometimes—made up crazy stories to see if the dumb kid would believe them. But Aleksander wasn't smiling or acting like he was telling a joke. His expression was just... matter-of-fact. Pleasant, even. Like I'd asked him what he did for work and he'd answered honestly.

And Soren was backing him up. Not in an obvious way, but he wasn't contradicting him either. He was just sitting there, completely calm, like this was the most normal conversation in the world.

Something about it seemed... not impossible. Which was weird, because everything about it should have been impossible. Nothing I'd learned in school, nothing anyone had ever told me, nothing that made any logical sense said I should believe this. If someone had been alive for over 130 years, they'd have to be like a vampire or something, and that was impos—

Oh.

Oh.

I looked back at Aleksander, really looked at him. He was just sitting there, waiting patiently for my reaction. Not scary or threatening or anything. Just... there. And Soren was watching me too, but his expression was kind. Like they were both waiting to see if I could handle this information.

They trusted me with this. Two adults who saw me as something more than just a stupid kid who needed to be lied to. They were treating me like I could handle the truth, whatever that truth was.

Soren Jensen

I watched Erik process what Aleksander had just revealed, saw the disbelief give way to consideration, then to something that looked like understanding. This fifteen-year-old kid was handling the revelation better than I had initially.

"Yeah," Erik said finally, his voice quiet but certain. "I get it."

He didn't really understand—how could he? But he believed us. More than that, he accepted what we were telling him without demanding proof or explanations that we couldn't give.

Erik Eriksson

I felt my face getting hot. "So you're like... you know..." I couldn't say the word 'vampire' out loud. It felt too weird. But I thought it.

And then I wondered if vampires could read minds, because Aleksander was looking right at me with this expression that seemed to see everything I was thinking. I looked away, embarrassed.

But when I glanced back, he just seemed... understanding. Not judgmental or amused by my awkwardness. Just patient.

"Maybe..." I said, trying to sound casual, "maybe I could visit you guys in London sometime. You know, see more of the world than this place." I paused, then added with a slight grin, "Maybe find someone cool like Aleksander. He's kinda hot anyway."

The words were out before I could stop them, and I felt my face turn even redder.

Aleksander Nordh

The boy's honesty was both endearing and familiar. Young people often wore their hearts on their sleeves in ways that adults had learned to guard against. I could see him struggling with his curiosity, his newfound understanding, and his very human teenager's concerns about fitting in and finding connection.

I knew my gamble had paid off. Sometimes you needed to extend a hand to those who felt marginalized. Erik might still need help developing his understanding of the world, but what he really needed was the opportunity to walk on his own path, knowing someone was around to catch him when he fell. And he would fall—we all did. But with guidance, he'd get back up and learn.

I had learned that lesson over centuries. Soren was learning it now. And Erik had just received his first real lesson in trust and acceptance.

"You're always welcome in London," I said simply. "Family looks out for family."

Erik nodded, and I could see something settle in his expression—a kind of peace that came from being truly seen and accepted for who you were, rather than who others expected you to be.

"That's pretty cool," he said, looking back at the photographs of Mikael. "What was he like?"

Soren Jensen

And just like that, the conversation transformed. Erik tucked his phone away entirely and leaned forward, suddenly engaged in a way his grandparents clearly hadn't seen in a while. Aleksander began sharing stories about Mikael—not the careful, edited versions he'd given me initially, but real memories filled with personality and warmth.

"He had this laugh," Aleksander said, his eyes distant with memory. "When something truly surprised him, he'd throw his head back and just... let go. It was infectious. Everyone around him would start laughing too, even if they didn't know what was funny."

"Did he ever talk about home?" Erik asked. "About here?"

"All the time. He told me about learning to swim in the lake, about helping with the harvest, about winter nights when the aurora borealis would light up the entire sky." Aleksander glanced around the kitchen. "He said the kitchen always smelled like cardamom and coffee, and that his mother sang while she worked."

When Marta returned from the kitchen carrying a traditional Swedish dessert, she stopped short at the sight of Erik actually participating in conversation.

"I am amazed," she said, setting down the platter. "He usually stares at his phone. How did you get him to actually speak?"

"We're telling him about Mikael," I explained. "About what he was like as a person, not just names and dates."

"Ah," Marta said, understanding immediately. "The stories. Yes, that is what makes family real."

TREASURES IN THE ATTIC

Aleksander Nordh

Before we prepared to leave, Lars insisted on showing us some items that had been preserved in the attic.

"Gustaf's things, mostly," he explained as we climbed the narrow wooden stairs. "When he died, his will said most should go to family. Books, some papers, small things."

The attic was cramped but organized, with wooden chests and boxes arranged carefully under the slanted roof. Lars opened an old trunk, revealing layers of carefully preserved items—quilts, cookware, some tools, and at the bottom, a collection of books bound with string.

"Could those be what Gustaf left to R. Jørgensen?" Soren asked quietly.

I lifted the books carefully, noting their age and condition. Most were in Danish—poetry, philosophy, a few novels. But it was the inscription in one of them that made my breath catch.

"To my beloved R, who gave meaning to these words. Forever yours, G."

"Gustaf wasn't just living in Copenhagen," I said softly. "He was in love there. Just like Mikael."

Soren Jensen

As we prepared to leave the farm, Erik surprised us by asking for our email addresses.

"Maybe I could visit London sometime," he said with studied casualness. "You know, see more of the world than this place."

"You're always welcome," I told him, meaning it completely. "Family looks out for family."

Walking back toward the village in the gathering dusk, I felt something I'd never experienced before—the deep satisfaction of belonging to something larger than myself. Not just the academic understanding of genealogy, but the lived reality of family connection spanning oceans and generations.

"Thank you," I said to Aleksander as we reached the village center.

"For what?"

"For bringing me here. For sharing Mikael with them. For helping me understand that family isn't just about names on a tree—it's about the stories that connect us."

Aleksander Nordh

As we made our way back to Stockholm for our evening flight, I realized that this trip had accomplished something I hadn't expected. It had transformed my relationship with Mikael's memory from something private and painful into something shared and celebratory.

And perhaps most importantly, it had shown me that love—in all its forms—had a way of persisting across generations, creating connections that transcended time and distance. Gustaf and his R. Jørgensen. Mikael and me. Soren and me. Erik, finding his own path to authenticity.

The Jensen family tree was more complex and beautiful than any of us had imagined. And somewhere in London, Rafael was waiting to discover that he too might be part of this legacy of love and courage that stretched back through the centuries.

"Ready to go home?" Soren asked as we settled into our seats for the flight back to London.

"Yes," I said, taking his hand. "Ready to go home."

21
SMALL TOWN DREAMS

JENSEN FAMILY FARM (HISTORICAL) SILJANSNÄS 47, 795 91 RÄTTVIK, SWEDEN

Erik Eriksson

The rooster's crow dragged me from dreams of neon-lit streets and coffee shops where people my age talked about art and books instead of crop rotation and livestock prices. I lay in my narrow bed for a few extra minutes, staring at the ceiling I'd memorized years ago, listening to the familiar sounds of Mormor moving around the kitchen below—the gentle clatter of dishes, the whistle of the kettle, the soft humming of songs she'd learned as a girl.

Five-thirty in the morning. Same as always.

I pulled on yesterday's jeans and a sweater that had seen better days, then padded downstairs to find breakfast waiting on the kitchen table. Mormor stood at the stove, her silver hair already neatly braided, wearing the same style of housedress she'd worn for as long as I could remember. She looked up when I entered, her face lighting up with the warm smile she reserved for mornings when it was just the two of us.

"God morgon, älskling," she said, using the endearment that meant beloved. "Sleep well?"

"Fine," I replied, settling into my usual chair and reaching for the coffee she'd already poured. At fifteen, I was probably too young for the strong brew Mormor made, but she'd been letting me drink it since I was twelve. One of the small freedoms that came with living in a household where your grandparents had given up trying to enforce conventional rules about child-rearing.

Outside, I could see Morfar moving around the barn, beginning the daily routine that had shaped his life for over sixty years. Feed the animals, check the equipment, assess what needed to be done based on weather and season. He'd been doing it so long that his body moved through the motions automatically, leaving his mind free to plan and calculate and worry about things beyond his control.

"Your parents called last night," Mormor said casually, buttering a piece of toast with practiced efficiency. "They send their love."

I looked up from my coffee, noting the careful neutrality in her voice that meant she was working hard not to express opinions about my parents' latest excuse for not visiting. They called every few weeks, usually when they were between business trips or social obligations, full of promises about coming to see me soon and apologies for being so busy with work.

Dr. Anna Eriksson and Dr. Björn Lindström—two successful urban professionals who had produced a child during a brief period when they'd thought parenthood might add meaning to their sophisticated lives. They'd discovered quickly enough that raising a child required sacrifices they weren't willing to make, so they'd shipped me off to the farm when I was ten and resumed their careers with minimal interruption.

"What did they want?" I asked, though I already knew the answer would be some variation of the same theme.

"To check on you. See how school is going. They're very proud of your grades."

My grades. The one aspect of my existence that still interested them, probably because academic achievement was something they understood and could brag about to their colleagues. Their brilliant son, excelling in his studies despite being raised by elderly relatives in the middle of nowhere.

"Did they say when they might visit?"

Mormor's pause was almost imperceptible, but I caught it. "They're very busy right now. Important research projects. But they're hoping to make time soon."

Soon. The word that had lost all meaning years ago.

I finished my breakfast in comfortable silence, watching Mormor move around the kitchen with the efficient grace of someone who'd been managing a household since before I was born. She never complained about the unexpected responsibility of raising a teenager, never made me feel like a burden or an imposition. But I could see the weariness in her movements sometimes, the way she paused to rest when she thought no one was looking.

She was eighty-one years old. She should be enjoying her retirement, traveling with Morfar, spoiling occasional grandchildren rather than raising one full-time. Instead, she was dealing with a fifteen-year-old who felt too old for his rural environment but too young to escape it.

. . .

SCHOOL AND SOLITUDE

The walk to school took me through countryside that postcard photographers loved but that I found increasingly suffocating. Rolling hills, traditional red buildings, forests that stretched to the horizon—all beautiful in their way, but also a constant reminder of how small my world had become.

The village school served students from a dozen farming communities, bringing together teenagers who'd known each other since childhood and had already sorted themselves into social groups that had little room for outsiders. I wasn't exactly an outsider—I'd been here for five years—but I wasn't quite an insider either. The other students treated me with polite distance, recognizing that I didn't quite fit their understanding of what a fifteen-year-old farm boy should be.

"Morning, Erik," called Lisa Andersson as I approached the school building. She was nice enough, though her idea of interesting conversation usually involved gossip about teachers or speculation about which couples might break up before graduation.

"Morning," I replied, offering the kind of smile that looked friendly but didn't encourage extended interaction.

Inside, I made my way to my usual desk in the back corner of our English classroom, where I could observe without being observed, participate without drawing too much attention. Our teacher, Herr Johansson, was enthusiastic about literature in a way that the other students found tedious but that I genuinely appreciated. He was the one person in this place who seemed to understand that books contained entire worlds worth exploring.

"Today we're discussing Strindberg's 'The Red Room,'" he announced, and I perked up despite myself. I'd read it twice already—once because it was assigned, and once because I'd actually enjoyed it. The story of young idealists in Stockholm, trying to make their mark on the world while navigating the corruption and compromise of adult society, felt more relevant to my life than anything else we studied.

"Erik," Herr Johansson said, making eye contact with me across the room. "What did you think of Arvid's relationship with the artistic community? Did his background help or hinder his acceptance?"

The question was exactly the kind I loved—complex enough to require real analysis, relevant enough to feel meaningful. As I organized my thoughts, I was vaguely aware of my classmates settling in for what they probably expected to be another of Erik's pretentious literary observations.

"I think his background was both an advantage and a barrier," I said, warming to the topic despite the audience. "He had the education and cultural knowledge to understand what the artists were trying to achieve, but he also had expectations about how art should function in society. The other characters could see that he was simultaneously one of them and separate from them."

"Interesting. Can you elaborate on that separation?"

"He was observing their world as much as participating in it. Like he was always conscious of being an outsider studying a culture he wanted to belong to but couldn't quite access naturally."

Several of my classmates exchanged glances that I caught in my peripheral vision. There goes Erik again, they were probably thinking, turning everything into some deep psychological analysis when it's just a story about people in Stockholm.

But I didn't care. For thirty minutes, I got to discuss ideas that actually mattered with someone who appreciated intellectual curiosity. It was the highlight of most of my school days.

After class, I packed my books slowly, hoping to avoid the usual cluster of students who gathered in the hallway to discuss weekend plans I wouldn't be invited to join. Not because they disliked me, exactly, but because I'd never learned the social skills that made casual friendship possible. I was too serious, too interested in things they found boring, too obviously different from the life path they were all following toward agricultural college or local apprenticeships.

"Erik," a voice called as I headed for the door. I turned to see Magnus Petersson approaching with the confident stride of someone who'd never doubted his place in the world. Magnus was everything I wasn't—effortlessly popular, naturally athletic, completely comfortable with the traditional masculinity that rural Sweden valued. He was also, I was fairly certain, the most beautiful boy I'd ever seen in person.

"Hey," he said, falling into step beside me as we left the building. "My family's having a party this weekend. You should come."

The invitation caught me completely off guard. Magnus and I had barely spoken beyond polite classroom interactions, and his social circle definitely didn't include awkward intellectual farm boys who read too much and talked too little.

"Thanks," I managed, "but I'll probably be busy helping Morfar with work around the farm."

It wasn't true—weekend chores never took all day—but I couldn't imagine a scenario where I'd fit in at a party with Magnus's friends. Besides, watching him laugh and flirt with girls while I nursed hopeless romantic feelings seemed like exactly the kind of torture I didn't need in my life.

"Maybe next time," he said with a shrug that suggested he'd expected the rejection.

As I watched him rejoin his friends, I wondered what would have happened if I'd been brave enough to say yes. If I'd been the kind of person who could walk into a room full of strangers and find my place naturally. If I'd been normal enough to have a chance with someone like Magnus, even though he was so obviously straight it almost hurt to look at him.

But I wasn't any of those things. I was Erik Eriksson, the strange boy who lived with his grandparents and read books for fun and had never kissed anyone, despite being out about his sexuality to anyone who cared to ask.

. . .

AFTERNOON CHORES

The work around the farm was familiar and oddly comforting, even when it left me exhausted and dirty. There was something satisfying about physical labor that produced visible results—hay bales stacked neatly in the barn, fences repaired to keep livestock secure, equipment maintained to last another season.

Morfar and I worked side by side most afternoons, and while he wasn't much for conversation, I appreciated his steady presence. He'd taught me everything I knew about taking care of animals, fixing machinery, reading weather patterns that determined when to plant and when to harvest. Practical skills that would serve me well if I chose to remain in rural Sweden, though we both knew that wasn't the life I was planning.

"You've been quiet today," he observed as we finished mucking out the horse stalls. "Everything alright at school?"

"Fine," I said, which was my standard response to most questions about my emotional state. "Just thinking."

"About what?"

I considered how to answer honestly without sounding ungrateful for everything he and Mormor had done for me. "About what comes next. After graduation."

Morfar leaned against his pitchfork, studying my face with the careful attention he usually reserved for evaluating livestock. "University?"

"Probably. If I can get into somewhere good." I paused, then decided to risk honesty. "Somewhere in Stockholm, maybe. Or even abroad."

"Abroad?" His eyebrows rose slightly. "That's expensive. And far from family."

"I know. But I want to see what else is out there, you know? I want to meet people who think about the world the way I do."

Morfar was quiet for a moment, processing what I'd said. Finally, he nodded slowly. "Your grandmother and I, we always knew you were different. Not better or worse than other children, just... different. With different needs."

"Different how?"

"Bigger dreams. Bigger questions. The kind of mind that needs more space to grow than this place can provide."

His understanding caught me off guard. I'd expected resistance, arguments about family loyalty and the importance of maintaining traditions. Instead, he was acknowledging what I'd barely dared to admit to myself.

"Would you be disappointed? If I left for university and didn't come back?"

"Disappointed, yes," he said honestly. "But not surprised. And not angry. Sometimes the best thing you can do for someone you love is help them find where they belong, even if it's not where you hoped they'd stay."

The conversation stayed with me as we finished the afternoon chores and returned to the house for dinner. Mormor had prepared one of my favorite meals—meatballs with lingonberry sauce, new potatoes, and the green beans she'd been preserving all summer. We ate in comfortable silence, the kind that comes from people who've shared countless meals and don't need constant conversation to feel connected.

After dinner, I helped with dishes while Mormor planned the next day's activities and Morfar reviewed the weather forecast. It was a routine we'd established years ago, each of us contributing to the household's smooth functioning without needing explicit direction or oversight.

But tonight felt different somehow. Maybe it was my conversation with Morfar, or Magnus's unexpected invitation, or just the accumulated weight of another day spent feeling like I was waiting for my real life to begin. Whatever the cause, I found myself restless in a way that made staying inside feel impossible.

"I'm going for a walk," I announced, grabbing a jacket from the hook by the door.

"Don't go too far," Mormor called after me. "And take a flashlight if you're going to be out after dark."

EVENING REFLECTIONS

The path around our property led through fields and along the edge of the forest, following routes that had been worn smooth by generations of feet. I'd walked these trails countless times, but tonight I found myself really looking at the landscape instead of just moving through it automatically.

The autumn air was crisp and clean, carrying scents of woodsmoke and dying leaves that would have inspired poetry in someone more romantically inclined. Above me, stars were beginning to appear in a sky unpolluted by city lights, creating the kind of view that urban people traveled hundreds of miles to experience.

It was beautiful, objectively. I could appreciate the aesthetic value of rural Sweden, understand why people chose this life, recognize the peace and simplicity that came with living close to the land. But beauty wasn't enough to make me want to stay. I needed more than scenic views and clean air. I needed intellectual stimulation, cultural diversity, the possibility of meeting someone who might actually understand me.

I needed to find my people, whoever they might be.

My phone buzzed with a text from one of my classmates, probably sharing some piece of social media drama that was supposed to be fascinating but would actually just depress me with its banality. I ignored it, preferring the silence of the evening to whatever digital noise was demanding my attention.

Instead, I found myself thinking about the books I'd been reading lately—stories about young people who'd left small towns for big cities, who'd found communities of artists and intellectuals and fellow outcasts who'd somehow created meaningful lives for themselves. Fiction, mostly, but fiction based on real possibilities that existed somewhere beyond the boundaries of my current world.

What would it be like to live in Stockholm? Or London? Or New York? To walk into a coffee shop and find people my age discussing philosophy or politics or art instead of farming equipment and local gossip? To attend university lectures taught by professors who'd published books I'd actually heard of? To maybe, possibly, find another gay teenager who read voraciously and thought deeply and wouldn't mind dating someone who talked too much about literature?

The fantasies were probably unrealistic—I had no idea what city life was actually like beyond what I'd seen in movies and television shows. But they felt more real than anything I experienced in my daily life, more relevant to who I was becoming than the practical skills I was learning on the farm.

As I walked, I composed mental letters to parents who would never read them.

Dear Mama and Papa,

I know you think you did the right thing by leaving me here while you pursued your careers. I know you believe that growing up with Mormor and Morfar has given me stability and traditional values and a strong work ethic. And you're right about some of that. But you've also given me five years to figure out that I don't belong in your world or this one. I'm floating between lives that don't quite fit, waiting for permission to go find where I actually belong.

The letters always ended the same way in my imagination: with forgiveness I wasn't sure I felt and understanding I definitely didn't possess. Because despite everything, I still wanted them to love me enough to fight for me. Still hoped they might someday choose me over their important research projects and prestigious conferences.

But hope was dangerous when it wasn't realistic. Better to focus on what I could control—my grades, my university applications, my plans for escape to somewhere that might have room for someone like me.

THE UNEXPECTED VISITORS

I was walking back toward the house, having worked through most of my restless energy, when I saw a car in our driveway that I didn't recognize. A rental, by the looks of it, with Stockholm plates. My first thought was that my parents had finally decided to surprise me with an unannounced visit, but the car was too modest for their usual preferences.

Through the kitchen window, I could see Mormor bustling around with the kind of excited energy she usually reserved for major holidays. Whoever our visitors were, she was treating their arrival as something special.

I approached the house quietly, partly from habit and partly from curiosity about who might have prompted such a reaction. Voices drifted through the open window—Mormor's accented English mixed with unfamiliar male voices that sounded educated, perhaps international.

"Erik!" Mormor called as I entered through the back door. "Come meet family. From America."

Family? I pulled out my earbuds and stuffed my phone in my pocket, preparing to endure whatever polite social interaction was required. Probably distant relatives I'd never heard of, passing through Sweden on vacation and feeling obligated to visit the old country connections.

But when I entered the sitting room, I found myself looking at two men who definitely didn't fit my expectations for random American tourists. One was tall and blonde with the kind of academic bearing that suggested university education and intellectual curiosity. The other was shorter, darker, and moved with a grace that seemed almost supernatural.

They were sitting close together on our sofa, not quite touching but clearly comfortable in each other's space. And there was something about the way they looked at each other—brief glances full of affection and understanding—that immediately triggered my gaydar.

"Erik," Mormor said with obvious pride, "these are your cousins from America. Soren and..." She paused, checking her pronunciation. "Aleksander."

I offered a halfhearted wave, still processing what I was seeing. These were supposed to be family? They looked nothing like the Swedish-American relatives I'd imagined, and there was something about Aleksander especially that seemed almost otherworldly.

For the next hour, I picked at my dinner and listened to the adults discuss genealogy and old photographs with the kind of enthusiasm I usually reserved for my favorite books. Normally I would have found the family history interesting, but something about these two men kept drawing my attention away from their research and toward their relationship dynamic.

After Mormor and Morfar disappeared into the kitchen to clean up, I finally gave in to curiosity.

"So how long have you guys been boyfriends?" I asked, figuring directness was the best approach.

The question clearly caught them off guard, though they tried to hide it. Soren went red around the ears—always a dead giveaway—while Aleksander looked genuinely surprised that I'd figured it out so quickly.

"How could you tell?" Soren asked. "We thought we were being discreet."

I almost laughed. "Please. It's obvious. The way you look at each other, the way you sit. I mean, it's not like you're holding hands or anything, but come on." I shrugged, trying to seem casual about what felt like a significant moment. "I'm cool with it. I mean, I'm gay too. Who cares?"

And just like that, the entire evening transformed. Instead of polite family small talk, we were having the kind of honest conversation I'd been craving for years. Aleksander began sharing stories about his relationship with my ancestor Mikael—stories that were so detailed and personal they almost seemed like firsthand memories rather than family history.

But it was when he casually mentioned being Mikael's lover over 130 years ago that everything clicked into place. The otherworldly grace, the anachronistic mannerisms, the way he spoke about historical events like personal experiences.

Oh.

I stared at him, processing implications that should have been impossible but somehow made perfect sense. If someone had been alive for over 130 years, they'd have to be something more than human. And if that something was sitting in my grandparents' kitchen, calmly discussing family history while my cousin treated it as completely normal...

"So you're like..." I couldn't quite say the word *vampire* out loud, but I thought it loudly enough that Aleksander seemed to hear it anyway.

"Maybe I could visit you guys in London sometime," I said, changing the subject before my nerve failed completely. "You know, see more of the world than this place."

The words tumbled out before I could stop them, followed by what was probably the most embarrassing admission of my teenage life: "Maybe find someone cool like Aleksander. He's kinda hot anyway."

I felt my face burn with humiliation, but instead of laughing or looking uncomfortable, Aleksander just smiled with the kind of understanding that suggested he'd been fifteen once too, despite whatever supernatural circumstances had extended his life far beyond normal human limits.

"You're always welcome in London," he said simply. "Family looks out for family."

And suddenly, for the first time in years, I felt like I might have found my people after all.

AFTER THEY LEFT

I lay awake long after the rental car disappeared down our driveway, staring at the ceiling while my mind raced through everything that had happened. In the space of a few hours, my understanding of the world had expanded to include possibilities I'd never imagined, and my conception of family had grown to encompass people who might actually understand what it felt like to be different.

Aleksander was a vampire. An actual, literal vampire who had been alive for over a century and had loved my ancestor in 1880s Copenhagen. And Soren was his boyfriend—a regular human who had somehow built a relationship with someone supernatural while researching his own family history.

It should have been terrifying. Everything I'd learned about vampires from books and movies suggested they were dangerous predators who viewed humans as food sources rather than potential romantic partners. But Aleksander hadn't seemed dangerous at all. He'd seemed... kind. Patient. Genuinely interested in my thoughts and feelings in a way that most adults weren't.

And he'd invited me to visit them in London. Not just polite family courtesy, but what felt like a genuine offer to help me explore the wider world I'd been dreaming about.

London. The city I'd imagined visiting since I was old enough to understand that there were places beyond Sweden where people like me might find their communities. The possibility of spending time with two men who were openly, comfortably gay, who had built a life together despite whatever challenges their unusual circumstances might present.

For the first time in years, I had something concrete to hope for beyond vague university plans and eventual escape from rural Sweden. I had an invitation to experience the kind of life I'd only read about in books—cosmopolitan, intellectual, diverse enough to include vampires and academics and teenagers who didn't quite fit conventional expectations.

I pulled out my phone and opened a new text to Soren, whose number I'd carefully entered before they left.

ERICK (THE GREAT!)

Thank you for tonight. For treating me like an adult and trusting me with the truth. I know I'm just a fifteen-year-old farm kid, but if you meant what you said about visiting London, I'd really like to take you up on that offer someday.

I deleted the message without sending it, then wrote another one:

It was really great meeting you both. I hope we can stay in touch.

That one felt too formal, too polite for what had actually happened between us. I deleted it too.

Finally, I settled on something that felt honest without being too desperate:

Thanks for tonight. I haven't had a conversation that interesting in years. Looking forward to staying in touch.

I hit send before I could change my mind again, then set the phone aside and tried to process everything that had changed in the space of a single evening.

Tomorrow I would return to school and pretend to care about assignments that suddenly seemed irrelevant compared to the larger questions about identity and belonging that my cousins had helped me begin to explore. I would sit through classes with students who had never met anyone like Aleksander, who couldn't imagine the kinds of lives that were possible beyond the boundaries of their small-town experience.

But I would also begin researching London universities with a new sense of purpose, start planning visits that might actually happen instead of remaining fantasies. I had connections now—family who understood what it felt like to be different, who had built successful lives despite not fitting conventional expectations.

Most importantly, I had proof that people like me could find love, even when that love took forms that the rest of the world might not understand or accept. If Aleksander and Soren could build a relationship that spanned species and centuries, maybe I could find someone who would appreciate my particular combination of intellectual curiosity and rural Swedish awkwardness.

Maybe someday I would walk into a London coffee shop and find my people waiting for me. Maybe someday I would have my own impossible love story to tell.

For the first time in years, the future felt like something to anticipate rather than simply endure. And it all started with two unexpected visitors who had seen something worth knowing in a fifteen-year-old farm boy who read too much and dreamed too big for his current circumstances.

I fell asleep planning the email I would write to them tomorrow, the careful message that would keep our connection alive until I was old enough and brave enough to take them up on their invitation to discover what kind of life might be waiting for me in London.

The farm would always be here. Mormor and Morfar would always love me. But for the first time, I could imagine a future that honored both my roots and my need to grow beyond them.

A future that might even include finding someone who thought I was worth crossing impossible distances to love.

22
COMING HOME

STOCKHOLM ARLANDA AIRPORT 190 45 STOCKHOLM-ARLANDA, SWEDEN

Soren Jensen

As our plane lifted off from Stockholm and climbed through the evening clouds, I found myself talking faster than usual, my mind racing with possibilities that hadn't existed just days ago. The view out the window showed Sweden growing smaller below us, but somehow the country felt larger in my mind now—not just a place my ancestors had left behind, but a living connection with family who were still there.

"I should call my parents as soon as we land," I said, pulling out my notebook to jot down ideas before I forgot them. "They're going to be absolutely amazed by what we found. And Marta and Lars—we should definitely put them in touch with my family in Minnesota. Maybe my dad could help coordinate some kind of reunion."

Aleksander listened with that patient attention he always gave my enthusiasms, but I could see something warm and amused in his expression.

"And Erik," I continued, my excitement building. "We should definitely follow through on that invitation. Maybe he could come for a summer program at one of the London universities? I bet there are exchange opportunities, or we could help arrange something. He's so smart, Alek, and he's clearly ready to see more of the world."

I paused, realizing I was probably talking too fast, but the ideas kept flowing. "Do you think we could help fly Marta and Lars over to Minnesota? I mean, they're family, and they've never been to America. My parents would love to meet them, and there's so much they could share about the family history..."

Aleksander Nordh

Watching Soren plan and dream was like watching someone discover they had wings. The shy graduate student I'd first met in the library had been replaced by someone confident in his connections, eager to build bridges across oceans and generations. It was beautiful to witness, and it made something in my chest tighten with an emotion I couldn't quite name.

What had begun as a research project had grown into something organic, yet that wasn't fully true. It was more like something had always been there, hidden beneath the surface, waiting to be rediscovered. Old and new, intertwined in ways that felt both surprising and inevitable.

Ironic—that was exactly how I felt about myself these days. Ancient beyond human comprehension, yet somehow renewed by love. Old and new.

As Soren continued planning ways to connect his newly expanded family, I reached across the small space between our seats and took his hand, causing him to pause mid-sentence. He looked at me with a questioning expression.

"Alek?" he asked, his voice almost silent above the aircraft's engines.

"Yes?"

There was something in his eyes—curiosity mixed with a different kind of longing than I'd seen before. "Do you have any images of you when you were younger?"

"Younger?" I laughed softly. "I look like I'm twenty-two."

"I mean... I know... well, this sounds silly... but..." He struggled with the words, a blush creeping across his cheeks. "I know photographs are only fairly recent, but was there ever a painting or drawing or something of you as a 'boy'? I think it would be fascinating to know what it would have been like to have known you as you grew up. Perhaps I'm not making any sense—I know time is different between us and all..."

He grew embarrassed, looking down at our joined hands.

Soren Jensen

I felt foolish asking the question, but I couldn't shake the curiosity. Here was someone I loved who had lived through centuries, who had experienced childhood in ways I could barely imagine. What had he looked like as a child? What had shaped him during those formative years that had lasted decades instead of the brief span of human childhood?

Aleksander squeezed my hand tighter, and the warmth in his voice made me look up again.

"Not in the least," he said gently. "I'm flattered you care about such things."

Aleksander Nordh

His question touched something deep in me—the recognition that he wanted to know all of me, not just the carefully curated version I presented to the world. The idea that he wished he could have known me through all my ages, all my experiences, was both moving and painful in the sweetest way.

"There was a painting, actually," I said, memories stirring. "When I appeared to be around ten years of age in human terms—though I was already quite mature intellectually by then. I was a 'student' at an academy in Bruges, and one of the masters there, a Flemish painter who was just beginning to make his reputation, needed subjects for portrait practice."

I could see the fascination in Soren's eyes as I continued. "The painter was particularly interested in capturing what he called 'the wisdom in young faces.' I sat for him several times over the course of a winter. He said I had unusual eyes for a child—that I looked as though I'd seen more of the world than most adults."

"Do you have it?" Soren asked eagerly.

I smiled, an idea forming. "Why don't I show it to you when we get back?"

"I'd like to see it very much."

MONDAY EVENING

Upon our return to London, we made our way back to my flat through the familiar streets that felt somehow different after our journey. Everything looked the same—the Victorian terraces, the warm glow of pub windows, the late commuters hurrying home—but something fundamental had shifted. I was no longer just Aleksander living in London; I was part of something larger, connected to a web of relationships that stretched across continents and centuries.

"Would you like to stay tonight?" I asked as we reached my door, noting the lateness of the hour. "Given how late it is..."

Soren looked tempted, and I could see him weighing the offer against his practical concerns. "I'd love to," he said finally, "but I have early classes tomorrow, and all my materials are back at my flat. I should probably head back."

I understood, though I felt a pang of disappointment. These past few days of constant companionship had spoiled me for solitude.

"In that case," I said, an idea suddenly illuminating my mind, "why don't you meet me at Trafalgar Square after your classes Wednesday? I have a little surprise in store."

Soren Jensen

The mystery in Aleksander's voice intrigued me. After everything we'd shared in Sweden, after all the revelations and discoveries, what could he possibly have left to surprise me with?

"What kind of surprise?" I asked, but he just smiled and shook his head.

"You'll see Wednesday. Trust me."

As we parted with a lingering kiss on his doorstep, I found myself already counting the hours until Wednesday evening. Whatever Aleksander had planned, I knew it would be something meaningful. He didn't do anything casually.

WEDNESDAY EVENING - TRAFALGAR SQUARE

I spotted Aleksander immediately when I emerged from the Underground at Charing Cross. He was standing by one of the lion statues at the base of Nelson's Column, looking perfectly at ease among the evening crowds of tourists and commuters. When he saw me, his face lit up with the kind of smile that made my heart skip.

"Ready for your surprise?" he asked, taking my hand as naturally as breathing.

"I've been curious all day," I admitted. "Where are we going?"

Instead of answering, he simply guided me across the square toward the imposing neoclassical facade of the National Gallery. "I thought it was time you met someone," he said cryptically.

Aleksander Nordh

Leading Soren through the familiar halls of the National Gallery felt like bringing two important parts of my life together. The gallery had been one of my refuges over the years—a place where I could spend hours among beautiful things, where the careful preservation of art across centuries felt like a mirror of my own existence.

I guided him past the more famous works—the Turners and Constables that drew the largest crowds—toward a smaller, quieter wing that housed the Northern European paintings. Here, in a room with fewer visitors, hung the smaller works that often went unnoticed by casual museum-goers.

"There," I said softly, stopping before a particular painting. "I'd like you to meet someone."

Soren Jensen

The painting was small, perhaps eighteen inches square, displayed in an ornate gilt frame that spoke of its age and value. The placard beside it read: "Portrait of a Young Scholar, c. 1485, attributed to Hans Memling, oil on wood panel."

But it wasn't the technical details that made my breath catch. It was the subject.

Staring back at me from the panel was a boy who couldn't have been more than ten years old, painted with the meticulous detail characteristic of Flemish masters. He had dark hair that caught the light, pale skin with just a hint of color in his cheeks, and eyes that seemed far too knowing for such a young face.

Eyes that I recognized immediately.

"Aleksander," I whispered, stepping closer to the painting. "It's you."

Aleksander Nordh

"Five hundred and twenty-eight years ago," I confirmed quietly. "Though the painter got my age wrong in his notes—I appeared ten, but I was already over sixteen hundred years old by then."

Soren studied the painting with the same intense focus he brought to all his research, but there was something deeply personal in his gaze now. He was looking at a version of me that had existed centuries before he was born, trying to reconcile the face in the painting with the man standing beside him.

"You look..." he started, then stopped, searching for words.

"Like I was thinking about something far beyond what a child should know?" I suggested. "That's what the painter said. He told me I had 'ancient eyes in a young face.' He wasn't wrong."

"You look lonely," Soren said softly, and the observation hit me harder than I'd expected.

Soren Jensen

There was something in the painted boy's expression that made my chest tight. Despite the masterful technique, despite the formal pose typical of the era, there was an unmistakable sadness in those familiar eyes. This child—this ancient being trapped in a child's body—looked profoundly alone.

"Were you?" I asked quietly. "Lonely?"

Aleksander was silent for a long moment, studying his own image from five centuries past. "Constantly," he said finally. "I'd already outlived several human friends by then. My parents were beginning their long period of traveling, leaving me to fend for myself more often. I was attending the academy because I needed to maintain the appearance of normal childhood development, but I was more intellectually advanced than my supposed peers, and far more emotionally isolated."

He paused, his voice growing softer. "I used to stare at that painting when I was older, wondering if I would always carry that expression. That sense of being fundamentally separate from everyone around me."

"And now?" I asked, though I thought I already knew the answer.

Aleksander turned from the painting to look at me, and the contrast was startling. Where the painted boy's eyes held centuries of accumulated loneliness, the man beside me looked... peaceful. Content. Connected.

"Now I know what it feels like to be truly seen," he said simply. "To be known and accepted completely. The loneliness isn't gone entirely—how could it be, after so many centuries? But it's no longer the defining feature of my existence."

Aleksander Nordh

Standing there with Soren in front of a portrait of my younger self, I realized why I'd wanted to share this with him. It wasn't just about showing him another piece of my history. It was about demonstrating how far I'd traveled—not just through time, but through the landscape of connection and isolation that had defined my existence.

The boy in that painting had been me, but he was also a version of myself I'd finally left behind. I would always be ancient, always carry the weight of centuries, but I no longer had to carry them alone.

"Thank you," Soren said quietly, still looking between me and the painting.

"For what?"

"For trusting me with this. For letting me see who you were before you became who you are." He reached for my hand, intertwining our fingers. "For letting me be part of your journey from that lonely boy to... this."

As we made our way out of the gallery into the London evening, I felt something settle in my chest—a sense of completeness I'd never expected to experience. The journey from Sweden had brought us home not just to London, but to an understanding of how past and present could coexist, how old wounds could heal, and how love could bridge any distance—whether measured in miles or centuries.

"Ready to go home?" Soren asked as we emerged into the bustling evening crowds of Trafalgar Square.

"Yes," I said, meaning it more deeply than he could know. "Ready to go home."

"Portrait of a Young Scholar" c. 1485 Oil on wood panel 12 x 16 inches (30.5 x 40.6 cm) Attributed to **Hans Memling** (c. 1430-1494) Flemish School This intimate portrait depicts an unidentified boy of approximately ten years, painted during the artist's mature period in Bruges. The subject's penetrating gaze and the painter's meticulous attention to psychological detail exemplify the Northern Renaissance tradition of portraiture. Contemporary records note the artist's fascination with capturing "ancient wisdom in young faces," and this work demonstrates his ability to convey profound psychological depth. The boy's expression suggests an intelligence and melancholy uncommon for his apparent age, characteristics that the artist reportedly found compelling enough to request multiple sittings throughout the winter of 1484-85.

23
THREE WORDS

CHARING CROSS STATION (NORTHERN AND BAKERLOO LINES), STRAND, LONDON WC2N 5HS

Soren Jensen

The tube ride back to Aleksander's flat passed in comfortable silence. We sat side by side, shoulders touching as the carriage swayed through the tunnels beneath London. Around us, the evening commuters embarked and disembarked in their familiar rhythms—students heading home from university, office workers finally finishing their long days, tourists consulting maps and guidebooks.

But I found myself lost in thought, my mind returning again and again to that portrait in the National Gallery. The lonely boy with ancient eyes, trapped in a child's body for decades while carrying the wisdom and pain of sixteen centuries. When that painting was created, Aleksander had already lived sixteen times longer than my entire life would ever span. The scope of it was almost incomprehensible.

I caught Aleksander sneaking glances at me, studying my face with that careful attention he always paid to my moods. When our eyes met, I smiled, and something warm spread through my chest. He wasn't just the missing puzzle piece I hadn't known I was looking for. He was something more fundamental than that—a pivotal part of my life that I couldn't have fully appreciated until I'd seen that window into his past, understood the depth of solitude he'd carried for so long.

Aleksander Nordh

Soren was quieter than usual on the journey home, but it wasn't the silence of discomfort or withdrawal. Rather, he seemed to be processing everything he'd seen and learned, turning it over in his mind with that same methodical approach he brought to his research. I found myself stealing glances at his profile, marveling at how naturally he'd accepted the reality of my extraordinary longevity, how he'd looked at that centuries-old portrait with compassion rather than fear.

When he caught me watching and smiled, something in my chest loosened—a tension I hadn't even realized I'd been carrying. Whatever thoughts were occupying his mind, they didn't seem to be driving him away from me.

A REQUEST

Soren Jensen

As we walked from the tube station through the quiet London streets toward Aleksander's flat, I found my nerves building. The evening air was crisp, carrying the scent of woodsmoke from nearby chimneys, and the familiar route felt different somehow—charged with possibility and anticipation.

"Alek," I said as we approached his building, my voice coming out more tentative than I'd intended. "Could I... would it be alright if I stayed tonight? I don't want to be presumptuous, but there are some things I'd like to talk about. Things I want to ask you."

He turned to look at me, his expression immediately attentive. "Of course. You never need to ask permission to stay, Soren. What's on your mind?"

Aleksander Nordh

The hesitation in Soren's voice caught my attention immediately. Over the months we'd been together, I'd learned to read the subtle variations in his tone, the way his voice changed when he was nervous or excited or working through something important. This was the sound of someone gathering courage for a significant conversation.

"Let's go upstairs," I said, unlocking the door to my building. "Whatever it is, we can talk about it properly."

. . .

CONFESSIONS

Soren Jensen

Once we were settled in Aleksander's flat, I found myself pacing to the window and back, my usual calm deserting me entirely. So many thoughts had been building over the past few weeks—about my family, about Rafael, about us—and they all seemed to demand attention at once.

"I've been thinking," I began, then stopped, laughing nervously at how inadequate the words sounded. "Actually, I've been thinking about several things, and I'm not sure where to start."

Aleksander settled onto the sofa, his expression patient and encouraging. "Start wherever feels right."

I took a deep breath. "First, I talked to my parents the other night. About the Swedish family we found, about Marta and Lars and Erik. They're absolutely thrilled. My dad's already looking into arranging some kind of reunion, maybe bringing the Swedish family to Minnesota next summer."

"That's wonderful," Aleksander said, genuine warmth in his voice.

"And I've been thinking about Rafael too," I continued. "About what we discovered in Sweden, about the connections we're still trying to understand. I know he didn't show up for dinner, but I keep hoping we'll find a way to reach him eventually."

"We will," Aleksander said quietly. "These things take time."

"But there's something else," I said, my voice growing more hesitant. "Something more personal. About us."

Aleksander Nordh

The shift in Soren's tone made me sit forward slightly. Whatever he was building toward, it felt significant—not alarming, but important in a way that demanded my full attention.

"I'm listening," I said gently.

Soren Jensen

"I want to come out to my family," I said in a rush, the words tumbling out before I could lose my nerve. "I want to tell my parents, my relatives, everyone.

About being gay, about having a boyfriend. But I want to do it in person, not over the phone. I'm thinking about going home for Christmas, maybe, or spring break."

I paused, watching Aleksander's face for his reaction. "I'm nervous about it, but I think they'll be okay. My family's always been pretty accepting, and they liked you when I told them about my research partner who's been helping me."

"They know about me?" Aleksander asked, surprise evident in his voice.

"Not about what you are," I clarified quickly. "Just that I have this incredibly knowledgeable friend who's been sharing family documents and helping with my research. They think you're just another graduate student."

I took another deep breath. "But that's what I wanted to ask you about. I'd like your permission to tell them about our relationship. I want to be proud of my boyfriend, not hide anything. I want them to know that I'm happy, that I've found someone who... who means everything to me."

Aleksander Nordh

The earnestness in Soren's voice, the way he called me his boyfriend with such obvious pride, made something warm bloom in my chest. After centuries of relationships that had to be hidden, disguised, or kept carefully compartmentalized, the idea of being openly acknowledged felt both thrilling and terrifying.

"Of course you have my permission," I said immediately. "I'm honored that you want to share our relationship with your family. Though you might want to keep the more extraordinary details to yourself."

Soren laughed, some of his tension easing. "I figured I'd stick to 'my boyfriend is older than he looks and really passionate about history.'"

"That should suffice," I agreed with a smile.

Soren Jensen

"There's one more thing," I said, my voice dropping to almost a whisper. "Something I've been wanting to say for weeks now, but I kept worrying it was too soon, that I might scare you away."

Aleksander went very still, his attention focused completely on me.

"I love you," I said simply. "I love you, Aleksander. I've felt it for so long, and I've said it in roundabout ways, but I've never just said it directly. And I was afraid it might be too early, but I decided to take the chance, hoping I wouldn't scare you."

Aleksander Nordh

The words hit me like a physical blow—not painful, but overwhelming in their simple perfection. I felt tears spring to my eyes before I could stop them, and I watched Soren's expression shift from nervous hope to concern.

"Alek?" he said, moving toward me. "Are you alright? Did I—"

Soren Jensen

The tears sliding down Aleksander's cheeks weren't like any I'd ever seen before. They caught the light differently, with an almost bluish, crystalline quality that made them seem otherworldly. Beautiful, but strange. I'd never seen him cry, had never even imagined what Elder tears might look like.

"I'm sorry," I said, panic rising in my voice. "I shouldn't have said it. I know it's too soon, I just—"

Aleksander Nordh

"No," I managed, reaching for him and pulling him down onto the sofa beside me. "No, Soren, you don't understand. I've been waiting centuries to hear those words. Centuries."

He looked confused, and I realized I needed to explain.

"Didn't Mikael ever say it?" he asked softly. "Didn't you two...?"

"We felt it," I said, my voice thick with emotion. "We both knew it. But we could never bring ourselves to say it out loud. It would have been too dangerous, too real. If we'd said those words to each other, leaving would have been impossible."

Soren Jensen

"Oh, Aleksander," I whispered, understanding flooding through me. The weight of centuries of unexpressed love, of feelings that had to be hidden even from each other, of a connection that could never be fully acknowledged.

"I love you too," he said, his voice breaking slightly. "I love you more than I thought possible. You've given me something I never expected to have—the chance to love completely, openly, without fear or reservation."

. . .

COMPLETION

What followed felt as natural and inevitable as breathing. Aleksander's hands found my face, his thumbs brushing away tears I hadn't realized were falling. When he kissed me, it was different from all our previous kisses—deeper, more urgent, filled with the weight of everything we'd just confessed to each other.

"Are you sure?" he whispered against my lips, even as his hands moved to the buttons of my shirt.

"I've never been more sure of anything," I replied, and meant it completely.

Aleksander Nordh

Making love to Soren felt like coming home after a journey of millennia. Every touch, every kiss, every whispered endearment was a revelation—not just of physical pleasure, but of emotional connection I'd thought lost to me forever.

I was tender with him, careful, making sure he was comfortable as we explored this new intimacy together. For all my centuries of experience, this felt like the first time I was truly making love rather than simply sharing physical comfort. This was what I'd been waiting for without knowing it—complete emotional and physical connection with someone who saw all of me and loved me anyway.

Soren Jensen

It was thrilling and overwhelming and a little uncomfortable at first, but Aleksander was so patient, so gentle, that any anxiety I felt melted away under his careful attention. He made sure I was cared for, that every moment was about us together rather than his experience or mine separately.

When we finally lay tangled together afterward, skin against skin, hearts beating in synchrony, I felt something profound settle into place. This wasn't just physical culmination—it was the completion of something that had been building since the moment we'd first met in the library. The Jensen lineage had found its way back to the love it had left behind, and somehow, incredibly, we had found our way to each other.

Aleksander Nordh

As Soren drifted off to sleep in my arms, I found myself thinking about patterns

—how love echoed across generations, how connection found a way to persist even when separated by time and death and impossible circumstances.

I had given myself over to Soren completely, in a way I'd never been able to do with anyone else, not even Mikael. And in return, I'd received something precious beyond measure—not just love, but acceptance, understanding, and the promise of a future I'd stopped daring to imagine.

The Jensen bloodline had indeed bonded with mine, but it was more than that. We had created something new together, something that honored the past while building toward a future neither of us could have anticipated.

For the first time in over two thousand years, I fell asleep without the weight of solitude pressing down on my chest. Instead, I slept with gratitude, love, and the quiet certainty that some waits—however long—were worth every moment when they finally came to an end.

24
HELIX

MINNEAPOLIS-ST. PAUL INTERNATIONAL AIRPORT 4300 GLUMACK DR, MINNEAPOLIS, MN 55111, USA

Soren Jensen

The familiar sights and sounds of Minneapolis hit me as soon as we emerged from the jetbridge—the distinctive Minnesota accent of the gate agents, the smell of coffee from Caribou stands, the easy midwestern friendliness that I'd forgotten I'd missed. After months in London's more reserved atmosphere, everything felt overwhelmingly warm and welcoming.

"Nervous?" Aleksander asked quietly as we made our way through the terminal toward baggage claim.

"Terrified," I admitted, though excitement was winning out over anxiety. "But good terrified. Ready-to-jump-out-of-an-airplane terrified."

I'd been rehearsing various versions of coming out to my family for weeks, but now that the moment was approaching, all my careful scripts felt inadequate. How do you casually work into conversation that you're gay and dating someone? Especially when that someone happens to be a two-thousand-year-old vampire, though obviously I'd be leaving that detail out.

Aleksander Nordh

Walking through an American airport felt surreal after so many decades away from this continent. The last time I'd been in the United States, commercial aviation was still in its infancy. Now passengers moved through gleaming terminals with casual efficiency, wheeling luggage that would have seemed impossibly advanced to travelers from earlier eras.

But more than the technological marvels, I was struck by the energy Soren radiated as we moved through familiar territory. This was his homeland, and I could see him relaxing into rhythms and customs that were second nature to him. The slight tension he always carried in London—the careful politeness of someone adapting to a foreign culture—was melting away with each step.

"There they are," Soren said suddenly, pointing toward the arrivals area where a crowd waited behind security barriers.

I followed his gaze and immediately spotted them—a middle-aged couple who could only be his parents, both scanning the emerging passengers with the intent focus of people watching for someone precious. The family resemblance was unmistakable: his father's height and build, his mother's expressive eyes, both carrying themselves with that distinctive Jensen combination of warmth and reserved dignity.

THE REUNION

Soren Jensen

"Soren!" My mother's voice carried across the terminal as she spotted us, and suddenly I was engulfed in arms that smelled like home—her familiar perfume mixed with something that might have been Christmas cookies.

"Oh, honey, look at you," she said, pulling back to study my face with maternal intensity. "You look so different. More mature. Happier." Her eyes were bright with unshed tears, the way they always got when she was emotionally overwhelmed.

My father appeared beside her, wrapping me in one of his crushing bear hugs that lifted me slightly off the ground despite my adult height. "Good to have you home, son," he said into my ear, his voice gruff with emotion.

Aleksander Nordh

Watching the Jensen family reunion stirred something deep in my chest—not jealousy, exactly, but a profound recognition of what I was witnessing. This was the kind of unconditional familial love that transcended distance and time, the bond that had sent Mikael across an ocean to fulfill family expectations over a century ago.

I hung back a respectful step, not wanting to intrude on their moment, but studying the family dynamics with fascination. Soren's mother had the same animated expressiveness I'd seen in him when he got excited about research. His father possessed that quiet strength that I recognized from Mikael's stories about his own family.

Then Soren's mother turned to me, and I found myself the focus of warm brown eyes that seemed to take in everything at once.

"You must be Aleksander," she said, stepping forward with arms already extended. "I'm Brigitta, but everyone calls me Britta. I'm a hugger!"

Before I could respond, I found myself enveloped in an unexpected embrace. After centuries of careful social distances and formal interactions, the spontaneous warmth caught me completely off guard.

"Mom, don't scare him," Soren protested with good-natured embarrassment, but I could see the affection in his eyes as he watched his mother's enthusiastic welcome.

Soren Jensen

Watching Aleksander's face as my mother hugged him was priceless. For just a moment, his carefully maintained composure cracked entirely, replaced by surprise and something that looked almost like wonder. It occurred to me that someone who'd lived for millennia might not have experienced many truly spontaneous displays of affection.

My father stepped forward with his hand extended, rescuing Aleksander from my mother's enthusiasm. "Lars Jensen," he said with that firm handshake he'd perfected through decades of meeting graduate students and academic colleagues. "Welcome to Minneapolis, Aleksander. How was the flight?"

"Quite comfortable, thank you," Aleksander replied, and I could see him settling into his practiced social mode. "And please, call me Henry. It's what most people use."

I caught his eye over my father's shoulder, and we shared a look that conveyed everything we couldn't say aloud: *Welcome to the family. This is what I come from. These are the people who shaped me.*

THE DRIVE HOME

Britta Jensen

I couldn't stop stealing glances at Soren's friend in the rearview mirror as Lars navigated the familiar route home from the airport. There was something intriguing about the young man—impeccable manners, a slight accent that suggested European education, and a quality of attentiveness that seemed unusual in someone his age.

"So Henry, Soren tells us you're also studying at King's College?" I asked, launching into what my family had long ago dubbed my "interview mode."

"That's right. I'm working on my master's in British literature," he replied smoothly. "Soren's been invaluable in helping me understand American perspectives on cultural preservation."

"And you're from...?"

"Originally from Scandinavia, though I've lived in London for several years now."

Aleksander Nordh

The interrogation was gentle but thorough, conducted with the kind of loving concern that only families can manage. Britta asked about my studies, my family, my interests, my plans—all while maintaining a running commentary about their holiday preparations and the various relatives who were eager to meet Soren's "friend from London."

What amused me most was how quintessentially American everything seemed after months in London. The scale of the landscape, the width of the highways, the casual abundance visible everywhere. And the Christmas decorations—entire neighborhoods blazed with lights that would have been visible from orbit.

"I hope you don't mind staying through New Year's," Britta was saying. "I was so surprised when Soren said he was bringing you for the whole winter break. It's wonderful, of course, but I want to make sure you have everything you need."

"It's very generous of you to welcome me," I replied, meaning it completely. "I'm looking forward to experiencing an American Christmas."

Soren Jensen

As we pulled into our subdivision, I saw Aleksander taking in the suburban landscape with carefully concealed amusement. Row after row of houses, each decorated with enough Christmas lights to power a small European village. Our neighbors had clearly engaged in their annual competition to see who could create the most elaborate display.

"Subtle," Aleksander murmured as we passed the Hendersons' house, which featured a life-sized nativity scene complete with animatronic angels.

"Wait until you see ours," I said, and watched his eyebrows rise as we turned into our driveway.

My mother had outdone herself this year. Every window blazed with warm light, garland wrapped every surface, and a twelve-foot inflatable Santa dominated the front lawn. The house looked like something from a Christmas movie.

"Your mother doesn't do anything halfway, does she?" Aleksander asked as we climbed out of the car.

"You have no idea," I replied, grinning at his expression.

THE JENSEN HOME

Aleksander Nordh

If the exterior decorations were impressive, the interior was overwhelming. Every surface seemed to hold some Christmas ornament, garland, or festive arrangement. The living room featured not one but two Christmas trees—a massive Norwegian spruce covered in family ornaments collected over decades, and a smaller tree that appeared to be dedicated entirely to Scandinavian decorations.

"Britta collects Christmas," Lars explained, noticing my expression as he set down our luggage. "Started when the kids were small and just... never stopped."

"It's beautiful," I said honestly. The warmth and abundance spoke of decades of family traditions, of creating magic for children who were now adults themselves.

Soren Jensen

"Connor! Maja! Come meet Soren's friend!" my mother called toward the family room, where I could hear the distinctive sounds of video game warfare.

My younger siblings appeared with the reluctant enthusiasm of teenagers who'd been told to be social. Connor had grown at least three inches since I'd seen him last spring—at eighteen, he was now taller than me, with the lanky build of someone still growing into his height. Maja, sixteen and in that phase where everything adults did was either embarrassing or amusing, looked up from her phone just long enough to offer a halfhearted wave.

That is, until they saw Aleksander step into the room behind me.

Connor straightened immediately, suddenly interested in something other than his game. Maja actually put down her phone, which was approximately equivalent to a miracle in our household.

"Who's this?" Maja asked, with the kind of direct curiosity that only teenagers can manage.

Aleksander Nordh

The younger Jensen siblings were studying me with unconcealed interest. The boy—Connor—had the same tall build as Soren and their father, but with an openness in his expression that suggested he hadn't yet learned to guard his thoughts. The girl—Maja—possessed her mother's expressive eyes and what appeared to be a healthy dose of teenage boldness.

I found myself at the center of attention from five pairs of Jensen eyes, all waiting for Soren to make introductions. The moment felt weighted with significance, though the family didn't yet understand why.

Soren Jensen

And then something came over me. Standing there in my childhood home, surrounded by my family, with Aleksander beside me looking perfectly comfortable and completely out of place at the same time, I felt a sudden rush of clarity.

This was my family. These were the people who had loved and supported me unconditionally for twenty-four years. If I couldn't trust them with this truth, who could I trust?

"Mom, Dad, Connor, Maja," I said, my voice coming out steadier than I felt. "Let me introduce you to Aleksander... my boyfriend. I'm gay."

THE REVELATION

Connor Jensen

"I KNEW IT!" I shouted, jumping up from the couch so fast I nearly knocked over the coffee table. "I totally called this! Didn't I say he was gay, Maja? I've been saying it for years!"

I practically bounced over to give Soren a high-five followed by the kind of enthusiastic hug that probably embarrassed him, but I didn't care. My big brother was finally being honest about something I'd suspected since I was old enough to notice that he never brought girlfriends home or showed interest in the girls who were obviously interested in him.

Maja Jensen

I stared at Aleksander—Soren's incredibly attractive boyfriend—with the kind of devastating disappointment that only a sixteen-year-old can experience. "You're gay?" I said to Soren, then turned to Aleksander. "Your hot boyfriend is not available? Figures! Why do all the good ones have to be gay?"

Aleksander Nordh

The teenagers' reactions were so genuinely delighted that I had to fight back laughter. Connor's enthusiastic celebration and Maja's theatrical disappointment felt wonderfully normal after all the careful politeness of adult interactions.

But it was the parents' responses that mattered most, and I watched with growing tension as Britta and Lars processed their son's announcement.

From Britta's perspective (briefly):

My son's words hit me like a gentle shock—not surprising, exactly, because mothers know things even when they don't admit to knowing them, but still momentous. I stood there watching Connor's celebration and Maja's dramatics, and felt my heart swell with pride at how naturally they'd accepted their brother's truth.

Walking over to Soren, I reached up to cup his face in my hands the way I had when he was small and needed comfort. "Honey, I love you no matter what you are," I said, meaning every word. "I think I always knew, but I'm happy you trust us enough to share this with us. But that's one hell of a way to come out, I must say!"

Soren Jensen

All eyes turned to my father, who had remained silent through the chaos of my siblings' reactions and my mother's emotional response. He stood there by our luggage, his expression unreadable in that way that had terrified me as a child when I wasn't sure if I was in trouble.

"Well?" my mother demanded when the silence stretched too long. "Aren't you going to say something?"

My father looked around the room—at Connor still grinning, at Maja rolling her eyes at the whole situation, at my mother with her hands on her hips in full protective mode, at me standing there trying not to look as nervous as I felt.

"You go, girl?" he said finally.

Aleksander Nordh

The deadpan delivery was so unexpected that Connor and Maja burst into laughter. Even Britta couldn't maintain her stern expression, though she still managed to scold her husband.

"Honey!" she protested, but I could see her fighting back a smile.

Lars set down the luggage and walked over to his son, pulling him into an embrace that spoke volumes about the relationship between them.

"Son, I love you," he said simply. "I always will. And if this fellow over here"—he pointed at me with a slight grin—"treats you well and loves you back, then I'm all for it."

Soren Jensen

The tears that had been threatening finally spilled over. These weren't the dramatic sobs of movie scenes, but the quiet tears of profound relief. My family—my wonderfully, perfectly imperfect family—had just accepted the most important truth about me with the kind of unconditional love I'd hoped for but hadn't dared to expect.

Aleksander Nordh

Watching this moment of family acceptance stirred emotions in me that I'd thought long buried. I'd witnessed countless human families across the centuries, but I'd never been privileged to see this kind of unconditional love offered so freely, so completely.

"Well," Britta said, breaking the emotional moment with characteristic practicality, "I was going to put you on a cot in the family room, Henry, but I think you'll be more comfortable sharing with Soren in his old room."

Soren Jensen

I felt my face burn with embarrassment at my mother's matter-of-fact assumption about our sleeping arrangements, but Aleksander smoothly redirected the conversation.

"That would be lovely, thank you," he said with perfect composure. "Could you show me around? I'm amazed by all the decorations. Everything is so festive for Christmas!"

"Oh, I love your accent!" Maja said immediately.

"You're so in heat!" Connor added with teenage bluntness.

"Toad!" Maja shot back.

Aleksander Nordh

As the family dissolved into familiar sibling banter and Britta began her enthusiastic tour of the Christmas decorations, I caught Soren's eye across the chaos. His smile was radiant, relieved, and full of a happiness that made my chest tight with affection.

This was his family. These were the people who had shaped the man I'd fallen in love with—generous, accepting, slightly chaotic, and completely, wonderfully human. And somehow, incredibly, they'd just welcomed me into their circle as if I belonged there.

For the first time in over two millennia, I was spending Christmas with a family. The novelty of it was both thrilling and terrifying, but as I watched Soren laughing with his siblings while his mother explained the historical significance of each ornament, I realized I was exactly where I wanted to be.

~

EVENING

Soren Jensen

"I can't believe I just blurted it out like that," I said later as we settled into the double bed in what had once been my childhood room. My mother had transformed it into a combination guest room and game room, but she'd kept some of my old things—debate team trophies, academic awards, a few carefully selected childhood photos that didn't embarrass me too much.

"It was perfect," Aleksander said, pulling me closer in the narrow bed. "Honest, direct, no room for misunderstanding. Very you."

"I'd planned this whole speech about gradual revelation and easing them into it," I admitted. "But standing there, looking at all of them, I just... I wanted them to know. I wanted them to know about us."

Aleksander Nordh

"They love you," I said simply. "All of them. That was immediately obvious."

"They love you too," Soren replied. "I could see it. Especially my mother—she's already adopted you."

As we lay there in the darkness, surrounded by the familiar sounds of Soren's childhood home, I found myself thinking about family in ways I hadn't for centuries. This was what Mikael had left behind when he chose love over expectation. This was what he'd given up to be with me, and what he'd ultimately returned to when duty called him back.

But this time was different. This time, love and family didn't have to be opposing forces. This time, I was being welcomed rather than hidden, accepted rather than rejected.

"Thank you," I whispered into the darkness.

"For what?"

"For trusting me with this. For letting me be part of your family, even temporarily."

Soren shifted to look at me in the dim light filtering through the window. "Not temporarily, Alek. For as long as you want to be."

As sleep finally claimed us both, I realized that somewhere in the span of a single evening, I had gained something I'd never expected to have again: a place at a family table, a spot in the circle of people who mattered, a home that had nothing to do with bloodlines or species and everything to do with love freely given and freely received.

25
AN UNEXPECTED PROPOSAL

FLAT 3B, 47 MARCHMONT STREET, BLOOMSBURY, LONDON WC1N 1AP

Soren Jensen

The winter had passed in a blur of contentment I'd never experienced before. After returning from Minneapolis, Aleksander and I had settled into a rhythm that felt both natural and extraordinary—library research sessions that stretched into dinner dates, quiet evenings in his flat discussing everything from vampire biology to my family's genealogy, weekends exploring London neighborhoods we'd never visited before.

The research had progressed steadily, if not dramatically. We'd made several more attempts to contact Rafael, each one politely but firmly declined. Aleksander had tried different approaches—casual coffee invitations, offers to help with research, even mentioning that we'd discovered potential family connections that might interest him. But Rafael remained elusive, maintaining his careful distance despite Aleksander's persistent kindness.

"Another polite rejection," Aleksander had said just last week after his latest attempt, though I could see the disappointment he tried to hide. "He's very gracious about it, but quite firm."

Still, neither of us was ready to give up entirely. There was something about the possibility of family—especially family who might need connection as much as Rafael apparently needed solitude—that kept us both hoping for eventual progress.

Aleksander Nordh

The months since Christmas had been among the happiest of my very long existence. Watching Soren integrate his identity as my boyfriend into his daily life, seeing him grow more confident and comfortable with who he was, had been a privilege I'd never expected to experience.

His family's acceptance had transformed him in subtle but profound ways. The careful reserve he'd carried in London had given way to an openness that extended to every aspect of his life. He laughed more easily, spoke up more freely in seminars, even seemed to take up more space physically—as if coming out had literally made him larger in the world.

And perhaps most remarkably, his family had embraced me with a warmth that still caught me off guard. The group email chain Britta had initiated after Christmas had become a weekly source of genuine joy—updates on Connor's college applications, Maja's latest teenage adventures, Lars's fishing expeditions, and general family news that somehow always included questions about how I was adapting to London weather or whether I'd tried some recipe Britta had suggested.

For someone who'd spent over two millennia carefully compartmentalizing relationships, being woven into the fabric of a human family felt miraculous.

SATURDAY AFTERNOON

Soren Jensen

"I just need to grab a few things," I said as we climbed the stairs to my flat in Bloomsbury. "Some books for Monday's seminar, and I want to pick up that sweater you like."

We'd been at the British Library all morning, making slow but steady progress on a new angle of research—investigating shipping records between Sweden and Denmark during the 1880s, hoping to find more evidence of the mysterious R. Jørgensen who'd inherited Gustaf's books. It was detailed, painstaking work, but Aleksander approached it with the same patient enthusiasm he brought to everything.

"Soren," Aleksander said as we reached my door, "if it's not too presumptuous, I was wondering... might I stay here tonight? With you?"

I paused with my key halfway to the lock, surprised by the request. While Aleksander and I spent most nights together, it was almost always at his flat. His space was larger, more comfortable, with better amenities and that impressive bed with Egyptian cotton sheets that probably cost more than I paid in rent.

"Of course," I said, trying to understand what had prompted the request. "Though I should warn you, my bed isn't exactly a luxury accommodation compared to yours."

"I'm not interested in the bed," Aleksander said with that gentle smile that always made my heart skip. "I'm interested in the experience. Your space, your neighborhood, your life. I've been so charmed by your family's warmth, and I suppose I'm curious about seeing where you've built your London home."

Aleksander Nordh

The truth was, I'd been thinking about this for weeks. Despite the time we'd spent together, I realized I knew surprisingly little about Soren's daily environment. His flat remained largely mysterious to me—a place we visited briefly to collect things before heading elsewhere. I'd met his flatmates only in passing, never long enough for real conversation.

There was something appealing about the idea of staying in his space, seeing how he'd arranged his books, what photographs he kept on his desk, how he moved through rooms he'd made his own. After being welcomed so completely into his family home, I found myself curious about the London life he'd built independently.

"If you're sure it's not an imposition," I added. "I know you value your privacy, and I don't want to intrude on your routine."

"No intrusion at all," Soren said, unlocking the door. "Though I should probably tidy up a bit—"

"No need, Soren. It'll be perfect just as it is."

MEETING THE FLATMATES

Soren Jensen

As if summoned by our conversation, Olivia Chen appeared in the hallway just as we entered. I'd mentioned her to Aleksander before—the fellow American graduate student I'd become friends with over our shared experience of navigating British academic culture.

"Soren!" she said, emerging from the kitchen with a cup of tea in hand. "I thought I heard voices."

Until this moment, my flatmates knew I had a boyfriend, but they'd never properly met Aleksander. Our encounters had been limited to brief nods in passing, polite "hellos" when he waited in the entry while I grabbed something from my room.

"Olivia, I'd like you to meet Henry properly," I said, suddenly feeling nervous about this introduction in a way I hadn't expected. "Henry, this is Olivia Chen. She's working on Chinese-American communities."

Aleksander Nordh

Olivia extended her hand with the confident friendliness I'd observed in many American graduate students. She was petite, perhaps five-foot-three, with short black hair and expressive eyes behind stylish glasses that suggested both intelligence and approachability.

"I'm Henry," I said, taking her hand with a smile that I hoped struck the right balance between polite and appropriately youthful. "Soren's boyfriend."

The words felt different saying them here, in Soren's space, to his friend. More real, somehow. More integrated into the fabric of his actual life rather than something that existed primarily in our private world.

Olivia's face immediately lit up with genuine delight. "Oh my God, finally! A proper introduction!" She turned to Soren with mock accusation. "You've been hiding him from us for months. That's so wonderful, Soren! I'm so happy to meet you properly, Henry."

Soren Jensen

The warmth in Olivia's response shouldn't have surprised me—she'd always been genuinely interested in my life and happiness. But hearing her excitement about meeting Aleksander made me realize how compartmentalized I'd kept different aspects of my London existence.

"Henry's been helping with my family research," I explained. "He has an amazing collection of historical documents."

"And Soren's been invaluable in helping me understand American perspectives on cultural preservation," Aleksander replied smoothly. "We make a good research team."

"That's amazing," Olivia said, and I could see her filing away details with the same analytical mind that made her such a good researcher. "How long have you two been together?"

"Since last fall," I said, reaching for Aleksander's hand without thinking about it. "About six months now."

The casual gesture felt significant in this context—claiming our relationship openly in front of my friend, in my home, without hesitation or explanation.

. . .

AN EVENING HOME

My room was exactly as I'd left it that morning—bed hastily made, desk covered with research notes and library books, laundry basket overflowing with items I'd been meaning to deal with for weeks. It was functional rather than elegant, a graduate student's space focused on necessity rather than aesthetics.

"This is it," I said, suddenly self-conscious about the modest accommodations. "Not exactly luxury accommodations."

Aleksander moved through the space with the same careful attention he brought to everything, but there was something different in his expression—a kind of gentle curiosity rather than his usual polite interest.

"It's perfect," he said, studying the photographs I'd pinned to a bulletin board above my desk. "Is this your family?"

"Christmas morning," I confirmed, pointing to a photo Maja had taken of all of us in our pajamas, opening presents around the tree. "And that's from Sweden—Marta and Lars and Erik at the farm."

He spent several minutes examining each image, and I realized he was seeing evidence of my life and connections in a way that felt oddly intimate. These weren't formal portraits or carefully curated displays, but the casual documentation of relationships that mattered to me.

Aleksander Nordh

Soren's room told stories I'd never heard—evidence of friendships from university, family photos spanning years of gatherings, ticket stubs from museums and concerts, books that revealed interests beyond his academic focus. It was unmistakably the space of someone building a life rather than merely occupying time.

"You have good taste in books," I observed, scanning the shelves that lined one wall. "And quite an eclectic collection."

"Occupational hazard," Soren replied with a slight blush. "I can't resist bringing things home from the library bookshop."

As evening settled over London, we ordered takeaway from a Thai restaurant down the street and ate sitting on Soren's narrow bed, talking about everything and nothing. There was something deeply comfortable about the ordinariness of it—no elegant restaurants or carefully planned activities, just the simple pleasure of being together in a space that belonged entirely to him.

EMAIL

Soren Jensen

We were discussing whether to watch a film or simply continue talking when my phone chimed with an email notification. I almost ignored it—Saturday evening emails were usually spam or university administrative updates—but something made me glance at the screen.

The sender's name made me sit up straight: Erik Eriksson.

"It's from Erik," I said, immediately getting Aleksander's attention. "Our cousin from Sweden."

I opened the email and began reading aloud, translating Erik's enthusiastic mixture of English and Swedish as I went:

```
Hey Soren and Alek (my favorite Guncles!!!)

Hope you guys are doing well in London.
Things here are... complicated as usual.
Parents still fighting about everything and
I'm getting tired of being the excuse for why
they can't sort out their problems. Mormor
and Morfar (Marta and Lars) are great but I
think they're getting worn out too.

So here's the thing - remember when you said
I could maybe visit London sometime? Were you
just being polite or were you actually
serious? Because if you were serious, I've
been looking at flights and I have school
break coming up in April and I've saved some
money from my part-time job and I really,
REALLY want to take you up on that offer.

I know I'm only 15 but I'm not a baby and I
can handle traveling by myself. Plus, you
guys are basically the coolest relatives I
have (sorry to all the other Jensens lol) and
I want to see what real life is like outside
this village.

So... can I come visit? Please? I promise I
won't be any trouble and I'll help with
cooking and cleaning and whatever you need. I
just need to get away from here for a while
and see something bigger than Swedish
farmland.

Love you both, Erik
```

PS - Mormor says hi and wants to know if you're eating enough vegetables, Alek. She worries about you being too skinny.

CONCERNS AND CONSIDERATIONS

I set down my phone and looked at Aleksander, feeling a mixture of excitement and panic. The idea of Erik visiting was wonderful in principle, but the practical realities were daunting.

"He's serious about this," I said. "But Alek, he's only fifteen. Traveling by himself from Sweden? What about visa requirements? And who would be legally responsible for him while he's here? We're not his guardians."

Aleksander was quiet for a moment, his expression thoughtful rather than concerned.

"Those are all solvable problems," he said finally. "I have connections that could help with travel arrangements and documentation. The more important question is whether we're prepared to take responsibility for a teenager who's clearly dealing with family stress."

"Are we?" I asked, suddenly feeling very young myself. "I mean, I'm only twenty-four. I've never been responsible for anyone else before. What if something happens? What if we're not equipped to help him?"

Aleksander Nordh

Watching Soren grapple with the weight of potential responsibility stirred something protective in me. He was approaching this with characteristic thoughtfulness, considering all the ways things could go wrong rather than focusing on the potential benefits.

"Soren," I said gently, "we're not being asked to be his parents. We're being asked to be his family—to provide a safe place for a few weeks while he experiences something beyond the limitations of his current situation."

I thought about Erik as I'd seen him at the farm—intelligent, mature for his age, but clearly struggling with the isolation of rural life and family dysfunction. Sometimes young people needed examples of different ways to live, different possibilities for their futures.

"His parents are in a 'complicated' situation, remember?" I continued. "And from what I observed, Erik needs stable influences in his life. As bizarre as it might sound, we might be among the most stable relationships he has access to right now."

Soren Jensen

The truth in Aleksander's words hit me immediately. Erik had mentioned his parents' ongoing conflicts both during our visit and in occasional family emails. Marta and Lars were wonderful, but they were elderly and dealing with their own challenges. We might indeed represent something Erik needed—evidence that life could be different, that there were other ways to build relationships and create stability.

"You're right," I said slowly. "And honestly, I'd love to have him visit. I just worry about all the practical details, the costs, the legal requirements..."

"Let me investigate those concerns," Aleksander said with the quiet confidence of someone who'd navigated bureaucracy across centuries. "I have resources that can help with travel arrangements and documentation. The financial aspects aren't a concern."

"Alek, a trip like this for a fifteen-year-old... that's thousands of pounds. Flights, accommodation, activities, food..."

"Soren," he interrupted gently, "this would be a once-in-a-lifetime opportunity for someone Erik's age. And given his circumstances, it might be exactly what he needs right now."

Aleksander Nordh

I could see Soren still wrestling with doubts, so I decided to address the deeper concern I sensed beneath his practical worries.

"You're worried about being responsible for him," I said. "But you're not alone in this. We're in this together, and honestly, you underestimate your own capabilities. You've handled far more complex challenges than hosting a teenage relative for a few weeks."

Soren looked at me with that direct gaze that always made my chest tighten. "We're not his parents, but..."

"We're his family," I finished. "You're his cousin, distant but genuine. And I..."

I paused, realizing I was about to make a claim I'd never made before, not with anyone in over two millennia.

"What?" Soren prompted gently.

UNEXPECTED DECLARATION

Soren Jensen

Something in Aleksander's expression had shifted, become more serious and somehow more vulnerable than I'd seen before.

"I was going to say that I'm just as much his uncle as you are," he said quietly. "But that's not quite accurate, is it? I'm not really part of the Jensen family, not officially. I'm just..."

"Stop," I interrupted, feeling something fierce rise in my chest. "Don't you dare finish that sentence."

Aleksander looked startled by the intensity in my voice.

"You are not 'just' anything, Aleksander. You're more a part of this family than I am, and don't you ever forget that. You may have been alone in this world for the longest time, but I'm claiming you as a member of the Jensens from here on out. You're not an outsider looking in. You're family. You're... you're *my family.*"

Aleksander Nordh

The passionate certainty in Soren's voice stopped me cold. For someone who'd spent over two thousand years carefully managing his place in human relationships, being claimed so completely, so unreservedly, was overwhelming.

"Soren," I said, my voice catching slightly, "its as if you are proposing."

The words came out more lightly than I'd intended, meant as gentle teasing to defuse the emotional intensity of the moment. But something shifted in Soren's expression, and I realized my jest had touched something deeper than either of us had expected.

"Well..." Soren said slowly, his eyes never leaving mine. "I... I... I guess *I am.*"

Time stopped.

The casual conversation, the practical concerns about Erik's visit, the comfortable domesticity of the evening—all of it faded into the background as the weight of his words settled between us.

PROPOSAL

"You... *you're what?*" I managed finally, my voice coming out rougher than intended.

In over two millennia of existence, I'd been caught off guard by wars, natural disasters, technological revolutions, and countless human behaviors that defied prediction. But nothing had prepared me for this moment—this beautiful, impossible young man looking at me with complete sincerity and offering me something I'd never dared to hope for.

Soren Jensen

I hadn't planned this. The idea hadn't even been in my consciousness when we'd walked into my flat that afternoon. But looking at Aleksander—this ancient, wonderful being who'd spent centuries alone, who'd loved my ancestor and now loved me, who'd been welcomed into my family with such warmth—something powerful and undeniable rose from the deepest part of my heart.

"Listen, Alek," I said, my voice growing steadier as I found my footing. "I'm not asking for anything drastic. I actually hadn't planned any of this. And sometimes, that's for the best. I can get too much in my head, you know that. But this is from my heart."

I reached for his hands, intertwining our fingers as I searched for the right words.

"You have so much history with our family. You've been so pivotal, so kind to all of us. So kind... to me. So patient, caring..." My voice dropped to almost a whisper, but I found my breath and continued. "I love you. And I have so much more I want to share. So many more questions and... well, you are a part of me. You are just as much a Jensen as I am."

Aleksander Nordh

Every word hit me like a physical blow—not painful, but overwhelming in their simple truth. This young man who'd stumbled into my carefully ordered existence had somehow seen past every barrier I'd constructed, past the impossible span of years that separated us, to something essential and unchanging at my core.

Soren Jensen

"And today is different from all those years ago," I continued, my voice growing stronger. "I'm sorry you weren't able to be who you truly were back then, but I know you can now. And... well, Aleksander... Henrik... will you be my husband?"

Calling him Henrik—his true name, the name Mikael would have known him by—felt like offering the most precious thing I possessed. It was vulnerability and acceptance and love all wrapped in four syllables that somehow contained centuries of history and the promise of a shared future.

Aleksander Nordh

The sound of my oldest name on his lips nearly undid me completely. Henrik—the name my parents had given me, the name Mikael had whispered in the darkness of Copenhagen nights, the name that connected me to who I'd been before centuries of careful disguises and managed identities.

"Yes," I said, the word coming out as barely more than breath. "Soren, forever as we may hold each other in embrace, I say yes. I shall honor your name and that of the Jensen family. I shall be yours."

AFTERMATH

Soren Jensen

The tears came immediately—joyful, overwhelming, accompanied by laughter that bordered on hysterical. We were engaged. I was engaged to a two-thousand-year-old vampire who'd loved my ancestor over a century ago, and somehow that was the most natural thing in the world.

"I can't believe I just proposed," I said between kisses that tasted like salt and happiness. "I can't believe you said yes."

"I can't believe it took you this long," Aleksander replied, his voice thick with emotion I'd never heard before. "I would have said yes the first night you stayed at my flat, if you'd asked."

Aleksander Nordh

Holding Soren against me, feeling his heartbeat against my chest, I realized that every loss I'd endured, every century of loneliness I'd carried, had led to this moment. All of it—the pain of losing Mikael, the isolation of endless years, the careful distance I'd maintained from human connection—all of it had been necessary to bring me here, to this place where I could receive and return love without reservation.

"Should we call your parents?" I asked when we'd finally caught our breath. "Our parents?"

. . .

Soren Jensen

The casual way he said "our parents" made my heart skip. After centuries of isolation, he now had in-laws who sent him recipes and worried about whether he was eating enough vegetables.

"We should," I agreed. "Though it's probably the middle of the night in Minnesota right now."

"They'll forgive us," Aleksander said with certainty. "Some news can't wait for convenient time zones."

PRACTICAL MATTERS

Aleksander Nordh

As we began to surface from the emotional intensity of the moment, practical concerns started reasserting themselves. My phone chimed with a reminder that we'd never actually responded to Erik's email.

"Our nephew is still waiting for an answer," I pointed out, and felt a warm glow at how naturally the possessive pronoun came.

"Our nephew," Soren repeated with wonder. "God, Alek, we're going to be married. We're going to have a family. We're going to host a fifteen-year-old Swedish relative who thinks we're the coolest people he knows."

Soren Jensen

The scope of what had just changed hit me all at once. An hour ago, I'd been a graduate student with a boyfriend. Now I was engaged to be married, with potential family responsibilities that extended across international borders.

"What do we do about Erik's visit?" I asked. "I mean, practically speaking?"

"Why don't I fly to Sweden and retrieve our nephew personally?" Aleksander suggested. "It would ease your concerns about him traveling alone, and I could coordinate with Marta and Lars about any necessary documentation."

The offer was so generous, so thoughtful, that I felt another wave of love crash over me.

"You'd do that?"

"Soren," he said gently, "Erik is family now. And family takes care of family, whatever that requires."

. . .

Aleksander Nordh

As we sat in Soren's narrow bed, surrounded by the modest accommodations of a graduate student's life, planning our engagement announcement and our nephew's visit, I realized that this was what I'd been searching for across millennia without knowing it. Not grand gestures or dramatic declarations, but the simple, profound joy of building a life with someone who saw all of me and chose to stay.

The Jensen bloodline had indeed found its way back to me, but not in the way I'd ever imagined. Instead of echoes of the past, I'd found the promise of a future I'd never dared to dream.

"So," Soren said, settling against my chest with a contented sigh, "engaged and about to become temporary guardians of a Swedish teenager. That's quite an evening's work."

"The best evening's work of my very long life," I replied, meaning every word.

Outside, London hummed with its usual Saturday night energy—traffic and laughter and the distant sound of music from nearby pubs. Inside Soren's small room, we held each other and planned a future that somehow managed to honor both the ancient past and the uncertain years ahead.

We were engaged. We were family. And for the first time in over two thousand years, I was exactly where I belonged.

26
MIDNIGHT CALL AND MORNING PLANS

2847 OAKWOOD LANE, EDINA, MN 55424, USA

Britta Jensen

The iPhone's insistent buzzing pulled me from deep sleep with the kind of jarring urgency that immediately triggered maternal panic. Three calls in succession at nearly 3 AM could only mean emergency—accident, illness, something terrible happening to one of my children.

I fumbled for the phone, my heart already racing as I squinted at the screen. The international number took a moment to register, but when I saw "Soren - London" my panic shifted into a different kind of alarm.

"Soren?" I answered, my voice thick with sleep and worry. "Honey, what's wrong? Are you okay?"

Beside me, Lars stirred, the urgency in my voice penetrating his deeper sleep. I could hear something in Soren's voice—excitement, not distress—but my mother's brain was still catching up.

"Wait, honey. Let me put you on speaker," I said, reaching over to shake Lars more fully awake while my thumb found the speaker button.

Lars rubbed his eyes, immediately alert in that way parents develop after years of midnight crises. "What's happening?" he whispered.

I held up a hand, wiping tears I hadn't realized were falling as Soren's voice filled our bedroom, clear and happy and completely alive.

"Hi Dad, sorry to call so late, but Henry and I wanted to share some news..."

The relief of hearing him safe and well, combined with the joy practically radiating through the phone, broke through my remaining confusion. Only one kind of news warranted a middle-of-the-night international call between people this happy.

"They're getting married!" I burst out, unable to contain myself.

Aleksander Nordh

Sitting on Soren's narrow bed in his London flat, listening to his mother's delighted shriek across the Atlantic, I felt something bubble up from deep in my chest—laughter, pure and unguarded, the kind I hadn't allowed myself in decades. The spontaneous joy in her voice, the immediate celebration without hesitation or questions, was so quintessentially American, so perfectly Jensen family.

"Good morning, Mrs. Jensen. Our apologies for waking you," I offered, trying to regain some semblance of proper manners while still grinning like a fool.

Britta Jensen

"You're our son now, call me Mom!" I practically sang into the phone, meaning every word. This wonderful young man who'd made my son so happy, who'd been welcomed into our family with such ease at Christmas—of course he was our son now. That's how family worked.

Soren Jensen

My mother's immediate, wholehearted claim of Aleksander as her son hit me harder than I'd expected. I felt the phone slipping from my suddenly shaky hands, but before I could even register the problem, Aleksander's fingers were there, steadying my grip with those impossibly quick reflexes that still caught me off guard sometimes.

Watching his face as he processed being claimed as someone's son after over two millennia of careful independence was worth every moment of middle-of-the-night nervousness about this call.

Aleksander Nordh

"You're much too kind... Mom," I managed, testing the word like a foreign language. And perhaps it was—in all my centuries, I'd never had occasion to use that particular term for anyone but my own ancient parents.

The word felt strange in my mouth, but not unpleasant. Americans really were a remarkable people, I reflected. Their capacity for immediate, generous acceptance never ceased to amaze me.

THE INTERROGATION

Lars Jensen

Once Britta had claimed another son and I'd managed to fully wake up, I found myself grinning at the familiar sound of my wife launching into what the kids had always called her "information gathering mode." Some things never changed, no matter the hour or the continent.

"Who proposed?" she was demanding. "How did it happen? When? Where? Do you have a ring? What are your plans?"

The questions tumbled out faster than either of the boys could answer, and I could hear Soren laughing as he tried to keep up with her enthusiasm.

"I proposed," Soren said, his voice carrying a pride that made my chest tight with emotion. "Just a few hours ago, actually. We were talking about family and I just... I couldn't imagine my life without him."

"And I said yes immediately," came Henry's voice, warm with affection. "Though I should mention we haven't discussed rings or dates or any of the practical details yet."

Britta Jensen

"Well, we have time for all that," I said, already mentally organizing guest lists and venue options. "The important thing is that you're both happy and you want to build a life together."

I paused, a thought occurring to me. "This isn't a secret, is it? Can I tell the family? Because Connor and Maja are going to be absolutely thrilled, and your aunt Susan will want to start planning something immediately..."

Soren Jensen

I looked at Aleksander, realizing we hadn't even considered the question of privacy. The idea of family celebrations, of sharing this news widely, felt both wonderful and slightly overwhelming.

"Sure, Mom," I said, making the decision for both of us. "It'll be easier than sending announcements. Besides, you know how you are with secrets."

"I am perfectly capable of keeping secrets when necessary," she protested, though her tone suggested she knew exactly what I meant.

"Of course you are, honey," my father's voice came through with gentle amusement.

WEDDING PLANS

Britta Jensen

"Soren, I think we should have the wedding here in Minnesota and it should have all the family and—" I began, my mind already racing through possibilities.

"Perhaps they want something quiet, honey?" Lars interrupted gently. "Maybe there in London? Or even in Sweden? Maybe in our old hometown?"

Aleksander Nordh

Lars's suggestion of Sweden made something warm bloom in my chest. The idea of being married in the country where I'd first fallen in love, where Mikael's family still lived, where we'd found such unexpected connection with the current generation... it felt like completing a circle that had been broken for over a century.

"Whatever you choose, I'll fly there with wings just to see," Britta's voice came through the speaker. "I'm so happy for you both!"

Soren Jensen

The realization that I hadn't given a single thought to wedding planning hit me suddenly. We'd gone from casual conversation to engagement to international phone calls without pausing to consider what marriage actually meant in practical terms.

But looking at Aleksander's face as he considered my father's suggestion about Sweden, I could see possibilities forming that hadn't existed an hour ago.

AFTER THE CALL

Soren Jensen

After we'd said our goodbyes and promised to call again with more details, I set the phone aside and looked at Aleksander. The reality of what we'd just done—not just getting engaged, but announcing it to my family, making it real in the wider world—was starting to sink in.

"They love you," I said, though I knew he already understood that.

"Your family is extraordinary," he replied, reaching for my hand. "I've never experienced anything like that kind of immediate acceptance."

"Before you go up to retrieve Erik, maybe we should float the idea of a wedding around... but... it's early," I said, my mind jumping ahead to all the decisions and plans that would need to be made.

Aleksander Nordh

"One thing at a time, puzzle boy," I said, using the endearment that had just occurred to me. Something about the way Soren approached life's complexities—methodically, carefully, fitting pieces together until the whole picture emerged—reminded me of someone working an intricate puzzle.

"Puzzle boy?" he asked, raising an eyebrow.

"My puzzle boy," I said, leaning in to kiss him, tasting happiness and possibility and the promise of a future I'd never dared to imagine.

As we settled back into the narrow bed, surrounded by the quiet sounds of London at night, I realized that in the space of a few hours, everything had changed. We were engaged. We had family who celebrated our love without reservation. We had a teenage nephew requesting to visit. We had wedding plans to make and futures to build.

But first, we had the rest of this perfect night to simply hold each other and marvel at the impossible good fortune that had brought us together.

The Jensen bloodline had indeed found its way home, and this time, nothing would tear it away again.

27
ERIK ARRIVES

HEATHROW AIRPORT TERMINAL 5, LONGFORD TW6 2GA, UNITED KINGDOM

Erik Eriksson

The black taxi wound its way from the airport and into London streets that seemed impossibly narrow after the wide roads of Sweden, and I couldn't stop staring out the window. Everything was so... much. More people, more cars, more buildings pressing together like they were all trying to share secrets. Stockholm had felt big when I'd traveled there with Alek yesterday, but London was something else entirely—a living, breathing organism that seemed to pulse with energy I could feel through the taxi windows.

"This is mental," I said, pressing my face closer to the glass as we passed a group of teenagers my age clustered around a bus stop, all looking impossibly sophisticated in ways that made my Swedish small-town clothes feel suddenly inadequate. "How do people not get lost every single day?"

Alek chuckled from beside me, and I still couldn't get over how strange it felt to be sitting next to someone who looked barely older than me but had lived for... well, centuries probably. On the plane, when he'd casually directed me to seat 2A in business class, I'd been amazed.

"We're not in the back?" I'd asked, surprised by the spacious seats and actual legroom.

"Most certainly not," he'd replied with that slight smile that suggested there was more to the story than he was sharing.

Aleksander Nordh

Watching Erik experience London for the first time reminded me why I loved this city so much. Through his eyes, the familiar streets became extraordinary again—the Victorian architecture, the layers of history visible in every corner, the casual diversity that made London feel like the center of the world.

The journey from Sweden had gone more smoothly than I'd expected. Erik was remarkably mature for sixteen, handling the travel documentation and airport procedures with minimal assistance. More importantly, he'd opened up during our conversations in ways that suggested he was hungry for adult company that took him seriously.

"Erik," I said as we passed through a particularly busy intersection, "if it's not too forward, when did you move in with your grandparents?"

Erik Eriksson

The question didn't surprise me—Alek had been asking thoughtful questions all day, never prying but showing genuine interest in understanding my situation. It felt good to have an adult actually listen instead of just telling me what I should think or feel.

"About two years ago," I said, settling back in the taxi seat. "My parents... well, they're not exactly on speaking terms anymore. Haven't been for years, really."

I found myself telling him the whole messy story—how my mother was a Jensen who'd married my father when she discovered she was pregnant, much against my grandmother's wishes. How the troubles had started before I was even born, with my father going away for months to work at sea and my mother resenting being stuck in our small village life.

"She wanted something bigger," I explained, watching London roll past the windows. "She knew about the old times when our ancestors went abroad and made something of themselves. She felt trapped, I think. And my father... well, he wasn't around enough to help make anything better."

Aleksander Nordh

The story Erik told was achingly familiar—family tensions, unfulfilled dreams, a young person caught in the middle of adult conflicts beyond his control. It reminded me of countless human families I'd observed over the centuries, each generation struggling with the balance between duty and desire, tradition and change.

"So I mostly raised myself," Erik continued with the matter-of-fact tone teenagers use when describing situations that would horrify most adults. "Between my mother's arguments with my father when he came home, and her arguments with my grandmother about how to raise me properly, it was easier to just... disappear into my room with books and music."

"Does anyone know you're gay?" I asked, then immediately regretted the directness of the question. "I'm sorry, Erik. That was too personal and not my business. I retract the question."

Erik Eriksson

"You're too uptight, Uncle Alek!" I said, grinning at his formal apology. Hearing myself call him uncle felt surprisingly natural, and I could see something warm and pleased cross his face at the title.

"No, I've never officially come out to them," I continued. "I figured they'd just argue more about it. But I never really denied it either. I just tried to be me, you know? I don't worry about it much, but I don't really have a boyfriend or anything, so it's not been an issue."

The truth was more complicated than that. I'd figured out I was gay around age fourteen, but living in a small Swedish village didn't exactly provide a lot of dating opportunities. Most boys my age were into football or skiing or girls—especially the cute ones, who were inevitably straight. I'd learned to keep my interests to myself: the gothic literature, the spooky stories, the bands that sang about darkness and mystery.

"I love all those vampire novels and horror movies," I said, then stopped abruptly, remembering who I was talking to. "Oh God, I'm sorry. I... well... you... well..."

Aleksander Nordh

"Oh... oh... that," I said, understanding immediately why he looked mortified. The irony of a teenager apologizing to an actual vampire for enjoying vampire fiction was not lost on me. "Why don't we chat about that later this evening when we're home, okay? And it's okay—I've read them all myself."

My reassurance seemed to relax him, though I could see him studying me with new curiosity. He was clearly intelligent enough to have pieced together more about my nature than Soren and I had explicitly shared, despite our careful avoidance of specifics.

As we turned into my neighborhood, I pointed out the window. "We're almost home."

"I wish I lived here," Erik sighed, taking in the tree-lined streets and elegant Victorian terraces.

THE FLAT

Erik Eriksson

Alek's flat was... well, amazing. Grand, at least by my standards, though he seemed to think it was nothing special. Everything looked expensive but comfortable, like it belonged in a magazine about sophisticated city living. I was afraid to touch anything at first.

"Relax, Erik," Alek said, noticing my hesitation. "It's fine. You're welcome here, always."

He showed me to a guest room that was larger than my bedroom back in Sweden, with tall windows overlooking the street and a bed that looked impossibly comfortable. The whole flat felt like Alek—elegant, timeless, carefully curated but somehow warm.

When Soren arrived a few minutes later, he smiled and waved but seemed uncertain about how to greet me. I could see the hesitation in his body language.

"What?" I asked. "Aren't you going to kiss him hello? He just got back from a long trip, after all!"

Soren Jensen

Erik's directness caught me off guard, but in the best possible way. Here was this teenager, in a foreign country for the first time, confidently telling me how to greet my own fiancé. There was something wonderfully uncomplicated about his perspective.

I gave Aleksander a proper kiss hello, then turned back to Erik. "Happy?"

"I don't know. Are you, Alek?"

"Very," Aleksander replied with genuine warmth.

Aleksander Nordh

After Erik had unpacked and settled in, I surprised both Jensens with an announcement I'd been planning since our flight landed.

"I've scheduled a special dinner tonight in Erik's honor," I said, enjoying their expressions of curiosity. "In fact, since your grandmother whispered to me that it's your seventeenth birthday in a few days..."

"Why didn't you tell us?" Soren whispered to Erik.

"I wanted to share a special place with you," I continued. "It's a Friday evening, and I know we've traveled today, but I thought it might be nice to celebrate properly."

Erik Eriksson

I felt my face burn with embarrassment. I didn't want anyone making a fuss about my birthday—I'd learned over the years that the less attention I drew to myself, the safer it felt. When people noticed me, they had expectations or disappointments. It was easier to stay invisible.

But looking at Alek and Soren's faces, I could see they genuinely wanted to celebrate with me. It wasn't obligation or duty; it was affection. Family.

"Our reservation isn't until nine-thirty," Alek said, "so why don't you freshen up a bit, Erik, and we'll leave soon."

"Where are we going?" Soren asked with curiosity.

"You'll see," Alek replied with that mysterious smile. "I don't know if this will work, but it came to me yesterday as I was getting to know Erik."

THE RESTAURANT

An hour later, we emerged from the Underground in what felt like a completely different world from central London. This was a small village tucked away in the northwest, all narrow streets and old buildings that looked like they'd stepped out of one of my gothic novels. The restaurant Alek led us to was dimly lit and atmospheric, exactly the kind of place I'd always imagined but never thought I'd actually experience.

"Good evening, Henry," the owner greeted Alek with obvious familiarity. "Your table is ready."

As we followed him deeper into the restaurant, past flickering candles and dark wood paneling, I felt like I was walking into one of my fantasies. This was the kind of place where mysterious things happened, where stories began.

And then we turned the corner into a private alcove, and I saw him.

He was the most beautiful boy I'd ever seen. Slightly older than me, definitely Asian—maybe Filipino?—with dark hair and clothes that looked like they belonged in a fashion magazine. But it was his eyes that stopped me cold. Dark, soulful, like they'd been painted on but somehow more real than anything else in the room. His skin was this incredible pale mocha color that seemed to shimmer in the candlelight.

When our eyes met, I saw something I recognized immediately—that look of someone prepared to run, to disappear before anyone could hurt them. But I wouldn't let him. Something passed between us in that moment, some understanding that neither of us had expected.

Aleksander Nordh

I exhaled visibly, relief flooding through me as I watched Erik and Rafael's first meeting unfold. This had been a tremendous gamble—bringing Erik here, hoping that somehow a sixteen-year-old Swedish teenager might be the key to reaching Rafael when months of adult diplomacy had failed.

"Soren, Erik," I said quietly, "let me introduce you to Rafael."

Rafael Mercado

I had agreed to this dinner against every instinct I possessed, driven by something I couldn't name—curiosity, loneliness, or perhaps simply exhaustion from my own isolation. Aleksander had been persistent but respectful in his invitations, and there was something about his mention of family, of connections I didn't understand, that had finally worn down my resistance.

But I hadn't expected this. Hadn't expected to look up from my nervous fidgeting with the menu and see a teenager with bright eyes and an expression of wonder that reminded me, suddenly and painfully, of myself at that age. Before everything had gone wrong. Before I'd become something that couldn't belong anywhere.

The boy—Erik—was staring at me with an intensity that should have made me uncomfortable but somehow didn't. Instead of the usual urge to flee, I felt something I hadn't experienced in years: curiosity about another person, genuine interest in what he might say or think or feel.

Soren Jensen

Watching the moment unfold between Erik and Rafael, I finally understood what Aleksander had been planning. This wasn't just a birthday dinner—it was an intervention, carefully orchestrated to bring together people who needed each other, even if they didn't know it yet.

Rafael looked exactly as Aleksander had described him—beautiful, guarded, carrying himself with the careful precision of someone who'd learned to be invisible. But there was something in his expression as he looked at Erik that suggested his walls might not be as impenetrable as they appeared.

And Erik... sixteen-year-old Erik was looking at Rafael like he'd found something he'd been searching for his entire life without knowing it.

Aleksander Nordh

As introductions began and we settled around the table, I realized that whatever happened next, we'd already crossed a threshold. Rafael was here, present in a way he hadn't been during our previous careful encounters. Erik was completely engaged, his usual teenage self-consciousness replaced by genuine fascination.

And for the first time in months… no, years of trying to reach Rafael, I felt hope that maybe, just maybe, family had a way of finding itself even across the most impossible circumstances. He had carefully boxed himself in a protective cage that neither Soren nor I could think to unlock. Tonight, perhaps Erik might.

28
THE TRANSFORMATION

ROOM 314, MAIN BUILDING, UNIVERSITY OF SANTO TOMAS, ESPAÑA BLVD, SAMPALOC, MANILA 1008, PHILIPPINES

Rafael Mercado

2002

The afternoon heat pressed against the tall windows of Professor Nazari's office, but the room remained surprisingly cool thanks to an ancient air conditioning unit that wheezed with determined efficiency. I sat across from his cluttered desk, surrounded by artifacts that seemed impossibly authentic for an academic's collection—Byzantine coins, medieval manuscripts, carved figures that looked like they belonged in museums rather than a university office.

"Your essay on iconographic symbolism was exceptional, Mr. Mercado," Professor Nazari said, his voice carrying the slight Eastern European accent that had always intrigued me. Czech, perhaps, or Slovak. Despite decades in the Philippines, it lingered in his pronunciation like an echo of distant mountains.

At his elbow, Eliza Chen sat with her usual efficient posture, taking notes in her precise handwriting. She'd been Professor Nazari's teaching assistant for as long as I'd been taking his classes—sharp, competent, and perpetually distant. Today, however, something seemed different about her demeanor. She kept glancing between the professor and me with an expression I couldn't quite interpret.

"Thank you, Professor," I replied, though his compliment felt heavier than it should have. "I find Byzantine art particularly fascinating—the way spiritual and political meanings layer together."

Professor Nazari leaned forward slightly, his dark eyes holding an intensity that made me suddenly self-conscious. He looked older than usual today, I noticed—paler, with a slight tremor in his hands that he tried to conceal. Colleagues whispered that he was fighting some sort of illness, probably cancer, though he'd never confirmed it publicly.

"Your understanding goes beyond academic analysis," he continued. "You seem to perceive things that others miss entirely. Where did you develop such... sensitivity?"

The question caught me off guard. Eliza's pen stopped moving, and I felt her attention sharpen on our conversation.

"I'm not sure what you mean, Professor," I said honestly. "I've always been drawn to art, especially older pieces. Sometimes I feel like I can sense the artist's intentions, but I assumed everyone experienced that to some degree."

"Show me," Professor Nazari said suddenly, gesturing toward a small bronze figure on his desk. "Tell me what you sense about this piece."

I glanced at Eliza, who was watching me with an expression that might have been warning, though I couldn't understand why. The bronze dancer seemed to call to me—a figure frozen in mid-movement, her surface worn smooth by countless hands.

"May I?" I asked, reaching toward the sculpture.

"Please," the professor encouraged, though I noticed Eliza's grip tighten on her pen.

The moment my fingers touched the bronze, the familiar shift in perception occurred. The office faded around me as images flooded my mind: afternoon sunlight streaming through tall windows, an artist's hands shaping clay with desperate precision, the weight of love and loss infusing every detail of the figure's expression.

"She was created as a memorial," I heard myself saying, though I had no conscious knowledge of the piece's history. "The artist was mourning someone he loved—a dancer who died young. He poured his grief into the bronze, trying to capture not just her appearance but the essence of her movement, the joy she had brought to the world before illness took her."

When the vision faded, I found Professor Nazari watching me with an expression that mixed satisfaction with something that might have been hunger. Eliza had gone completely still, her face pale.

"Remarkable," Professor Nazari murmured. "And how do you explain this ability?"

"I can't," I admitted, suddenly uncomfortable under his intense scrutiny. "It's not something I learned. It's just... something I've always been able to do."

Professor Nazari was quiet for a long moment, his gaze distant as if he were calculating possibilities I couldn't imagine. When he spoke again, his voice carried a weight that made the hair on my neck stand up.

"Mr. Mercado, how would you feel about participating in a more intensive research project? Something that would allow you to develop your natural gifts to their fullest potential?"

I felt excitement flutter in my chest—the opportunity to work closely with the university's most renowned professor seemed like a dream come true. But something in Eliza's expression gave me pause. She was looking at Professor Nazari with what I could only describe as pleading, though she said nothing.

"What would that involve?" I asked.

"Evening sessions at my private residence, where we have access to more... specialized materials. Ancient texts, artifacts that require careful handling, consciousness expansion techniques that could enhance your natural sensitivity." His eyes never left my face. "It would be intensive work, Mr. Mercado. Not everyone is suited for such... deep exploration."

The phrase sent an odd chill through me, but the academic opportunity was too significant to dismiss based on vague unease.

"I'd be honored, Professor," I said, ignoring the way Eliza's hand had moved to cover her mouth as if suppressing words she couldn't speak.

"Excellent." Professor Nazari's smile was warm, paternal, but something flickered behind his eyes that I couldn't identify. "We'll begin tomorrow evening. Eliza will provide you with the address."

As I gathered my things to leave, I caught Eliza's eye. For just a moment, her composed mask slipped, and I saw something that looked remarkably like fear.

"Is everything alright?" I asked quietly as Professor Nazari turned to organize papers on his desk.

"Everything's fine," she said, but her voice sounded strained. "Just... be careful, Rafael. Some opportunities come with costs that aren't immediately apparent."

Before I could ask what she meant, Professor Nazari looked up with that intense smile.

"Until tomorrow evening, Mr. Mercado. I believe you're going to find our work together quite... transformative."

I left the office with excitement buzzing through my veins, completely unaware that I had just agreed to something that would destroy everything I thought I knew about the world—and about myself.

PROFESSOR NAZARI'S PRIVATE RESIDENCE, MALATE DISTRICT, MANILA

Professor Ibrahim Nazari

The afternoon heat pressed against the tall windows of my study, but inside remained surprisingly cool. I stood before my desk, reviewing the materials I'd assembled for tonight—surgical instruments, monitoring equipment, sedatives carefully measured for Rafael's body weight.

Nine hundred and eighty-seven years of existence, and still the secret had eluded me.

I pulled out my leather-bound journal, opening to entries I'd written across centuries. Florence, 1456. Prague, 1634. Shanghai, 1892. Page after page documenting my failed attempts to prove what I knew must be true: that knowledge resided in the blood, transferable through consumption or exchange.

But Rafael... Rafael was different.

I moved to the wooden chest beneath my desk, withdrawing the surgical supplies I'd been gathering for months. My hands shook slightly as I arranged the instruments—not from fear, but from the cellular degeneration that marked my approaching millennium. I could feel my body beginning its final decline, metabolism faltering in ways that no amount of feeding could reverse. I had perhaps months left, maybe a year.

If my theory was correct, if the knowledge-rich blood I'd accumulated over centuries could be transferred successfully to someone with Rafael's natural psychometric gifts, then my work wouldn't die with me. He would become the perfect vessel—my academic passion combined with his innate sensitivity, enhanced by nearly a millennium of carefully selected feeding.

I pulled out Rafael's academic records, studying essays that demonstrated not just intelligence but genuine insight. His paper on Byzantine iconography had shown understanding that typically required decades of study to achieve. His analysis of medieval manuscript illumination revealed perception that went beyond mere academic training.

This wasn't coincidence. This was evolutionary potential waiting to be unlocked.

The scholar in Córdoba whose blood I'd taken in 1187—his expertise would enhance Rafael's linguistic abilities. The Renaissance artist from Venezia in 1511—his understanding would deepen Rafael's aesthetic perception. The Chinese calligrapher from Guangzhou in 1899—his mastery would expand Rafael's psychometric range.

Centuries of knowledge, waiting to be transferred to someone worthy of carrying it forward.

The process would likely kill me. The blood transfer ritual required replacing nearly the entirety of the subject's circulatory system while maintaining perfect cardiac rhythm. Few Regulars survived performing it, and those who did were typically left so weakened that death followed within days.

But I was dying anyway. At least this way, death would have meaning.

I opened Rafael's student file, studying the photograph attached to his enrollment documents. Twenty-one years old, brilliant, sensitive to beauty in ways that suggested supernatural potential. The perfect candidate for receiving nearly a millennium of accumulated knowledge.

My fingers traced the surgical instruments one final time.

Tomorrow evening, Rafael Mercado would arrive expecting an academic research session. He would leave as something far more significant—the inheritor of wisdom spanning centuries, the vessel through which my life's work would continue long after my body returned to dust.

The scholar's ultimate achievement: creating an intellectual legacy that transcended the boundaries of individual mortality.

I closed the journal and began preparing the ritual space, humming softly as I worked—the same melody I'd hummed in Prague when I was young and certain that knowledge could be captured, contained, and transferred through the simple act of consumption.

Tomorrow, I would finally test whether nine centuries of faith in that principle had been justified.

Rafael Mercado

The professor's house surprised me—a Spanish colonial structure tucked away on a quiet street in Malate, surrounded by high walls and tropical gardens that muffled the constant noise of Manila traffic. As I approached the heavy wooden door, I felt a flutter of excitement mixed with nervous energy. This was the opportunity I'd been hoping for since beginning my studies—intensive mentorship with someone of Professor Nazari's reputation.

Eliza answered the door before I could knock, as if she'd been watching for my arrival. She looked even more tense than she had in the office yesterday, her usual composed efficiency replaced by something that seemed almost like dread.

"Rafael," she said, her voice carefully neutral. "Professor Nazari is waiting for you in his study."

I followed her through rooms lined with books and artifacts that made his university office seem sparse by comparison. Medieval manuscripts rested in climate-controlled cases, ancient pottery filled glass shelves, and paintings that looked suspiciously authentic hung from every available wall space.

"This is incredible," I breathed, pausing before a Byzantine icon that seemed to glow with inner light. "How did he acquire all of this?"

"Professor Nazari has been collecting for a very long time," Eliza replied, but something in her tone suggested that was an understatement. She paused at the entrance to what appeared to be his private study. "Rafael... if you feel uncomfortable at any point this evening, you don't have to stay. You can leave whenever you want."

The warning puzzled me. "Is everything alright? You've seemed concerned since yesterday."

"I don't really know what the professor has planned," she said quietly, and for the first time since I'd known her, Eliza sounded uncertain rather than efficient. "He's been... different lately. More secretive. I think his illness is affecting his judgment."

Before I could ask what she meant, Professor Nazari's voice called from within the study.

"Mr. Mercado! Please, come in. We have much to accomplish this evening."

The study was dimly lit by table lamps that cast pools of warm light across Persian rugs and leather furniture that looked centuries old. Professor Nazari sat behind an enormous desk covered with open books and what appeared to be medical texts, which struck me as odd for a classics professor.

"Punctual as always," he said, gesturing toward a chair positioned directly across from his desk. "Eliza, would you prepare the tea? The special blend we discussed."

I settled into the indicated chair while Eliza moved to a side table where an ornate tea service waited. She seemed uncertain about the preparation, referring to handwritten notes the professor had apparently given her.

"I trust you're excited about our work together," Professor Nazari continued, his eyes never leaving my face. He looked even more unwell than yesterday—skin pale and slightly waxy, hands trembling almost imperceptibly. Whatever illness he was fighting seemed to be progressing rapidly.

"Very excited," I replied honestly. "I've been reading about consciousness expansion techniques in preparation. The intersection of meditation and aesthetic perception is fascinating."

"Indeed. Though I should warn you that tonight's session will be more intensive than anything you've experienced in my regular classes." He accepted a cup of tea from Eliza, who then prepared one for me with obvious nervousness, checking and rechecking the professor's written instructions. "We'll be working with materials that require... deeper levels of receptivity."

The tea she handed me was aromatic, carrying scents of cardamom and something else I couldn't identify—something that seemed almost medicinal. As I raised the cup to my lips, I caught Eliza's eye. She was watching me with an expression that looked remarkably like confusion mixed with fear, as if she knew something terrible was about to happen but didn't understand what.

"Is the tea alright?" Professor Nazari asked, noting my hesitation.

"It's fine," I said, taking a careful sip. The flavor was complex, warming, with an undertone that seemed to make my thoughts feel strangely distant even as the professor's voice remained perfectly clear. "Just different from what I'm used to."

"Ancient recipe," he said with a smile that didn't quite reach his eyes. "The preparation is quite specific—Eliza has been practicing the blend for weeks now."

I noticed Eliza glance at him sharply, as if this wasn't entirely true, but she said nothing.

I took another sip, then another, finding the warmth oddly comforting despite the unusual taste. The room seemed to take on a dreamlike quality, edges softening as if viewed through gauze.

"You have such an unusual sensitivity to beauty, Mr. Mercado," Professor Nazari was saying, his voice seeming to come from very far away. "Not just appreciation—true sensitivity. The ability to perceive layers of meaning that escape most observers."

"Thank you," I managed, though forming words felt increasingly difficult. The teacup seemed to weigh more than it should, and I had to concentrate to keep my grip steady.

"Your essay on iconographic symbolism demonstrated understanding that typically requires decades of study to achieve. Where did you develop such insight?"

I tried to answer, but my thoughts felt wrapped in cotton. The professor's face seemed to swim slightly before my eyes, and I became aware that Eliza had moved to stand behind my chair, though I couldn't remember seeing her cross the room.

"I don't..." I started, then stopped as a wave of dizziness washed over me. "I feel strange. Perhaps I should—"

"It's perfectly normal," Professor Nazari said, his voice gentle but somehow more distant than before. "The tea helps lower mental barriers that typically interfere with psychometric perception. You're perfectly safe, Rafael. Perfectly safe."

Eliza Chen

"Professor," I said quietly, "he seems very disoriented. Are you sure this is—"

"Everything is proceeding exactly as it should," he interrupted, though I noticed his own hands were shaking more than usual. "This is simply the first stage of a process I've... studied extensively."

But there was something in his voice that suggested he was less certain than he wanted to appear. Over the weeks leading up to tonight, I'd noticed him poring over ancient texts written in languages I couldn't identify, making notes in margins with the desperate intensity of someone trying to remember half-forgotten details.

Rafael's head lolled forward, and I instinctively moved to steady him, my heart racing with fear about what we were about to attempt.

"Is he ready?" Professor Nazari asked, rising from his chair with obvious effort.

"I think so," I replied, though I had no real idea what "ready" meant in this context. "His breathing is deep, pulse seems steady."

"Good. Help me move him to the preparation room."

As we carried Rafael's unconscious form to the smaller adjacent room, I couldn't shake the feeling that neither Professor Nazari nor I truly understood what we were about to attempt. The medical equipment he'd assembled looked professional enough, but his explanations of the procedure had been filled with phrases like "based on historical accounts" and "theoretically sound."

"Professor," I said as we positioned Rafael on the makeshift surgical table, "you've actually done this before, haven't you?"

He paused in his preparations, and for a moment his confident facade slipped entirely.

"I witnessed it once, in Florence in 1489," he admitted quietly. "I assisted another Regular who was attempting to transform his chosen successor. It failed catastrophically—both the Regular and his subject died during the procedure."

My blood ran cold. "So you've never actually performed it yourself?"

"No Regular who performs this ritual survives long enough to do it again," he said, his voice carrying the weight of centuries. "And as for my own transformation..." He paused, looking suddenly older. "Like Rafael now, I was unconscious throughout the entire process. I have no memory of what was done to me."

The full horror of what he was planning settled over me like ice water. "Then you're..."

"Dying either way," he finished quietly. "My metabolism is already failing—I have months left, perhaps less. But this way, my death serves a purpose. This way, something of value survives me."

I stared at him, understanding finally why he'd been so secretive, so desperate. This wasn't just about transforming Rafael—it was Professor Nazari's planned method of death, disguised as academic legacy.

"What I learned assisting in Florence," he continued, "and what you're learning now—it's all anyone can know. The ritual can only be performed once, by someone willing to die for it."

The last thing I saw before we began was Rafael's peaceful expression, unmarked by any awareness that his human existence was about to end—one way or another.

THE ANCIENT RITUAL

I had never seen anything like this before, and the clinical precision Professor Nazari demanded felt impossible when my hands wouldn't stop shaking. He'd explained the process to me in theoretical terms over the past weeks, but witnessing it unfold was entirely different from understanding the concept.

"Steady, Eliza," Professor Nazari murmured as he made the first incision along Rafael's neck, exposing the carotid artery with surgical precision. "I need you to monitor his pulse constantly. If it drops below sixty beats per minute or rises above one hundred, alert me immediately."

The blood that welled from the cut was darker than I'd expected, and I fought the urge to partake as the coppery scent filled the small room. Professor Nazari moved with careful efficiency, though I could see the uncertainty in his movements—the slight hesitation before each step that suggested he was working from fragmentary memory rather than experience.

"How exactly did the Florence procedure fail?" I asked, my voice barely steady as I watched him prepare the second incision site.

"The Regular moved too quickly," he replied, making a precise cut near Rafael's groin where major blood vessels ran close to the surface. "Tried to replace too much blood at once. The subject's heart couldn't handle the sudden change in blood chemistry—it began beating irregularly, then stopped entirely."

My chest tightened with fear. "And the successful transformation you mentioned?"

"I only know my procedure was successful because I exist," Professor Nazari said grimly. "My maker died within hours of completing my transformation. I woke up three days later, alone and confused, with no understanding of what had been done to me."

The weight of our ignorance settled over me like a suffocating blanket. We were attempting something that had killed most people involved, guided only by his century-old memories of a failed procedure.

"Insert the IV line," Professor Nazari instructed, handing me surgical tubing with a needle attachment. "Into the vein running alongside the femoral artery. This will carry my blood directly to his heart while I drain his through the carotid."

My hands trembled as I followed his instructions, carefully inserting the line where it could access the major vein that would pump blood directly to Rafael's heart.

"The timing is critical," he said, positioning himself beside Rafael's neck. "I must remove his blood at exactly the rate mine is being pumped in. Too fast, and his heart will pump empty chambers. Too slow, and the pressure buildup could cause cardiac failure."

He leaned down and began drinking Rafael's blood directly from the carotid artery, while his own blood flowed through the tubing into Rafael's femoral vein, carried by the young man's heartbeat throughout his circulatory system.

"Pulse?" he asked after several minutes.

"Eighty-five beats per minute," I reported. "Blood pressure dropping but stable."

"Good. The balance is everything."

~

Hours passed in this delicate dance. Professor Nazari's movements grew increasingly labored, and I began to understand why so few Regulars survived performing this ritual. The physical strain was enormous—maintaining perfect timing while his own blood supply was systematically depleted and replaced.

I watched Rafael's vital signs shift into entirely new patterns on the monitoring equipment. Heart rate stabilizing at a significantly higher baseline than human normal. Blood pressure elevated but steady. His metabolism was clearly changing at the fundamental level, even though outwardly he looked much the same—just paler, as if recovering from a long illness.

But Professor Nazari was failing. His skin had taken on a grayish pallor, his movements increasingly unsteady. The ritual that was giving Rafael supernatural life was draining the life from his maker with every minute that passed.

"It's working," Professor Nazari whispered, wonder in his voice despite his obvious exhaustion. "After nine centuries, it's finally working. He's accepting the blood, integrating it, becoming something more than himself."

The new blood coursing through his system—Rafael's young, healthy blood—couldn't reverse the damage being done by the procedure itself. Professor Nazari's cells seemed to be breaking down faster than they could regenerate, his metabolism unable to cope with the strain of the blood exchange.

"The blood carries it all," he whispered, his voice filled with conviction despite his failing strength. "Nine centuries of knowledge. He'll inherit everything I've learned."

I wanted to tell him the truth—that blood didn't work that way. But watching him pour his life into this final act of misguided hope, I couldn't bring myself to destroy his last comfort.

"Eliza," he said softly as he began the final disconnection procedures, "when this is finished, you must guide him. He'll wake transformed but with no memory of how it happened. Help him understand what he's become."

"Professor—"

"Promise me," he insisted, his voice barely above a whisper.

I nodded, tears I hadn't shed in decades threatening to spill over. "I promise."

The transformation was complete—Rafael Mercado was no longer human, and Professor Ibrahim Nazari was dying from the effort of making him something more.

"Nine hundred and eighty-seven years," he murmured as he collapsed into a chair beside the makeshift surgical table. "And finally, finally, I've created something worthy of surviving me."

Within minutes, his breathing grew shallow, then stopped entirely. Professor Ibrahim Nazari, ancient Regular vampire and devoted scholar, died believing he'd successfully transferred nine centuries of accumulated knowledge to the unconscious young man whose life he'd irrevocably transformed.

I was left alone with a dead professor and a student who would wake with no memory of what had been done to him—and no understanding of what he'd been forced to become.

For three days, I'd known this moment was coming. I'd tried to think of ways to prevent it—warning Rafael directly, sabotaging the preparations, even leaving Manila entirely. But I owed Professor Nazari my existence. He'd found me in Kowloon fifty years ago, starving and half-mad from my own transformation, and given me purpose when I had nothing left.

I couldn't betray him, even as I watched him destroy an innocent young man's life in pursuit of an impossible dream.

The morning sun was already threatening to creep through the heavy curtains when I finally finished cleaning the ritual site and disposing of the evidence. Rafael's vital signs had stabilized in their new supernatural patterns, but he would likely sleep for another day or two while his body completed the final stages of transformation.

I had perhaps forty-eight hours to decide how much of the truth to tell him when he woke up—and how to help him survive becoming something he'd never chosen to be.

AWAKENING

Rafael Mercado

I woke up drowning in pain.

Not the sharp, localized agony of injury, but something deeper and more pervasive—as if every cell in my body was screaming in harmony. My head felt like it was splitting apart from the inside, and my limbs burned with fire that seemed to originate in my bones themselves.

"Rafael? Rafael, can you hear me?"

My mother's voice, tight with fear and exhaustion. I tried to open my eyes, but even the dim morning light filtering through closed curtains felt like knives stabbing into my brain.

"Mama?" My voice came out as barely a whisper, my throat raw as if I'd been screaming for hours.

"Thank God." I felt her hand on my forehead, cool against what must have been fever. "Gabriel! Gabriel, come quickly—he's awake!"

Footsteps rushing up the stairs, and then my father's voice, carrying the controlled panic of a medical professional trying not to alarm his family.

"How are you feeling, iho?" he asked, and I could hear him shifting into doctor mode even as parental worry leaked through his clinical tone.

"Everything hurts," I managed. "What happened? I remember going to Professor Nazari's house, and then..." Nothing. A complete blank where memory should have been.

"You collapsed," my father said, and I could hear papers rustling—probably medical charts. "Professor Nazari... I'm sorry, Rafael. He died that same evening. His teaching assistant, Eliza Chen, found both of you. She called for help immediately."

The professor was dead? The information felt distant, filtered through layers of pain and confusion that made it impossible to process properly.

"You've been unconscious for three days," my mother added, her hand still stroking my forehead. "We've been so worried."

Three days? I tried to sit up, but my body refused to cooperate. Every muscle felt simultaneously too weak and too tense, as if my nervous system couldn't decide whether to shut down or go into overdrive.

"Don't try to move yet," my father said. "Your body has been through significant trauma. We're still running tests to understand exactly what happened."

I noticed his careful phrasing—"significant trauma," not "illness" or "infection." My father's medical training made him precise with language, and his choice of words suggested he didn't understand my condition any better than I did.

"There are some... unusual symptoms," he continued, and I could hear the frustration in his voice. "Elevated heart rate, altered blood chemistry, heightened sensitivity to light and sound. Nothing that appears immediately dangerous, but we're monitoring everything carefully."

My mother squeezed my hand. "The important thing is that you're awake and you're here. We'll figure out the rest together."

Through the haze of pain and confusion, I felt a surge of love for them both —their unwavering determination to help me, their refusal to give up even when medical science couldn't explain what was wrong.

If only I'd known then what I would learn over the coming weeks: that their love and dedication couldn't save me from what I'd already become.

The pain had settled into something more manageable, though "manageable" was relative. I could sit up now, could tolerate soft lamplight, could speak in full sentences without feeling like my skull was splitting apart. But something was fundamentally wrong in ways that went beyond physical discomfort.

Food tasted like ash. Water did nothing to ease the constant, gnawing sensation in my gut that felt almost like hunger but wasn't satisfied by eating. And the sunlight—even the indirect glow from my bedroom window—caused searing pain on any exposed skin after just a few moments.

"Rafael?" Eliza's voice from my doorway, cautious and careful. "Your parents said you were feeling well enough for a visitor."

I looked up to see her standing there, holding a small gift bag that probably contained fruit or some other useless offering. She looked exactly as I remembered—composed, efficient, her expression carefully neutral. But something in her eyes seemed different. Worried. Almost... guilty?

"Eliza," I said, my voice still hoarse despite days of recovery. "What happened at Professor Nazari's house? I can't remember anything after the tea he gave me."

She glanced toward the hallway, checking that my parents weren't within earshot, then stepped inside and closed the door partway.

"You collapsed during your research session," she said carefully, her words sounding rehearsed. "Professor Nazari had been feeling unwell all day—his illness was progressing faster than anyone realized. When he collapsed, the stress of seeing it may have triggered some kind of... sympathetic medical episode in you."

It was a terrible explanation, and even through my fog of pain and confusion, I could tell she was lying. But why? What had really happened that night?

"But the pain," I said. "The way my body feels like it's changing. This isn't normal illness, Eliza. What aren't you telling me?"

She met my eyes directly then, and I saw the conflict there—the desire to tell me truth warring with something else. Fear? Obligation? I couldn't tell.

"Sometimes trauma affects people in unexpected ways," she said finally.

"Your father's tests show that your body is under significant stress, but nothing that appears dangerous. You just need time to recover."

Before I could press further, my mother's voice called from downstairs: "Eliza? Would you like some tea?"

"I should go," Eliza said quickly, backing toward the door. "But Rafael—if you need anything, anything at all, please call me. I'll check on you again in a few days."

She left before I could ask the questions piling up in my mind. Questions about why her explanation didn't make sense, why she looked so afraid, why I could still feel her pulse from across the room like a drumbeat calling to something deep in my chest that I didn't understand.

Questions that would take weeks of increasing horror to answer—and the truth, when it finally came, would be worse than anything I could have imagined lying there in my childhood bedroom, surrounded by the love of parents who couldn't protect me from what I'd already become.

UNIVERSITY OF SANTO TOMAS LIBRARY

Rafael Mercado

I sat hunched over a table in the library's most isolated corner, surrounded by medical journals and texts on rare blood disorders that I'd been desperately searching through for any explanation that made sense. The pain had subsided somewhat over the past two weeks, but everything else was getting worse.

The sensitivity to light had become impossible to ignore—even the fluorescent bulbs in the library made my eyes water and my skin feel like it was burning. I'd taken to wearing sunglasses indoors and long sleeves despite Manila's heat, claiming a skin condition to anyone who asked.

Worse was the hunger. Not for food—regular meals had become nauseating, leaving me sick and weak. But there was something else, some craving I couldn't name that grew stronger every day. Sometimes I caught myself staring at other students' throats when they leaned close to help with research, fighting urges that horrified me but seemed to be growing stronger.

"You look terrible," Eliza said, dropping into the chair across from me with her usual efficiency.

I looked up to see her studying me with an expression I couldn't interpret. Over the past two weeks, she'd been checking on me regularly, but our conversations had felt strangely formal, as if she were carefully monitoring what she said.

"I feel terrible," I admitted. "My parents are talking about taking me to specialists in Singapore, maybe even flying to the United States for consultation. They're convinced something serious is wrong with me."

"And what do you think?"

The question felt loaded somehow, as if she were testing my response rather than simply asking for information.

"I think something happened to me in Professor Nazari's office that night," I said, watching her face carefully. "Something you're not telling me about."

Eliza was quiet for a long moment, her fingers drumming silently on the table. She looked like someone wrestling with a difficult decision.

"Rafael," she said finally, "what I'm about to tell you is going to sound impossible. Insane, even. But I need you to listen to the entire explanation before you react."

My chest tightened with both hope and dread. "What happened to me?"

"Professor Nazari didn't just collapse from his illness that night. He... he did something to you. Something he'd been planning for months." She leaned forward, lowering her voice. "He believed that his blood carried knowledge—centuries of accumulated wisdom from everyone he'd ever... fed from. He thought that by transforming you, he could transfer all of that to you."

"Fed from?" The phrase sent a chill through me. "What do you mean, fed from?"

"Rafael," Eliza said, her voice steady despite the impossibility of what she was saying, "Professor Nazari was a vampire. A Regular, we call ourselves. And that night, he transformed you into one as well."

The words hit me with more than simple incredulity—they carried the weight of impossible truth. I stared at her, waiting for a laugh, to explain that this was some sort of elaborate psychological experiment or academic exercise.

"That's impossible," I whispered. "Vampires don't exist. They're myths, stories, movie monsters."

"Look at yourself," she said quietly. "Really look. When did you last eat a full meal? When did you last go outside in direct sunlight? When did you last feel normal?"

The accuracy of her observations made my stomach clench. I hadn't been able to eat solid food for days. Sunlight had become painful to the point where I'd started avoiding windows. And normal... I couldn't remember feeling normal since waking up from whatever had happened that night.

"This is insane," I said, but even as I spoke, fragments of memory began surfacing. The strange tea, Professor Nazari's intense interest in my psychometric abilities, Eliza's obvious fear that evening.

"The hunger you're feeling," she continued relentlessly, "the craving you can't name—that's your body demanding blood. Mammalian blood. *Human* blood. It's the only thing that will sustain your new metabolism."

"Stop." I stood up so abruptly that my chair fell backward. "Stop talking. This isn't real. This isn't happening."

"Rafael—"

"No!" The word came out louder than I'd intended, causing other students to look in our direction. I lowered my voice but couldn't control the desperation in it. "You're talking about monsters. About things that kill people. About—"

"About what you are now," Eliza interrupted, her tone gentle but implacable. "Whether you want to believe it or not."

I felt the world tilting around me as the implications crashed over me. If what she was saying was true, then I was no longer human. I was something that fed on blood, something that would have to hurt people to survive.

"The professor," I said, my voice barely above a whisper. "He did this to me?"

"He believed he was giving you a gift," Eliza replied. "He thought his blood carried nine centuries of knowledge and experience. He died convinced that he'd created the perfect scholar-vampire, someone who could continue his work with all his accumulated wisdom."

"And you helped him." The accusation came out more bitter than I'd intended.

"I assisted because I owed him my existence. He found me fifty years ago during the war in Kowloon, when I was starving and half-mad from my own transformation. He gave me purpose when I had nothing left." Her voice carried decades of complicated loyalty and guilt. "But I never agreed with what he planned to do to you."

"Then why didn't you stop him?"

"Because I was a coward," she said simply. "And because I didn't fully understand what he intended until it was too late."

I slumped back into my chair, overwhelmed by the magnitude of what she was telling me. "My parents. They think I'm sick, but I'm actually..."

"You're something they could never understand or accept," Eliza said quietly. "Which brings us to the choice you have to make."

"What choice?"

"You can tell them the truth about what you are and try to figure out how to make it work with your family. Or..." She paused, her expression growing more serious. "You can disappear from their lives entirely. Let them believe you died rather than burden them with the truth of what you've become."

The bluntness of her words hit me like a slap. "You're talking about my family."

"I'm talking about your survival," she corrected. "And theirs. Regulars need blood, Rafael. Human blood. You can supplement with animal blood for a while, but eventually, you'll need to feed from people. Can you imagine your parents' faces when they discover their son has become something that has to hurt others to survive?"

The thought made me physically ill. My parents—Dr. Gabriel Mercado and Dr. Sofia Santos-Mercado, two people who'd devoted their lives to healing—discovering that their son was now something that fed on the blood of innocent people.

"There has to be another way," I said desperately. "Medical alternatives, synthetic substitutes, something—"

"I've been a vampire for over two hundred years," Eliza said with clinical detachment. "I've tried everything. There is no alternative that works long-term."

"Two hundred years?" The casual way she mentioned her age drove home the reality of what she was claiming. "You're really..."

"Really a vampire, yes. Really transformed against my will, like you. Really forced to choose between telling my family the truth or letting them believe I was dead." She met my eyes directly. "I chose to disappear. It was the kindest thing I could do for them."

I thought about my parents, who'd spent the past two weeks frantically trying to find medical explanations for my condition. Who'd scheduled appointments with specialists, researched rare diseases, maintained hopeful smiles while privately fearing they were losing their son to something they couldn't understand.

"If I disappear," I said quietly, "they'll never stop looking for me."

"They will if they believe you're dead," Eliza said with the efficiency that had marked all our interactions. "I can help you stage something convincing. An accident, a suicide—something that will give them closure while protecting them from the truth."

The word 'suicide' made my blood run cold. "You want me to fake my own death."

"I want you to choose the option that causes the least harm to everyone involved," she corrected. "Your parents will grieve, but they'll heal. They'll remember their son as the brilliant, sensitive young man he was rather than discovering he'd become something they'd fear."

"And me? What happens to me?"

"You disappear. New identity, new city, new life. I have contacts who can help with documentation and travel arrangements. You learn to survive as what you are now, away from anyone who knew you before."

I stared at her, trying to process the magnitude of what she was proposing. Erase my entire existence. Let my parents believe their son was dead. Become someone else entirely.

"There's no other choice?" I asked, though I could already hear the defeat in my own voice.

"Not if you want to protect them," Eliza said gently. "Not if you want to give them the chance to heal and move on with their lives."

I thought about my father's determination to find medical answers for my condition, my mother's prayers for my recovery, their complete faith that love and science could overcome whatever was wrong with their son.

They would never stop fighting for me. Never stop trying to save me from something they couldn't understand. Never stop believing that their brilliant, sensitive boy could be healed if they just found the right treatment.

The cruelest truth was that Eliza was right. The kindest thing I could do for the people I loved most in the world was to let them believe I was dead.

"When?" I asked quietly, tears starting to form in my shallow eyes.

"Soon," she replied. "Before your condition deteriorates further. Before the hunger becomes unmanageable and you accidentally hurt someone."

"How?"

"Manila Bay," she said, her voice steady and practical. "Apparent suicide by drowning. We stage it carefully, leave evidence that will be found, create a plausible narrative about psychological strain from Professor Nazari's death and your mysterious illness."

The clinical way she discussed erasing my existence made something cold settle in my chest. But underneath the horror was a terrible relief. No more lying to my parents. No more pretending I was getting better when I was becoming something that would terrify them. No more watching their hope die a little more each day as conventional medicine failed to help me.

"And after?"

"After, Rafael Mercado dies in Manila Bay, and someone else begins learning how to survive as a vampire in a world that doesn't believe in monsters."

I closed my eyes, feeling the weight of the decision settling over me like a shroud. When I opened them again, Eliza was watching me with something that might have been compassion.

"I'll help you," she said quietly. "With the transition, with learning what you need to survive, with getting established somewhere safe. You won't be completely alone."

"Why?" I asked. "Why would you help me?"

"Because someone helped me once, when I had nothing left. Because Professor Nazari asked me to guide you, and despite everything, I owed him that much." She paused. "And because no one should have to face becoming a monster entirely alone."

Monster. The word hung in the air between us like a verdict.

"Tomorrow night," I said finally, wiping my eyes, trying to maintain a sense of composure in this very public of buildings. "We do this tomorrow night."

Eliza nodded. "I'll make the preparations. Be at Roxas Boulevard at eleven PM. Bring nothing you can't afford to lose, because Rafael Mercado won't be needing any of it after tomorrow."

As I sat there in the university library, surrounded by medical texts that contained no answers for what I'd become, I realized I was planning my own death in order to become someone—something—else entirely. And I wanted to weep. I wanted to scream for my own loss. But I needed to remain cool. I needed to pretend.

The boy who had trusted his professor, who had believed in human goodness and rational explanations, was going to die tomorrow night in Manila Bay. What emerged would be harder, more suspicious, something that had learned the terrible lesson that the people who care for you most can destroy you in the name of love.

ROXAS BOULEVARD, MANILA BAY

Rafael Mercado

11:00PM

The lights of Manila Bay stretched out before me like fallen stars, reflecting off water that looked black and infinite in the darkness. I stood at the designated meeting point, carrying nothing but the clothes on my back and a letter I'd written to my parents—an explanation they would never see, words I needed to write but couldn't bear to leave behind.

Eliza appeared out of the shadows with the efficiency that marked everything she did, carrying a small waterproof bag and what looked like police evidence markers.

"You came," she said, though there was no surprise in her voice.

"Did you think I wouldn't?"

"I thought you might change your mind. Most people would." She gestured toward a secluded section of the seawall where fewer streetlights reached. "We need to move to a more private area."

I followed her along the concrete barrier that separated the boulevard from the bay, each step feeling like walking toward my own execution. The irony wasn't lost on me—I was about to kill myself in order to survive.

"Your parents?" Eliza asked as we walked.

"I told them I was going for a walk to clear my head. That I'd been feeling overwhelmed by everything that's happened." My voice sounded strange to my own ears, flat and distant. "They were worried, but they thought fresh air might help."

"Good. That fits the narrative we're creating." She stopped at a section of seawall that offered both privacy and clear water access. "Have you been feeling the hunger more strongly today?"

The question was practical rather than sympathetic, but I appreciated her directness. "Yes. Worse than ever. I kept staring at my mother's throat during dinner, imagining..." I couldn't finish the sentence.

"It will only get worse," she said matter-of-factly. "Another few days and you might not be able to control it around people you care about. This is the right choice, Rafael. The only choice that protects them."

She began unpacking her bag, revealing items that made the reality of what we were doing hit home: my university ID, a suicide note written in handwriting that looked remarkably like mine, personal items that would suggest I'd planned this carefully.

"How did you—"

"I've been preparing for this possibility since the night you were transformed," she said. "I knew there was a chance you'd choose this option, so I made sure everything would be convincing."

The note was brief but devastating in its authenticity:

I can't continue living with this illness that no one can cure. The pain is unbearable, and I can't watch my parents suffer anymore trying to save me. Please know that this isn't anyone's fault. Sometimes there are problems that love and medicine cannot solve. Take care of each other.
Rafael

"You forge handwriting?" I asked, though the signature looked exactly like my own.

"Among other skills you develop over two centuries of existence." She placed the note in a plastic evidence bag. "This will be found tomorrow morning, along with your ID and shoes. The conclusion will be obvious."

I stared at the forged suicide note—my death certificate written in my own hand by someone else. "My parents will blame themselves," I said through repressed sobs.

"They'll grieve," Eliza corrected. "But they'll also understand. Your father is a doctor—he's seen terminal cases before. Your mother is a teacher—she understands that some battles can't be won through determination alone. They'll remember you as someone who fought bravely against an impossible situation."

The practical way she discussed my parents' future grief made something cold settle in my stomach. But she was right. This narrative would give them closure, a reason they could eventually accept, a way to heal and move forward.

"The water," I said, looking out at the dark expanse of Manila Bay. "How do I—"

"You swim," she said simply. "Out to the coordinates I'll give you, where a boat will be waiting. The current patterns and search protocols mean your body will never be found, which supports the suicide theory. People will assume you were swept out to sea."

"And the boat?"

"Transport to a freighter heading for Singapore, then connections to London. By the time the search for your body is called off, you'll be establishing a new identity in a city where no one knows Rafael Mercado ever existed."

London. The city I'd dreamed of visiting seemed like a different universe now—not a destination for academic adventure, but exile from everything I'd ever known.

"Your transformation," I said suddenly. "In China. Did you... did you do this too?"

"Something similar," she replied. "Though the circumstances were different. War makes disappearances easier to arrange." Her expression grew distant. "I was nineteen when I was transformed. My family thought I died in a raid on our village. In a way, I suppose I did."

"Do you ever regret it? Letting them think you were dead?"

"Every day for the first fifty years," she said honestly. "But I've lived long enough now to see what happened to their lives afterward. My parents had other children, found happiness again. My siblings grew up without the shadow of a monstrous older sister haunting their family. They lived better lives because they believed I was dead."

The matter-of-fact way she discussed decades of loss and sacrifice made me realize how much strength it would take to survive what I was about to become. Not just the physical demands of vampirism, but the emotional weight of complete isolation from everyone I'd ever loved.

"Are you ready?" she asked, checking her watch.

I looked back toward the lights of the city where my parents were probably lying awake worrying about their son who had gone for a walk and hadn't returned yet. By morning, they would be receiving the worst news of their lives. By the time they held my funeral, I would be thousands of miles away, learning to survive as something they would never understand.

"No," I said honestly. "But I don't think anyone could be ready for this," I said to myself mostly as I couldn't hold back my tears.

I removed my shoes and placed them beside the seawall where they would be found, along with my university ID. The suicide note went into a plastic bag weighted to stay in place but visible to investigators.

"The coordinates are two miles due west," Eliza said, pointing out into the darkness. "The boat will flash a light three times when you're close enough. Your new lungs should handle the swim easily—enhanced capacity is one of the benefits of transformation."

Enhanced capacity. Benefits. The clinical terms she used to describe supernatural abilities that would help me fake my own death.

"Eliza," I said as I prepared to enter the water. "Thank you. For helping me, for giving me a choice, for..." I gestured helplessly at the elaborate deception she'd arranged. "For all of it."

"Don't thank me yet," she replied, echoing words she'd spoken before. "Thank me when you've figured out how to live with what you are without killing anyone."

I looked back at her one final time—this harsh, efficient woman who was saving my life by helping me destroy it—and tried to find words for what I was feeling.

"Will I see you again?"

"In London, eventually. I have business there that will take me away from Manila for several years. When you're ready, when you've learned to manage what you've become, we'll cross paths again."

She gestured toward the water. "Now go. We've got a timeline to maintain."

The water was warm against my skin as I waded into Manila Bay, following Eliza's instructions with mechanical precision. Leave the evidence on the rocks. Swim to the predetermined coordinates. Surface only when the patrol boats have passed. Trust that she'd thought of everything, because there was no room for improvisation now.

"Rafael Mercado drowns here," she called out as I prepared to dive beneath the surface. "What comes up is someone else entirely. Don't forget that."

I looked back at her one last time, then dove beneath the dark water of Manila Bay, leaving Rafael Mercado to drown while something nameless and new began the swim toward an uncertain future.

Behind me, Eliza was already implementing the next phase of her plan—placing evidence, preparing to make anonymous calls in a few hours, setting in motion the discovery and investigation that would convince my parents their son was dead. By morning, Dr. Gabriel Mercado and Dr. Sofia Santos-Mercado would be receiving a phone call.

But they would survive it. They would grieve, but they would heal. They would remember their son as the brilliant, sensitive young man he had been rather than learning he had become something that fed on blood to survive. I kept reminding myself of this. It had to be true.

It was the cruelest gift I could give them—and the only one that might keep them safe.

MANILA BAY TO LONDON

I surfaced two miles from shore, my transformed lungs easily handling the extended submersion that would have killed the human I had been just weeks before. The swim that should have been impossible felt effortless—my body moving through the water with efficiency I'd never possessed, my enhanced metabolism providing strength that seemed limitless despite the distance.

In the darkness ahead, I could see the lights of the freighter that would carry me away from everything I had ever known, toward a future I couldn't imagine. Three flashes, just as Eliza had promised. The signal that meant my new life was waiting.

As I swam toward those lights, I felt the last threads connecting me to Rafael Gabriel Mercado dissolving in the salt water of Manila Bay. That young man—the literature student who trusted his professors, who believed in human goodness and rational explanations, who loved his parents and dreamed of academic achievement—was drowning behind me.

What pulled itself up the rope ladder onto the freighter's deck was something harder, more suspicious, something that had learned he was now a monster, never again to know the love of his parents or the life he had so longed for.

The Captain

The young man who emerged from the bay looked like a refugee from his own life—pale, exhausted, carrying nothing but the clothes on his back and an expression of complete desolation. But his payment had been arranged in advance through channels that suggested discretion was more important than curiosity.

"Welcome aboard," I said in English, noting his obvious relief at hearing a familiar language. "Your passage to Singapore has been paid for. No questions, no documentation required."

He nodded silently, water still dripping from his dark hair. In thirty years of running discrete transport for people who needed to disappear, I'd learned to recognize the look of someone leaving everything behind. This one had it worse than most.

"There's a cabin prepared for you below deck. Food if you want it, though..." I paused, noting his obvious illness or exhaustion. "Though you might want to rest first."

"Thank you," he said quietly, his voice carrying an accent that suggested education and privilege. Whatever had driven him to fake his own death in Manila Bay, it hadn't been poverty.

Rafael Mercado

The cabin was small but clean, with a narrow bunk and a porthole that showed nothing but endless ocean. I sat on the edge of the bed, finally allowing myself to process what I had done.

My parents would be waking up soon. When I didn't return from my "walk," they would start calling friends, checking hospitals, growing increasingly frantic as hours passed without word. By afternoon, someone would find the evidence Eliza had left at the seawall. By evening, they would be identifying my belongings and accepting the impossible news that their son had taken his own life.

The grief would destroy them initially. My father would blame himself for not recognizing the depth of my psychological distress. My mother would blame herself for not fighting harder to keep me safe. They would replay every conversation from the past weeks, searching for signs they had missed, words they should have said.

But eventually, they would heal. They would remember me as the son who had fought bravely against an impossible illness, not the monster I was becoming. They would be able to mourn cleanly, completely, without the horror of discovering their child had become something that fed on blood to survive. Or so I kept telling myself.

Over the three weeks it took to reach Singapore, then book passage to London, I learned the first harsh lessons of vampire existence. Food became nauseating, leaving me weak and sick whenever I tried to eat normal meals. The hunger grew stronger each day, becoming a constant ache that no amount of water or rest could ease.

By the time we reached Singapore, I was desperate enough to try feeding from the ship's stores of medical blood supplies, meant for emergency transfusions. The relief was immediate and overwhelming—like a starving man finally finding food, like an addict getting their first fix after weeks of withdrawal.

But even as the blood eased my physical symptoms, it confirmed what Eliza had told me. I was no longer human. I was something that required blood to survive, something that would have to... hurt people.

ARRIVAL

The city that had once represented adventure and academic opportunity now felt like exile from everything I had ever known. The contacts Eliza had arranged provided me with documentation identifying me as Rafael Thompson, a Filipino-British citizen returning to London after family business in the Philippines.

The story was simple and plausible: my father had been British, my mother Filipino, and I had been living in Manila caring for elderly relatives until their recent deaths freed me to pursue opportunities in London. It explained my accent, my familiarity with both cultures, my lack of extensive local connections.

The flat they found for me was in a converted warehouse in East London—six stories up, with large windows that could be covered completely and neighbors who valued privacy above curiosity. It was perfect for someone who needed to avoid sunlight and maintain odd hours.

But the practical arrangements couldn't address the deeper challenges of what I had become. The hunger was constant now, requiring me to feed every few days to maintain basic functionality. The contacts had provided me with access to medical blood supplies, but even that felt like a temporary solution to a permanent problem.

More difficult was the isolation. For twenty-one years, I had been surrounded by family, friends, classmates, professors—a network of people who knew and cared about Rafael Mercado. Now I was completely alone in a city of millions, with no connections to my past and no idea how to build meaningful relationships when my very existence was built on a fundamental deception.

I spent the first month in London barely leaving the flat, learning to manage the basic requirements of vampire existence while wrestling with the psychological weight of what I had lost. Every night, I thought about my parents. Every morning, I wondered if they were healing or if the grief was destroying them as thoroughly as the transformation had destroyed me. Every day, I sobbed uncontrollably.

The newspapers I had shipped from Manila carried brief mentions of the search for my body, interviews with university officials expressing shock at the promising student's apparent suicide, statements from my parents asking for privacy during their time of grief. Reading about my own death in clinical newspaper language made the loss feel both more real and more surreal.

Dr. Gabriel Mercado and Dr. Sofia Santos-Mercado requesting privacy to mourn their son. Rafael Mercado, 21, a literature student at University of Santo Tomas, whose body was never recovered from Manila Bay.

THREE MONTHS

By winter, I had learned the basic mechanics of survival. Blood from medical sources sustained me physically. Careful scheduling allowed me to avoid sunlight. Forged credentials got me access to university libraries where I could continue some semblance of intellectual life.

But I was still fundamentally alone, still struggling with the knowledge that I would never again be able to maintain the kind of close relationships I had taken for granted as a human. How could I explain to potential friends why I never ate food? Why I couldn't meet during daylight hours? Why I sometimes stared at their throats with hunger I had to fight to control?

The contacts Eliza had arranged included an address for other vampires in London—a discrete community of people who understood the challenges of supernatural existence in a human world. But I wasn't ready for that yet. I wasn't ready to accept that this isolation, this careful management of monstrous appetites, would be the rest of my existence.

I was still mourning the death of Rafael Mercado, still grieving for the life I had lost and the family I would never see again. Still hoping that somehow, this was temporary, that there might be a way back to something resembling normal human existence.

But as months passed in the warehouse flat, as the hunger became routine and the isolation became familiar, I began to understand that Rafael Mercado was truly dead. What remained was something else—something that shared his memories and his face but had been fundamentally changed by blood and loss and the terrible knowledge that love could be more destructive than hate.

The boy who had trusted his professor, who had believed in human goodness and rational explanations, was gone. What survived was a monster now: harder, more suspicious, determined to survive even if survival meant accepting a loneliness so complete it felt like death itself.

But it was survival. And began to welcome death.

. . .

SIX MONTHS

The letter from Eliza arrived on a gray London morning, forwarded through channels I didn't fully understand but had learned to trust. Brief, practical, typically efficient:

> Rafael - I will be traveling to London next year on business. When you are ready to learn more about what you are and how to manage it properly, contact the address below. There are others like us who have learned to build lives despite what we've become. You don't have to remain alone forever. - E

I read the letter three times, then placed it carefully in the desk drawer where I kept the few possessions that had survived my transformation. Someday, I thought, I might be ready to learn what she was offering. Someday, I might be strong enough to risk building connections with others who understood the weight of monstrous existence.

But not yet. For now, I was still learning the most basic lesson of vampire survival: how to live with what you had become without losing whatever remained of what you had once been.

The process, I was discovering, could take decades.

29
FAMILY REVELATIONS

THE BLACKSMITH'S ARMS 47 HIGH STREET, HAMPSTEAD VILLAGE, LONDON NW3 6RS

Aleksander Nordh

I guided everyone to our table with the careful precision of someone who'd spent centuries observing human dynamics. Erik to Rafael's right—close enough for conversation but not overwhelming. Soren to Rafael's left, providing the steady, calming presence that came so naturally to him. And I positioned myself directly across from Rafael, where I could monitor his comfort level while ensuring he had a clear view of the entire restaurant.

No blocked exits. No feeling trapped. Every detail calculated to make this as easy as possible for someone who'd spent over a decade avoiding exactly this kind of social interaction.

Rafael Mercado

I noticed immediately how deliberately Aleksander had arranged the seating. The consideration was both touching and mortifying—clear evidence that he understood exactly how fragile my composure was, how close I always sat to the edge of flight. When I caught him watching me with that careful attention, heat rose to my cheeks. I was being managed, however kindly.

But then his gaze shifted to Erik, and I found myself studying the boy beside me instead of cataloging escape routes. There was something about his openness, his genuine curiosity about everything around him, that made my hypervigilance feel almost... unnecessary.

THE ANNOUNCEMENT

"Rafael, thank you for joining us tonight," I began, then immediately shifted focus before he could feel too spotlighted. "But this evening is really about celebration. Erik, this is your birthday dinner—seventeen years old in just a few days!"

Erik Eriksson

I felt my face burn with the familiar embarrassment of being the center of attention, but watching Rafael's shoulders relax as the focus moved away from him made it easier to bear. When he actually smiled—small, but genuine—at my obvious discomfort, something warm spread through my chest.

Aleksander Nordh

Seeing Rafael's first real smile in months, watching him unconsciously lean slightly toward Erik as the spotlight shifted, confirmed what I'd hoped. But I couldn't let either of them feel too exposed.

"Actually," I continued, reaching for Soren's hand, "we have our own announcement to make. Soren and I are engaged."

Erik Eriksson

"What?!" The word exploded out of me before I could stop it, followed by a grin so wide it hurt my cheeks. "Are you serious? That's amazing! When? How?"

Rafael Mercado

The joy in Erik's voice was infectious, and I found myself smiling more broadly than I had in years. Watching Aleksander and Soren together—the way they looked at each other, the obvious love and contentment—stirred something in me I'd thought permanently buried. Hope, perhaps. Or simply recognition that love was still possible in the world, even if not for me.

THE WEDDING PLANS

Aleksander Nordh

"And we've been thinking about having two weddings," I continued, enjoying their puzzled expressions.

"Two?" Erik and Rafael said almost simultaneously, then looked at each other with surprise at their synchronization.

"Well," Soren added, his excitement evident, "we know the families in America want to participate, and then there are the families in Sweden..."

Erik Eriksson

I nodded eagerly, but noticed Rafael looking slightly confused. Of course—he didn't know about our Swedish connections, about the extended family we'd discovered.

"We thought," Aleksander continued, "it might be meaningful for all the families to learn about each other, about their origins, if we held the first wedding at your farm in Sweden, Erik. With your grandparents' permission, of course. We'd fly everyone from America over."

I couldn't believe what I was hearing. A wedding at the farm? In our tiny village? "Can you imagine, Rafael?" I said, reaching out instinctively to touch his shoulder as I laughed. "That small village will double in size! A gay wedding there!"

Rafael Mercado

Erik's hand on my shoulder sent shock waves through my entire body—not fear, but the overwhelming sensation of human touch after years of careful isolation. When he pulled away, I found myself touching the spot where his hand had been, amazed that the contact had felt warm and safe rather than dangerous.

Aleksander was watching me carefully, and I could see him cataloging my reaction, ready to intervene if I showed signs of panic. But I felt... happy. Unexpectedly, impossibly happy.

. . .

THE DEEPER REVELATION

Aleksander Nordh

"But we'd also like to have a smaller, more intimate wedding for our 'other' family," I said, choosing my words carefully.

"Other?" Erik asked, while Rafael simply held my gaze, understanding beginning to dawn in his eyes.

"Yes, I have parents. Soren hasn't met them yet. Erik knows a little about me, and we'll discuss more during his visit, but he's aware that I'm older than this city we live in."

Rafael Mercado

My eyes widened as the implications hit me. Aleksander was revealing his nature, here, in front of Erik. The boy knew. Somehow, this sixteen-year-old Swedish teenager knew about vampires and was completely comfortable with it.

Erik Eriksson

I smiled as Rafael looked between Alek and me, seeing his surprise and maybe a little relief. "It's okay, Rafael," I said, though I wasn't entirely sure what I was reassuring him about. There were clearly layers to this conversation I didn't fully understand yet.

Aleksander Nordh

"He's family," I continued, looking at Soren, who squeezed my hand encouragingly. "And we're his uncles."

I took a deep breath, preparing for the most delicate part of this conversation.

"I love Soren more than in all the lonely centuries I've lived. I've told my parents about him, and I'd like them to meet the man I'm going to marry." I turned to Erik. "Erik, if you'd like to attend, we'd be honored to have you as our guest."

Then I looked directly at Rafael, my voice becoming softer, more personal. "And Rafael, I'd like to know if you'd consider being my best man. It would be a tremendous honor."

Rafael Mercado

The request hit me like a physical blow. Best man. Aleksander wanted me—damaged, isolated, monstrous me—to stand beside him at his wedding. To be part of the most important moment of his life.

"Before you answer," Aleksander continued gently, "this will be small. At night. In our home. Private. And with the people I love."

I stared into his eyes, then looked at Soren, whose expression held nothing but warmth and acceptance. But Erik... if he knew what I was, what I'd done, what I was capable of...

THE MOMENT OF TRUTH

Erik Eriksson

The silence stretched on, and I could see Rafael struggling with something deep and painful. Without really thinking about it, I spoke into the quiet.

"Rafael," I said, my voice softer than I'd intended, startling everyone at the table. "I may be just turning seventeen, but... if you want to go with me to their wedding, I'll... well, I'll be your date. I mean... I hope... well, I'd like to, if you would."

Rafael Mercado

I couldn't believe what I was hearing. This beautiful, innocent boy was asking me to be his date. Did he understand what he was saying? Did he know what he was asking? Did he know he was talking to a monster?

Aleksander Nordh

I could see Rafael's thoughts spiraling toward panic and self-recrimination. "Rafael," I said gently, drawing his attention back to me. "Erik can be trusted. Believe me. He understands."

Erik Eriksson

After what felt like forever, I decided to take a chance. Slowly, carefully, I reached over with my left hand and lightly touched Rafael's fingertips. He flinched—just a little—but he didn't pull away.

Gradually, tentatively, our fingers intertwined. His hand was cooler than I'd expected, but it felt right somehow. Safe.

"It'll be okay, Rafael," I said quietly. "I'm figuring this out too."

Rafael Mercado

The simple touch, the gentle acceptance in Erik's voice, the lack of fear or revulsion—it was more than I'd dared hope for in over a decade. For the first time since my transformation, I wasn't the most lost person at the table.

Looking around at Aleksander's patient expression, Soren's kind eyes, and Erik's hand warm in mine, I realized something extraordinary was happening. I wasn't being tolerated or managed or pitied.

I was being included. Wanted. Maybe even loved.

"Yes," I whispered, my voice barely audible. "Yes, I'd be honored to be your best man, Aleksander. And Erik..." I turned to look at this remarkable boy who'd somehow seen past everything I thought made me unworthy of human connection. "I'd love to be your date."

Aleksander Nordh

As Rafael's walls finally began to come down, as Erik's face lit up with genuine joy, as Soren reached across to clasp both our hands in celebration, I felt something I hadn't experienced in centuries: the perfect contentment of watching a family come together.

The Jensen bloodline had worked its magic once again, creating connections that transcended every barrier we'd thought insurmountable. Tonight, we were no longer just individuals navigating separate struggles.

Tonight, we had become exactly what we'd all been searching for without knowing it: home.

AFTER THE ACCEPTANCE

Soren Jensen

Watching this moment unfold—Rafael's quiet "yes," Erik's radiant smile, the way their hands remained linked even after the formal acceptance—I felt something profound settle in my chest. This was what family looked like when it worked. Not the family you were born into, necessarily, but the family you chose and built through love and acceptance.

"Well then," I said, raising my water glass with a grin, "I think this calls for a toast. To unexpected family, to love in all its forms, and to weddings that are going to be absolutely unforgettable."

Rafael Mercado

As we raised our glasses—water for most of us, though I noticed Aleksander had quietly ordered wine for himself—I felt something I hadn't experienced since before my transformation: belonging. Not just tolerance or charity, but genuine welcome into something precious and rare.

"To family," I managed, my voice steadier than I'd expected. "And to second chances."

Erik Eriksson

"To the coolest uncles in the world," I added, squeezing Rafael's hand gently, "and to whatever this is between us, because I have no idea what I'm doing but I really, really want to figure it out."

Rafael's laugh—surprised and genuine—was the most beautiful sound I'd ever heard.

Aleksander Nordh

As our glasses clinked together over the small table, surrounded by the warm light of candles and the quiet hum of other diners, I realized that all my careful planning had led to something I couldn't have orchestrated: the moment when four separate people became something larger than the sum of their parts.

We had become family. Chosen, complicated, spanning species and centuries and continents, but family nonetheless.

And for the first time in over two millennia, I was no longer the loneliest person in any room.

30
FIRST STEPS HOME

CHESTER ROAD, REGENT'S PARK, LONDON NW1 4NR

Soren Jensen

The black taxi felt like a cocoon of warmth against the London night, its leather seats and polished interior a stark contrast to our usual tube journeys. Aleksander had arranged everything with his characteristic attention to detail—not just the car, but the entire evening's careful orchestration. As I settled into the rear-facing seat, positioning myself so my knees touched his, I could see the satisfaction in his eyes. Tonight had gone better than any of us had dared hope.

"Right then," I said, launching into stories about our Christmas in Minneapolis, partly to fill the comfortable silence and partly to give Rafael time to process everything that had happened. "You should have seen Aleksander's face when he first saw my mother's Christmas decorations. I thought his eyes might actually fall out of his head."

Erik Eriksson

I couldn't stop stealing glances at Rafael as Soren told stories about America. In the dim light of the taxi, Rafael looked even more beautiful—the way the streetlights caught his features as we passed under them, the small smile that appeared when Soren described Aleksander's shock at twelve-foot inflatable lawn ornaments. Our hands were still linked from the restaurant, hidden in the shadows between our seats, and I was terrified to move in case he remembered he was supposed to be guarded and pulled away.

Rafael Mercado

The warmth of Erik's hand in mine was an anchor in the swirling confusion of the evening. I'd agreed to come back to Aleksander's flat—something I would have considered impossible just hours ago—and now I was sitting in the back of a hired car, listening to stories about American Christmas celebrations while holding hands with a sixteen-year-old Swedish boy who somehow made me feel less monstrous than I had in over a decade.

The cab driver's laughter at Soren's impression of Aleksander trying to navigate a Walmart on Christmas Eve made something tight in my chest loosen. This felt normal. Human. Like I might actually belong somewhere again.

Aleksander Nordh

Watching Rafael's gradual relaxation, seeing the way he unconsciously leaned closer to Erik as the stories continued, confirmed every instinct I'd had about bringing them together. The careful distance Rafael maintained from the world was crumbling in the face of Erik's uncomplicated acceptance.

As we pulled up outside my building, I turned to address the concern I could sense in Rafael's posture as the evening's reality reasserted itself.

"Rafael, I know this has been quite a heavy evening, but we can keep it low-key for a few moments before you go," I said softly, allowing him space on the stoop before pausing. "You are always welcome in my home."

ENTERING THE SANCTUARY

Erik Eriksson

The moment we stepped inside Aleksander's flat, I could see Rafael taking in everything with wide eyes. The elegant furniture, the walls lined with books, the carefully placed art that looked like it belonged in museums—it was even more impressive in the full light than it had been when I'd arrived that afternoon.

"This is mental," I said, grinning as I pulled Rafael further into the room. "Look at this place! It's like living in a palace."

. . .

Rafael Mercado

Aleksander's flat was extraordinary—centuries of careful curation evident in every corner. But what struck me most wasn't the obvious wealth or sophistication. It was how lived-in everything felt despite its elegance. Books with worn spines, a coffee cup left casually on a side table, the comfortable indentations in the sofa cushions that spoke of countless evenings spent reading or thinking.

This wasn't a museum or a showplace. This was a home.

Soren Jensen

I could see Rafael hesitating just inside the doorway, his eyes darting between the room's elegance and the exit behind him. For a moment, I thought he might bolt—politeness warring with the instinct that had kept him isolated for so long.

But then Erik simply took his hand and pulled him toward the settee, settling them both as if they'd been coming here together for years. The casual confidence of the gesture, the way Rafael allowed himself to be led, made something warm bloom in my chest.

"Soren, could you help me provide some refreshment?" Aleksander asked, excusing us to the kitchen.

THE MOMENT OF TRUTH

Rafael Mercado

Alone with Erik in the elegant sitting room, the weight of the evening finally caught up with me. This beautiful, innocent boy was looking at me with such open affection, such genuine interest, and he had no idea what he was doing. What he was risking.

"Why... why are you so nice to me?" I finally managed to ask, the question emerging from somewhere deep and frightened inside me.

Erik Eriksson

Rafael's question caught me completely off guard. The vulnerability in his voice, the way he asked it like he genuinely couldn't understand why anyone would want to be kind to him, made my chest tight.

"I am? I'm just being me. I mean... sorry... I thought you knew I was gay... Oh my god. I'm sorry. I didn't know. Oh... you're straight! Oh, I am sooo embarrassed! I'm sooo sorry! I didn't..."

The words tumbled out faster than I could stop them as panic set in. I'd misread everything. I'd been holding his hand, asking him to be my date, and he was straight. He was just being polite. I was such an idiot.

Rafael Mercado

Watching Erik's face crumple with mortification, seeing him start to pace as anxiety overtook him, stirred something I'd thought permanently buried. Empathy. The protective instinct that had once made me want to shield others from pain.

"Erik, no no no... It's not that. Erik... It's okay," I said, my own worries cast aside in the face of his distress.

Erik Eriksson

"I'm so sorry Rafael, I didn't realize... I thought... I should go. I didn't mean..." The tears were coming now, hot and embarrassing, and I couldn't stop them. I'd ruined everything. I'd made him uncomfortable, pushed too hard, assumed too much.

Rafael Mercado

I couldn't bear to watch him fall apart over a misunderstanding. Without thinking, I grabbed Erik by the shoulders and pulled him against my chest, his tall frame folding into my smaller one. He was so warm, so solid and real, and for the first time in over a decade, I was the one offering comfort instead of needing it.

Erik Eriksson

Rafael was stronger than he looked—much stronger. And colder than I'd expected, like he'd been standing in the snow and needed someone to warm him up. But he was holding me, whispering something in my ear, his voice soft and urgent.

Rafael Mercado

"Erik... you're doing fine. I'm... I was... gay. It's... complicated. I... like you," I whispered against his ear, the words feeling foreign after so many years of silence.

Erik Eriksson

"Really?" I pulled back just enough to look at his face, hope and confusion warring in my chest.

"Yes... It's... hard to be with someone... but... yes... I do... Just... give me some... time... okay?"

Something about the way he phrased it—"I was gay," "it's hard to be with someone"—made pieces click into place. The same careful distance I'd noticed in Aleksander, the way Rafael seemed to exist slightly apart from the normal world.

"Are... you bi?" I asked, trying to understand.

"What?"

"You said... you were gay."

"Oh... well... I mean... sorry... it's a long story... it's... well... no, I'm not bi... I'm gay... it's just..."

"Rafael... It's okay... I think I know... and it's okay," I said, still holding onto him, never wanting to let go.

From Rafael's perspective:

Every muscle in my body tensed. He knew. Somehow, this sixteen-year-old boy had figured out what I was. The terror that had kept me isolated for over a decade crashed over me like a wave.

"You know?"

Erik Eriksson

I could feel him pulling away, see the fear creeping back into his eyes. But I wasn't afraid. Whatever Rafael was, whatever had happened to him, it didn't change how I felt.

"I don't know much, but I know you're more like Alek... and that's cool. I'm okay with that."

Rafael Mercado

"You... you are?"

The acceptance in his voice, the complete lack of fear or disgust, broke something inside me that had been holding back tears for over a decade. I buried my face against his shoulder and wept—for the family I'd lost, for the years of isolation, for the simple, impossible gift of being seen and accepted exactly as I was.

IN THE KITCHEN

Aleksander Nordh

I stood quietly in the kitchen, holding Soren by his hips, his head rested against my chest. We both knew there was a moment we couldn't witness happening just on the other side of the door. My enhanced hearing meant I could follow every word, every breath, every tear, but I kept my attention focused purely on ensuring both boys were safe.

"It's working," Soren whispered against my chest. "They're really connecting."

"Yes," I replied softly, stroking his hair. "I think they are."

Soren Jensen

Standing there in Aleksander's arms, listening to the muffled voices from the sitting room, I felt something profound settling into place. This was how family worked—not just the bonds of blood or law, but the choice to care for each other, to create space for healing and connection.

"Should we go back in?" I asked.

"In a moment," Aleksander replied. "Let them have this. Rafael's been alone for so long, and Erik... Erik understands more than we might have expected."

As we held each other in the warm light of the kitchen, surrounded by the quiet sounds of two young men discovering they weren't as alone as they'd thought, I realized we weren't just witnessing the beginning of something between Erik and Rafael.

We were watching our family truly begin.

31
SATURDAY DISCOVERIES

CENTRAL LINE, OXFORD CIRCUS STATION, OXFORD STREET, LONDON W1B 3AG

Soren Jensen

The tube carriage was moderately crowded for a Saturday morning, filled with tourists clutching maps and locals heading into central London for weekend shopping. Erik practically vibrated with excitement beside me, his head swiveling to catch every glimpse of anything he could through the windows as we raced through tunnels toward Tower Hill.

"This is mental," he said for the third time since we'd left Aleksander's flat, his voice carrying that particular enthusiasm only teenagers could manage. "I can't believe I'm actually here. In London! On the Underground!"

I smiled, remembering my own first impressions of the city when I'd arrived for graduate school. Everything had seemed impossibly historic, impossibly sophisticated, impossibly... much. But seeing it through Erik's eyes reminded me why I'd fallen in love with this place.

Erik Eriksson

I couldn't contain my curiosity, and sitting next to Soren on the tube felt like the perfect opportunity to get answers to all the questions that had been building since last night.

"How did you two meet?" I asked, not bothering to lower my voice despite the other passengers nearby.

Soren glanced around, then leaned closer. "At the library, actually. King's College. I was having trouble with a microfilm machine, and he offered to help. Turned out he was much better with the equipment than I was."

"Did you think he was hot when you first saw him?"

Soren Jensen

I felt heat rise to my cheeks as Erik fired off questions with typical teenage directness. A middle-aged woman across the aisle was trying not to smile at our conversation, and I found myself both embarrassed and amused by my cousin's complete lack of filter.

"Erik," I said quietly, but he was already moving on to his next question.

"Wait? You didn't know you were gay until you met him?"

"No, I... well, I'd suspected, but I'd never really..." I fumbled for words that wouldn't scandalize our fellow passengers. "I'd never acted on it before."

"Did you two do it on the first date?"

The woman across the aisle was now openly grinning, and I wanted to disappear into my seat. "Erik!" I hissed, but he just looked at me with that innocent expression that suggested he genuinely didn't understand why I was embarrassed.

"What? I'm curious! I've never had a boyfriend before. What's it like to do it?"

I took a deep breath and decided honesty was the best approach. "Erik, we can talk about all of this, but maybe... quietly? And not on public transport?"

But he was already moving on to his next question, this one delivered in a stage whisper that was somehow even more conspicuous.

"Okay, so what's it like to fall in love? I mean, how do you know? Can you be in love like instantly?"

This question was easier to answer, and I found myself speaking more seriously despite our very public venue.

"You feel... seen," I said quietly. "Like someone understands parts of you that you didn't even know were there. And you want to make them happy more than you want anything for yourself."

Erik was quiet for a moment, absorbing this. "Is that how you feel about Rafael?"

The question caught me off guard. "Rafael?"

"I mean... do you think that's how I feel about Rafael?"

THE WHITE TOWER

The Tower of London was impressive as always, its ancient walls rising against the London sky like something from a fairy tale. Erik was suitably awed by the obvious tourist attractions—the Crown Jewels, the Beefeaters, the ravens—but I had something more personal to share with him.

"Come on," I said, steering him away from the crowds toward the White Tower at the complex's heart. "I want to show you something most tourists don't bother to see."

We climbed the narrow stone stairs to the second story, past displays of ancient weapons and armor, until we reached the back of the building where a small doorway led into what looked like a simple stone room.

"It's a Norman chapel," I explained as we stepped inside. "Built around 1080. Most people walk right past it."

Erik Eriksson

The chapel was nothing like the elaborate churches back home in Sweden. No ornate decorations, no gilt or stained glass. Just simple stone arches, plain wooden benches, and an altar that looked like it had been carved from a single block of stone. But there was something about the space that made me want to whisper.

"It's beautiful," I said, meaning it completely.

"I discovered it by accident once, before I met Alek," Soren said, settling onto one of the wooden benches. "It was a weekday afternoon, not many tourists around. I sat here for the longest time."

I joined him on the bench, feeling the weight of centuries in the stone around us. "What did you think about?"

Soren Jensen

"About what I was doing with my life. Who I was. What I was in our family," I said, the memory still vivid despite everything that had changed since then.

"What do you mean?"

"Well... I suppose I was feeling like everyone around me seemed to have a plan. Grow up. Go to school. Marry. Start a family. And it's a new branch of the family tree, right? I didn't feel that. Or think I did. I didn't know what I felt. And I didn't really know what the 'Jensen family' was, other than a bunch of crazy people in Minnesota who went to ice hockey and football games and put up weird Christmas decorations and ate too much food."

Erik Eriksson

I laughed, recognizing the description. "Swedes are similar, but simpler, different. Yet, they have similar problems." My amusement faded as I thought about my own situation. "But family is important. But... I didn't feel like I had one. Or at least one that wanted me. It made me feel like I didn't belong."

Soren Jensen

"So," I continued, "I would sit here and stare up at this simple little altar and listen to the tourists on the floor below and imagine life 500 years ago and what it would have been like..."

I got lost in my thoughts about Aleksander. Had he ever been here? Five hundred years ago, a thousand years ago? Had he sat in this same space, perhaps thinking about Mikael, about love and loss and the weight of time?

"Uncle Soren... are you okay?"

"Yeah, I was just thinking..."

"If Uncle Alek ever came here?"

Erik's perceptiveness startled me. "How... how did you know?"

"I'm not a dumb kid. And... I know Uncle Alek could probably have been around when this place was built."

I paused and lowered my voice. "Erik, does that not bother you? Are you not frightened?"

"No, Uncle Soren. I could never be frightened of Uncle Alek. I'd be more frightened of my mum than him. He's... why he's... he's the most loving man I've ever seen. I don't know how he's survived living as long as he has and having to put up with all of these... assholes."

"Erik!" I laughed, but shushed him nonetheless.

"It's true. How old do you think he is? 600, 700 years old?"

"I believe he's 2200."

"Whhhhhaaa??"

"There's much to the man, but it's best he shares what he'd like to you personally. It's his story to tell."

"Yeah... I guess. But... did he bite you?"

"Erik!" I nudged my cousin, but we both laughed at the joke we shared. "Let's go. We've more to see."

MIDDAY DREAMS

Rafael Mercado

While Soren and Erik explored the city, I rested in my East London flat, typical for this hour. While I could be awake and about during the day, I didn't enjoy the bright light, and it was a labor to slather on all the sun protection, clothing, and accouterments just to make myself comfortable. Best to rest and arise somewhere closer to midday to begin my work. Or, in the case of a Saturday, my weekend.

However, I spent my morning drifting in and out of a dream. This dream involved Erik. Holding his hand as we walked through town. Only this town was Makati back in Manila. It was on Ayala Avenue. We were simply walking, taking in the day, going shopping at Rustan's up at the mall. Perhaps lunch. Normal. Fun. Something boyfriends would do. I felt so comforted. So warm. So... human.

So different from what I became. Erik said he knew what I was, but did he really? Perhaps he meant he knew I was gay? Maybe he didn't really know I was a monster? Maybe he thought I was an Elder like Alek? If only I could be an Elder! At least I'd be respected. I wouldn't have to hunt for my food. I wouldn't be... oh, it hurt to even think about. Maybe I'd been foolish to believe this whole business with Erik would go anywhere? Maybe I should just call everything off before I hurt anyone? How could I be so foolish?

Just then, I heard a knock. And then another. Scrambling, I arose and discovered Aleksander at my door.

"Rafael, please pardon my intrusion. I do not need to disturb your sleep and will not beg to come in, but I would like to ask you to meet me later today when the sun is lower. I'd like to talk. Just the two of us. Please. At Harry's. Will you join me?"

How could he know that I'd been thinking about...

"Rafael?"

"Yes, Aleksander," I said from behind the darkened door. "I will join you at 4:30. Harry's."

FISH AND CHIPS

Erik Eriksson

Soren and I had just stepped off a tourist boat on the Thames, sharing a laugh about the tour guide's terrible jokes, when I caught sight of a fish and chips shop. "We have to try that, right? Isn't it some sort of English tradition?"

"I'm American, so I'm not the person to ask, but we can have a bite," Soren replied. "I think I'll just have a drink of something cool if you don't mind. You can compare the fish to what you have up north."

Soren Jensen

As Erik amused himself with mediocre fried fish at a tourist trap, he began another round of questioning, this time about Rafael.

"He seems so fragile. Did something happen to him?"

I considered how to answer. "It's complicated, and it's better if Rafael chooses to tell you himself. But please be gentle with him."

"I know he's like Uncle Alek. How old do you think he is?"

"Well, Erik—again, it's complicated. He sort of is like Uncle Alek... but it's his story to tell. They're not quite the same. I don't fully understand myself. And he's not that old. He... well, let's just say you two aren't that far apart."

"Oh, wow. You mean..."

"Well, he's definitely older than you, but not by much... at least by Alek's standards, for sure. But he's been through a lot. It was a miracle he even came to dinner. It was the first time I even met him, and we've been trying to get him to come for months."

Erik Eriksson

"Really? And he even let me hold his hand!"

"Well, that was a miracle too—I admit, I nearly fainted upon seeing you two, but I'm happy you both found each other. I think he really needs a friend, and I know you do too. But I want you to know there's a lot going on there. Just be sensitive to it. And know you can always come talk with me. Or Alek anytime. Okay? We want to give you both your privacy, but we want to ensure you're both safe."

"Safe? You mean like sex?"

. . .

Soren Jensen

"Well, sure... but that's not what I was thinking, although now that you mention it, you should be safe when you choose to have sex. But..."

"You think he's going to hit me or something?"

"No... nothing like that. It's just... he's fragile, and I don't want him to get his heart broken."

"Or mine too!"

"Yes... yours too, but something tells me you're pretty tough."

"Yeah... maybe, but I'm a teddy bear inside sometimes, too."

We laughed and people-watched before Erik asked one last question.

"Soren?"

"Yeah?"

"Ummm... I feel awkward asking, but I don't know who else to ask..."

"It's okay. Ask me anything..."

"Well... how do I... uh... kiss him? I mean... do I start it first or... wait... or what?"

I wanted to laugh a little, but I knew Erik was serious. So, I gave a serious answer.

"If the moment is right, you can simply ask politely."

"Really?"

"Yes."

"So, you just say 'Can I kiss you?' like that?"

"Yes."

"Huh."

~

HARRY'S BAR

Rafael Mercado

Across town at Harry's, I made good on my promise. I didn't know why, but it felt right to keep my word. Aleksander was at his usual spot.

I sat down, back to the wall so I could see everything, as usual, but I didn't feel quite as nervous. The edge was slightly off compared to normal.

"Thanks for coming to join me, Rafael. I'm very pleased to see you."

"Mmm."

"Rafael, I'd like you to consider something. I'll keep it short. I can only say that I empathize with your feelings, but will never pretend to fully appreciate them. To say so would be to dishonor you. And that I would never do. But I do believe there is a young man staying with us who has taken to you strongly."

"Does he know I'm a monster?"

"I believe he knows you're one of us, but he does not yet understand the differences."

"So, he doesn't know I feed or hunt or have been condemned to a life like this? He doesn't know that to love me, he must accept that I'm a killer?"

"He's seventeen, Rafael. He knows he's falling in love—sees a young man who's beginning to steal his heart. This boy recognizes that the man with the deep brown eyes and timid hands is not human, yet accepts that truth. Erik looks beyond what you are to *who* you are. Curious and welcoming and loving."

"And naive."

"Yes. He is that. But he is a Jensen. He is part of us. He is part of you."

I looked at Aleksander and paused. "What do you mean?"

"Rafael, I believe you both have a very, very distant relative. Too far back to be of concern, but close enough to make it important."

"I don't follow."

Aleksander Nordh

"Rafael, my love Mikael..." I paused, allowing myself to expose my emotions ever so slightly. This was unusual for me, and I could see Rafael taking note. I was being vulnerable.

"Mikael was the love of my life 130 years ago. And I pushed him away. I've regretted it ever since. But... he set forth a generation of people that blossomed across the globe. And I believe you... yes, you, are a descendant."

Rafael Mercado

"What? How? I was born in Manila. How could I be?"

"It's rather complicated, and I'm still researching it with Soren."

"Isn't that how you and he met?"

"Well, yes..."

"So, Soren is a descendant, which makes me a cousin of..."

"Soren. Yes. Distant."

"Really?"

"Yes."

"And Erik?"

"He's from Mikael's older sister's lineage... many generations down."

"So, everyone's related?"

"In some ways."

"And... you're getting married to Soren, so you'll be related... but you were lovers with Mikael, so..."

"It's all come full circle. Yes."

"I... I'm so confused."

Aleksander Nordh

"It is rather confusing, isn't it?" We both laughed, easing the tension of the conversation.

"Rafael, the point I'm making is for you to be open. If you and Erik are friends or not is entirely up to you both. However, please do not rule out the possibility. He is in need of a friend, and I know you could use one yourself. Go slow. He is new to all of this as well. And I'm happy to help in any way, especially guiding with the questions. He's a smart young man. Trust him. Take your time. But please, give him a chance. Give yourself one."

32
SUNDAY SANCTUARY

FLAT 6, 84 VYNER STREET, LONDON E2 9DG

Erik Eriksson

The tube carriage rumbled through tunnels beneath London as we traveled east, each station taking us further from the elegant neighborhoods I'd grown accustomed to during my stay with Aleksander. Through the windows, I caught glimpses of a different London—industrial estates, converted warehouses, streets that felt grittier but somehow more alive than the polished areas around King's College.

Rafael sat beside me, one hand resting lightly on the small overnight bag I'd packed, his fingers occasionally brushing mine when the train swayed. He'd been quiet since collecting me from Aleksander's flat, but it wasn't the tense silence of yesterday. This felt more like anticipation, nervous energy building as we approached his private sanctuary.

"Are you sure about this?" he asked softly, his voice barely audible above the train's rhythm. "Having me stay overnight, I mean. We could just have dinner and I could return to my uncles'."

Rafael Mercado

I'd been asking myself the same question since yesterday evening, but watching

Erik's face as he took in the changing landscape outside, seeing his genuine excitement about experiencing my world, made the answer clear.

"I want you to stay," I said, surprised by my own certainty. "I want to share this with you."

The smile that spread across Erik's face made my chest tight with an emotion I'd almost forgotten how to feel. Hope, perhaps. Or simply the quiet joy of being wanted exactly as I was.

THE WAREHOUSE DISTRICT

Erik Eriksson

We emerged from the Underground into a neighborhood that felt like stepping into an entirely different city. Where central London was all Georgian terraces and tourist crowds, this area pulsed with creative energy—converted warehouses housing artist studios, industrial buildings repurposed as trendy restaurants, young professionals cycling home from work through streets lined with galleries and independent shops.

"This is incredible," I said, taking in the mixture of old and new, industrial and artistic. "It's like a whole secret London."

"Not so secret anymore," Rafael replied with a slight smile. "The area's been discovered by property developers. But it still maintains some of its character."

Rafael Mercado

Seeing the neighborhood through Erik's eyes reminded me why I'd chosen to live here. When I'd first arrived in London, this area had felt like neutral ground —neither fully human nor fully other, but something in between. A place where unusual was normal, where no one looked too closely at their neighbors' habits or schedules.

We walked through streets that were busy enough to provide anonymity but not so crowded as to feel overwhelming. Erik's hand found mine as we navigated the sidewalks, and I marveled at how natural the contact felt despite my years of careful isolation.

"There," I said, pointing to a six-story brick building with large industrial windows. "That's home."

ENTERING THE SANCTUARY

Erik Eriksson

Rafael's building was everything I'd hoped for and nothing I'd expected. The exterior maintained its warehouse character—red brick, metal fire escapes, loading dock entrances that spoke of the building's industrial past. But the lobby was clearly modern, with polished concrete floors and security systems that suggested the conversion had been expensive and thoughtfully done.

"Top floor," Rafael said as we entered a lift with the original freight elevator's industrial aesthetic but obviously updated mechanics. "I wanted the most space and the best light control."

Rafael Mercado

As the elevator rose, I found myself growing increasingly nervous about Erik's reaction to my flat. It was the most personal space I had, carefully designed for my specific needs but also reflecting years of solitary living. What if he found it cold? Unwelcoming? Too obviously the home of someone who'd forgotten how to live with others?

"Rafael," Erik said quietly, his hand squeezing mine, "whatever it's like, I'm honored that you're sharing it with me."

His words, so simple and genuine, eased some of my anxiety. Whatever his reaction, I realized, he would be kind about it.

THE FLAT

Erik Eriksson

When Rafael unlocked his door and led me inside, I stopped short, overwhelmed by the sheer scale and beauty of the space. The flat stretched across what must have been the entire floor, with soaring ceilings, exposed brick walls, and enormous windows that had been fitted with what looked like specialized glass to filter harsh light.

"This is... Rafael, this is amazing," I breathed, taking in the carefully curated combination of modern comfort and industrial character.

The space was divided into distinct areas—a kitchen with professional-grade appliances, a sitting area with furniture that looked both expensive and comfortable, a dining space, and what appeared to be a library with floor-to-ceiling bookshelves along one entire wall. Everything was immaculate, elegantly arranged, but somehow felt lived-in rather than sterile.

Rafael Mercado

Erik's obvious delight in the space sent warmth through me that had nothing to do with the flat's heating system. I'd designed this place as a refuge from the world, but having him here made it feel like something more—a home I could share rather than simply inhabit.

"The windows are specially treated," I explained, noting his curiosity about the glass. "UV filtering. Essential for... my condition."

"It's brilliant," Erik said, moving to examine the bookshelves with obvious excitement. "And you have so many books! This is like having a private library."

SHARED INTERESTS

Erik Eriksson

Rafael's book collection was extraordinary—thousands of volumes spanning centuries, languages I recognized and others I didn't, first editions mixed with well-worn paperbacks that spoke of being read and reread. When I found the Dracula first edition he'd mentioned, prominently displayed but accessible, I couldn't help but grin.

"May I?" I asked, gesturing toward the volume.

"Of course," Rafael replied, moving to stand beside me as I carefully opened the book.

Rafael Mercado

Watching Erik handle the precious volume with appropriate reverence, seeing his genuine appreciation for the craftsmanship and history it represented, confirmed what I'd hoped. He understood that books weren't just possessions but connections to ideas, stories, and experiences that transcended time.

"I acquired it shortly after moving to London," I said. "There's something... amusing about owning the definitive vampire novel when you are one."

"Does it bother you?" Erik asked, his expression curious rather than pitying. "Reading about vampires in fiction when you know the reality?"

The question was thoughtful, respectful of my experience without tiptoeing around it. I found myself giving an honest answer rather than a deflection.

"Sometimes. The myths are so far from reality that it's almost like reading about an entirely different species. But Stoker... he captured something true about isolation, about being fundamentally different from the world around you."

EVENING SETTLES IN

I prepared dinner while Erik continued exploring the flat, giving him time to process the space and myself time to adjust to having someone else in my carefully ordered environment. The kitchen had been designed for someone who enjoyed cooking but rarely entertained—high-end equipment but scaled for one or two people.

"Can I help?" Erik asked, appearing at my elbow as I arranged ingredients for a simple but elegant meal.

"You could open the wine," I suggested, gesturing toward a bottle I'd selected earlier. "Though I should mention I can't actually drink alcohol. My metabolism doesn't process it properly."

Erik Eriksson

"That's okay," I said, studying the wine label with interest. "I've never had wine anyway. Is it alright if I try just a little? I won't tell my uncles if you won't."

Rafael's laugh—genuine and spontaneous—was the most beautiful sound I'd heard all day.

"I think a small glass with dinner would be perfectly reasonable," he said. "Though you should eat something substantial with it."

Rafael Mercado

Cooking for someone else felt strange after so many years of solitary meals, but Erik's presence in the kitchen was companionable rather than intrusive. He asked questions about the ingredients, offered to help with simple tasks, and generally made the process feel less like a performance and more like... domesticity.

The thought should have terrified me. Instead, it felt like coming home to a life I'd thought lost forever.

. . .

DINNER CONVERSATION

Erik Eriksson

We ate at Rafael's dining table, positioned near the windows to take advantage of the evening light filtering through the specialized glass. The food was exceptional—Rafael clearly knew his way around a kitchen—but what I loved most was the conversation.

"Tell me about Manila," I said, genuinely curious about his life before London. "What was it like growing up there?"

Rafael Mercado

The question caught me off guard. Most people who knew my story focused on what I'd become rather than who I'd been before. But Erik seemed genuinely interested in understanding my entire history, not just the dramatic parts.

"Beautiful," I said slowly, remembering. "Complicated. My parents are—were—both academics. We lived in a privileged bubble, really. Private schools, university connections, household staff. I was incredibly sheltered."

"Do you miss it?"

"Sometimes. The warmth, both climate and cultural. Filipino families are... demonstrative in ways that took me years to appreciate. Everything is shared, celebrated, mourned together." I paused, swirling the water in my glass. "It's the opposite of how I live now."

Erik Eriksson

I could hear the longing in Rafael's voice, the grief for connections he'd chosen to sever rather than complicate with his transformation. It made me want to reach across the table and take his hand, to offer whatever comfort my presence could provide.

"Maybe you don't have to live that way forever," I said quietly.

Rafael Mercado

The gentle certainty in Erik's voice, the way he said it like my isolation was a choice rather than an inevitability, stirred something I'd thought permanently buried.

"Erik," I said carefully, "you need to understand what you're saying. What you're suggesting. I'm not... I can't be part of a normal life. There are things about what I am, what I need to survive, that make ordinary relationships impossible."

THE DIFFICULT CONVERSATION

Erik Eriksson

I could see Rafael retreating, building walls again just when we'd been making progress. But I wasn't ready to let him disappear behind his fears.

"What things?" I asked directly.

"Erik..."

"No, really. What specific things? Because so far, everything about you seems pretty wonderful to me."

Rafael Mercado

His directness, his refusal to let me hide behind vague warnings, forced me to articulate fears I'd carried silently for over a decade.

"I need blood to survive," I said bluntly. "Human blood. Not constantly, but regularly. That means I have to... hunt, essentially. Take what I need from people who don't know what I am."

I watched his face carefully, waiting for the disgust, the fear, the inevitable withdrawal.

Erik Eriksson

Rafael's confession hung between us in the quiet dining room. I could see him braced for my reaction, expecting horror or revulsion.

For a moment, I couldn't process what he'd just said. My brain seemed to stutter, trying to reconcile the gentle man across from me with the words that had just come out of his mouth.

"Du..." I started in Swedish, then caught myself. "You... you need human blood?"

"Yes."

The simple confirmation hit me like a physical blow.

"And you..." My voice cracked slightly. "Fan, this is... you actually hunt people? Like, real people?"

Rafael's eyes filled with pain at my tone, and I realized I'd pulled back slightly in my chair without meaning to.

"Erik, I can explain—"

"Nej, wait." I pressed my palms against my eyes, trying to think. "Sorry, I mean... no, just... just give me a second here, okay?"

Rafael Mercado

Watching Erik struggle with my confession was agony. I could see him retreating, could hear the way his accent got thicker when he was upset, could see the exact moment when the boy I'd fallen in love with started looking at me like I was a stranger.

"I target people who deserve it," I said carefully, my own voice sounding foreign to my ears. "Criminals, usually. People who hurt others—"

Erik Eriksson

"But how do you... shit, how do you know?" The curse slipped out before I could stop it, and I felt my face burn. "I mean, how can you be sure someone deserves to... to die? What if you're wrong? What if they look bad but they're actually..."

I couldn't finish the sentence. The English words felt clumsy in my mouth when everything inside me was screaming in Swedish.

"I watch them, Erik. Sometimes for weeks. I don't act unless I'm certain."

"Certain hur då? Based on what?" I could hear myself mixing languages and tried to slow down. "You're not like... police or judge or something. You just decide who lives and who... who doesn't?"

Rafael Mercado

The way Erik's voice cracked on the last words nearly broke me. I wanted to reach for him, to comfort him, but I could see he needed space.

"Hindi ganun... it's not that simple," I said, my own careful English beginning to fracture under the stress. "Erik, please, if you could just let me explain—"

"It sounds exactly that simple!" Erik pushed back from the table, his chair scraping loudly. "You're talking about... about murder, Rafael. Maybe okay murder, but still murder, right?"

The word hit me like a physical blow. Murder. That's what he saw when he looked at what I did to survive. What I was.

Erik Eriksson

I realized I was shaking—not from being cold, but from something deeper, something scared. My body was doing things without asking my brain first, which was really confusing because I knew Rafael wouldn't hurt me. Right? I knew that. But my hands were still shaking.

"I need... jag behöver..." I stopped, frustrated with myself. "I need a minute. Just to think, okay?"

I walked to the window, putting distance between us while trying to figure out what the hell I was supposed to think about all this. Behind me, I heard Rafael's chair move, and my shoulders went tense without meaning to.

"Erik, please don't—"

"Don't what?" I spun around, and seeing how hurt he looked made my chest tight. "Don't be scared? Don't ask questions? Don't be a normal person about learning that my... that you kill people?"

Rafael Mercado

"I don't kill them," I said, my voice barely above a whisper. The way he'd started to say 'my' and then stopped—like he couldn't bring himself to call me his anything anymore—felt like dying. "I take what I need and leave them alive."

"But you could kill them." His voice was flat now, matter-of-fact in that way teenagers got when they were trying not to cry. "If you wanted. If you made mistake or just... decided to."

The silence stretched between us because we both knew the answer.

Erik Eriksson

"I think..." I wiped my nose with the back of my hand, a gesture that would have mortified me yesterday but seemed unimportant now. "Shit, I think I need some time to... to understand this. What it means and stuff."

Rafael Mercado

My heart felt like it was stopping. "Of course. I can take you back to your uncles, or call them, or whatever you need—"

"No." The word came out sharper than I'd meant. "I don't want to leave, okay? I just... can we just sit quiet for a bit? Maybe you could.. I don't know.. just sit or something?"

The relief that flooded through me was so intense I had to blink back tears. He wasn't running. He was staying, even scared, even upset.

"Sige... yes, of course. Would you like tea? Or I could just... I'll just read quietly."

Erik Eriksson

I sat curled up in the corner of Rafael's sofa, hugging a cushion to my chest while watching him pretend to read. He'd positioned himself across the room—far enough that I didn't feel trapped, close enough that he could still see me. Whether he'd done it on purpose or not, I couldn't tell, but it helped.

My brain kept going in circles. Like, okay, Rafael was gentle with me. Super careful about everything—consent, boundaries, making sure I felt safe. He'd spent a whole week being nothing but kind and sweet, never making me feel weird or pressured about anything.

But he was also... väd fan, he hunted people. Actual people. His hands—the same hands that held me and made me dinner and touched me so carefully—those hands had hurt people. Made them unconscious. Took their blood.

It was making me feel sick.

But then I'd look at him sitting there, trying so hard not to crowd me, looking absolutely miserable, and I'd think: this is still Rafael. Same person who worried about me drinking too much wine. Same person who made sure I had blankets when I was cold.

How could someone be both things at once?

. . .

GRADUAL ACCEPTANCE

After what felt like forever, I finally worked up the courage to talk.

"Raf?"

His head snapped up like he'd been waiting for me to say something for hours. Which, shit, he probably had been.

"Yeah?"

"I need to ask you some stuff, okay? And it might be... hard questions. But I need you to be honest with me. Like, completely honest."

"Of course. Whatever you need."

I took a deep breath. "Have you ever been wrong? About someone deserving what you did?"

Rafael Mercado

The question felt like a knife to the chest, but I'd promised honesty.

"I... hindi ko alam. I don't know." The admission came out in a mixture of languages, my carefully maintained English crumbling. "I choose people whose crimes are documented, obvious. But you're right—I could be wrong. That possibility... it keeps me awake sometimes."

Erik Eriksson

Something in my chest unclenched a little at hearing how scared he sounded when he said it. "Do you... do you like it? The hunting part?"

"No," he said immediately, then stopped. "The feeding itself... oo, yes. It's like nothing else, the energy it gives. But the hunting, having to take from others..." He shook his head, and I could see his hands trembling. "It's something I have to do, not something I want to do."

"What if you stopped? Found another way?"

"I'd die," he said simply. "But Erik, if there was another way, I would take it immediately. The hiding, the guilt, the weight of these choices—I wouldn't wish this on anyone."

I believed him. You could hear it in his voice—how tired he was, how much he hated what he had to do.

"And you never..." I had to stop and swallow hard. "You never hurt someone who didn't deserve it?"

"Never on purpose," he whispered. "But I can't promise I've never made a mistake. I can only promise I try to be as careful as possible."

I sat there for a long time, just thinking about his answers. Finally, I asked the question that scared me most.

"Could you hurt me? By accident or if you lost control or something?"

"Aldrig. Never." His voice was fierce now, stronger. "My control around you is absolute. And even if it wasn't... Erik, I would rather die than harm you. That's not romantic bullshit—that's truth."

Looking at his face, seeing how much he meant it, I felt something settle in my chest. Not like everything was okay—I was still scared and confused and kind of sick to my stomach. But maybe... maybe I could work through this.

"I believe you," I said quietly.

The way his whole face crumpled with relief almost made me cry.

"But I need time," I added quickly. "To really get what this means. About you and about us and everything."

"All the time you need," he said, and his voice sounded thick like he might cry too.

I got up slowly and walked over to him. When I reached for his hand, he let me take it but didn't grab or anything—just waited to see what I wanted.

"I'm scared," I admitted. "Not of you exactly, but of... what you have to do. What that means about everything."

Rafael Mercado

"I'm terrified too," I said softly. "I've been scared since I started caring about you this much. Scared you'd learn what I was and run. Scared I'd lose the best thing that's happened to me in years."

Erik Eriksson

"You're not losing me," I said, squeezing his hand. "But you gotta be patient with me while I figure out how to... how to be okay with all this stuff, yeah?"

"However long it takes."

We stood there for a moment, just holding hands in the middle of his sitting room. It felt weird—like we were both afraid to move, afraid to break whatever fragile thing we'd just built between us.

"So..." I said finally, because the silence was getting heavy. "What happens now?"

Rafael Mercado

Erik's question hung between us. What did happen now? We'd crossed some kind of bridge tonight, but I had no idea what waited on the other side.

"I don't know," I admitted. "I've never... this is new territory for me."

"Yeah, same." Erik looked around the room, seeming suddenly young and uncertain. "Should we like... sit down or something? I feel weird just standing here."

Erik Eriksson

We ended up on his sofa, but not close like before dinner. I sat in one corner, him in the other, both of us being careful not to crowd each other. It was awkward as hell, but also kind of necessary.

"This is så konstigt," I muttered, then caught myself. "Sorry, I mean... this is really weird."

"What's weird about it?"

"Everything?" I laughed, but it came out shaky. "Like, an hour ago I was freaking out about you being a... you know. And now we're just sitting here like we're gonna watch TV or something."

Rafael Mercado

The way Erik was struggling with the normalcy of the moment after everything we'd discussed made perfect sense. We'd just blown up his entire understanding of who I was, and now we were supposed to... what? Pretend it was fine?

"We don't have to pretend everything's normal," I said carefully. "If you need space, or time to think more, or—"

"No, that's not..." Erik rubbed his face with both hands, a gesture that made him look even younger. "I don't want space. But I also don't know how to just... be around you now. Like, how do I talk to you? How do I act?"

Erik Eriksson

The question came out more desperate than I'd meant it to, but it was true. Everything felt different now, but I didn't know what the new rules were supposed to be.

"The same way you did before?" Rafael suggested, but he sounded uncertain too.

"But it's not the same, is it?" I shifted on the sofa, pulling my knees up to my chest. "Before, you were just... Rafael. Nice guy who makes good food and worries about me drinking wine. Now you're Rafael who also... does other stuff."

I couldn't bring myself to say 'hunts people' again. It was too big, too scary.

"I'm still the same person who worries about you drinking wine," Rafael said softly.

"I know. That's what's confusing." I looked at him across the sofa. "How are you both things at the same time?"

Rafael Mercado

It was such an honest question, asked with the kind of directness only teenagers possessed. Adults would dance around it, but Erik just asked what he needed to know.

"I don't know," I said. "I've been trying to figure that out for eleven years."

"Does it get easier? Living with... being two different people?"

"Some days." I shifted position, mirroring his posture unconsciously. "Other days it feels impossible."

Erik Eriksson

We sat like that for a while, just looking at each other across the sofa. It should have been uncomfortable, but somehow it wasn't. It was like we were both trying to figure out who we were now, after everything that had changed.

"Raf?" I said finally.

"Yeah?"

"Can I... would it be okay if I moved closer? Not for kissing or anything, just..." I gestured vaguely. "I don't want to sit so far away anymore."

The relief on his face was obvious. "Of course."

I scooted over until we were sitting closer, not quite touching but close enough that I could feel his warmth. It felt better, less like we were strangers.

"Thanks," I said.

"For what?"

"For telling me the truth. Even though it was scary as hell."

"Thank you for staying," he said. "For trying to understand instead of just running."

We looked at each other for a moment, and I felt something shift between us.

Not back to what we were before—that was gone forever. But maybe something new was starting.

Without really planning it, I reached for his hand again. This time, when he took it, it felt less desperate and more... hopeful.

"We're gonna figure this out," I said, though I wasn't sure if I was trying to convince him or myself.

"Yeah," Rafael said, squeezing my fingers gently. "We are."

We sat there holding hands for a while, neither of us talking much. It wasn't the same comfortable quiet we'd had before dinner—this was different, more careful. But it was okay. Better than okay, actually.

I must have yawned or something, because Rafael looked at me.

"You're tired," he said.

"Yeah, I guess." I was exhausted—not just tired, but like... emotionally wiped out. Everything that happened tonight felt like it lasted forever instead of just a few hours.

"I should show you the guest room," Rafael said, starting to get up. "Get you some blankets and stuff—"

"Wait." I held onto his hand. "Do I have to sleep in there?"

Rafael Mercado

The question made my stomach drop. Was he afraid to be in the same room as me now?

"Erik, if you're worried about being safe, I can sleep in the guest room instead. You can lock the door—I swear on my life, you have nothing to worry about with me, but if it would make you feel better—"

"No, that's not..." Erik shook his head quickly. "That's not what I meant."

Erik Eriksson

"I meant like... do you want me to sleep in there? Because honestly, after everything we talked about tonight, being alone in a room thinking about all this stuff sounds really shitty."

Rafael looked confused, like he was trying to figure out what I actually wanted.

"I don't know what the right thing is," he said quietly. "After everything I told you..."

"The right thing is what feels okay for both of us," I said. "And sleeping by myself sounds awful right now. But if you think it's weird or whatever—"

"It's not weird," Rafael said quickly. "I just... I want you to feel safe. That's all."

Rafael Mercado

Looking at Erik's face, I could see he meant it. Even after learning what I was, what I did, he still wanted to be close. Still trusted me that much.

"You're sure you're okay with it?" I asked. "Because I can set up anywhere. The couch, the guest room, whatever makes you comfortable."

"I'm sure," Erik said. "Unless you don't want to. Which is fine too, I just—"

"I want you to stay close," I admitted. "I was scared you'd want to be as far away from me as possible."

Erik squeezed my hand. "I'm still scared about some stuff. But not about you hurting me or anything like that."

"Good," I said, relief flooding through me. "Because I'd rather die than—"

"I know," Erik said softly. "I believe you."

And so we settled into my bedroom together—Erik in a t-shirt and his underwear, me in silk pajamas that suddenly felt absurdly formal. He curled up on his side of my large bed while I propped myself against the headboard with a book, both of us maintaining careful distance while reveling in the simple pleasure of shared space.

As the minutes passed, I could feel Erik gradually relaxing beside me, though he wasn't quite asleep yet. At first we maintained careful distance on opposite sides of my large bed, but slowly—tentatively—he began to shift closer. First just his hand drifted toward the center of the bed, then gradually his whole body migrated across the space until he was curled against my side, one arm draped across my waist.

I set my book aside, unable to concentrate on anything but this extraordinary boy who, despite everything he'd learned about me tonight, still chose to be close. In this vast bed, in this carefully constructed sanctuary, Erik had somehow found his way to me—not in unconscious sleep, but in conscious trust.

Watching him there, still awake but peaceful, allowing himself to be vulnerable with me after everything we'd discussed, I couldn't help but feel overwhelmed by the magnitude of what he was offering.

"Rafael?" Erik's voice was soft in the darkness.

"Yes?"

"Thank you. For telling me the truth tonight. Even though it was scary as hell."

"Thank you," I replied, "for staying. For trying to understand."

Erik Eriksson

Rafael's breathing had gotten quiet and steady, and I thought maybe he'd fallen asleep. But I was still wide awake, my brain spinning with everything that had happened tonight.

"Raf?" I whispered.

"Mmm?"

"Are you gonna be okay? Like, with me knowing everything now?"

I felt him shift slightly in the darkness. "What do you mean?"

"I don't know. Like... are you worried I'm gonna freak out tomorrow when I really think about it? Or tell someone, or—"

"No," Rafael said immediately. "I'm not worried about any of that."

"Then what are you worried about?"

He was quiet for so long I thought maybe he'd decided not to answer. Then: "That you'll realize what you've gotten yourself into and decide it's too complicated."

Rafael Mercado

Lying there in the darkness with Erik warm and trusting beside me, I felt the weight of everything I'd shared tonight. Not regret—I was glad he knew the truth. But fear about what it meant for us going forward.

"This isn't gonna be simple," Erik said softly, like he'd read my thoughts.

"No," I agreed. "It's not."

"But maybe that's okay," he said, his voice getting sleepy. "Maybe simple is overrated anyway."

I felt him settle more comfortably against my side, his breathing starting to slow toward sleep.

"Rafael?" he mumbled.

"Yeah?"

"I'm glad you trusted me."

"I'm glad you stayed," I whispered back.

Erik Eriksson

As I drifted toward sleep in Rafael's elegant bedroom, surrounded by the scent of his cologne and the quiet sounds of pages turning, I felt something I'd never experienced before: the certainty that I was exactly where I was supposed to be.

Tomorrow would bring new questions, new challenges, new things to figure out about this extraordinary person who'd somehow chosen to trust me with his biggest secrets.

But tonight, we were together in the sanctuary Rafael had built, and neither of us was alone anymore.

33
MONDAY MORNING REVELATIONS

FLAT 6, 84 VYNER STREET, LONDON E2 9DG

Rafael Mercado

I woke to unfamiliar warmth pressed against my side and the quiet sound of steady breathing that wasn't my own. For a moment, disorientation clouded my thoughts—in over a decade of solitary existence, I'd never shared sleeping space with another person. Then memory flooded back: Erik, our difficult dinner conversation, his shock at learning what I was, the tentative way we'd reconnected afterward, and his choice to stay close despite everything.

Erik was still curled against me, one arm draped across my waist, his face peaceful in sleep. But even unconscious, there was something different about his posture—less the complete abandon of trust I might have expected, and more the careful closeness of someone who had chosen to be here despite his fears.

Sunlight filtered through the specialized glass of my bedroom windows, creating a soft golden glow that illuminated his features. For the first time in years, I didn't want to get up. But not because everything was perfect—because everything was complicated, and somehow that made it more precious.

Erik Eriksson

I woke slowly, consciousness returning in gentle waves accompanied by the unfamiliar sensation of silk pajamas against my cheek and the scent of expensive cologne. It took a moment to remember where I was—Rafael's flat, Rafael's bed, Rafael's arms around me.

When I lifted my head to look at him, I found dark eyes already watching me with an expression that was... careful. Hopeful but cautious, like he was trying to read whether I'd changed my mind overnight.

"Good morning," he said softly.

"Morning," I replied, suddenly aware of how awkward this might be. I mean, what were the rules here? After everything we'd talked about last night, after learning he was a vampire who hunted people, after somehow deciding to stay anyway—what was I supposed to say now?

"Did you sleep okay?" Rafael asked.

"Yeah, actually. You?"

"A little. More than I usually do." His hand came up like he might brush hair away from my face, then hesitated. "Are you... how are you feeling? About everything?"

THE MORNING AFTER REALITY

The question made my stomach do a little flip. Because honestly? I wasn't sure how I felt. Everything from last night felt sort of... surreal in the morning light.

"I don't know," I said, which was probably the most honest answer I could give. "Like, I'm still here, right? That has to mean something. But everything feels... I don't know how to describe it."

Rafael's face fell slightly, and I immediately felt bad.

"It's not that I want to leave or anything," I added quickly, trying to find better words. "It's just... shit, this is hard to explain in English. Det är bara... it's like my head knows you're the same person, but also not the same person, you know?"

Rafael Mercado

His mix of languages when he was struggling to express something complex was endearing, and also reminded me how young he was—not just in years, but in experience with navigating complicated emotions.

"I think I understand," I said carefully. "It's a lot to process."

"Yeah." Erik rubbed his face with both hands. "But I don't want you to think

I'm gonna freak out and run or something. I'm just... still figuring out how to think about all this."

I nodded, trying not to let my relief show too obviously. He was staying. He was processing, but he wasn't running.

"Take all the time you need," I said.

Erik Eriksson

"Can I ask you something?" I said.

"Always."

"Last night, when I was freaking out... were you scared I was gonna leave?"

Rafael Mercado

The question hit closer to home than I'd expected. "Terrified," I admitted, my voice barely above a whisper. "I kept thinking I'd just destroyed the only good thing that had happened to me since... since I became what I am."

"But you told me anyway. Even though you were scared."

"You deserved to know the truth," I said, then hesitated. "And I... I couldn't keep lying to you. Not if we were going to keep spending time together."

Erik was quiet for a moment, thinking. "Can I ask you something else?"

"Sure."

"Are you always this scared of everything?"

The question was so direct, so honest, that it caught me completely off guard. "What do you mean?"

"I mean like... last night you seemed scared to tell me, scared I'd leave, scared of what I'd think. And right now you seem scared that I'm gonna change my mind or freak out or whatever." Erik shifted to look at me more directly. "Are you always waiting for something bad to happen?"

His observation was uncomfortably accurate. "I... yes, I suppose I am."

"Why?"

"Because for eleven years, something bad was always happening. Or about to happen. I learned to expect it."

"That sounds exhausting."

"It is."

Erik Eriksson

"Look, I know this is all fucked up and complicated," I said, getting frustrated with trying to find the right words. "But I don't want you to treat me like some kid who doesn't know shit about anything."

Rafael Mercado

The flash of anger in his voice caught me off guard, but he was right. I had been treating him like he was too young to understand, when really it was my own fear making me cautious.

"I'm sorry," I said quietly. "I didn't mean to... it's just that you're seventeen, and I'm..." I struggled with how to explain it. "I may look young, but I'm actually thirty-two. That's... that's a big difference in life experience. And I've spent the last eleven years being terrified of my own shadow, basically. I don't really know how to do... this. Whatever this is."

Erik Eriksson

"So because I'm seventeen, what?" I said, feeling my frustration building again. "You think I can't handle complicated stuff? That I don't know what I want?"

"That's not what I meant—"

"That's exactly what you meant." I could feel myself getting worked up. "You're doing it again, using my age as some fucking excuse." The curse slipped out with my frustration, along with my accent getting thicker. "I'm not some little kid who doesn't know vad fan he wants. I'm seventeen, not seven, okay?"

I could hear myself getting heated, mixing languages the way I always did when I was upset.

"And yeah, I'm still trying to figure shit out, but so are you, right? So don't act like you've got everything sorted just because you're older."

Rafael Mercado

The way Erik's careful English completely fell apart when he got angry was both jarring and oddly reassuring. It reminded me that underneath his thoughtful questions and mature responses, he really was just a teenager trying to navigate something impossibly complicated. But he was also right—I was using his age as a shield for my own fears.

"You're right," I said softly. "I'm sorry. I was being unfair."

"Ja, you were," Erik said, still heated. "And I don't... jag vill inte... fuck, why is English so hard when I'm mad?"

Despite everything, I almost smiled. "Because you're thinking faster than you can translate."

"Whatever. Point is, don't treat me like I'm stupid, okay? Just because you're scared doesn't mean I am."

"I don't think you're stupid," I said. "And you're right—I am scared. But that's not your fault."

Erik Eriksson

The way he said it—so quietly, like he was afraid I'd judge him for being scared —made my anger deflate a little. This wasn't about him thinking I was too young. This was about him being terrified of everything.

"Look," I said, my voice calming down. "I get that thirty-two and seventeen is weird, okay? I'm not stupid. But you hiding behind that, pretending like it's about protecting me or whatever—that's not fair either."

"You're absolutely right," Rafael said. "It's not about protecting you. It's about protecting myself."

The vulnerability in his voice made something click for me. This wasn't about him being older or more experienced. This was about him being just as scared as I was, just in different ways.

"Okay," I said.

"Okay?"

"Yeah, okay. We're both scared and don't know what the hell we're doing. At least we're honest about it."

MORNING CONVERSATIONS

After that, things felt a little easier between us. Not normal—I didn't think anything between us would ever be normal. But more honest, maybe.

Rafael told me about what it was like waking up in different places for eleven years, never staying anywhere long enough to feel settled. I told him about what it was like growing up in a place where everyone expected you to be happy with a life that felt too small.

"Do you miss it?" I asked. "Home, I mean."

"Every day," he admitted. "But it's complicated. The place I miss doesn't exist anymore, you know? And the people who made it home..." He trailed off.

"Your parents," I said carefully.

He nodded. "They think I'm dead. They buried me, grieved for me. What kind of person comes back from that?"

"Maybe the kind of person who found a reason to want to live again?"

The quiet way I said it made his eyes fill with something I couldn't identify.

"Erik..."

"I'm not saying you should or shouldn't," I said quickly. "Just that maybe having a reason to want to live is different than actually being dead."

Rafael Mercado

Eventually we had to get up and face the real world. I needed to prepare for whatever I did during the day, and Erik had to get back to his uncles' place before they started worrying.

"What do we tell them?" Erik asked as we got dressed. "About last night, about... whatever this is?"

His question made me pause. What were we, exactly? We'd had an incredibly intense conversation, reconnected tentatively, slept in the same bed, and agreed to be honest with each other. But defining it felt both premature and insufficient.

"We tell them we're... taking it one day at a time," I said finally. "That we care about each other and want to see where this goes."

"Even though we've only known each other for three days?"

"Even though," I agreed. "Because sometimes three days can change everything."

Erik nodded, looking thoughtful. "Are you nervous? About telling them?"

"Terrified," I admitted. "But not because I think they'll disapprove. Because it makes it real, you know? Talking about it with other people means we can't pretend it's not happening."

"Do you want to pretend it's not happening?"

"No," I said immediately. "Do you?"

"No. But I'm still scared."

"Me too."

~

Erik Eriksson

The tube journey back to central London was weird. Not bad weird, but definitely different from yesterday. Rafael sat beside me, and sometimes our hands would brush when the train rocked, and we'd both get sort of self-conscious about it.

"Can I ask you something?" I said as we got close to our stop.

"Sure."

"Last night, when you were telling me about... the hunting stuff... were you trying to scare me away?"

Rafael looked surprised. "No. Why would you think that?"

"I don't know. Maybe part of you thought it would be easier if I just ran."

"Erik, the last thing I wanted was for you to run. But I also couldn't keep lying to you."

"Even if the truth might drive me away?"

"Especially then."

~

Rafael Mercado

Looking at Erik as we approached Aleksander's building, I realized something had shifted between us overnight. Not into something defined or certain—we weren't ready for labels or promises. But into something more honest. More real.

"Ready?" Erik asked as we climbed the stairs.

"Not even close," I admitted. "But I guess we're doing it anyway."

"Yeah," he said with a shaky laugh. "We are."

Soren Jensen

I was grading papers at Aleksander's dining table when I heard voices in the hallway—Erik's laugh followed by a quieter response that had to be Rafael. When they entered the flat together, something in their body language immediately caught my attention.

Not the easy intimacy of an established couple, but something more tentative. More careful. Like they were still figuring out how to exist in the same space.

"Good morning," I said, looking up from my work. "How did everyone sleep?"

Erik Eriksson

I felt my face go red immediately. "Uh, good. Yeah. Fine."

Smooth, Erik. Really smooth.

Soren raised an eyebrow but didn't comment on my obvious awkwardness. "Rafael, you look... different. More rested."

"I am," Rafael said simply. "We had some... important conversations last night."

"The kind that needed privacy?" Aleksander asked, appearing from the kitchen with coffee.

Rafael Mercado

I could feel all three of them watching us, trying to figure out what had changed. The attention made me want to shrink into myself, to find the nearest exit, but Erik shifted slightly—not touching me, but close enough that I could feel his presence like support.

"Erik knows," I said, my voice coming out smaller than I'd intended. "About what I am. About... everything."

The relief in Aleksander's expression was immediate. "How are you handling it, Erik?"

Erik Eriksson

"Still figuring that out," I said honestly. "It's a lot to process, you know? But I'm not going anywhere."

The way Rafael's shoulders relaxed slightly when I said that made something warm spread through my chest.

"We're just... taking it one day at a time, I guess," I added. "Seeing how it goes."

Aleksander Nordh

Looking at them standing there—Erik unconsciously protective, Rafael cautiously hopeful—I felt something settle in my chest that I hadn't realized was tense. They were going to be okay. Not immediately, not without challenges, but they were going to figure it out.

"That sounds very wise," I said. "And if you need anything—advice, support, someone to talk through complications—you know we're here."

"Thank you," Rafael said, and for the first time since I'd known him, he seemed to really mean it.

It wasn't romantic or dramatic. But somehow, it felt like the most honest thing any of us could have said.

Soren Jensen

As I watched them settle into the morning routine—Erik helping with coffee, Rafael accepting inclusion with cautious gratitude—I realized we were witnessing something remarkable. Not a love story, exactly, not yet. But the beginning of something that could become one, built on honesty and mutual choice rather than fantasy.

And maybe that was the best kind of beginning there was.

34
MYTHS AND TRUTHS

FLAT 6, 84 VYNER STREET, LONDON E2 9DG

Rafael Mercado

The afternoon light filtered through my specially treated windows, casting everything in that soft golden glow that had become one of my favorite aspects of this flat. Erik had arranged himself on my sofa with the unconscious comfort of someone who belonged there, his long legs stretched out, one arm draped along the back cushions in an invitation I couldn't resist.

I settled beside him, close enough that our thighs touched, and felt something I hadn't experienced in over a decade: the simple pleasure of domestic intimacy. No performance, no careful management of distance, just... us.

"So," I said, turning to face him fully, "you said you wanted to understand everything about what I am. I meant what I said earlier—nothing is off the table. Ask me anything."

Erik Eriksson

The seriousness in Rafael's voice made me understand this wasn't just casual conversation. This was him offering me complete honesty about the most difficult parts of his existence. The trust implicit in that offer made my chest tight with affection.

"Anything?" I asked, settling more comfortably against the sofa cushions.

"Anything. The transformation, the biology, the feeding, the limitations—all of it. Better to know now than discover it later when it might cause problems between us."

I could see the vulnerability beneath his matter-of-fact tone, the fear that knowing the complete truth might change how I felt about him. But I'd already decided that wasn't possible.

"Alright," I said, taking his hand. "How long ago were you turned?"

THE TRANSFORMATION STORY

Rafael Mercado

"Eleven years ago. 2002. I was twenty-one, in my final year at University of Santo Tomas." The memories still carried weight, but telling Erik felt different from the careful recitations I'd given Aleksander over the years. "I was studying literature, completely focused on my academic work and my friendship with someone named Luke."

"Luke?"

"My best friend since we were thirteen. I was... well, I was in love with him, though I'd never told him. He was straight, charming, everything I wasn't confident enough to be."

Erik Eriksson

I could hear the old pain in Rafael's voice, but also something new—the ability to speak about loss without being consumed by it.

"Did you know who did it to you?" I asked.

"Professor Ibrahim Nazari. Ancient Regular vampire, over 2,500 years old. He taught classics at the university." Rafael's expression grew thoughtful. "I was one of his favorite students. We'd have these long discussions about literature and philosophy after class."

"Why did he choose you?"

Rafael Mercado

"I've wondered about that for eleven years," I said honestly. "Nazari was dying—well, reaching the natural end of his extraordinarily long life. His metabolism was failing. I think... I think he saw something in me that reminded him of himself when he was young. My love of beauty, perhaps. My intensity about ideas."

"Was it instant? The transformation?"

"God, no. It was horrific." I felt Erik's hand tighten in mine, offering comfort for something that had happened before he was even born. "He drugged my tea one evening, then performed the blood exchange at his private residence. The actual transformation took nearly six months."

Erik Eriksson

"Six months?" I couldn't hide my shock. "That sounds awful."

"It was. My father—he's a hematologist, ironically—took charge of my medical care. They ran every test imaginable, tried every treatment they could think of. Nothing worked, obviously, because they were trying to cure something that wasn't actually a disease."

Rafael Mercado

"The worst part was watching my parents' desperation. They never gave up, never stopped believing they could save me. My mother took a sabbatical from teaching to care for me personally. They maintained twenty-four-hour vigils during the worst periods."

"Did you know what was happening to you?"

"Not at first. Nazari died just weeks after the initial exchange, before he could explain much. I thought I was dying of some rare blood disorder. It wasn't until I met another vampire—Eliza Chen—that I learned the truth."

THE DIFFICULT QUESTIONS

Erik Eriksson

"When did you decide to stage your own death?"

Rafael was quiet for a long moment, his thumb tracing patterns on my hand. "When I realized I couldn't control the hunger anymore. When I understood that staying would mean either revealing what I'd become or accidentally hurting someone I loved. My parents thought I was recovering, getting better. How could I tell them I was becoming something that would have to feed on blood to survive?"

"How did you actually do it?"

"Eliza helped. We staged a suicide—left a note about psychological strain from the prolonged illness, created evidence suggesting my body was lost in Manila Bay. I couldn't bear to watch them grieve, but I observed the memorial service from a distance."

Rafael Mercado

The memory of that day still hurt, but sharing it with Erik somehow made it more bearable.

"The last time I saw them together was at the service. Luke gave this beautiful eulogy about friendship and all the things he'd wished he'd said while I was alive. I wanted to run to him, to tell him I was there, but..."

"But you couldn't."

"No. It would have destroyed everything—their healing, their ability to move forward, their memories of who I'd been before."

Erik Eriksson

"How did you get to London?"

"Eliza had connections. There's an informal network among Regular vampires for helping newly transformed individuals. Someone owed her a favor, and that person helped me establish a new identity and relocate."

"And money?"

Rafael actually smiled at this. "Carefully managed investments, mostly. Vampires tend to accumulate resources over time, and there are... discreet financial services that cater to our community's unique circumstances."

. . .

THE BIOLOGY LESSON

"Okay, now for the really important stuff," I said, grinning to lighten the mood. "Will you really burn up in the sun?"

Rafael Mercado

Erik's deliberate shift toward curiosity rather than sympathy made me laugh —actually laugh—for the first time in years.

"Not exactly burst into flames, but yes, UV radiation causes severe burns very quickly. Think of the worst sunburn you've ever seen, but happening in minutes rather than hours."

"Do you have fangs?"

I opened my mouth slightly, showing him the subtle changes to my canine teeth. "They're more pronounced than human teeth, but not the dramatic things you see in movies. More... efficient."

Erik Eriksson

"Would you accidentally bite me?" I asked, then felt my face burn with embarrassment. "I mean, if we were... you know... kissing or whatever..."

Rafael Mercado

His blush was absolutely adorable, and his practical concern touched something deep in my chest. "No, Erik. I have complete control over my feeding responses. They're not triggered by normal physical affection."

"Can you run really fast or disappear?"

"Enhanced speed and strength, yes. Nothing supernatural, just... optimized biology. And no disappearing, though I am very good at moving quietly."

"Levitation?"

"Absolutely not," I said, laughing again. "I'm not a magic trick."

Erik Eriksson

"Do you have a heartbeat?"

"Yes, though it's faster than yours due to accelerated metabolism." I guided his hand to my chest, letting him feel the rapid rhythm. "See?"

The simple contact sent warmth through both of us, and I found myself reluctant to move his hand away.

THE EMBARRASSING QUESTION

"I know this is embarrassing," I said, my face burning, "but... did it change anything... you know... down there?"

Rafael Mercado

Erik's mortification was so complete that I couldn't help but smile. The question was perfectly reasonable, even if asking it clearly wanted to make him disappear into the sofa cushions.

"No, everything functions normally," I said gently. "Enhanced stamina, perhaps, but otherwise completely typical."

"Enhanced stamina?" Erik squeaked.

"Enhanced everything, Erik. It's part of the accelerated metabolism."

Erik Eriksson

I buried my face in my hands, but I was grinning despite my embarrassment. "I can't believe I asked that."

"I'm glad you did. These are important things to know."

LONGEVITY AND SUSTENANCE

"How long will you live?"

Rafael Mercado

"Regular vampires typically live between 300 and 500 years. Some reportedly have lived longer. The professor was older, but I think he was an exception. We don't age physically in the same way, but our bodies do eventually... wear out, I suppose. It's hard to explain. Our cells regenerate quickly, I guess."

"And you really need human blood? You can't just get it from animals?"

"I can supplement with animal blood, and I do, but it's not sufficient long-term. I need human blood approximately twice a month, give or take, for complete nutrition."

"What about medical alternatives? Iron injections or something?"

I smiled at his hopeful expression. "I've tried everything, Erik. Synthetic alternatives, concentrated supplements, different animal sources. Nothing provides the specific nutrients my metabolism requires. Believe me, if I could find an alternative..."

Erik Eriksson

I could see this was one of the hardest aspects of his existence for Rafael to accept. The biological imperative that forced him to take something from others, even if he did it ethically.

"But you're careful about it. You choose people who... deserve it."

"I try to target criminals, people who hurt others. But Erik..." His expression grew serious. "I need you to understand that this makes me dangerous. Not to you, but to others. There's always the possibility that I might make a mistake, hurt someone innocent."

"Have you ever?"

"Not that I know of. But the risk is always there."

TURNING THE TABLES

Rafael Mercado

After two hours of patient answers to Erik's questions, I found myself curious about this remarkable boy who'd somehow decided to love me despite knowing exactly what I was.

"My turn," I said, shifting so I was facing him more directly. "English or Swedish—which is easier for you to speak?"

Erik Eriksson

"Swedish for emotion, English for ideas," I said without hesitation. "When I'm angry or really happy, I think in Swedish. But for academic stuff or talking about complex things, English feels more natural."

"What about next year? University?"

"I've been accepted to Uppsala, but..." I hesitated, suddenly uncertain. "That was before. Before you. I don't know what I want anymore."

Rafael Mercado

The admission that I'd already changed his life plans sent both warmth and worry through me. I never wanted to be the reason he limited his opportunities.

"What did you want to study?"

"Literature, like you did. Gothic literature specifically, with a focus on how folklore reflects cultural anxieties." Erik grinned. "Turns out I was more interested in the reality than I knew."

"And your dreams? What do you want to do with your life?"

Erik Eriksson

"I want to write," I said, the admission coming easier than it ever had before. "Novels, probably. Stories about people who don't fit into normal categories, who have to create their own definitions of family and belonging."

"Do you play any instruments?"

"Piano, though I'm not very good. I'm better with words than music."

Rafael Mercado

"Places you want to visit?"

"Everywhere. But especially places with complicated histories—Prague, Istanbul, New Orleans. Cities where different cultures have layered on top of each other for centuries."

"Your dream date?"

Erik blushed again, but answered seriously. "Wandering through a bookshop together, then dinner somewhere we can talk for hours without being interrupted. Maybe walking along a river at night, just... being together without having to perform for anyone else."

The simplicity of his answer, the way it perfectly matched my own desires, made my chest tight with affection.

THE SERIOUS QUESTIONS

Rafael Mercado

"Erik," I said, my voice growing more serious, "I need to ask you something difficult. What happens as you age and I don't? You'll be thirty, forty, fifty, and I'll still look exactly like this."

Erik Eriksson

I'd been wondering when this question would come up. It was the obvious problem with our relationship, the thing that made it seem impossible to outside observers.

"I don't know," I said honestly. "But Rafael, I can't live my life based on problems that might happen decades from now. I'd rather have however many years we can have together than spend them worrying about what comes after."

Rafael Mercado

His maturity, his willingness to face uncertainty with hope rather than fear, reminded me why I'd fallen for him so quickly.

"Do you ever want to get married? Really married, not just... whatever this is?"

"This isn't just whatever," Erik said firmly. "This is real, and yes, I want everything with you. Marriage, a life together, whatever we can build."

"Are we going too fast?"

Erik Eriksson

I considered the question seriously. Three days ago, I'd been a lonely teenager on a Swedish farm. Now I was living with my vampire boyfriend in London, making plans for a future I couldn't have imagined.

"Maybe," I said finally. "But fast doesn't mean wrong. And honestly? Being with you feels like the first time anything in my life has made complete sense."

Rafael Mercado

"Can you handle being in school for another year while we're apart?"

The question hung between us, heavy with implications. Erik's expression grew thoughtful, and I could see him working through possibilities I'd been afraid to voice.

"What if I didn't go to Uppsala?" he said slowly. "What if I took a gap year, or applied to universities in London instead?"

EVENING FALLS

Erik Eriksson

We'd been talking for hours, alternating between serious conversations and lighter moments, sometimes jumping up to get water or snacks, other times pulling each other in for spontaneous kisses when the discussion grew too intense. The afternoon had melted away without either of us noticing.

I was curled against Rafael's side, his arm around my shoulders, when I realized the light outside had faded to evening.

"I don't know how you did it," Rafael said quietly, his voice filled with wonder.

"Did what?"

"Made me not afraid of myself anymore. Made me remember who I used to be before everything went wrong."

Rafael Mercado

Looking down at Erik—this beautiful, impossible boy who'd somehow seen past every wall I'd built to something worth loving—I felt tears threaten for the second time in as many days.

"Why would I be afraid of you?" Erik asked, tilting his head to look at me directly.

"If I were you, I'd be scared shitless," I said honestly.

Erik Eriksson

I shifted so I could see his face properly, noting the genuine confusion in his expression.

"Rafael, you're the least frightening person I've ever met. You're gentle, you're careful with everyone around you, you think more about ethics than most humans I know. You've told me about every single thing that makes you different, and none of it makes me want to run away."

Rafael Mercado

"But I'm a predator, Erik. I hunt. I take blood from people to survive."

"You're selective about it. You target people who hurt others. And you do it as carefully as possible." Erik's voice grew firmer. "You know what scares me? The idea that you might still think you're a monster when you're obviously not."

Erik Eriksson

I leaned up and kissed him, tasting the salt of tears I hadn't realized were falling.

"You're not a monster," I whispered against his lips. "You're just Rafael. And Rafael is exactly who I want to be with."

As London settled into evening outside our windows, I realized that somewhere in the span of an afternoon filled with questions and answers, we'd moved past the careful politeness of new love into something deeper. We knew each other now—really knew each other—and somehow that only made what we felt stronger.

Rafael Mercado

Looking down at Erik—this beautiful, impossible boy who'd somehow seen past every wall I'd built to something worth loving—I felt my chest tighten with an emotion so powerful it almost stopped my breath. The words rose in my throat, three simple syllables that would change everything between us.

I love you.

But even as the phrase pressed against my lips, desperate to be spoken, I couldn't quite release it. Not yet. Not when he was still processing everything I'd told him, still reconciling the gentle man he'd fallen for with the predator I'd revealed myself to be.

Holding Erik as darkness fell over the city, listening to his steady heartbeat against my chest, I felt something I'd thought lost forever: hope for a future that included not just survival, but happiness. Real, uncomplicated, impossible happiness.

For the first time in eleven years, I wasn't afraid of what I was. I was grateful for it, because it had brought me here, to this moment, to him.

And that changed everything.

35
BEFORE THE DAWN

FLAT 6, 84 VYNER STREET, LONDON E2 9DG

Rafael Mercado

I stood in my kitchen, surveying the preparations with the kind of nervous energy I hadn't felt in over a decade. The dining table was set with my best china —pieces I'd acquired over the years but never had occasion to use. Candles flickered throughout the flat, casting warm light that reflected off the exposed brick walls and made everything feel more intimate than usual.

It was Erik's last night in London, and I'd insisted on hosting a proper celebration. His seventeenth birthday dinner, even though we'd already acknowledged the milestone. But I wanted—needed—to give him something special, something that marked this moment as significant. Our first time entertaining as a couple. Our first time welcoming family into our shared space.

"It looks perfect," Erik said, appearing at my elbow with the wine glasses I'd asked him to arrange. "Though you know they'll be happy just to be here with us, right?"

Erik Eriksson

Rafael had been adorably anxious all afternoon, adjusting place settings and rearranging flowers like he was hosting royalty instead of our uncles. But I understood the significance of this evening for him. After years of careful isolation, he was choosing to open his sanctuary to family, to celebrate rather than simply endure.

"I know," he said, his hand finding mine automatically. "But I want this to be special. For you, yes, but also... I've never had the chance to share this space with people who matter. It feels important."

The simple honesty in his voice made my chest tight with affection. I leaned in to kiss his cheek, tasting the hint of expensive cologne he'd applied earlier.

"They already love you," I reminded him. "Just like I do."

THE ARRIVAL

Aleksander Nordh

The transformation in Rafael's bearing was immediately apparent when he opened the door to welcome us. Gone was the careful distance, the polite reserve that had characterized our previous interactions. In its place was genuine warmth, the relaxed confidence of someone comfortable in his own space with people he cared about.

"Aleksander, Soren," he said, stepping back to gesture us inside. "Welcome. Thank you for coming."

"Thank you for having us," I replied, offering the bottle of wine I'd selected for the evening. "This is quite an honor."Soren Jensen

Rafael's flat was even more impressive than Erik had described. The combination of industrial architecture and elegant furnishings created an atmosphere that was both sophisticated and welcoming. But what struck me most was how clearly it had become a shared space—Erik's presence was evident in small details that spoke of domestic harmony.

"This is extraordinary," I said, taking in the soaring ceilings and carefully curated art. "Erik wasn't exaggerating when he said it was like a private museum."

"One that's finally being lived in properly," Rafael replied, his eyes finding Erik across the room. The look that passed between them carried such obvious affection that I felt almost intrusive witnessing it.

DINNER CONVERSATION

Erik Eriksson

We settled around Rafael's dining table as the sun set over London, the conversation flowing as easily as the wine Rafael had allowed me to share. Aleksander regaled us with stories of his various university experiences across the centuries, while Soren shared updates from his thesis research and news from his family in Minneapolis.

"My mother sends her love," Soren told me, raising his glass. "She's already planning care packages for when you start university, wherever that ends up being."

Rafael Mercado

Watching Erik laugh at Soren's stories about American family dynamics, seeing him engage with Aleksander's historical anecdotes with genuine curiosity, reinforced what I'd come to understand about his character. He had this remarkable ability to make everyone feel heard, valued, included. It was a gift that had drawn me to him from our first meeting.

"Speaking of university," Aleksander said, his tone carefully casual, "have you given more thought to your plans for next year?"

Erik Eriksson

I glanced at Rafael, noting the slight tension that entered his posture at the question. We'd discussed this extensively over the past week, weighing options and possibilities that would have seemed impossible just days ago.

"I've decided to defer Uppsala for a year," I said, my voice steady despite the magnitude of what I was announcing. "I want to apply to universities here in London instead."

Soren Jensen

The silence that followed Erik's announcement was heavy with implications. I could see Aleksander processing the decision, weighing its wisdom and practical challenges. Across the table, Rafael looked stunned, as if he hadn't quite believed Erik would actually choose to uproot his entire life plan.

"That's... quite a significant change," Aleksander said carefully. "Are you certain it's what you want?"

"I've never been more certain of anything," Erik replied, reaching for Rafael's hand. "I know it seems impulsive, but this feels right. More right than any plan I've ever made."

THE SMALL DETAILS

Aleksander Nordh

As the evening progressed, I found myself cataloging the small intimacies that marked Erik and Rafael as a genuine couple. The way Rafael automatically refilled Erik's wine glass before his own. The way Erik unconsciously adjusted his position to stay within Rafael's reach. The countless tiny gestures that spoke of comfort and consideration.

It was when Erik reached for the bread that I noticed it—a simple silver band on his right ring finger that definitely hadn't been there when he'd arrived in London.

"Erik," I said, curiosity getting the better of diplomatic restraint, "that's a lovely ring."

Soren Jensen

I followed Aleksander's gaze and immediately spotted what he'd noticed. The ring was understated but clearly significant—not expensive enough to be an engagement ring, but meaningful enough to mark some kind of commitment.

Erik's face flushed slightly, but he didn't try to hide his hand. "Rafael gave it to me yesterday. A early birthday present, he said, though I think it was really a promise."

"What kind of promise?" I asked gently.

Erik Eriksson

I looked at Rafael, seeing the same mixture of nervousness and hope in his expression that I felt in my chest. We hadn't planned to announce this tonight, but somehow it felt right to share it with family.

"That we're serious about this," I said simply. "About each other, about making this work despite all the complications. It's not an engagement ring—we're not that impulsive—but it's a promise that we want to build something together."

Rafael Mercado

The ring had been an impulse purchase, something I'd seen in a small shop near my flat and immediately known was perfect. Simple, elegant, durable enough to last. When I'd given it to Erik, I'd struggled to explain what it meant—not a proposal, but not nothing either. A marker of intent, perhaps. A visible reminder that he was chosen, claimed, loved.

"It's beautiful," Aleksander said warmly. "And remarkably appropriate. You two move together like you've known each other for years."

"Old souls," Soren added with a grin. "Both of you. It's like you were waiting for each other without knowing it."

THE EVENING WINDS DOWN

As we moved to the sitting area for dessert and coffee, I found myself marveling at how natural this felt. Having family in my space, sharing conversation and laughter, playing host instead of carefully maintained guest. Erik had transformed more than just my personal life—he'd made me remember who I'd been before fear and isolation had redefined me.

"This has been lovely," Soren said as the evening began to wind down. "Thank you for sharing your home with us, Rafael. It's been an honor."

"The honor has been mine," I replied, meaning it completely.

Aleksander Nordh

As we prepared to leave, I found myself genuinely reluctant to end the evening. The warmth of Rafael and Erik's hospitality, the easy domesticity of their shared space, the obvious contentment they'd found in each other—all of it reinforced my belief that some connections transcended logic or convenience.

"We'll collect you at ten tomorrow morning?" I said to Erik, though the practical question felt heavy with unspoken emotion.

"Actually," Rafael said quietly, "I'd like to come to the airport as well. If that's alright."

. . .

Soren Jensen

The request caught me slightly off guard, though it shouldn't have. Of course Rafael would want to see Erik off personally, to have those final moments together before the separation.

"Of course," I said immediately. "That would be lovely."

UNEXPECTED AFFECTION

Rafael Mercado

As we reached the door, something inside me shifted. Maybe it was the wine, or the warmth of the evening, or simply the recognition that these people had become genuinely important to me. But when Soren leaned in for what I expected to be a polite handshake goodbye, I found myself pulling him into a proper embrace instead.

"Thank you," I whispered against his ear. "For accepting me. For welcoming me into your family."

Soren Jensen

Rafael's unexpected hug caught me completely off guard, but in the best possible way. This was the first time he'd initiated physical contact with anyone other than Erik, and the trust implicit in the gesture made my throat tight with emotion.

"Thank you for making Erik so happy," I whispered back. "And for letting us be part of this."

Aleksander Nordh

When Rafael turned to me with the same open affection, I felt something settle in my chest that I hadn't realized was tense. Over the months I'd known Rafael, I'd respected his boundaries, his need for distance and control. Having him choose to embrace me—literally and figuratively—felt like a profound gift.

"Take care of him tomorrow," Rafael said quietly as we held each other. "And take care of yourself. You're precious to all of us now."

Erik Eriksson

Watching Rafael say goodbye to my uncles with such genuine warmth made my heart swell with pride and love. This was the man I'd fallen for—not the carefully controlled vampire he presented to the world, but the loving, generous person he'd been before circumstances forced him into isolation.

"He's always been like this," I said as Aleksander and Soren headed down the stairs. "Loving, I mean. He just needed to remember it was safe to show it."

ALONE AGAIN

Rafael Mercado

After the door closed behind them, the flat felt strangely quiet despite Erik's presence. The evening had been perfect—exactly what I'd hoped for—but now reality was reasserting itself. Tomorrow, Erik would be gone. Tomorrow, I would be alone again.

"Hey," Erik said softly, appearing beside me as I stood staring at the closed door. "What's wrong?"

I turned to face him, this beautiful boy who'd somehow transformed my entire existence in the span of a week, and felt tears threaten.

"I wasn't sure I wanted to meet you," I said quietly. "And now I can't stand the idea of you leaving."

Erik Eriksson

The vulnerability in Rafael's voice, the way he was struggling not to cry, made my own throat tight with emotion. I reached for him, pulling him close until his head rested against my shoulder.

"I'll visit," I said, my voice muffled against his hair. "And you'll visit me. Right?"

"Yes, of course. It's not that far."

"And we'll call and email and text constantly," I continued, trying to convince both of us that distance was manageable.

"Don't make me cry," Rafael warned, though his voice was already thick with tears.

"Too late," I said, feeling my own tears start to fall. "I already am."

THE QUESTION

Erik Eriksson

We stood holding each other in the soft light of Rafael's flat, both of us trying to memorize the moment before tomorrow changed everything. But gradually, the sadness began to transform into something else—urgency, perhaps, or simply the recognition that we had tonight before we had to face separation.

"Raf?" I said softly.

"Yes?"

"Can I... kiss you?"

Rafael Mercado

The question, asked with the same careful politeness Erik had shown me from our first evening together, made me smile despite my tears.

"Yes," I whispered, tilting my face up to meet his.

Erik Eriksson

The kiss was salt-sweet with tears and desperate with the knowledge that we had limited time. When we broke apart, both breathing harder, I found the courage to ask for what I'd been wanting all week.

"Can I..." I began, then stopped, suddenly shy despite everything we'd shared.

"What?" Rafael asked gently.

"Do more?" The words came out in a rush, followed immediately by doubt.

"Really? You're sure?"

Rafael Mercado

Erik's nervous hopefulness, the way he asked rather than assumed, reminded me of all the reasons I'd fallen for him so quickly. But his question also stirred anxiety I'd been trying to ignore.

"Yes," I said, meaning it completely. "Although... I have something to confess."

"What?"

"I'm a virgin," I said, the admission coming out smaller than I'd intended. "So I don't really know what to do."

THE CONFESSION

Erik Eriksson

Rafael's confession caught me completely off guard, though it shouldn't have. He'd been transformed at twenty-one, and his life since then had been marked by isolation and careful distance from human connection. Of course he wouldn't have had the opportunity for physical intimacy.

"It's been a long time since I even thought I'd be...." Rafael continued, his cheeks flushed with embarrassment. "But I promise, we'll figure it out together."

The tenderness in his voice, the way he was offering to guide me despite his own inexperience, made love bloom even stronger in my chest.

"No fangs!" I said suddenly, then burst into laughter at my own joke.

Rafael Mercado

Erik's unexpected humor, his ability to find lightness even in vulnerable moments, reminded me why I'd felt safe enough to love him in the first place. His laughter was infectious, and soon we were both giggling like the young people we were despite everything that made our situation extraordinary.

"No fangs!" I promised, pulling him closer. "Just us."

Erik Eriksson

"Just us," I agreed, and let Rafael lead me toward his bedroom, toward whatever waited for us in the gentle darkness of our last night together.

. . .

TENDERNESS AND PASSION

Rafael Mercado

What followed was everything I'd dreamed of but never dared to expect—gentle discovery mixed with urgent need, careful exploration tempered by desperate affection. Erik was beautiful in his nervousness, trusting in his vulnerability, generous in ways that took my breath away.

We learned each other slowly, patiently, with the kind of attention that transformed physical intimacy into something approaching worship. Every touch was deliberate, every kiss a promise, every whispered endearment a declaration of love that transcended species and circumstance.

Erik Eriksson

Rafael's hands were cool against my skin but warmed quickly under my touch. His enhanced strength meant he could lift and position me effortlessly, but he used that power with such careful gentleness that I never felt anything but cherished. When he whispered my name against my neck, when he guided me through discoveries that made my entire body sing, I understood for the first time what it meant to be completely, thoroughly loved.

Rafael Mercado

Afterward, we lay tangled together in the darkness, Erik's head on my chest, his breathing gradually slowing toward sleep. The reality of his departure tomorrow felt distant and manageable in the cocoon of post-intimacy contentment.

"Jag älskar dig," he whispered against my skin, the words vibrating through my chest in the musical cadence of his native tongue.

The Swedish phrase washed over me like a baptism I didn't fully understand but could feel in my bones. Though I didn't speak the language, the tenderness in Erik's voice, the way the words seemed to pour from somewhere deep inside him, made their meaning unmistakable. This was love spoken in its purest form—unguarded, unthinking, coming from a place so genuine he'd forgotten to translate.

I remained perfectly still, not wanting to break the spell of this moment, watching his face in the darkness as the reality of what he'd said seemed to dawn on him.

Erik's eyes fluttered open, and I saw the exact moment he realized what had happened. A soft smile spread across his features, shy but unashamed.

"Sorry," he whispered, his cheeks warming against my chest. "I said... jag älskar dig. It means..." He lifted his head to look at me directly. "I love you."

The simple phrase hit me like a revelation, like sunlight breaking through storm clouds after eleven years of darkness. Hearing it first in Swedish—the language of his heart, his childhood, his truest self—and then offered again in English like a gift meant specifically for me, made something inside me crack open completely.

"Jag... jag ahl-skar..." I stumbled over the unfamiliar sounds, my accent mangling the beautiful phrase he'd spoken so naturally.

Erik's face lit up like sunrise, his eyes bright with delighted surprise. "Oh, Rafael," he breathed, sitting up slightly. "Say it again, but softer on the 'ahl'—jag *EHL*-skar dig."

"Jag EHL-skar..." I tried again, concentrating on the shape of the words in my mouth.

"Dig," Erik finished gently, his hand coming up to cup my cheek. "Jag älskar dig."

"Jag älskar dig," I repeated, finally getting the pronunciation right. The foreign words felt strange on my tongue but somehow perfect, like they carried a weight that English couldn't match. "Jag älskar dig, Erik."

His smile was radiant in the darkness. "You said it perfectly."

"I love you too," I added in English, my fingers stroking through his hair. "More than I thought possible. More than I ever thought I deserved."

"You deserve everything," Erik murmured sleepily, settling back against my chest. "Every good thing."

After over a decade, lying there with this extraordinary boy in my arms, I almost believed him.

Erik Eriksson

I settled back against Rafael's chest, but something occurred to me. The way he'd tried so hard to say "I love you" in Swedish, stumbling through the unfamiliar sounds just to meet me in my own language—it touched something deep inside me.

"Rafael?" I whispered.

"Mmm?"

"How do you say 'I love you' in... in your language? From home?"

I felt his breath catch, his entire body going still beneath me. The silence stretched so long I worried I'd said something wrong.

Rafael Mercado

From home.

The simple phrase hit me like a physical blow. For eleven years, I'd avoided thinking of Manila as home, had trained myself to think of it as my past, my former life, something I'd lost access to forever. The language of my childhood, my parents, my culture—I'd buried it all along with my human identity, convinced it belonged to someone who no longer existed.

But here was Erik, asking me to share something from *home*. Not my past, not my former life, but home. As if that part of me wasn't dead, wasn't lost, but simply waiting to be invited back into the light.

"Mahal kita," I whispered, saying the words aloud after so many years of silence felt like coming back to life. The Tagalog flowed from my lips with a musical quality I'd forgotten I possessed, carrying with it the warmth of tropical afternoons, my mother's laughter, my father's gentle corrections of my pronunciation when I was small.

"But Erik, you don't need to—" I started, overwhelmed by the flood of memories and emotions.

Erik Eriksson

"Mahal kita," I repeated carefully, testing the sounds. Something about the way Rafael had gone so quiet, the way I could feel tension in his entire body, told me this meant more to him than I'd understood. "Is that right?"

Rafael Mercado

"Yes," I whispered, my voice breaking slightly. "Yes, that's... that's perfect."

For the first time in eleven years, someone was learning words from my true home not out of academic curiosity or casual interest, but out of love. Erik was asking for these words because he wanted to love me in the language my parents had taught me, in the sounds that had shaped my earliest understanding of affection.

Erik Eriksson

"Mahal kita, Rafael," I said again, more confidently this time, lifting my head to look at him in the darkness. "I wanted to say it in your language too."

Rafael Mercado

The way he said my name after those precious words—*mahal kita, Rafael*—nearly broke me completely. I pulled him closer, unable to speak for a moment as eleven years of careful separation from my Filipino identity crumbled in the face of this generous, loving gesture.

He wasn't just reciprocating my attempt at Swedish. He was offering me a bridge back to the part of myself I'd thought was lost forever, making my heritage part of our love story instead of something I had to hide or mourn.

Erik Eriksson

The way his face crumpled with emotion, the way he pulled me closer like he couldn't believe what he was hearing, told me I'd just given him something he hadn't expected to receive. Not just love returned, but something deeper.

As I drifted toward sleep in Rafael's arms, surrounded by his scent and the steady rhythm of his heartbeat, I felt something settle deeply within. The exchange of "I love you" in both our native tongues had created something sacred between us—a bridge that honored both our cultures, both our hearts, and, I suspected, somehow helped Rafael find his way back to parts of himself he'd thought were gone forever.

Whatever challenges tomorrow bring, whatever difficulties we'd face in the coming months, this moment was ours. This love was real—proven not just in words but in our willingness to seek out each other's languages, creating something beautiful from what had once been sources of pain and separation.

And that was enough to face anything.

36
DEPARTURES AND PROMISES

HEATHROW AIRPORT TERMINAL 5, LONGFORD TW6 2GA, UNITED KINGDOM

Erik Eriksson

Heathrow at ten in the morning hummed with the efficient chaos of international travel—families reuniting, business travelers checking phones, tourists dragging oversized luggage toward check-in counters. But standing in the departure hall with Rafael, Aleksander, and Soren, everything else felt distant and irrelevant.

"I hate this," I said quietly, my hand firmly linked with Rafael's as we watched the departure board update flight information. "I know it's only a few months until the wedding, but it feels like forever."

Rafael Mercado

Erik's words echoed my own thoughts exactly. Three months until we would see each other again at the Swedish wedding celebration. Twelve weeks. Ninety-one days. The numbers felt simultaneously manageable and impossible.

"It will go faster than you think," I said, trying to convince both of us. "University applications will keep you busy, and I have..." I paused, realizing I didn't actually know what I would do to fill the time. For over a decade, time had simply passed. Now I would need to actively live through it.

"You'll have us," Soren said gently, understanding my hesitation. "Wedding planning, family dinners, probably more research projects than you bargained for."

Aleksander Nordh

Watching Erik and Rafael navigate this first separation reminded me painfully of my own farewell to Mikael over a century ago. But there was something fundamentally different about this goodbye—it carried hope rather than finality, plans rather than resignation. These two were choosing temporary separation to build a sustainable future together.

"Erik, they're calling for boarding," I said softly, noting the announcement echoing through the terminal.

THE LETTER

Rafael Mercado

I reached into my jacket pocket and withdrew the envelope I'd been carrying since early morning—cream-colored paper with Erik's name written in my careful script.

"I have something for you," I said, pressing the letter into his hands. "But you have to promise not to read it until you're in the air. Really promise."

Erik Eriksson

The envelope felt substantial in my hands, and I could see the care Rafael had taken with the presentation. Whatever was inside, it mattered to him.

"I promise," I said solemnly. "But Rafael, you don't need to—"

"I wanted to," he interrupted. "Something for you to have when you're feeling uncertain about any of this."

I tucked the letter carefully into my carry-on bag, already anticipating the moment when I could finally read his words.

GOODBYE

Erik Eriksson

When the final boarding call came, the reality of leaving hit me with unexpected force. I turned to Aleksander and Soren first, embracing each of them with gratitude that felt too large for words.

"Thank you," I said to Aleksander. "For bringing me here, for introducing me to Rafael, for making me part of your family."

"Thank you for reminding us what family really means," he replied, his voice thick with emotion.

Rafael Mercado

Watching Erik say goodbye to his uncles gave me time to compose myself, to find the words I needed for our own farewell. When he finally turned to me, I saw my own mix of sadness and hope reflected in his eyes.

"This isn't goodbye," I said firmly, taking his hands in mine. "This is 'see you soon.'"

"See you soon," Erik agreed, leaning down to kiss me one last time.

The kiss was gentle, careful of our public location but unmistakably loving. When we broke apart, I could see tears threatening in his eyes that matched my own.

"Go," I whispered. "Before I change my mind and kidnap you."

Erik Eriksson

I squeezed Rafael's hands one final time, memorizing the feel of his fingers intertwined with mine, then forced myself to walk toward the boarding gate. At the entrance, I turned back for one last look.

Rafael stood between Aleksander and Soren, their hands on his shoulders in a gesture of support that spoke volumes about how our family had grown. He raised his hand in a small wave, and I could see him mouth the words "I love you" across the distance.

I mouthed it back, then disappeared into the jetbridge.

AFTER THE DEPARTURE

Aleksander Nordh

Rafael stood perfectly still for several minutes after Erik disappeared from view, staring at the boarding gate as if he could will the plane to bring Erik back. I could see him struggling with the impulse to retreat into the careful isolation that had protected him for so long.

"Right," I said briskly, making the decision for all of us. "I know exactly what we're doing today."

Rafael Mercado

I turned to look at Aleksander, noting the determined expression that suggested he'd already made plans I wasn't going to be consulted about.

"I should head back to my flat," I said automatically. "I have things to—"

The words died as I realized what I was doing. Retreating into isolation, the same way I had eleven years ago when pain became too much to bear. When I'd left Manila, I'd told myself that disappearing was noble self-sacrifice. Now I could see it for what it had always been: the desperate attempt of someone who had never learned that love could survive difficulty.

Erik was gone for three months, not three lifetimes. He was returning to family who loved him, not fleeing from someone he could no longer bear to see. This separation had an end date and a purpose, unlike the permanent exile I'd chosen in Manila.

"No," Soren interrupted firmly. "Absolutely not. You're spending the day with us."

Aleksander Nordh

"There's a new exhibition at the Tate Modern I think you'd find fascinating," I said, already guiding Rafael toward the airport exit. "Contemporary artists exploring themes of transformation and identity. Quite relevant, actually."

I could see Rafael processing the suggestion, part of him wanting to accept the distraction while another part clung to the familiar comfort of solitude.

"And there's this little club I know," I continued. "Very quiet, very sophisticated. Perfect for afternoon drinks and conversation."

"You two don't have to babysit me," Rafael said, though his protests lacked conviction.

"We're not babysitting," Soren said with a grin. "We're selfishly claiming your company because we enjoy it."

EXHIBITION

Rafael Mercado

The Tate Modern's newest exhibition was exactly the kind of thoughtful, challenging art I'd always gravitated toward—pieces that explored the boundaries between human and other, traditional and transformed. Standing before a particularly striking sculpture that seemed to shift and change depending on the viewing angle, I found myself thinking about my own transformation in new ways.

"It's about becoming rather than being," I murmured, studying the artist's statement. "The process rather than the result."

Soren Jensen

Rafael's engagement with the art was immediate and profound. I watched him move through the gallery with the kind of focused attention that suggested the pieces were speaking to something deep in his experience.

"That resonates with you," I observed, joining him in front of a painting that depicted figures caught between states of existence.

"I've spent so long thinking of my transformation as an ending," Rafael said quietly. "The end of my human life, the end of my family connections, the end of who I used to be. But maybe it was actually a beginning."

Aleksander Nordh

Rafael's words struck me with unexpected force. After centuries of viewing my own transformation as simply the starting point of an extended existence, hearing him frame it as a beginning rather than an ending offered a perspective I'd never considered.

"Erik sees it that way," I said gently. "Not as what you lost, but as what you became."

"Yes," Rafael agreed, a smile playing at the corners of his mouth. "He does."

THE CALL

Rafael Mercado

We were settled at a quiet table in Aleksander's club—a sophisticated space that felt like a gentleman's library crossed with an art gallery—when my phone rang. Erik's name on the display made my heart skip.

"Excuse me," I said, stepping away from the table to take the call.

"Rafael!" Erik's voice, slightly distorted by the international connection but unmistakably cheerful, filled my ear. "I'm home safe. The flight was fine, and Mormor and Morfar are so excited to hear about everything."

Erik Eriksson

Hearing Rafael's voice, even through the phone, made the distance between us feel temporarily manageable. I was sitting in the farmhouse kitchen where I'd grown up, surrounded by familiar sights and sounds, but all I wanted was to be back in London.

"I read your letter," I said, settling into the chair by the window. "Rafael, it was beautiful. I'm going to keep it forever."

"I meant every word," Rafael's voice came through warm and certain. "Especially the parts about our future."

Rafael Mercado

The happiness in Erik's voice, the obvious joy he took in simply talking to me, sent warmth through my chest that had nothing to do with the club's fireplace.

"Tell me about your grandparents' reaction," I said, settling back into the conversation. "Did they take the news about university plans well?"

Erik Eriksson

"Better than I expected," I replied honestly. "Mormor cried a little, but happy tears, I think. And Morfar just said that if London makes me happy, then London is where I should be."

"And your application plans?"

"I'm meeting with my guidance counselor on Monday to discuss the process. King's College, UCL, Imperial... I want to apply to several programs so we have options."

HEART-TO-HEART

Aleksander Nordh

After Rafael finished his call with Erik, he returned to our table with a smile that transformed his entire face. The careful control he'd maintained during Erik's departure had given way to genuine happiness.

"He's safely home," Rafael reported, settling back into his chair. "And apparently his grandparents are supportive of his London plans."

"That's wonderful news," I said, then decided it was time for the conversation I'd been planning all day. "Rafael, there are some things I'd like to discuss with you. About Erik, about your relationship, about the challenges ahead."

Rafael Mercado

Aleksander's tone was gentle but serious, and I could see him choosing his words carefully. I braced myself for concerns about the speed of our relationship, warnings about the complications of cross-species love.

"I'm listening," I said.

Aleksander Nordh

"Erik is seventeen," I began, then quickly continued before Rafael could interpret this as criticism. "Which means he's at a crucial point in his development—university decisions, career planning, figuring out his place in the world. These are significant pressures even without adding a relationship that spans countries and species."

"I'm aware of that," Rafael said quietly.

"I'm sure you are. But I want you to know that Soren and I are committed to helping both of you navigate these challenges. Erik's family situation is...

complicated. His parents' ongoing conflicts have left him feeling displaced, uncertain about where he belongs."

I paused, choosing my words carefully. "What's interesting is how similarly you both respond to separation. Most seventeen-year-olds, even in serious-looking relationships, don't react to temporary distance with quite this level of... intensity."

Rafael Mercado

I could hear the concern in Aleksander's voice, the protective instinct that had made him such a thoughtful uncle to Erik.

"What are you asking me to do?" I said carefully.

"Nothing except what you're already doing," Aleksander replied. "Love him, support him, be patient with the process of building a life together across distance and difference. But also know that you're not alone in this. We're here to help—with university applications, with travel arrangements, with family negotiations, with whatever obstacles arise."

Soren Jensen

I could see Rafael processing Aleksander's words, and I realized this was my moment to add my own perspective.

"Rafael," I said, leaning forward, "what Aleksander is trying to say is that family helps family navigate difficult paths. And sometimes that means accepting help even when you're used to handling everything alone."

"You and Erik understand each other in a way that goes deeper than typical romantic connection," I continued thoughtfully. "You've both experienced abandonment by the people who should be there unconditionally. Erik's parents chose their careers over raising him. You were forced to abandon your family to protect them. Both of you know what it feels like to be cut off from home."

I exchanged a glance with Aleksander. "I'd wager, that shared understanding of displacement... it's probably part of what created such an immediate bond between you."

Rafael Mercado

Soren's words hit me with unexpected force. I could see the truth of what he was describing in Aleksander's face, the way his expression softened as Soren spoke about their relationship.

"Being part of this family," Soren continued, "being a Jensen, even by choice rather than blood—it means you don't have to face challenges alone anymore. It means there are people who want to help you succeed, who celebrate your happiness, who'll stand with you when things get difficult."

Aleksander Nordh

Watching Rafael's reaction to Soren's words, seeing the emotion building in his eyes, I realized my fiancé had found exactly the right approach. Rafael needed to understand that accepting help wasn't weakness—it was what families did for each other.

"What Soren is saying," I added gently, "is that love—real love—creates networks of support. Your relationship with Erik doesn't exist in isolation. It's part of a larger web of connections that includes all of us."

Rafael Mercado

I felt tears threatening as the full weight of what they were offering hit me. Not just tolerance for my relationship with Erik, but active support. Not just acceptance of what I was, but celebration of who I was becoming.

"Thank you," I managed, my voice thick with emotion. "Both of you. I've spent so long thinking I had to handle everything alone that I'd forgotten what it felt like to have people care about my happiness."

"You'll never have to handle anything alone again," Soren said firmly. "That's what family means."

EVENING REFLECTIONS

Soren Jensen

Later that evening, as Aleksander and I settled into bed in his flat, I found myself reflecting on the day's events. Seeing Rafael laugh at the gallery, watching him light up during Erik's phone call, witnessing his emotional response to our offer of support—all of it reinforced my belief that love really could transform everything.

"Today went well," I said, curling against Aleksander's side. "Rafael seemed genuinely happy."

"He did," Aleksander agreed, his fingers stroking through my hair. "It's remarkable what love can accomplish. A week ago, he could barely tolerate social interaction. Today he spent the entire day with us and seemed to enjoy every moment."

Aleksander Nordh

"Speaking of transformation," I said, an idea that had been building all day finally crystallizing, "there are some things I'd like to discuss with you as well."

"Oh?" Soren tilted his head to look at me, curiosity evident in his expression.

"Several things, actually. The wedding timeline, my family's schedule, and a personal request I've been wanting to make."

WEDDING PLANS

Soren Jensen

I settled more comfortably against Aleksander's chest, recognizing the tone that meant he'd been thinking seriously about logistics and timelines.

"Tell me about the wedding schedule first," I said. "June will be here before we know it."

Aleksander Nordh

"The Swedish celebration is all arranged," I began. "June 21st, midsummer, at the farm with both our families. Your parents are thrilled, Connor and Maja are planning to make a documentary of the entire event, and your extended family is treating it like the reunion of the century."

"And the Minnesota families?"

"Everyone is booked for Stockholm, though some needed assistance with travel costs. I've found some creative ways to help without making anyone feel like charity cases." I paused, smiling at the memory of the conversations I'd had with various Jensen relatives. "Your great-aunt Susan thinks I'm 'that lovely European boy with excellent manners,' and she's already planning to adopt me officially."

Soren Jensen

I laughed, imagining Aunt Susan's reaction to Aleksander's old-world courtesy. "She's going to love you. But what about your family? When are we doing the second ceremony?"

Aleksander Nordh

"October," I said, noting how Soren's body tensed slightly at the mention of my parents. "They've decided autumn would be ideal—better weather than summer, and it gives us time to recover from the Swedish festivities."

"And they're... they're alright with you marrying a human?"

The vulnerability in Soren's voice made my chest tight with protective affection. After all these months together, he still worried about acceptance from my family.

"Soren," I said gently, turning so I could look at him directly, "my parents are over four thousand years old. They've seen empires rise and fall, watched countless species evolve and adapt. The idea that love transcends species boundaries is not shocking to them—it's simply reality."

Soren Jensen

"But they've never met me," I said quietly. "What if they think I'm too young, too inexperienced, too... human?"

Aleksander Nordh

"Then they'll spend five minutes in your company and realize what I realized the first time we met," I said firmly. "That you're extraordinary. That you're exactly what their son needs. That you make me happier than I've been in over two millennia."

I paused, then added with a slight smile, "Besides, my mother has been pestering me to find a partner for centuries. She's so relieved I've finally chosen someone that she would accept anyone, but the fact that it's you—someone she can already tell makes me happy—has her absolutely delighted."

"But first," I said, "there's something practical we should discuss about the

Sweden trip. Rafael's been trying to plan everything himself, but I think he could use some assistance."

I paused, choosing my words carefully. "The duration of the stay, the rural location... have you considered how he'll manage his dietary requirements there?"

Soren looked puzzled for a moment before understanding dawned. "Oh. That's... that would be much more challenging than London, wouldn't it?"

"Exactly. Fewer people, and in a small community, any unusual behavior gets noticed quickly. I wanted to offer my assistance with the practical arrangements."

"That's really thoughtful of you, Alek. I bet he's been worried about it."

"Family helps family," I said simply. "And frankly, I'm better equipped to handle these logistics discreetly."

THE REQUEST

"Which brings me to my personal request," I said, suddenly feeling nervous in a way I hadn't experienced since our early days together.

"What kind of request?" Soren asked, though I could see him bracing for something significant.

"I would like you to move in with me," I said simply. "Officially. Permanently. Make this our home rather than just my flat where you happen to spend most nights."

Soren Jensen

The request caught me off guard, though it shouldn't have. We'd been spending nearly every night together for months, and most of my belongings had gradually migrated to Aleksander's flat anyway.

"What brought this on?" I asked, though I thought I already knew the answer.

Aleksander Nordh

"Watching Rafael and Erik," I admitted. "Seeing how naturally they created a shared space, how they moved around each other like they'd been living together for years rather than days. It made me realize I've been unfairly hesitant about asking you to fully commit to sharing a life with me."

"Unfairly hesitant?"

"I was protecting myself," I said honestly. "Holding back some small part of domestic intimacy as insurance against loss. But watching those two boys choose complete vulnerability with each other made me realize I was being foolish."

Soren Jensen

Aleksander's honesty about his own emotional defenses touched something deep in my chest. After centuries of self-protection, he was choosing to be completely open with me.

"I'd love to move in with you," I said immediately. "Though I should probably warn you that I come with a lot of books and a complete inability to keep plants alive."

"I have enough space for infinite books," Aleksander replied with obvious relief. "And I've been successfully maintaining houseplants for decades."

THE MISSING PIECE

"There is one other thing I wanted to discuss," I said, my academic mind shifting to the research puzzle that had been nagging at me for months. "My dissertation is nearly complete, but I'm still missing that crucial connection between Rafael's family and ours."

Aleksander Nordh

"Ah yes, the genealogical mystery," I said, my interest immediately piqued. "Have you had any new thoughts about how to approach it?"

Soren Jensen

"Actually, yes. Now that Rafael is talking openly about his past, perhaps he has access to family documents we haven't considered. Photographs, letters, certificates—anything that might shed light on the connection between the Mercado and Jensen lines."

"That's an excellent point," Aleksander agreed. "Rafael mentioned that his grandfather Emilio kept detailed records. There might be documentation that survived his move to London."

"It's worth asking," I said. "And honestly, I think Rafael might enjoy being part of the research process. It could give him another reason to feel connected to the family, another project we're working on together."

Aleksander Nordh

"Plus," I added with a smile, "it would provide him with excellent distraction while Erik is in Sweden. Nothing better for managing separation anxiety than a compelling research project."

Soren Jensen

"Exactly. And if we can prove the family connection definitively, it adds another layer of meaning to Rafael and Erik's relationship. Not just chosen love, but family finding its way back to family across time and continents."

"Like us," Aleksander said softly.

"Like us," I agreed, settling back against his chest with a contentment that felt deep and permanent.

LOOKING FORWARD

Aleksander Nordh

As Soren's breathing gradually deepened toward sleep, I found myself thinking about the extraordinary changes that had occurred in such a short time. A month ago, we'd been a couple planning a wedding. Now we were the center of a chosen family that spanned species, generations, and continents.

Rafael was no longer isolated but embraced. Erik had found love and purpose beyond his wildest expectations. Soren and I were building something that honored both our individual natures and our shared dreams. And somehow, all of it felt like the natural culmination of patterns that had been building for over a century.

Soren Jensen

Just before sleep claimed me entirely, I realized that my dissertation—if I could solve the final genealogical puzzle—would tell a story far more extraordinary than anything I'd originally envisioned. Not just the tale of Swedish-American cultural preservation, but the saga of how love transcends every boundary humans think is insurmountable.

Blood and choice. Time and distance. Species and mortality. All of it connected by the simple truth that family, in its deepest sense, isn't about what you inherit but what you choose to build together.

"Good night, my love," I whispered against Aleksander's chest.

"Good night, puzzle boy," he whispered back, and I drifted off to sleep planning research strategies and dreaming of June weddings in Swedish villages where impossible love stories finally got their happy endings.

37
WORDS ACROSS THE DISTANCE

28,000 FEET NORTH SEA, INTERNATIONAL WATERS

Erik Eriksson

The seat belt sign had been off for twenty minutes, the London skyline long disappeared beneath a carpet of clouds, but I still hadn't moved to retrieve Rafael's letter from my carry-on bag. My hands kept returning to the envelope's location—top compartment, left side, nestled between my passport and the university brochures I'd been studying—but something held me back from actually opening it.

Maybe it was the weight I'd felt when Rafael pressed it into my hands. The careful way he'd watched my face as he asked me to promise not to read it until I was airborne. The slight tremor in his voice when he'd said it was "something for you to have when you're feeling uncertain about any of this."

Uncertain about what, exactly? About leaving London? About our relationship? About the future we were trying to build across countries and species and the kind of complications that most nineteen-year-old university applicants never had to consider?

Or maybe he meant uncertain about him. About whether someone who'd spent nearly a decade building walls around his heart could really tear them down for a Swedish teenager he'd known for less than three weeks.

The flight attendant passed by with the drinks cart, and I requested coffee—something to occupy my hands while I worked up the courage to read whatever Rafael had written. The woman next to me was reading a romance novel, occasionally sighing at particularly dramatic moments, while the businessman across the aisle typed furiously on his laptop, completely absorbed in whatever crisis required his attention at thirty thousand feet.

Normal people living normal lives, none of them carrying letters from vampire boyfriends or trying to figure out how to explain supernatural love to elderly Swedish grandparents.

I pulled out the envelope.

The paper was expensive—cream-colored with a subtle texture that spoke of Rafael's attention to quality in everything he touched. My name was written across the front in his careful script, each letter formed with the precision that marked everything he did. Even his handwriting was beautiful, elegant in a way that suggested countless hours of practice rather than the natural penmanship of someone barely into his twenties.

Inside, I found three pages covered in the same careful script, the ink slightly darker in places where he'd paused to think or perhaps to gather courage for whatever he was trying to say.

My dearest Erik,

I am writing this at four in the morning, sitting in the flat that has been my sanctuary for over a decade, trying to find words for feelings I had convinced myself I would never experience again. You are sleeping in my room—though it has become "our" room without either of us quite deciding when that happened—and I can hear your quiet breathing through the walls. Even unconscious, you make this place feel less like a hiding spot and more like a home.

By the time you read this, you will be somewhere over the North Sea, traveling away from me toward a life and family I have never seen but already love because they shaped you into the extraordinary person you are. You will be returning to people who knew you before London changed you, and I wonder if they will see the differences I see when I look at you now.

Three weeks ago, you were a lonely teenager visiting London for the first time, trying to understand your place in a family that had been scattered by circumstances beyond anyone's control. Now you are someone who has fallen in love with a monster and somehow managed to convince that monster he might be worthy of love in return. The transformation is remarkable, and it has nothing to do with the supernatural elements of our situation. You have simply become more yourself—braver, more confident, more open to possibilities that would have seemed impossible just days ago.

I need you to understand what you have given me, because I am not certain I will ever find the courage to say these things aloud. For nearly ten years, I have existed rather than lived. I built walls so high and so thick that I convinced myself they were protection rather than prison. I told myself that isolation was safety, that feeling nothing was better than risking the kind of pain that love can bring.

But you have torn down those walls with a gentleness that makes their destruction feel like liberation rather than assault. You have reminded me that isolation—whether chosen or forced—is not protection. It is merely another form of death.

When I left Manila eleven years ago, I told myself I was protecting my family by disappearing from their lives. I convinced myself that letting them mourn me was kinder than asking them to love a monster. But watching you leave today, feeling this ache of separation even though I know you will return, I finally understand the truth: I wasn't protecting them from me. I was protecting myself from the pain of their potential rejection.

You have shown me that love—real love—requires the courage to risk everything, including the possibility of loss. You have chosen to love me knowing exactly what I am, what I need to survive, what loving me will cost you in secrecy and complexity. And in making that choice, you have given me permission to believe I might be worthy of such a gift.

You walked into my carefully constructed world and demolished those walls simply by seeing me—really seeing me—and choosing to stay anyway. You looked at what I am, understood the reality of what that means, and your response was not fear or revulsion but curiosity and acceptance. You asked questions not to judge but to understand. You offered affection not despite my nature but as recognition of who I am beneath the supernatural complications.

I have spent a decade believing I was a monster. You have made me remember that I am a person.

The night you first stayed here, when you curled against me in sleep with such complete trust, I lay awake until dawn marveling at the simple miracle of your presence. No one had touched me with affection since my transformation. No one had shared my space without calculation or fear. No one had looked at me and seen someone worth loving rather than someone to be managed or avoided.

You changed that in a single evening, and you have continued changing it every day since.

I know that returning to Sweden means facing questions about your time in London, about your plans for university, about the future you are building that your family doesn't yet understand. I know that explaining any of this will be complicated, and I would not blame you if you decided the complications outweighed the benefits. What we have is extraordinary, but it is also difficult in ways that most relationships never have to navigate.

But I hope—I hope with every part of my heart that learned to beat properly again because of you—that you will find the courage to fight for what we have built together. Not because it is easy, but because it is real and precious and worth whatever challenges we must face to protect it.

I am writing this letter because my protective instincts are already screaming at me to retreat, to build new walls, to disappear back into the safety of isolation before you can decide that loving me is more trouble than it's worth. Every learned response from the past decade is telling me to run before you can leave, to end this before it can hurt me.

But you have taught me that love is not about avoiding pain—it is about choosing connection despite the risks. You have shown me that the courage to be vulnerable is not weakness but strength. You have proven that some things are worth fighting for even when the odds seem impossible.

So I am fighting my instincts by writing these words. I am choosing trust over fear, hope over self-protection, love over safety. I am promising you that I will not run, no matter how frightened I become or how loudly my defenses scream at me to retreat.

I love you, Erik Eriksson. I love your curiosity and your

kindness and your remarkable ability to see beauty in things others have labeled monstrous. I love the way you laugh at my nervous jokes and the careful attention you pay when I share difficult parts of my past. I love your determination to build a future that includes both your dreams and mine, your willingness to fight for love even when it requires crossing oceans and species lines.

I love that you chose me, and I promise to spend every day proving worthy of that choice.

Apply to every university in London that interests you. Accept the challenges of international study and cross-cultural relationships and all the complications that come with loving someone like me. Build the future you want, and know that I will be here working to build it with you.

When you doubt—and you will doubt, because doubt is natural when attempting something this extraordinary—remember that you are not alone in this. You have uncles who have navigated their own impossible love story and emerged stronger for it. You have family who have learned that the heart recognizes truth even when the mind struggles to understand it. You have me, fighting every defensive instinct I possess because you are worth the battle.

Most importantly, you have your own courage and wisdom and remarkable capacity for love. Trust those gifts. They have brought you this far, and they will carry you through whatever comes next.

I will call tonight after you have had time to settle in with your grandparents. I will send terrible texts at inappropriate hours because I miss you already. I will research British university programs with the dedication of someone whose happiness depends on your academic success. I will count the days until June, when we can stand together at your uncles' wedding and celebrate love that transcends every barrier others think should separate us.

And I will work every day to become the kind of person who deserves the extraordinary gift of your love.

Come back to me, Erik. Come back to London and let us build something beautiful together.

With all my love and every hope I thought I had lost forever,

Rafael

SOMEWHERE OVER THE NORTH SEA

I read the letter three times before the tears blurred my vision too much to continue. The businessman across the aisle was studiously ignoring my obvious emotional reaction, while the woman beside me had abandoned her romance novel entirely in favor of offering tissues from her purse.

"Bad news, dear?" she asked gently, her accent marking her as Yorkshire born and raised.

"No," I managed, accepting the tissue gratefully. "The best possible news, actually. Just... overwhelming."

She smiled with the understanding of someone who'd lived long enough to recognize the difference between tears of joy and tears of sorrow. "Love letter?"

"Something like that."

I folded the pages carefully, returning them to their envelope with the kind of reverence reserved for precious documents. Which, I realized, was exactly what this was—the most precious document I'd ever received. Rafael's promise, written in his own hand, that he would fight his protective instincts for our relationship. His declaration that I was worth the battle against a decade of defensive habits.

The magnitude of what he'd shared hit me all over again. This wasn't just a love letter—it was a manifesto of vulnerability from someone who had spent ten years believing that emotional safety required emotional isolation. He had opened his heart completely, laid bare his fears and hopes and desperate love, trusting me with the kind of honesty that could destroy him if I chose to misuse it.

I wouldn't misuse it. I would treasure it, protect it, prove worthy of the trust he'd placed in me.

The flight attendant announced that we were beginning our descent into Stockholm, and I found myself looking out the window at the familiar landscape of my homeland with entirely new eyes. Three weeks ago, I'd left Sweden as a confused teenager running toward possibilities I couldn't name. Now I was returning as someone who had found love, family, and purpose beyond anything I'd dared to imagine.

REFLECTING ON TRANSFORMATION

The Sweden spreading out beneath the plane looked exactly the same as when I'd left—forests and lakes and the orderly countryside that had shaped my childhood. But I felt fundamentally different, as if some essential part of my identity had been rewired during my weeks in London.

I thought about the first time I'd seen Rafael in Aleksander's flat, the way he'd held himself with careful reserve that had made me want to prove I could be trusted. Now I understood that reserve differently—not as him being standoffish or anything, but as someone protecting himself because he'd been hurt before.

Every memory reinforced what Rafael had written in his letter— that we were starting to build something extraordinary together, something worth fighting for despite the complications it would bring to both our lives.

The teenager who had left Sweden three weeks ago would have been overwhelmed by the challenges ahead. But sitting there on the plane, I realized something: maybe Rafael and I understood each other so well because we'd both been through similar shit, just in different ways.

His parents thought he was dead—something he'd done to protect them but which meant he'd been alone for eleven years. My parents were very much alive —successful and living three hours away who had simply chosen their work over raising me. Different situations, but the same basic thing: we both knew what it felt like when your own family doesn't really want you around.

Maybe that's why we'd both been so scared about this separation, why three months feels like forever instead of just a normal break. When people have already left you once, every goodbye feels like it might be permanent. When you've learned that love can just... disappear without warning, holding onto it when you find it again takes guts that most people probably never have to develop.

But we'd found each other despite all that mess. And we'd decided to build something together that acknowledged the painful stuff we'd both been through without letting it ruin what we were trying to create.

The person I think I'm becoming—the person Rafael's love is helping me become—saw those same challenges as problems to solve rather than reasons to give up. Uncle Aleksander and Uncle Soren had made their impossible love story work. Rafael had survived being turned into a vampire and eleven years of isolation and losing everything. I was part of a family now that specialized in making impossible things work through sheer stubborn determination to stick together.

If they could do it, so could we.

PLANNING CONVERSATIONS

As the plane touched down at Arlanda Airport, I found myself mentally rehearsing the conversations I would need to have with Mormor and Morfar. They deserved honesty about my plans, about the relationship that had reshaped my entire future, about the family I'd found in London that had welcomed me with such warmth.

But how did I explain falling in love with someone whose very existence challenged everything they understood about the world? How did I tell them that their grandson was planning to move to London to be with a vampire without revealing the supernatural elements that would terrify them?

I thought about Rafael's approach to his own family—the terrible choice he'd made to let them believe he was dead rather than burden them with truths they couldn't handle. The sacrifice he'd made to protect people he loved from knowledge that would destroy their peace.

I wouldn't need to make such an extreme choice, but I would need to be strategic about how much truth I shared and when. Mormor and Morfar loved me unconditionally, but they were practical people rooted in traditional values. The idea of their nineteen-year-old grandson planning his entire future around a three-week romance would concern them regardless of any supernatural complications.

So I would start with the basics: I had met someone special in London. I was considering university applications that would allow me to spend more time in England. I had found family connections through Uncle Aleksander and Uncle Soren that made London feel like a place where I could build a meaningful life.

All true, if incomplete. The rest could come gradually, as they learned to trust my judgment and saw evidence that my London plans were making me genuinely happy.

DREAMS OF THE FUTURE

As I waited for my luggage in the familiar chaos of Stockholm's airport, I found myself imagining the future Rafael and I were working toward. Not just the immediate challenges of university applications and visa paperwork, but the longer arc of a life built together.

I imagined introducing Rafael to Mormor and Morfar—carefully, gradually, in ways that would let them see his kindness and intelligence before worrying about the complications. I imagined showing him the Sweden that had shaped me, the farms and forests and small communities where I'd learned about love and loyalty and the importance of family.

I imagined us finding a flat in London that belonged to both of us rather than being his space that I visited. I imagined studying at university while he worked on his import business, both of us building careers that complemented rather than competed with each other. I imagined Sunday mornings in bed and dinner parties with Uncle Aleksander and Uncle Soren and the comfortable domesticity of a relationship that had weathered its early challenges.

Most of all, I imagined Rafael gradually learning to trust that love didn't have to mean loss, that opening his heart didn't inevitably lead to having it broken. I imagined him meeting my extended family and understanding that he was welcomed not despite his differences but because of the happiness he brought to someone they loved.

The future I envisioned wasn't without challenges—cross-species relationships would always require careful navigation, and Rafael's feeding requirements would demand ongoing discretion. But those challenges felt manageable when balanced against the love we'd already proven we could build together.

HOMECOMING

Mormor and Morfar were waiting in the arrivals area, both looking exactly as I'd left them but somehow smaller, more fragile than I remembered. Three weeks in London, surrounded by the supernatural confidence of Uncle Aleksander and the academic energy of Uncle Soren, had given me a different perspective on age and vitality.

"Erik, älskling!" Mormor called out, using the endearment that had comforted me through childhood fears and teenage uncertainties. "You look so grown up! London has been good to you."

I embraced them both, breathing in the familiar scents of Mormor's perfume and Morfar's aftershave, feeling the profound comfort of unconditional love that had anchored my entire life. But I also felt the difference in myself—the way I stood straighter, spoke with more confidence, carried myself like someone who had found his place in the world.

"London was extraordinary," I said honestly as we made our way toward the car. "Life-changing, actually. I have so much to tell you both."

"And we have time to hear everything," Morfar said with the gentle patience that had made him such an effective confidant throughout my growing up. "The farm is quiet, the weather is beautiful, and we've cleared our schedules to spend time with our grandson."

As we drove through the familiar countryside toward the farm where I'd found safety after my parents' abandonment, I found myself seeing everything through Rafael's eyes. What would he think of the endless forests, the red wooden houses, the simple beauty of a landscape shaped more by nature than by human intervention? Would he understand why this place had formed me, why the values learned here had made me someone capable of seeing past supernatural differences to the person beneath?

I thought about his letter, folded carefully in my jacket pocket, and the promise it contained. He would fight his protective instincts. He would choose trust over fear. He would build a future with me despite every reason his past gave him to retreat into isolation.

The least I could do was match his courage with my own.

"Mormor, Morfar," I said as we turned into the farm's familiar driveway, "I need to tell you about someone very important I met in London. Someone who... well, someone who's changed everything about what I want for my future."

They exchanged a glance that spoke of decades of shared understanding, and I could see them preparing for whatever revelation their grandson was about to share.

"His name is Rafael," I continued, feeling my heart race with the magnitude of what I was beginning to reveal. "And I think I'm going to spend the rest of my life loving him."

The smile that spread across Mormor's face was radiant with recognition and joy. "Tell us everything, älskling. We want to know all about the person who has made you so happy."

As we parked beside the barn where I'd learned to drive the tractor, where Morfar had taught me about responsibility and hard work and the satisfaction that came from caring for something larger than yourself, I realized that coming home didn't mean returning to who I used to be.

It meant bringing who I had become back to the people who had made that becoming possible.

Rafael's letter had promised he would fight for our future. Now it was time for me to prove I was ready to fight for it too.

38
THE WEDDING THAT WASN'T

STOCKHOLM ARLANDA AIRPORT 190 45 STOCKHOLM-ARLANDA, SWEDEN

Rafael Mercado

Arlanda Airport buzzed with the familiar chaos of international arrivals, but I barely noticed the crowds or the announcements echoing through the terminal. My eyes were fixed on the gate where passengers from the London flight were beginning to emerge, searching for three familiar faces among the stream of travelers.

It had been two months since Erik's return to Sweden—two months of daily calls, constant messages, and an ache in my chest that no amount of London distractions could ease. The plan had been simple: we would arrive today, rest at our Stockholm hotel, and meet Erik and his grandparents tomorrow for the journey to the farm. Civilized. Organized. Manageable.

But Erik had other ideas.

I spotted them before they saw us—Aleksander with his careful traveler's composure, Soren looking slightly overwhelmed by the journey, both scanning the arrivals area with the patient attention of people expecting to navigate to ground transportation and check into hotels. They weren't looking for a reception committee.

Which made Erik's surprise all the more perfect.

Soren Jensen

"Soren! Aleksander! Rafael!"

The voice cut through the airport din like a bell, and I spun toward the sound to see Erik pushing through the crowd with the single-minded determination of someone who refused to wait another moment for reunion. Behind him, moving with more dignity but equal warmth, came Marta and Lars Eriksson.

My heart swelled at the sight of him—taller somehow, more confident, radiating happiness in a way that made every passerby smile involuntarily. This was Erik as I'd never seen him: completely, utterly joyful.

Erik Eriksson

I couldn't contain myself any longer. The moment I saw Rafael emerge from the crowd, everything else faded away—the other passengers, the noise, even my grandparents' gentle protests that we should let them settle in first. I had waited sixty-three days for this moment, and I was done waiting.

"Rafael!" I called out, breaking into a run.

Rafael Mercado

Erik hit me like a beautiful hurricane, his arms wrapping around me with such force that I had to use my enhanced strength to keep us both upright. He was warm and solid and real after months of video calls and carefully timed phone conversations, and for a moment I forgot we were in a public place surrounded by strangers.

"I missed you," he whispered against my ear, his voice thick with emotion. "I missed you so much."

"I missed you too," I managed, my own voice barely steady. "Every day."

Aleksander Nordh

Watching Rafael and Erik's reunion—the pure, uncomplicated joy of it—stirred something profound in my chest. But it was the sight of Marta and Lars Eriksson approaching with familiar warmth that filled me with gratitude. After months of separation, their easy acceptance of our unusual family remained as strong as ever.

"Aleksander," Marta said warmly, her English more confident than it had been during our first meeting. "Welcome back to Sweden. Erik has missed you all so much."

"It's wonderful to see you again," I replied, genuinely moved by their continued acceptance. "Thank you for arranging all of this."

"Family takes care of family," Lars added with that same gentle smile I remembered from our first visit. "And you are family now."

THE JOURNEY NORTH

Soren Jensen

The drive from Stockholm to the farm took us through countryside that looked like something from a fairy tale—rolling green fields dotted with red wooden buildings, forests that seemed to stretch to the horizon, lakes that reflected the June sky like mirrors. But what made the journey magical wasn't the scenery. It was listening to Erik chatter excitedly about everything that had happened since his return, his hand never leaving Rafael's, his face animated with the kind of happiness that was impossible to fake.

"You should see what Mormor and Morfar have done to prepare," he was saying, switching between English and Swedish as his excitement built. "The whole farm is transformed. And wait until you meet everyone who's coming—second cousins and great-aunts and family friends I've never even heard of."

Rafael Mercado

I found myself relaxing in ways I hadn't expected as we drove deeper into the Swedish countryside. Marta kept turning around from the front seat to ask questions about London, my work, my interests—not the careful probing of someone trying to assess a threat, but the genuine curiosity of someone who wanted to understand her grandson's chosen family.

"Erik says you have beautiful flat," she said as we passed through a small village. "He shows us pictures. Very modern, very elegant."

"Thank you," I replied. "Though I have to admit, seeing this countryside makes me understand why Erik missed home so much."

"Sweden is beautiful," Lars agreed from behind the wheel. "But family makes any place home, yes?"

The casual wisdom in his observation hit me harder than I'd expected. Family makes any place home. For someone who'd spent over a decade in carefully constructed isolation, the concept felt both foreign and achingly appealing.

THE FARM TRANSFORMED

Erik Eriksson

As we turned into the familiar driveway, I felt a surge of pride at my grandparents' preparations. The farm had been transformed from its usual working agricultural appearance into something that could host an international wedding celebration. White tents dotted the yard, strung with lights that would create magic once the sun set. Tables and chairs were arranged in careful configurations that I knew Soren's mother had probably spent hours planning via video calls with Mormor.

"This is incredible," Soren breathed, taking in the scope of the preparations. "How did you manage all this?"

"Many hands," Marta replied with satisfaction. "Family helps family."

Aleksander Nordh

The transformation was indeed remarkable, but what struck me most was the seamless integration of Swedish and American elements. Traditional Midsummer decorations mingled with touches that were clearly inspired by Minnesota celebrations—a fusion of old world and new that perfectly captured what this wedding represented.

"Aleksander!" A familiar voice called out in accented English, and I turned to see Britta Jensen approaching with arms already extended, just as enthusiastic as she'd been during our first meeting in Minneapolis. "There's my honorary son! Look at you—even more handsome than I remembered!"

Soren Jensen

"Mom!" I protested, though I was grinning as Britta Jensen—who had somehow made it from Minneapolis to rural Sweden and immediately taken charge of everything—swept Aleksander into an embrace that he accepted with bemused grace.

"And you must be Rafael," she continued, turning to my cousin's boyfriend with the same unqualified warmth. "Erik's told us so much about you. Welcome to the family, honey."

I watched Rafael's face as he processed my mother's immediate, wholehearted acceptance. After months of careful integration into our unusual family structure, he still seemed surprised when people simply chose to love him without reservation.

DAYS BLUR TOGETHER

Rafael Mercado

The next few days passed in a whirlwind of activity that left me both exhausted and exhilarated. I had never experienced anything like the controlled chaos of a large family preparing for celebration—the constant stream of arriving relatives, the endless negotiations over seating arrangements and meal preparations, the way decisions seemed to emerge from group discussions that appeared to have no clear structure but somehow always reached consensus.

Erik's great-aunt Astrid, a formidable woman in her eighties, had taken it upon herself to teach me traditional Swedish drinking songs. Soren's cousin Marcus from Wisconsin spent hours explaining the finer points of American football to anyone who would listen. Children ran between the adults, switching effortlessly between languages as they played games that seemed to require no translation.

And through it all, Aleksander moved with the easy grace of someone who had spent centuries adapting to new cultures and customs. I watched him charming Erik's elderly relatives with stories that were probably more historically accurate than anyone realized, helping with preparations that utilized his strength without calling attention to its supernatural nature, and generally making himself so indispensable that it was impossible to imagine the celebration without him.

DINNER PREPARATIONS

Erik Eriksson

I knocked softly on Rafael's door, finding him adjusting his shirt in front of the small mirror with the careful precision he brought to all social situations.

"Hey," I said, settling on the edge of the bed. "I was thinking about the wedding feast tonight. All those courses Mormor has planned for the celebration, everyone toasting and watching to make sure you try everything..."

Rafael's hands stilled on his collar. "I'll manage."

"What if you don't have to? What if you felt a bit unwell from the travel? Stomach still adjusting to the time change, maybe needing some fresh air?" I watched his expression carefully. "It would give you an easy excuse to eat lightly during the celebration, step outside when needed. No one will question it on such a happy day—they'll just be glad you're trying to participate."

Rafael Mercado

The thoughtfulness behind Erik's suggestion made my chest tight with affection. He was thinking ahead, trying to protect me from awkward situations during what should be one of the most joyful nights of our family's life, learning to anticipate challenges I hadn't even voiced.

"That... that could work," I said softly. "Thank you for thinking of that."

"I'm learning," Erik said with a small smile. "Learning how to help."

Aleksander Nordh

There was something profoundly moving about being welcomed into the heart of a family celebration that honored traditions stretching back centuries. But it was the modern adaptations that touched me most deeply—the way Swedish customs had evolved in American soil, the way old songs had acquired new verses, the way children who had never seen Sweden nonetheless carried pieces of its culture in their voices and gestures.

On the second evening, as I helped Lars arrange seating for the growing crowd of guests, he paused in his work to study me with the careful attention of someone trying to solve a puzzle.

"You seem familiar," he said finally, his English slower than usual as he searched for the right words. "Like someone I should know, but cannot place."

The observation sent a chill through me that had nothing to do with the June evening air. In my long life, I had learned to be careful about such moments—times when human intuition penetrated the careful personas I maintained.

"I have one of those faces," I said lightly. "People often think they recognize me."

But Lars continued to study me with eyes that held the accumulated wisdom of eight decades of life, and I found myself wondering if somewhere in the deep history of this family, our paths had crossed before.

THE MORNING OF

Soren Jensen

I woke on the morning of June 21st to the sound of voices speaking rapid Swedish and the smell of coffee drifting up from the kitchen below. For a moment, I was disoriented—the guest room in Marta and Lars's farmhouse bore no resemblance to my London flat or my childhood bedroom in Minneapolis. Then memory flooded back: today was my wedding day.

The thought should have triggered anxiety, but instead I felt only a deep sense of rightness. Somewhere in this house, Aleksander was probably already awake, helping with the endless last-minute preparations that seemed to multiply despite everyone's best efforts. Outside, our families were gathering for a celebration that would officially unite two people who had been connected across centuries by love, loss, and the strange workings of fate.

Erik Eriksson

I found Rafael in the kitchen before dawn, moving quietly around the space as he prepared coffee with the careful precision he brought to everything. He looked up when I entered, his face lighting up with the smile I had missed so desperately during our separation.

"Couldn't sleep?" I asked, settling beside him at the table.

"Too much anticipation," he admitted. "Plus, my metabolism doesn't really do well with all the carbohydrates from yesterday's preparations. I needed something to settle my system."

It was such a perfectly Rafael response—practical concern dressed up as casual observation—that I couldn't help but grin.

"Nervous?" I asked.

"About the ceremony? No. About having this many people focused on our family? Terrified."

From Rafael's perspective:

The honesty came easier now, after months of learning to trust Erik with my fears and uncertainties. The boy—man, really, as his seventeenth birthday had marked some fundamental shift in how he carried himself—had this remarkable ability to make vulnerability feel safe rather than dangerous.

"They love you," Erik said simply, reaching for my hand. "All of them. I've watched them these past few days, and you're not an outsider they're tolerating. You're family they're celebrating."

The words settled something anxious in my chest that I hadn't fully acknowledged was there.

THE CEREMONY THAT WASN'T

Aleksander Nordh

By late afternoon, the farm had filled with a crowd that seemed to represent every branch of the extended Jensen family tree. Swedish relatives mixed with American cousins, elderly great-aunts chatted with young professionals from Minneapolis, and children who had never met before were already forming the kind of instant friendships that seemed to happen naturally in the presence of so much familial warmth.

But it was the seating arrangement that revealed the true genius of this celebration. Instead of traditional wedding formation—bride's side, groom's side, formal rows facing an altar—the tables had been arranged in a great spiral, each one positioned so that no one sat exclusively with people they already knew. Swedish farmers found themselves beside American academics, elderly relatives shared stories with young professionals, and everyone was forced to become acquainted with distant branches of their extended family.

"It's beautiful," Soren said, appearing at my elbow as we surveyed the scene. "Look at them. They're not just attending our wedding—they're discovering each other."

Soren Jensen

The realization that our wedding had become something larger than we'd planned filled me with a contentment I hadn't expected. This wasn't just about Aleksander and me making promises to each other. It was about weaving together all the scattered threads of family that had somehow led us to this moment.

"Are you ready?" I asked, though I wasn't sure what exactly we were supposed to be ready for. We had deliberately rejected most traditional wedding elements—no processional, no formal vows, no officiating clergy. Just family, food, and whatever words felt right when the moment came.

"I've been ready for this my entire life," Aleksander replied, his voice carrying the weight of centuries. "I just didn't know what I was waiting for until I found you."

Erik Eriksson

From my position at one of the center tables, I watched as various family members stood to share stories, songs, and memories that painted a picture of the Jensen lineage across time and geography. Some spoke in Swedish, with creative and often hilarious translation attempts for the Americans. Others shared stories in English that had the Swedish relatives nodding along despite the language barrier.

There was Uncle Nils, who recounted the family legend of great-great-grandfather Gustaf's mysterious friend in Copenhagen. Cousin Sarah from Wisconsin, who sang a song she'd learned from her grandmother about leaving home for distant shores. Great-aunt Astrid, who told stories of the farm during wartime that had everyone alternately laughing and wiping away tears.

But it was when Aleksander stood to speak that the entire gathering fell silent.

Aleksander Nordh

I had not planned to speak. Public addresses had always been carefully calculated affairs for me—opportunities to perform humanity rather than reveal it. But looking out at this crowd of faces, seeing the way they had all somehow become woven together over the past few days, I felt something stir in me that demanded expression.

"I would like to tell you a story," I began, my voice carrying easily across the gathering. "About a young man who grew up not far from this very place, many generations ago."

I let my gaze drift across the crowd, seeing nods of recognition, anticipation. Everyone loved a family story.

"This young man was raised to understand duty, tradition, the weight of family expectations. He learned early that love was a luxury that might conflict with obligation, that personal desires must sometimes be set aside for the greater good of those who depended on you."

A few of the older relatives were nodding now, recognizing universal themes that had shaped their own families' journeys.

"When this young man came of age, he found himself torn between the life his family needed him to live and the life his heart called him toward. Like so many before and after him, he chose duty. He crossed an ocean to build the kind of future his family could be proud of, leaving behind the person who had made him feel most himself."

I paused, letting the weight of that choice settle over the gathering.

"He built a good life in America. A respectable life. He married, raised children, established himself as the kind of man his family had always hoped he would become. But he carried with him always the memory of what he had left behind—not with regret, but with the kind of bittersweet gratitude that comes from having been truly known by another person."

Soren Jensen

I realized with growing amazement that Aleksander was telling Mikael's story—our story—in a way that let every person in the gathering see themselves reflected in it. The relatives who had emigrated from Sweden, the ones who had stayed behind, the children who had chosen unconventional paths, the parents who had sacrificed personal dreams for family stability—all of them were nodding along, recognizing their own experiences in his words.

"That young man's children grew up to make their own choices about love and duty, tradition and change. Some stayed close to home, others scattered across the globe. Some built the kinds of lives their parents had envisioned, others blazed entirely new trails. And some—" his eyes found mine across the gathering "—some discovered that love and duty need not be opposing forces, that tradition can evolve to embrace what was once thought impossible."

Aleksander Nordh

"The threads that connect us all—bloodlines, family lines, the bonds of choice and circumstance—they form a pattern more complex and beautiful than any of us can see from our individual perspectives. But when we come together like this, when we weave ourselves into the same story, the pattern becomes clear."

I gestured toward the spiral arrangement of tables, the way families that had been separated by ocean and time had somehow found their way back to each other.

"I have had the extraordinary privilege of witnessing many things in this world, in many times and places. But there is nothing more precious than what I see before me now—a young man who has worked tirelessly to trace the connections that bind you all together, who has dedicated himself to understanding how individual stories become family legacy."

My voice grew softer, more personal, as I turned to face Soren directly.

"Our vows of faith and love to each other are only possible through your support, through the foundation you provide. If you look around yourselves—all intertwined, interconnected—you are what will sustain us, support us as we endeavor to celebrate our commitment, our love for each other as Jensens and Nordhs."

Soren Jensen

Something shifted in the gathering as Aleksander's words moved from story to present moment. The relaxed celebration atmosphere gave way to something more formal, more sacred, without anyone quite realizing the transition was happening.

"For I, Aleksander Henrik Johan Nordh," he continued, his voice clear and strong, "take you, Soren Mikael Jensen, as my husband, my forever spouse, my lover, my life, my witness, my family."

The words hung in the summer air like a blessing, and I felt the weight of two millennia of solitude being lifted from the man I loved. But more than that, I felt the presence of everyone who had shaped our path to this moment—Mikael's love that had waited 131 years for completion, my parents' unconditional acceptance, Erik and Rafael's reminder that family could be chosen as well as inherited.

"And I, Soren Mikael Jensen," I heard myself say, stepping forward until we stood face to face in the center of the gathering, "take you, Aleksander Henrik Johan Nordh, as my husband, my forever spouse, my lover, my life, my witness... my family."

Rafael Mercado

It happened before anyone fully realized what was occurring. There had been no processional, no formal declaration of intent, no officiant asking for consent. But somehow, in the space between story and promise, between past and future, Aleksander and Soren had married themselves in front of everyone who mattered to them.

The kiss that sealed it was simple, pure, solemn—nothing theatrical or performative, just two people acknowledging the commitment they had already made to each other long before this day.

For a moment, the entire gathering held its breath. Then Britta Jensen burst into joyful tears, and the farm erupted in applause that scattered birds from the nearby trees and sent children running in circles, their laughter mixing with the cheers of adults who had just witnessed something they would talk about for the rest of their lives.

Erik Eriksson

Looking down at the crowd from my position at one of the elevated tables, I saw something that made my breath catch. The spiral arrangement of seating, which had seemed like simple practical planning, now revealed its deeper design. From above, the gathered families formed a perfect helix—two intertwining lines that supported and strengthened each other, separate but inseparable, ancient but ever-renewing.

It was exactly what Soren had been researching all along. The bloodline helix. Family lineages that seemed distinct but were actually part of the same larger pattern, connections that transcended time and species and geography to create something stronger than any individual thread.

Aleksander Nordh

As the applause died and normal conversation gradually resumed, as relatives began moving between tables to share congratulations and stories prompted by the ceremony, I found myself overwhelmed by a sense of completion I had never expected to experience.

For over two thousand years, I had moved through the world as an observer, careful to remain apart even when I seemed most integrated. But here, surrounded by Soren's family—our family—I was not performing belonging. I was simply belonging, accepted not despite my differences but because of my love for the person who connected us all.

Soren Jensen

Later, as the evening light began to fade and someone started a fire in the great stone pit Lars had constructed for the occasion, I found myself sitting with Aleksander on the old wooden swing that overlooked the farmyard. The celebration continued around us—children chasing fireflies, adults sharing stories that grew more elaborate with each telling, teenagers clustered around someone's guitar.

"No regrets?" Aleksander asked softly, his hand finding mine in the gathering dusk.

"Only one," I replied.

"What?"

"That it took us this long to get here."

Aleksander's laugh was soft and warm and full of the kind of contentment that comes from finding your way home after a very long journey.

"Some waits," he said, "are worth every moment when they finally end."

Above us, the first stars were beginning to appear in the Swedish summer sky, and somewhere in the distance, someone was singing an old song in a language that seemed to belong to the land itself. We were married now, officially and completely, surrounded by family that spanned continents and generations and species, held together by love that had proved stronger than time.

We were exactly where we belonged.

NIGHT WALKS

Erik Eriksson

We walked in comfortable silence through the crisp Swedish night, the wedding celebration finally winding down behind us. The excuse I'd suggested earlier had worked perfectly throughout the evening—Rafael's "travel-related stomach issues" had given him reason to "eat lightly" during the feast and step outside when needed, and everyone had been too focused on the joyful ceremony to pay much attention.

But as we walked away from the warm glow of the farmhouse, I felt the weight of everything unsaid between us.

"Rafael," I began, then stopped, unsure how to voice what I was feeling.

"Yes?"

"I want to help you. With... with everything. When you need to... you know. I want to be there. I want to help."

Rafael Mercado

The request hit me like ice water. "No," I said immediately, more sharply than I intended. "Erik, no. You can't."

Erik Eriksson

His instant rejection, without even hearing me out, lit something angry in my chest.

"Why not?" I demanded, my careful English already starting to fray. "I'm not some child who can't handle—"

"You don't understand what you're asking," Rafael interrupted.

"Then explain it to me!" My voice was rising, frustration spilling over. "I want to help you, and you just... nej! No explanation, no discussion, just no!"

Rafael tried to speak, but I was beyond listening now, switching rapidly between languages as emotion took control.

"I know you need... jag vet att du behöver... I know you need to eat, and I can't... jag kan inte bara stå och titta på medan du..."

(I know you need... I can't just stand and watch while you...)

I stopped walking entirely, turning to face him with tears in my eyes.

"If vi ska hålla, we need to help each other!" I said, my voice breaking as Swedish and English collided. "Varför kan jag inte—why can't I help you with this too?"

(If we're going to last... Why can't I...)

Rafael Mercado

Seeing Erik fall apart, watching him struggle between languages because I'd shut him down so quickly, made me feel sick with guilt. But the thought of him witnessing what I had to do...

"Erik, please," I whispered, my own tears starting. "You can't... I can't let you see that part of me. It would change how you look at me, and I couldn't bear—"

Erik Eriksson

"Det är farligt!" I continued in broken Swedish, too upset to maintain English. "Jag förstår att det är farligt, men jag vill ändå hjälpa dig!"

(It's dangerous! I understand it's dangerous, but I still want to help you!)

"Förlåt."

(Excuse me.)

Aleksander's quiet voice emerged from the darkness, and I realized he'd been approaching—probably coming to find Rafael because he knew it was time.

My anger faltered for a moment, replaced by confusion and something like awe. Aleksander had just gotten married hours ago. This was his wedding night, and instead of celebrating with Soren, he was here in the Swedish countryside, ready to help Rafael with something I couldn't even fully comprehend. The depth of his commitment to family, his willingness to put Rafael's needs above his own celebration, made me understand even more clearly how serious this was.

Aleksander Nordh

I could hear Erik's broken Swedish from quite a distance, could sense the emotional turmoil radiating from both of them. This conversation had been inevitable, but the timing was unfortunate. Still, Rafael's needs didn't pause for celebrations, and family responsibilities didn't stop for wedding nights.

"Erik," I said gently, switching to Swedish so he could understand me completely while Rafael could not. "Du är ädel och god för att vilja hjälpa Rafael. Men det finns alltid några saker som ofta är bäst att lämna ifred."

(You are noble and good for wanting to help Rafael. But there are always some things that are often better left alone.)

"Matning är en av dem. Även om jag vet att du förstår och sympatiserar med att vilja se Rafael, din kärlek, vara frisk och ha vad han behöver för att överleva, så kan det att stödja honom i den ansträngningen och att faktiskt bevittna det ibland fungera emot varandra."

(Feeding is one of them. While I know you understand and empathize with wanting to see Rafael, your love, be healthy and have what he needs to survive, supporting him in that effort and actually witnessing it can sometimes work against each other.)

"Det handlar inte om att du är för ung - du är ganska mogen. Det är helt enkelt för att du är människa. Och oavsett hur mycket kärlek du har för Rafael, skulle du inte kunna brottas bort de dystra realiteterna av matning från förståelsen att det måste göras. Förstår du?"

(It's not about you being too young - you're quite mature. It's simply because you're human. And no matter how much love you have for Rafael, you could not wrestle away the grim realities of feeding from the understanding that it must be done. Do you understand?)

Erik Eriksson

Through my tears, I nodded. The way Aleksander explained it in Swedish made it clearer than any English could have.

"Jag förstår," I managed. "Jag känner bara så mycket för honom..."

(I understand. I just feel so much for him...)

"Ja, det vet jag... vi ser det alla. Och det är bra att du känner. Men snälla... låt mig hjälpa Rafael medan vi är här med det här... och du... var där för honom när vi kommer tillbaka? Kan du göra det för mig? För honom?"

(Yes, I know that... we all see it. And it's good for you to feel. But please... let me help Rafael while we're here with this... and you... be there for him when we return? Can you do that for me? For him?)

"Ja," I whispered, understanding now that there were different ways of helping.

Aleksander Nordh

I returned to English, including Rafael in the conversation again. "Thank you, Erik. You're a very loving man, and Rafael, I think he understands the situation a little better now."

Erik Eriksson

I grabbed Rafael into a fierce hug, not caring that Aleksander was watching, and kissed him deeply.

"Jag älskar dig," I whispered against his lips.

Rafael Mercado

Hearing those words he taught me in Swedish, seeing the love and understanding in Erik's eyes despite his tears, made my heart swell with gratitude and wonder.

"Jag... jag älskar dig också," I managed, stumbling through the pronunciation but meaning every syllable.

(I... I love you too.)

Aleksander Nordh

I stepped back discretely, allowing them their moment, before gently suggesting, "Erik, perhaps you could warm some hot cider for our return? We shan't be too long... perhaps an hour."

I placed a hand on Rafael's shoulder as we prepared to disappear into the night.

Erik Eriksson

Our eyes met one final time - Rafael's filled with gratitude and love for my understanding, mine with the certain knowledge that this was the right path. As I turned toward the house, I realized I'd never known how much my heart had to give before tonight. And somehow, that made me love him even more.

39
AN UNEXPECTED ARRIVAL

JENSEN FAMILY FARM (HISTORICAL) SILJANSNÄS 47, 795 91 RÄTTVIK, SWEDEN

Soren Jensen

The celebration had settled into that perfect rhythm that marks the best kind of family gathering—children finally tired enough to stay in one place, adults relaxed by good food and better company, the kind of conversation that flows like music between tables. Aleksander and I had claimed the old wooden swing that overlooked the farmyard, content to watch the evening unfold around us rather than be at its center.

Music drifted from the main tent where someone had convinced Great-aunt Astrid to demonstrate traditional Swedish folk dances, her movements still graceful despite her eighty-plus years. Laughter punctuated the melody as younger relatives attempted to follow her lead, their modern sensibilities no match for steps passed down through generations.

"Look," Aleksander said softly, nodding toward the dance area.

I followed his gaze to see Erik leading Rafael onto the makeshift dance floor, his hands gentle but insistent as he coaxed his clearly reluctant boyfriend into the circle of swaying couples.

Rafael Mercado

"Erik, I don't know how to dance," I protested for the third time, my feet refusing to move despite his encouraging tugs toward the music. "I've never... this isn't something I learned."

"It doesn't matter," Erik replied, his smile radiant in the string lights that had transformed the farm into something magical. "No one's judging. Look around —half these people are making it up as they go along."

He was right. The "dancing" was really just couples swaying together, arms around each other, moving to whatever rhythm felt natural. Nothing formal or complicated. Nothing that required years of training or perfect technique.

Erik Eriksson

"Please?" I asked, my hands finding Rafael's waist, drawing him closer despite his obvious nervousness. "When will we ever get another chance like this? Our family's wedding, this music, all these lights... I want to dance with my boyfriend."

I could see the war playing out across Rafael's features—social anxiety battling with desire to make me happy. When he finally nodded, the smile that spread across my face felt like it might split my cheeks.

Rafael Mercado

Erik's joy was infectious, impossible to resist. And once we began moving together, his arms around me, my hands resting on his shoulders, everything else faded away. The other couples, the watching relatives, my own self-consciousness—none of it mattered. There was only Erik's heartbeat against my chest, the warmth of his body, the way he hummed along to the music in my ear.

For the first time in over a decade, I felt purely, simply happy. Not grateful or relieved or carefully content, but genuinely, completely happy. This was what I'd been missing all those years of isolation—not just love, but the ability to share joy openly, to be part of something larger than my own careful existence.

"See?" Erik whispered, his lips brushing my ear. "You're perfect at this."

Erik Eriksson

Rafael was beautiful when he let his guard down—the way his face softened when he stopped worrying about appearances, the grace that emerged when he trusted his instincts rather than overthinking every movement. We swayed together in the gentle light, surrounded by the warm hum of family conversation, and I felt like we were in our own private world.

This could have been our wedding reception, I found myself thinking. Someday, maybe it would be. The thought made my chest tight with happiness rather than anxiety. Rafael and me, dancing at our own celebration, surrounded by all these people who had learned to love us both.

The music shifted to something slower, more intimate, and I drew him closer, feeling his arms tighten around me in response. Perfect. Everything was perfect.

THE DISRUPTION

Rafael Mercado

The shouting cut through the music like broken glass, harsh Swedish words that I didn't understand but recognized immediately as profane. Every muscle in my body went rigid as a figure stumbled into the light—a woman, clearly intoxicated, her clothing rumpled and inappropriate for the celebration.

But it was Erik's face that told me everything I needed to know. The color drained from his features as recognition hit, followed immediately by a mixture of mortification and fear that made my heart clench.

Erik Eriksson

"Vad fan håller du på med med min pojke, din perversling?"

The words hit me like a physical blow, not just because of their vulgarity but because of who was speaking them. My mother stood swaying at the edge of the dance floor, her voice carrying across the suddenly silent gathering as she hurled obscenities that made several elderly relatives gasp.

"Mom!" I called out, my voice cracking with shock. "What are you doing here?"

Rafael Mercado

I backed away instinctively, my hands rising as if to shield myself from attack. The woman—Erik's mother, who I knew from his stories but had never met—was clearly drunk and furious, her eyes fixed on me with undisguised hatred. Those who understood Swedish looked appalled by whatever she was saying, while others simply reacted to her obvious hostility.

I felt the familiar urge to disappear, to remove myself from a situation that could only escalate. But beneath that instinct, something else stirred—a slow-burning anger at her behavior, at the way she was treating Erik, at her complete disrespect for this celebration.

Soren Jensen

The commotion pulled Aleksander and me from our peaceful observation instantly. I could hear my mother's voice raised in concern, see Lars and Marta moving toward the disturbance with expressions of deep distress. But it was Aleksander's reaction that caught my attention—the way he went absolutely still beside me, his enhanced hearing obviously picking up details I couldn't catch.

"Stay here," he said quietly, rising from the swing with fluid grace.

But I was already following, my academic mind cataloging the scene even as my heart raced with concern for Erik and Rafael.

Aleksander Nordh

I moved with supernatural speed toward the confrontation, arriving at the dance floor before most humans could fully process what was happening. The woman—clearly Erik's mother based on physical resemblance and his horrified reaction—was continuing her drunken tirade in Swedish that grew more offensive with each word.

When her gaze fixed on me, her hostility shifted targets immediately.

"Och vem fan tror du att du är?" she snarled, her words slightly slurred but clearly venomous.

Rafael Mercado

Aleksander appeared beside us as if from thin air, causing more than one gasp from onlookers. I knew immediately what was happening—he'd used his enhanced speed without thinking, responding to a perceived threat with reflexes honed over millennia.

Aleksander Nordh

Speaking in perfect Swedish, I introduced myself with calm politeness that stood in stark contrast to her aggressive tone. "God kväll. Jag heter Aleksander. Du måste vara trött efter resan. Varför sätter du dig inte ner?"

When she began to protest, I stepped closer and lowered my voice, letting just a hint of my true nature shine through my eyes as I spoke directly to her.

"Du kommer att sitta ner nu. Du kommer att dricka vatten. Och du kommer att behandla dessa människor med respekt, eller så kommer du att lämna. Förstår du mig?"

Erik Eriksson

My mother's entire demeanor changed in an instant. The drunken aggression melted away, replaced by something approaching sobriety as she stared into Aleksander's eyes. Whatever he'd said to her, however he'd said it, had cut through her intoxication like a knife.

She sat down without another word, accepting the water and food that materialized from nowhere as relatives sprang into action to manage the crisis.

Aleksander Nordh

Turning to Erik and Rafael, I could see the tremor in Erik's hands, the way Rafael held himself ready to flee. This was their moment of trauma, their celebration tainted by cruelty, and no amount of supernatural intervention could completely undo that damage.

I took both their hands, drawing them together, feeling the way they clung to each other and to me.

"Why did she come?" Erik whispered, his voice breaking. "How could she be so cruel?"

"It's her fear, Erik," I said gently. "It's not her true self speaking."

"But she... she hates us."

Rafael Mercado

Aleksander's hands on ours were steady, grounding, exactly what I needed to keep from spiraling into panic or rage. When he spoke, his voice carried the weight of centuries of understanding human pain.

"Erik... Rafael," he said, looking between us with infinite compassion. "She doesn't know you. She doesn't know herself. It will always hurt, hearing those things. I cannot change that. It hurts me. It hurts Soren. It hurts us all. Words mean things. But they're meaningless if we don't let them continue to be."

Aleksander Nordh

"She needs help, Erik. But you aren't the one to give it to her. You're not in the position to be able to, nor at the right stage of your life. You and Rafael have other matters to work on. But you will always have her, so long as you don't give up on her memory even when she has forgotten herself."

I could see my words settling into both young men, offering not false comfort but honest acknowledgment of a complex situation. Erik's mother would always be his mother, but that didn't make her behavior acceptable or something they had to endure.

Rafael Mercado

I had always admired Aleksander from a distance—his grace, his obvious intelligence, his careful kindness. But this was different. This was protection offered without hesitation, wisdom shared without judgment, family claimed and defended with quiet authority.

For the first time since meeting him, I truly understood why Soren had fallen in love with this ancient, extraordinary man.

AFTERMATH

Soren Jensen

As Aleksander melted away from the center of the commotion, moving toward me with the fluid grace that marked his supernatural nature, I opened my arms to receive him.

"What did you say to calm her so instantly?" I asked quietly, noting how the entire gathering was slowly returning to normal conversation, the crisis managed with typical Scandinavian efficiency.

"Not here, my love," Aleksander replied, his arms coming around me. "I'll tell you everything tonight. For now, let's see to it that Erik and Rafael are loved."

Rafael Mercado

The next hour passed in a blur of gentle attention from relatives I barely knew but who treated me like family nonetheless. Great-aunt Astrid appeared with a cup of strong coffee and a plate of traditional pastries, chatting about the weather as if nothing unusual had happened. Lars clapped me on the shoulder and invited me to help him tend the fire, giving me something practical to focus on. Marta fussed over Erik with the determined care of someone who would not let anyone hurt her grandson on her watch.

And through it all, Aleksander and Soren moved through the gathering like gracious hosts, ensuring that one woman's cruelty didn't poison the celebration they'd worked so hard to create.

Erik Eriksson

As the evening wound down and relatives began the slow process of goodbyes and promises to stay in touch, I found myself sitting with Rafael on the same swing where our uncles had been earlier. The crisis had passed, but its effects lingered in the careful way people spoke around us, the extra attention that felt both comforting and exhausting.

"I'm sorry," I said for the tenth time. "I'm so sorry she ruined tonight."

"She didn't ruin anything," Rafael replied firmly. "She tried to, but she didn't succeed. Look around, Erik. Everyone's still here. People are still celebrating. Your uncles are still married, your families are still connected, and I'm still completely in love with you."

Rafael Mercado

The truth of my words settled something anxious in my chest that I hadn't fully acknowledged. Erik's mother had been cruel, but she hadn't broken anything that mattered. Our love was stronger than her fear, our family bonds deeper than her hatred.

And I had learned something important about myself tonight—I didn't have to run from conflict or cruelty. I could stand my ground, accept protection when it was offered, and trust that the people who truly knew me would see past whatever poison others tried to spread.

"What happens now?" Erik asked quietly.

"Now we keep building what we started," I said, surprising myself with my certainty. "Together."

THE LAST DANCE

Hours later, when the last guest had been settled and the lights extinguished, when the fires had been banked and the cleanup completed, Erik and I found ourselves alone in the farmyard under a canopy of stars that seemed close enough to touch. The old wooden swing creaked gently as we swayed together, the only sound the distant murmur of night insects and the soft rustle of hay in the evening breeze.

"I'm sorry," Erik said for what felt like the tenth time. "I'm so sorry about my mother—"

"She didn't ruin anything," I interrupted gently, my hand finding his in the darkness. "She tried to, but she didn't succeed. She needs help, Erik. Just like Aleksander said."

"Yeah," Erik agreed, his voice soft with understanding. "She does."

We sat in comfortable silence, the swing moving in its ancient rhythm, when suddenly Erik popped up and grabbed my hands, pulling me to my feet with surprising force.

"What's happening?" I asked, startled by the sudden movement.

Erik Eriksson

"We never got to finish our dance," I said, looking into Rafael's confused face.

He let out an embarrassed laugh. "Oh... it's okay. I mean, given the circumstances..."

"No, it's not okay," I said firmly, taking his hands. "I wanted to dance with my boyfriend, and what's more romantic than out here under the stars?" I gestured toward the night sky, where the Milky Way stretched like scattered diamonds across the darkness.

Rafael Mercado

I wanted to beg off again, to retreat into the safety of the farmhouse, but I could see the determination in Erik's face. This mattered to him, and increasingly, what mattered to Erik mattered to me.

"Well," I said, grasping for excuses, "we don't have any music."

Erik Eriksson

Without hesitation, I stepped closer and pulled Rafael into my arms, positioning us as we had been on the dance floor before the interruption. Then I began to hum softly in his ear—a melody that came from nowhere and everywhere, something my heart composed in the moment.

The sound was slight and subtle, but I felt Rafael shiver as my breath tickled his ear, sending what I could only hope were the good sort of shockwaves through his body.

Rafael Mercado

Erik's improvised song wrapped around us like silk, and gradually we began to sway together, finding our rhythm under the vast Swedish sky. In the moonlight, I realized Erik's eyes held flecks of gold that caught the starlight, making him look almost otherworldly in his beauty.

This was perfect. More perfect than any formal dance floor or elaborate celebration could have been. Just the two of us, the night, and love so tangible I could feel it humming in the air between us.

WITNESSES

Aleksander Nordh

Soren and I had retreated to our guest room, exhausted by the evening's events and ready to collapse into each other's arms in the privacy of darkness. But as we stood by the window, nearly ready to surrender to sleep, my enhanced hearing caught something that made me pause.

The faintest melody drifted across the night air—a hummed love song coming from somewhere outside.

"What is it?" Soren asked, noting my stillness.

Instead of answering, I took his hand and led him quietly to the farmhouse's front door, pulling him out onto the porch.

Soren Jensen

Aleksander positioned himself behind me, his arms wrapping around my waist for warmth against the night air, and together we gazed out into the moonlit farmyard. There, in the distance, Erik and Rafael swayed together in perfect harmony, lost in their private dance under the canopy of stars.

The sight was so beautiful, so intimate and pure, that I felt tears prick my eyes. This was what we had all been working toward—not just our own happiness, but the creation of space where love could flourish in all its forms.

Aleksander Nordh

We stood witness to something sacred—the last dance of the night, the most special one. It belonged entirely to Rafael and Erik, under the stars, in the aftermath of crisis and the promise of tomorrow. The honor of witnessing it was ours to share, a gift as precious as any wedding blessing.

"Beautiful," Soren whispered against my chest.

"Perfect," I agreed, pressing a kiss to the top of his head.

The bloodlines continued their eternal spiral, weaving love into patterns more intricate and beautiful than any of us could have imagined. And there, in the Swedish summer night, under ancient stars that had witnessed countless love stories across the centuries, our family danced on.

40
THE DEAD END

KING'S COLLEGE LONDON - MAUGHAN LIBRARY CHANCERY LANE, LONDON WC2A 1LR

Soren Jensen

The microfilm reader hummed with its familiar electronic whine as I scrolled through yet another roll of shipping manifests from the Philippine-American period, my eyes burning from hours of squinting at faded typescript. The British Library's genealogy section had become my second home over the past month, but today the familiar routine felt more like imprisonment than research.

"Nothing," I muttered, ejecting the reel with more force than necessary. "Absolutely nothing."

Across the table, Aleksander looked up from his own stack of documents—immigration records from the early 1900s that we'd requested from three different archives. His expression held the patient sympathy of someone who'd watched me grow increasingly frustrated over the past several weeks.

"Still no connection between the Mercado family and John's military unit?" he asked quietly, mindful of the other researchers working nearby.

"Oh, there are connections," I said, rubbing my temples where a headache was building. "Plenty of them. John was stationed in Makati during the exact period when the Mercado family was most prominent in that district. He attended social functions where they were present. His commanding officer's reports mention him forming 'beneficial relationships with local intellectual leaders.'"

I gestured at the scattered photocopies covering our table. "But none of it proves he had a relationship with a specific Mercado family member. None of it proves he fathered children. None of it proves Rafael is actually connected to our family line."

Aleksander Nordh

Watching Soren's mounting frustration was painful, not just because I loved him but because I understood the deeper significance of what he was trying to accomplish. This research had begun as academic curiosity but had evolved into something far more personal—an attempt to create official family bonds that would validate what we all felt intuitively about Rafael's place in our lives.

"Perhaps," I said carefully, "the absence of official documentation is itself significant. If John did have a relationship with a local woman, particularly one from a prominent family, discretion would have been essential. Such connections rarely appeared in official military records."

"I know that," Soren replied, his voice sharper than usual. "That's exactly the problem. I can prove circumstantial connections all day long, but circumstantial isn't enough for my dissertation committee. And it's certainly not enough to help Rafael understand his own family history."

Soren Jensen

The real source of my frustration wasn't academic—it was deeply personal. Rafael had shared his family's story with such pain, such carefully controlled grief over the connections he'd severed when he'd chosen to let them think he was dead. If I could prove he was part of our extended family, if I could show him that he belonged to something larger than his own isolated existence, maybe it would ease some of that burden.

But after months of research, I was no closer to definitive proof than when I'd started. Every lead terminated in incomplete records, every promising connection dissolved under closer examination.

"There has to be something I'm missing," I said, more to myself than to Aleksander. "Some approach I haven't considered, some source I haven't explored."

Aleksander was quiet for a moment, considering. When he spoke, his voice carried the careful tone he used when he was about to suggest something significant.

"There is one option we haven't discussed," he said. "Though it would require Rafael's participation, and I'm not certain he'd be comfortable with it."

"What kind of option?"
"DNA testing."

THE SUGGESTION

Rafael Mercado

The conversation had moved to Aleksander's flat by evening, takeaway containers from our favorite Thai restaurant scattered across his dining table as the four of us discussed Soren's research challenges. I'd been listening with growing discomfort as he detailed the dead ends he'd encountered, the gaps in historical records that seemed to mock his efforts.

When Aleksander mentioned DNA testing, something cold settled in my stomach that had nothing to do with my vampire physiology.

"I know it's not ideal," Soren was saying, his excitement obvious despite his earlier frustration. "Commercial DNA testing has significant limitations for genealogical research, especially when you're trying to trace connections across multiple continents and ethnic backgrounds. But if we could establish even a distant relationship..."

"No," I said quietly, interrupting his analysis.

The single word cut through the conversation like a blade, leaving silence in its wake. All three of them turned to look at me, varying degrees of surprise and confusion on their faces.

"Rafael?" Erik said gently, his hand finding mine across the table. "What's wrong?"

I struggled to find words that would explain without revealing the full scope of my fears. How could I tell them that the thought of submitting biological samples terrified me? That I wasn't entirely certain what my transformation had done to my genetic markers, whether my altered DNA would flag abnormalities that would raise questions I couldn't answer?

"It's complicated," I said finally, aware how inadequate the explanation sounded.

"Because of what you are?" Soren asked, his academic mind immediately jumping to the most logical conclusion. "Because vampire genetics might show anomalies in commercial testing?"

The relief I felt at his understanding was immediately replaced by new anxiety. If Soren could recognize the problem so quickly, how many others might draw similar conclusions if unexpected results appeared?

"Among other reasons," I admitted.

Erik Eriksson

I could see Rafael withdrawing into himself, that familiar defensive posture that appeared whenever he felt cornered or exposed. After nearly a year together, I'd learned to recognize the signs—the way his shoulders tensed, the careful neutral expression that masked deeper fears.

"What other reasons?" I asked, keeping my voice soft and non-threatening.

Rafael was quiet for a long moment, his eyes fixed on his hands. When he finally spoke, his voice was barely above a whisper.

"What if we're wrong? What if there's no connection at all, and this whole... fantasy we've built about being family is just wishful thinking?"

Aleksander Nordh

Rafael's confession hit me with unexpected force. In all our months of building these connections, of welcoming him into our family structure, I'd never considered that he might doubt the reality of those bonds. The vulnerability in his voice reminded me powerfully of my own fears when I'd first allowed myself to love Soren—the terror that something so precious might prove illusory.

"Rafael," I said gently, "your connection to this family isn't dependent on genetic testing or historical documentation. You're part of us because we've chosen each other, because we've built something together. That's not wishful thinking—it's reality."

"But if Soren could prove it officially..." Rafael began.

"Then it would be a lovely bonus," I interrupted. "But it wouldn't change anything fundamental about who we are to each other."

Rafael Mercado

Aleksander's words were kind, logical, probably even true. But they didn't address the deeper fear that had been growing in me over the past months. The fear that my presence in their lives was somehow fraudulent, that I'd inserted myself into a family story where I didn't belong based on coincidence and hope rather than genuine connection.

"I understand why you want proof," I said to Soren, trying to find words for feelings I'd never voiced. "I want it too. But what if the proof goes the other way? What if testing shows conclusively that there's no blood relationship at all?"

"Then we'll know," Soren replied simply. "And we'll decide what that means to us. But Rafael, not knowing isn't making any of this easier for you."

THE ALTERNATIVE

Erik Eriksson

The conversation had reached an impasse, with Rafael clearly uncomfortable about DNA testing and Soren frustrated by research limitations. I found myself thinking about practical alternatives, ways to approach the problem that might satisfy everyone's concerns.

"What if we didn't do genetic testing here?" I suggested. "What if we went to the source?"

Three pairs of eyes turned to me with varying degrees of confusion.

"Manila," I clarified. "Rafael, you know the city, the culture, the language. You'd know how to navigate archives that might have records Soren can't access from London. And if there are family members still alive who remember the old stories..."

Rafael Mercado

Erik's suggestion hit me like a physical blow. Return to Manila. Face the place I'd fled from over a decade ago, the life I'd abandoned, the family I'd chosen to let grieve rather than burden with the truth of what I'd become.

"I can't," I said immediately, the response automatic and absolute.

"Why not?" Erik asked, his voice gentle but persistent. "I'd go with you. We'd all go with you, if you wanted."

"Because..." I began, then stopped, overwhelmed by the complexity of emotions the suggestion stirred. Fear, longing, guilt, hope—all warring in my chest until I could barely breathe.

Aleksander Nordh

I could see Rafael spiraling toward panic, his careful control beginning to fracture under the weight of possibilities he'd spent years trying not to consider. This was exactly the kind of moment that had driven him into isolation before

—when emotional pressure became too intense to bear, when flight seemed like the only viable option.

"Rafael," I said quietly, drawing his attention away from the impossible future Erik was suggesting toward the manageable present. "No one is asking you to make any decisions tonight. We're just exploring options."

"But it's not just an option," Rafael said, his voice tight with suppressed emotion. "It's the only option that makes sense. The church records, the family histories, the local knowledge—it's all there. Everything Soren needs to prove or disprove the connection."

He looked up at me with eyes that held too much pain for someone who appeared barely out of his teens.

"And I'm the only one who could access it."

Soren Jensen

Watching Rafael grapple with the implications of Erik's suggestion, I felt a profound guilt settle in my chest. In my academic excitement about solving research puzzles, I'd lost sight of the human cost of what I was asking. Rafael wasn't just a source of information or a subject for genetic analysis—he was family, someone I cared about, someone whose pain mattered more than any dissertation or historical curiosity.

"We don't have to do this," I said firmly. "Rafael, if the idea of returning to Manila is too difficult, we'll find another way. Or we'll accept that some questions don't have answers."

"But you need this research for your dissertation," Rafael replied. "And I... I need to know. Even if it's difficult. Even if it's terrifying."

Rafael Mercado

The truth was, Erik's suggestion had awakened something in me that I'd been trying to suppress for years—the desperate desire to return home, to see my family again, to somehow bridge the gap between the life I'd lost and the life I'd built. But it had also awakened every fear I'd carried since my transformation: that I was no longer the person my family had loved, that my presence would bring them pain rather than joy, that the monster I'd become had no place in their world.

"If we went," I said slowly, testing the words, "it would have to be carefully planned. I couldn't... I couldn't risk my family discovering I'm alive. The pain that would cause them, the questions..."

"Of course," Aleksander said immediately. "We would structure it as purely academic research. You would be our guide and translator, nothing more."

"And if we found family members who are still alive? People who might recognize me despite the years?"

"Then we'd adapt," Erik said with quiet confidence. "Whatever happens, we'd handle it together."

Erik Eriksson

I could see Rafael wavering between fear and hope, between the safety of his carefully constructed London life and the possibility of answers that might change everything. It was a decision only he could make, but I wanted him to know that whatever he chose, he wouldn't face the consequences alone.

"Rafael," I said, reaching for his hand across the table, "I've never been to your homeland. I've never seen the places that shaped you before you became who you are now. If you're willing to share that with me, I'd be honored to experience it with you."

The smile that appeared on Rafael's face was small and uncertain, but it was real.

"You have no idea what you're volunteering for," he said softly.

"Try me."

THE DECISION

Aleksander Nordh

An hour later, after the initial shock of the proposal had settled and we'd begun discussing practical considerations, I found myself marveling at the transformation in Rafael's demeanor. The panic had given way to careful planning, the fear replaced by cautious anticipation. Once he'd accepted the possibility of return, his mind had immediately begun working through logistics with the kind of precision that came from intimate knowledge of the city and culture we'd be navigating.

"September would be ideal," he was saying, sketching notes on a pad that had appeared from somewhere. "After the worst of the rainy season but before the holiday rush. Tourist visas would be sufficient for a research trip, and the universities would be in session if we need to access academic archives."

"How long would we need?" Soren asked, his academic enthusiasm once again overriding his sensitivity to Rafael's emotional state.

"Three weeks, minimum," Rafael replied without hesitation. "Possibly longer, depending on what we find and how cooperative the various institutions are."

Rafael Mercado

Planning the trip felt surreal, like organizing a journey to a past life rather than a simple international research expedition. But focusing on practical details—visas, accommodations, archive access, linguistic challenges—helped keep the emotional weight of the decision manageable.

"I should warn you," I said, looking around the table at three people who had never experienced the Philippines, "Manila isn't like London. The heat, the humidity, the population density, the cultural differences—it can be overwhelming for first-time visitors."

"We'll adapt," Aleksander said with the quiet confidence of someone who'd spent millennia adapting to new environments.

"And the research itself won't be straightforward," I continued. "Record-keeping practices, bureaucratic procedures, family privacy concerns—it's all quite different from what you're accustomed to in British archives."

"That's why we need you," Soren said simply. "Not just as a translator, but as someone who understands how things work there."

Erik Eriksson

Watching Rafael transform from frightened refugee to knowledgeable guide was fascinating and moving in equal measure. This was a side of him I'd never seen—confident, authoritative, clearly at home with navigating complex cultural and logistical challenges. It reminded me that before his transformation, before his years of isolation, he'd been a young man raised in a sophisticated urban environment, someone with education and social connections and practical skills.

"What about your feeding requirements?" I asked quietly, addressing the one concern that hadn't been openly discussed. "Will that be... manageable in Manila?"

Rafael's expression grew more serious, but he didn't seem surprised by the question.

"More challenging than London, certainly. But not impossible. The city has areas where... where someone like me can find what they need without drawing attention."

The careful euphemism reminded me that despite all our domesticity, despite how normal our relationship had become, Rafael was still fundamentally different from the rest of us. The trip would require planning around needs that went far beyond tourist logistics.

Aleksander Nordh

As the evening wound down and practical details gave way to excited speculation about what we might discover, I found myself reflecting on the extraordinary journey that had led us to this point. A year ago, Rafael had been an isolated figure on the periphery of Regular society, Erik had been a lonely teenager in rural Sweden, and Soren had been pursuing academic research with no idea it would transform his entire life.

Now we were planning international travel as a family unit, pooling resources and expertise to solve mysteries that connected all of us to something larger than our individual stories.

"There's one more thing we should consider," I said as we prepared to part ways for the evening. "The cost of this expedition. International travel for four people, extended accommodation, archive fees, local transportation—it won't be inexpensive."

"I can contribute," Rafael began, but I held up a hand to stop him.

"I'll handle the expenses," I said firmly. "This research benefits all of us, and I have resources specifically intended for family needs."

Soren Jensen

Aleksander's casual assumption of financial responsibility reminded me once again of the vast differences in our circumstances—not just the supernatural elements, but the accumulated wealth that came from over two millennia of careful investment and resource management. It still made me slightly uncomfortable, the ease with which he could solve problems that would represent major financial challenges for most people.

But I was learning to accept his generosity as an expression of love rather than charity, to understand that for someone with his resources, paying for family travel was equivalent to my offering to cook dinner or Erik volunteering to handle research translation.

"Thank you," I said simply, meaning it completely.

"When do we leave?" Erik asked, his excitement now undisguised.

Rafael looked around the table at three faces filled with anticipation and affection, taking a deep breath before committing to a course of action that would change everything.

"Three weeks," he said. "I'll need three weeks to make the necessary arrangements, contact the right people, prepare for what we might find."

"Three weeks," Aleksander confirmed, reaching for my hand across the table. "Our first international research expedition as a family."

Rafael Mercado

As I walked back to our flat with Erik later that evening, his hand warm in mine despite the London chill, I found myself marveling at how completely my life had changed. A year ago, the thought of returning to Manila would have sent me into paralyzing panic. Tonight, surrounded by people who had somehow chosen to love me despite knowing exactly what I was, it felt like the most natural thing in the world.

Terrifying, yes. Emotionally challenging, certainly. But natural nonetheless.

"Are you really okay with this?" Erik asked as we climbed the stairs to our flat. "The trip, I mean. I know it wasn't your idea originally."

"I'm terrified," I admitted, unlocking our door. "But I'm also... excited. For the first time in over a decade, I'm going home. And I'm not going alone."

The smile Erik gave me was worth every moment of anxiety the decision had cost me.

"No," he said, pulling me close as we stepped into the sanctuary we'd built together. "You're definitely not going alone."

41
GHOSTS AND MEMORIES

NINOY AQUINO INTERNATIONAL AIRPORT (NAIA) - TERMINAL 1, PASAY CITY, METRO MANILA 1300, PHILIPPINES

Rafael Mercado

The humid Manila air hit me like a physical embrace as we emerged from Ninoy Aquino International Airport, thick and warm and laden with scents that transported me instantly back thirteen years. Diesel fumes mixed with tropical flowers, street food vendors competing with expensive cologne from passing businessmen, the underlying sweetness of overripe fruit and the salt tang from Manila Bay—it was exactly as I remembered and completely overwhelming.

"Jesus," Erik breathed beside me, his fair Swedish skin already flushing in the heat despite the evening hour. "How do people function in this humidity?"

"You adapt," I said automatically, then caught myself. When had I stopped thinking of this as normal? When had London's temperate climate become my baseline instead of this tropical intensity that had shaped the first twenty-one years of my life?

Soren was studying a guidebook with typical academic thoroughness, while Aleksander moved through the airport chaos with the fluid grace of someone who'd navigated countless unfamiliar environments over the centuries. But it was the looks we were drawing that made my chest tight with anxiety—four foreigners, clearly tourists despite my Filipino features, obviously wealthy enough to afford international travel.

"The hotel is in Makati," I said, steering us toward the taxi queue. "It'll give us easy access to the business district and the older residential areas where the research needs to happen."

As our taxi wove through traffic that defied every traffic law I remembered from London, I found myself cataloging changes and continuities with the intensity of someone returning from the dead. New skyscrapers pierced the skyline where empty lots had been, but the basic rhythm of the city remained unchanged—jeepneys painted in brilliant colors weaving between sleek sedans, street vendors setting up for the evening rush, families crowded onto single motorcycles with casual disregard for safety regulations.

"It's incredible," Soren said, his face pressed to the window as we passed a street market that had transformed an entire block into an outdoor shopping center. "The energy, the density—it's like nothing I've ever experienced."

"Wait until tomorrow," I replied, my voice carefully neutral despite the emotions churning in my chest. "This is nothing compared to the districts we'll need to visit for the research."

But underneath my practical observations, something else was stirring—a recognition so profound it made my hands shake. This was home. Despite thirteen years of absence, despite the transformation that had changed everything about who I was, some fundamental part of me still belonged to these streets, these sounds, these impossible contradictions of poverty and wealth existing side by side.

Erik Eriksson

I'd studied photographs of Manila, read travel guides, tried to prepare myself for what Rafael's homeland would be like. But nothing had prepared me for the sheer intensity of it—the way every sense was constantly bombarded with new information, the way the city seemed to pulse with life at a frequency that made London feel sleepy by comparison.

But more than the sensory overload, I was watching Rafael's face as he processed returning to a place he'd never expected to see again. His expression was carefully controlled, but I'd learned to read the subtle signs of his emotional state over the past year. The slight tension around his eyes that meant he was fighting back tears. The way his hands clenched and unclenched in his lap when he thought no one was looking. The careful neutrality of his voice that meant he was working very hard not to fall apart.

"Are you okay?" I asked quietly, my hand finding his under the cover of the taxi's dim interior.

"No," he replied honestly, his fingers intertwining with mine. "But I will be."

THE FIRST RECONNAISSANCE

Rafael Mercado

The next morning, after a restless night spent adjusting to the time difference and the unfamiliar sounds of a city that never truly slept, I prepared for our expedition with the careful attention to protection that my condition demanded. The tropical sun was already intense at nine AM, streaming through our hotel windows with the kind of UV radiation that would leave me with painful burns within minutes of exposure.

I applied sunscreen with the methodical thoroughness I'd learned over years of managing my sensitivity, covering every inch of exposed skin with SPF 50+ before adding long sleeves, a wide-brimmed hat, and the compact umbrella I'd packed specifically for this trip. The routine was familiar but felt strange in this context—returning to my homeland while hiding from the very sun that had once been as natural to me as breathing.

"Ready?" I asked as we prepared to leave the hotel lobby, then paused as I saw Soren unfurling his own umbrella.

"For the heat," he explained with a slight smile that didn't quite hide his real motivation. "Erik mentioned that umbrellas are common here for sun protection, not just rain."

The gesture was so thoughtful, so quietly supportive, that I felt my throat tighten with emotion. He was right that umbrellas were common in Manila—businessmen, students, vendors all used them to shield themselves from the intense tropical sun. But I knew he was carrying one primarily so I wouldn't feel conspicuous, so I wouldn't have to navigate my limitations alone.

Erik Eriksson

Watching Rafael prepare for the Manila sun was a stark reminder of how different his needs were from ours, how carefully he had to manage every aspect of his existence to accommodate his Regular physiology. In London, his UV sensitivity was manageable—cloudy skies, shorter days, the ability to time activities around optimal light conditions. Here, the equatorial sun was unforgiving, turning something as simple as walking down the street into a calculated risk.

But it was Soren's immediate adaptation that made me proud of our family. Without fanfare or discussion, he'd acquired his own umbrella and was carrying it with the casual ease of someone accustomed to the local customs, making

Rafael's necessary protection seem like a natural choice rather than a medical requirement.

Rafael Mercado

As we ventured into the heart of Makati, I led our small expedition through streets that held decades of memory while staying carefully in whatever shade was available. The business district had transformed beyond recognition—gleaming towers housing international corporations, shopping centers that rivaled anything in London or New York, the kind of urban sophistication that spoke of the Philippines' growing economic influence.

But it was the older residential areas on the district's edges that we needed to explore, the neighborhoods where families like the Mercados would have lived during the American colonial period. Streets that had maintained their character despite the modernization surrounding them, though now I navigated them under the protection of my umbrella, ducking between awnings and covered walkways with the practiced efficiency of someone who'd learned to live within certain limitations.

"The church records will be our best starting point," I explained as we moved through sidewalks crowded with vendors, office workers, and school children in crisp uniforms. "Catholic parishes were meticulous about documentation, especially for prominent families."

"And you know which parishes to check?" Soren asked, his academic excitement obvious despite the challenges of the climate. He'd already soaked through his first shirt and we'd only been walking for thirty minutes, but he kept his umbrella positioned to provide me with additional shade whenever we stopped to talk.

"I know which ones existed during the relevant period," I confirmed. "Though finding priests who have access to century-old records, who are willing to share them with foreign researchers, who speak sufficient English..." I shrugged. "That's where things become complicated."

Erik Eriksson

Watching Rafael navigate the city was like seeing him transform into someone entirely new, though I was acutely aware of how he moved with constant attention to shade and shelter. Gone was the careful reserve that characterized his interactions in London, replaced by an easy confidence that suggested deep familiarity with the complex social codes that governed Filipino urban life. He moved through crowds with the unconscious grace of someone who understood exactly how much space to claim, which vendors to acknowledge, how to signal respect for elders while maintaining appropriate distance from strangers—all while keeping his umbrella positioned for optimal sun protection.

When he paused to ask directions from an elderly woman selling flowers under a colorful awning, their rapid Tagalog exchange was punctuated by laughter and the kind of warm familiarity that spoke of shared cultural understanding. She gestured approvingly at our umbrellas, clearly recognizing the practical wisdom of protecting ourselves from the intense midday sun. For the first time since I'd known him, Rafael looked completely at ease in his own skin, even while managing his physical limitations.

"She says Father Martinez at Santa Ana Parish has been there for forty years," Rafael translated as we continued down the street. "If anyone would have access to historical records, it would be him."

"And she just... told you that?" Soren asked. "A complete stranger?"

"Filipinos are hospitable people," Rafael replied with the first genuine smile I'd seen from him since we'd landed. "Especially when they think you're trying to trace family history. Everyone has stories about relatives who disappeared into America or Europe. Everyone understands the importance of connection."

SANTA ANA PARISH

Soren Jensen

Santa Ana Parish was a study in architectural evolution—the original Spanish colonial structure overlaid with decades of additions and renovations that told the story of the Philippines' complex history. Modern air conditioning units jutted from ancient stone walls, fluorescent lighting illuminated hand-carved wooden saints, and the sound of contemporary praise music drifted from speakers that competed with traditional church bells.

Father Martinez was exactly what I'd expected from Rafael's description—elderly, dignified, possessed of the kind of gentle authority that came from decades of shepherding a community through celebrations and tragedies. His English was careful but clear, and his eyes held the sharp intelligence of someone who'd learned to assess visitors quickly and accurately.

"You are researching American military families?" he asked, gesturing for us to sit in chairs arranged around his modest office. "From the colonial period?"

"Specifically, we're trying to trace connections between American servicemen and local Filipino families," I explained, offering him the credentials Rafael had suggested would be most persuasive. "Academic research focused on cultural exchange and community integration. It's part of a Doctoral program for King's College in London; a multi-year, multi-continent effort." Father

Martinez seemed impressed, if not a bit puzzled how his humble church might fit into their work.

Rafael Mercado

I sat in careful silence as Soren explained our research objectives, fighting the strange sensation of watching my past and present collide in ways I'd never imagined. This church was blocks from where I'd grown up, where my family had attended mass every Sunday for generations. Father Martinez might have known my parents, might have baptized children I'd played with as a boy.

The possibility of recognition was both thrilling and terrifying. Thirteen years had changed me—not just the supernatural transformation, but the simple passage of time, the different life I'd built in London. Would anyone see Rafael Mercado in the composed young man translating academic questions about century-old parish records?

"The Mercado family," Father Martinez said thoughtfully when Soren mentioned the name we'd been researching. "Yes, I remember stories about them. Very prominent in this district during the American period. The father was a professor, I think. Very learned man."

My heart stopped entirely. Stories. He remembered stories about my family.

Erik Eriksson

I saw Rafael's reaction to Father Martinez's words—the way his already pale skin went completely white, the slight tremor in his hands that he tried to hide by clasping them in his lap. Whatever the priest was about to tell us, it was going to affect Rafael more deeply than any of us had anticipated.

Instinctively, I shifted my chair closer to his, not quite touching but close enough to offer support if he needed it. Aleksander caught my eye from across the room, his expression alert in the way that suggested his enhanced senses were monitoring Rafael's stress levels.

"You knew the family personally?" Soren asked, his researcher's instincts overriding any sensitivity to Rafael's emotional state.

"Not personally, no," Father Martinez replied. "But there are records, stories passed down through the parish. The Mercados were generous benefactors, very involved in community affairs. Tragedy, what happened to the family eventually."

"What kind of tragedy?" I asked, my voice carefully neutral despite the way Rafael had gone rigid beside me.

Rafael Mercado

"The son," Father Martinez said, shaking his head with the sorrow of someone who'd witnessed too much human suffering over the decades. "Brilliant young man, educated at University of Santo Tomas, full of promise. Found dead in Manila Bay. Suicide, they said. The family never recovered from the loss."

The words hit me like physical blows. The story I had fabricated, the elaborate deception I had orchestrated with my friend's help to give my family closure, spoken aloud by someone who treated it as historical fact rather than my desperate fiction. I had created evidence of my own death—staged my body being found in Manila Bay, crafted a suicide narrative because I couldn't let them see what I had become. I had become a cautionary tale, a tragedy that old priests shared to illustrate the fragility of human happiness.

I had chosen this lie rather than burden my family with the truth of my transformation. With my friend's help, we had fabricated physical evidence, created a story that would allow them to grieve and move forward rather than spend eternity wondering what had happened to their son. The guilt in that choice was staggering—not just the grief I had caused them, but forcing them to live with a fabricated suicide story that carried social stigma in Filipino Catholic culture.

"The parents?" Soren asked gently, though I could see him glancing at me with growing concern.

"Mother passed several years ago. The grief, you understand—losing a child in such a way. Father is still alive, I believe. Lives quietly, keeps to himself. Understandable, given the circumstances. Lost his wife to grief over their son's death."

Soren Jensen

The change in Rafael was immediate and alarming. What little color had remained in his face drained away entirely, and I could see him struggling to maintain composure as the implications of what we'd just learned sank in. His father was alive. Living alone. Still grieving not just the son he believed had killed himself over a decade ago, but the wife who had died from that grief.

"Father," I said, instinctively moving to redirect the conversation before Rafael broke down entirely, "about the historical records we're researching. Would the parish archives have documentation from the 1900-1910 period?"

"Certainly. Though accessing them would require..." Father Martinez paused, studying our group with renewed attention. "Forgive me, but the young man appears unwell. Perhaps we should continue this conversation another time?"

I felt Erik's hand touch mine, Aleksander's concerned gaze, Soren's protective instinct to shield me from further emotional damage. But underneath the panic and grief, something else was stirring—a desperate, overwhelming need to know more. To understand what had become of the life I'd abandoned, the family I'd chosen to hurt rather than burden with the truth.

"I'm fine," I managed, my voice stronger than I'd expected. "Please, continue. The records—would it be possible to review documents from that period?"

Father Martinez studied me for another moment, then nodded slowly. "I will need to make some arrangements. These are historical documents, you understand. Very delicate. But for legitimate academic research..." He turned to Soren. "You have proper credentials from your university?"

"Of course," Soren replied immediately.

"Then return tomorrow afternoon. I will have what you need."

WALKING THROUGH GHOSTS

After leaving the parish, I found myself walking without conscious destination through streets that held the weight of my entire childhood, my umbrella creating a small circle of shade that had become as essential as breathing. Erik stayed close beside me, his own umbrella tilted to provide additional coverage when we stopped to rest, while Soren and Aleksander followed at a respectful distance. All of them understanding that I needed space to process what we'd learned while still having their support available.

The afternoon sun was brutal, even by Manila standards, but the familiar rhythm of seeking shade, timing movements between covered areas, brought back muscle memories from my youth. This was how people lived here—in harmony with the climate rather than fighting it, understanding that the sun demanded respect and accommodation. Erik became a lifeline in protecting me from its rays, seemingly knowing where to go to keep me safe. The umbrella was a shield he used in battle. I had never thought before of someone protecting me in such a way as pure, loving.

"Your father," Erik said quietly as we paused at an intersection that led toward the neighborhood where I'd grown up. "He's alive."

"Yes."

"And your mother died from grief."

"Because of me. Because they thought I was dead." The words came out harder than I'd intended, but the guilt was overwhelming. My mother had died believing her son had committed suicide, and my father was living alone with that double loss.

"Do you want to..." He didn't finish the question, but I understood what he was asking.

Did I want to see him? Did I want to risk the possibility of recognition, of having to explain thirteen years of absence and deception? Did I want to face the man who had lost both his son and his wife to grief, who was living with the fabricated story of a body pulled from Manila Bay?

"Not yet," I said finally. "Maybe not ever. I need to understand what seeing me would do to him before I make that choice."

Erik Eriksson

The neighborhood Rafael led us through was clearly middle-class by Manila standards—well-maintained houses with small gardens, tree-lined streets that provided some relief from the tropical sun, the kind of community where families knew each other and children played together in the evenings. It was easy to imagine a young Rafael growing up here, walking these same streets on his way to school, learning to navigate the complex social dynamics of Filipino family life.

But what struck me most was how he moved through the familiar landscape —not with nostalgia or joy, but with the careful attention of someone visiting a crime scene. Every corner held memories, but they seemed to cause him pain rather than comfort.

"That was my school," he said, nodding toward a building that had clearly been expanded since his childhood. "And there—" He pointed to a corner house with an elaborate garden. "The Sandoval family. They had seven children and Mrs. Sandoval made the best lumpia in the district."

His voice was carefully neutral, but I could see the effort it cost him to maintain that emotional distance from memories that were clearly precious despite their current pain.

"Rafael," I said softly, stopping in the middle of the sidewalk. "We can leave. We can go back to the hotel, or even back to London. You don't have to put yourself through this."

"Yes, I do," he replied with quiet certainty. "I've been running from this for thirteen years. If I'm ever going to have peace, if I'm ever going to be able to love you and our family completely, I have to face what I left behind."

Soren Jensen

The next morning brought a breakthrough that transformed our entire understanding of the research puzzle we'd been trying to solve. Father Martinez had arranged for us to examine parish records dating back to the 1890s, and within hours of careful examination, we'd found exactly what we'd been looking for.

"Here," I said, pointing to an entry in the baptismal register dated March 15, 1904. "Maria Elena Mercado, daughter of Professor Antonio Mercado and Elena Santos Mercado. Godfather listed as..." I paused, double-checking the faded ink. "Johannes Jensen, Captain, United States Army."

The silence that followed was profound. After months of circumstantial evidence and speculation, here was documentary proof of the connection we'd theorized. John Mikael Jensen—my great-great-great-grandfather—had been close enough to the Mercado family to serve as godfather to their daughter.

"That's not the end of it," Rafael said quietly, his finger tracing another entry several lines down. "Look at this."

The entry he'd found was dated two years later: "Rafael Antonio Mercado, son of Professor Antonio Mercado and Elena Santos Mercado." But it was the notation in the margin that made my breath catch—"Padre ausente, registro por familia."

"Father absent, registered by family," Rafael translated unnecessarily. "Born in 1906, two years after his sister. And look at the date of birth."

I did the calculation quickly. If Maria Elena's brother Rafael had been born in 1906 and lived a normal lifespan, he would have died sometime in the 1980s or 1990s. But if he'd had children...

"Your grandfather," I said, understanding flooding through me. "Your grandfather was Rafael Antonio Mercado, named after his uncle. Who was..." I gestured at the baptismal record. "Who was connected to our family through John Jensen's relationship with the Mercados."

Rafael Mercado

The chain of connection was suddenly, brilliantly clear. My great-great-uncle, the original Rafael Antonio Mercado, had been born into a family that had intimate connections with John Jensen during his military service. Those connections had been significant enough for an American army captain to serve as godfather to their daughter, suggesting a relationship that went far beyond military courtesy.

And now, over a century later, his descendant had found his way to the Jensen family descendants in London, drawn by circumstances that had seemed like chance but were actually the working out of connections forged generations ago.

"The bloodlines," I whispered, the phrase that had become shorthand for our family's complex interconnections taking on new meaning. "It really is all connected."

"What happens now?" Erik asked, his hand finding mine as we sat surrounded by century-old records that had just rewritten our understanding of our own family history.

I looked around the quiet parish office, at these three people who had become my family, at the documentary evidence that we belonged together not just by choice but by blood. And for the first time since we'd arrived in Manila, I felt something other than fear about the possibilities that lay ahead.

"Now," I said, "we find out what other stories these records have to tell us. And then..." I paused, gathering courage for what I was about to suggest. "Then maybe it's time to meet the family that's been waiting for me to come home."

42
RECOGNITION

THE PENINSULA MANILA CORNER OF AYALA AND MAKATI AVENUES, MAKATI CITY 1226, METRO MANILA, PHILIPPINES

Rafael Mercado

The morning of our planned visit, Erik had surprised me by producing a small cosmetics kit he'd quietly purchased from the hotel's boutique shop.

"Just enough to change your features slightly," he'd explained, his artistic eye studying my face with professional assessment. "A little contouring here, some highlighting there. Combined with your sun protection and Western clothes, you'll look like a mixed-heritage academic from London rather than a local Filipino."

Soren had contributed by selecting the most obviously European outfit from my luggage—a tailored blazer that screamed expensive London fashion, paired with perfectly pressed trousers that no local would wear in Manila's heat. The wide-brimmed hat I needed for UV protection was stylish enough to complete the image of a sophisticated foreign researcher.

The subtle makeup Erik applied worked exactly as intended. Combined with my naturally pale complexion from years of avoiding sunlight, I looked distinctly mixed-race—Filipino features softened and refined in ways that suggested European ancestry. When I practiced speaking in my most pronounced British accent, the transformation was complete. I was no longer Rafael Mercado, local boy. I was Rafael the London academic, foreign enough to be interesting but Filipino enough to warrant respect.

. . .

THE DECISION

Rafael Mercado

For three days after our breakthrough at the parish archives, I'd wrestled with the knowledge that my father was still alive, still living in our old neighborhood. The documented proof of our family's connection to the Jensens had given Soren everything he needed for his research, but it had also made avoiding the personal implications impossible.

I'd walked past our street twice, never quite gathering the courage to turn down the familiar block. Erik had been patient, understanding that this decision couldn't be rushed or forced. But this morning, watching him carefully pack our belongings for tomorrow's departure, I realized I was running out of time.

Now I stood at the end of the tree-lined street where I'd grown up, my umbrella providing necessary shade as I stared down the familiar block toward the house I'd called home for the first eighteen years of my life. Thirteen years of absence hadn't changed the basic layout—I could see our old house from here, smaller than I remembered but unmistakably the same coral-colored walls and red tile roof that had sheltered my childhood. Erik stood beside me, patient and supportive, while Aleksander and Soren had returned to the hotel hours ago, understanding that this conversation could take considerable time and that we would meet them there later.

The house was smaller than I remembered, though still well-maintained. The garden my mother had tended with such care showed signs of neglect—not abandonment, but the simpler maintenance of someone without the energy or heart for elaborate landscaping. The mango tree I'd climbed as a boy had grown enormous, its canopy providing shade for the entire front yard.

"Are you ready?" Erik asked softly, his hand finding mine despite the public setting.

I wasn't. I would never be ready for this. But I'd come too far to turn back now.

"Let's go," I said, and started up the familiar walkway toward the front door of my childhood home.

THE KNOCK

The sound of my knocking echoed through the house with a hollow quality that suggested emptiness—not physical vacancy, but the acoustic signature of a home where voices were rare and laughter even rarer. I could hear movement inside, slow and careful, the shuffle of elderly feet navigating furniture in rooms that had probably remained unchanged for years.

When the door opened, my world stopped entirely.

My father had aged decades in the thirteen years since I'd last seen him. His hair, once thick and black like mine, had gone completely white. His shoulders curved inward with the weight of grief and time, and his clothes hung loose on a frame that had clearly lost significant weight. But his eyes—those warm brown eyes that had read me bedtime stories and helped me with mathematics homework and looked at me with such pride when I'd been accepted to university—those eyes were unmistakably the same.

"Kumusta po kayo," I said carefully, deliberately emphasizing my British accent to make the English greeting sound foreign on my tongue. "Good afternoon, sir. I am... we are... researchers from London. My name is Rafael Thompson, and this is my colleague Erik. Father Martinez suggested we might speak with you about family history."

Erik Eriksson

The man who opened the door was clearly Rafael's father—the bone structure, the eyebrows, even the way he tilted his head when listening were identical despite the dramatic aging that grief had wrought. But what struck me most was the immediate change in his expression when he saw Rafael. Confusion flickered across his features, followed by something approaching recognition before settling into the careful politeness of someone accustomed to managing difficult emotions.

"Researchers?" he said in careful English, his voice carrying the slight rasp of someone who didn't speak often. "About my family?"

"About connections between Filipino families and American military personnel during the colonial period," Rafael Thompson replied, his voice steady despite the tremor I could feel in his hand. "We've been studying the Mercado family particularly, and their relationship with Captain Jensen."

The name had an immediate effect. Professor Mercado's eyes sharpened with interest, and he stepped back to gesture us inside.

"Please, come in. It has been... it has been some time since anyone asked about those old stories."

INSIDE THE HOUSE OF MEMORY

Rafael Mercado

Walking into my childhood home was like stepping through a photograph. Everything was exactly as I remembered—the wooden floors my mother had insisted on keeping polished to mirror brightness, the built-in bookshelves that lined the living room from floor to ceiling, the family portraits that chronicled decades of birthdays and graduations and celebrations.

But it was the additions that broke my heart. A shrine to my mother in the corner where her sewing machine used to sit, complete with candles and flowers and the rosary she'd carried to mass every Sunday. And beside it, smaller but no less significant, a memorial to me—my university graduation photo surrounded by academic awards and certificates from my time at University of Santo Tomas, frozen in time before everything went wrong.

My father noticed me staring at the memorial display and his expression grew heavy with familiar grief.

"My son," he said quietly. "He would have been about your age now, if..." He trailed off, unable to finish the sentence even after all these years.

"I'm very sorry for your loss," I managed, the words feeling like glass in my throat.

"He had just finished university when..." Professor Mercado paused, then seemed to gather himself. "But you are here about the historical research, yes? About Captain Jensen and the Mercado family?"

For the next hour, my father shared stories that brought our documentary research to vivid life. Captain Jensen hadn't just been a military acquaintance—he'd been a complicated figure in the family's history, someone who'd formed deep connections but ultimately caused pain through his departure.

"My grandfather told many stories about Captain Jensen," my father explained, settling into the chair that had clearly become his usual spot since my mother's death. "He spoke well of him in some ways—said he was different from the other American officers. He understood that we were people with our own culture, our own dignity. He learned to speak Tagalog, can you imagine? A U.S. Army captain taking time to learn the local language."

My father's expression grew more complex as he continued. "But there were also feelings of... disappointment. Betrayal, perhaps. When Captain Jensen left, he simply disappeared. No letters, no contact, no acknowledgment of the relationships he'd formed here. My grandfather said it was typical of the Americans—they made friends when it served them, then forgot us when they returned to their real lives."

"Did anyone ever try to contact him?" I asked, my British accent carefully maintained. "In America, I mean?"

Professor Mercado shook his head sadly. "This was before the great wars, you understand. Before modern communication. My grandfather was proud—he said if Captain Jensen had wanted to maintain contact, he would have found a way. Then came the Japanese invasion, the war years, so much destruction. By the time things settled, entire generations had passed. People moved on. It became just another story of how foreigners used our kindness and then abandoned us."

As he spoke, I found myself studying his face with desperate intensity, memorizing every line and shadow. This was my father—older, sadder, marked by losses I had caused, but still fundamentally the man who had shaped my childhood. The way he gestured when explaining complex ideas, the slight pause he took before sharing family anecdotes, the warmth that entered his voice when discussing people he'd loved—all exactly as I remembered.

Erik Eriksson

Watching Rafael listen to his father's stories was almost unbearable. I could see the war playing out across his features—desperate love and crushing guilt, the desire to reveal himself and the knowledge that doing so might cause more pain than joy. Every time Professor Mercado mentioned his lost son, Rafael's composure cracked a little more.

But it was the stories themselves that made the afternoon feel sacred. This elderly man, isolated by grief and time, was sharing family history with obvious pleasure at having an interested audience. The academic curiosity that had defined his career was still there, emerging as he described documents and photographs and oral traditions that painted a picture of genuine cross-cultural friendship.

"You remind me of someone," Professor Mercado said suddenly, his gaze fixed on Rafael Thompson with uncomfortable intensity. "The way you ask questions, the expressions you make when thinking. Very familiar."

Rafael Mercado

My heart stopped entirely. After three hours of conversation, the recognition I'd both hoped for and dreaded was finally surfacing. I could see my father's mind working, trying to place the familiarity he was feeling.

"I... I have one of those faces," I said, echoing Aleksander's strategy from similar situations. "People often think they recognize me."

But Professor Mercado continued to study me with the careful attention of someone trying to solve a puzzle that felt important beyond simple curiosity.

"Rafael," he said suddenly, and I felt a complex mix of relief and sadness at hearing my real first name spoken in his voice, even though he was addressing me by my false surname. "You said your name was Rafael, yes?"

"Yes, sir."

"My son was named Rafael as well. Family tradition—we name the first son after the great-uncle who died young." His voice grew soft with memory. "Such a beautiful name. It means 'God has healed,' you know."

The irony was devastating. A name that meant divine healing, carried by someone who'd chosen to break his family's hearts rather than burden them with an impossible truth.

THE WEIGHT OF RECOGNITION

As the afternoon wore on, my father's sense of familiarity seemed to deepen rather than fade. He began sharing more personal stories—about my mother's death, about the loneliness of living with double grief, about the small comforts that helped him navigate each day. It was as if my presence had awakened something in him, some need to connect with another person after years of careful isolation.

"You know," he said during a lull in conversation, "I have not spoken this much about family in... years, perhaps. But there is something about you that makes it feel... safe. Natural."

Erik secretly squeezed my hand gently, a reminder that I wasn't navigating this emotional minefield alone.

"Sometimes," I replied carefully, "we meet people who feel like family even when they're strangers."

"Yes," my father said, his eyes brightening with recognition of a truth he felt but couldn't name. "Exactly like that. As if... as if Rafael is somehow still present in the world, helping me connect with good people."

Erik Eriksson

The conversation was becoming increasingly emotional, and I could see Rafael struggling with the weight of his father's words. Professor Mercado clearly felt a deep connection to this mysterious young researcher who shared his lost son's name and somehow made him feel less alone in the world.

Rafael Mercado

"Excuse me for a moment," I said, rising from my seat with practiced composure. "Could I use your comfort room?"

"Of course," my father said, gesturing down the familiar hallway. "Second door on the left. Just as it's always been."

Just as it's always been. The casual phrase hit me harder than it should have. Of course it was still in the same place—this was my childhood home. But hearing those words from my father, directed at a stranger he didn't recognize, felt like being erased and remembered simultaneously.

I walked down the hallway on autopilot, my feet finding the path they'd traveled thousands of times before. The wooden floorboards still creaked in exactly the same spots—two steps from the living room, then again just before the bathroom door. I'd learned as a teenager which boards were silent when sneaking back from late-night reading sessions, which ones would alert my parents that I was still awake past curfew.

The comfort room door opened with the same slight squeak it had always had. My father had never fixed it, claiming he liked being able to hear when people were using it. "Preventive awareness," he'd called it with his doctor's logic, wanting to know if someone was sick in the night.

I stepped inside and closed the door, leaning against it as the carefully maintained composure finally cracked. The bathroom was exactly as I remembered—white tiles my mother had chosen because they were easy to keep clean, the wooden medicine cabinet my father had installed himself, slightly crooked despite his best efforts. But it was the additions that made my chest tight.

My mother's toiletries were still arranged on the counter. Her favorite coconut-scented soap in the ceramic dish she'd bought at the Quiapo market, the particular brand of lotion she'd used every evening after her shower, her reading glasses sitting beside the sink where she'd left them the last morning of her life. Everything untouched, preserved like a shrine to daily routines that would never happen again.

I picked up the soap dish with shaking hands. It was dusty—years of accumulated dust on an object my father couldn't bring himself to move. The coconut scent was still faint underneath the must, and suddenly I was eight years old again, sitting on the bathroom counter while my mother washed her face, telling me stories about her own childhood while I swung my legs and tried to stay awake past bedtime.

"Rafael, iho, you need to sleep. School tomorrow."

"Five more minutes, Mama? Please?"

"Always five more minutes with you. Just like your father—never wanting the day to end."

The memory was so vivid I could almost hear her voice, feel her cool fingers brushing my forehead as she checked for fever the way she did every night, convinced that children's illnesses always arrived after sunset. That protective instinct, that mother's certainty that vigilance could prevent all harm—and I'd repaid it by making her believe her son had killed himself in Manila Bay.

I set the soap dish back exactly where it had been and turned to the medicine cabinet. Inside, I found my father's meticulously organized medications—blood pressure pills, vitamin supplements, the omega-3s he'd always said every hematologist should take to practice what they preached. But there were also newer bottles. Antidepressants. Sleep aids. The pharmaceutical evidence of a man trying to manage grief that wouldn't heal.

Behind those were older items, and my breath caught when I saw them. My childhood asthma inhaler, expired for over a decade but still kept in its designated spot. The children's vitamins I'd taken every morning until I was twelve and declared myself too old for them. A small bottle of antihistamine with my name written on the label in my mother's careful handwriting: *Rafael - use only as needed.*

He'd kept everything. Every small piece of his son's existence, preserved in a bathroom medicine cabinet like relics of a lost civilization.

I closed the cabinet and caught my reflection in the mirror. The makeup Erik had applied made me look different enough—mixed heritage, European influence, definitely not the local boy who'd grown up in this house. But underneath, I could see traces of the person I'd been. The shape of my eyes was the same as in my university graduation photo displayed in the living room. The way I tilted my head when thinking was identical to that eighteen-year-old who'd believed the world made sense, that professors could be trusted, that transformation was something that happened to other people.

I turned away from the mirror and noticed the towels. They were new—my father had needed to replace things over the years—but they were hung exactly where towels had always hung in this bathroom. Two hooks on the back of the door, a decorative rack my mother had installed because she'd thought it made the space feel more elegant. Everything had its place, maintained by a man who found comfort in keeping routines alive even when the people who'd established them were gone.

The waste basket beside the toilet still had my mother's favorite liner—a cheerful floral pattern she'd insisted made even a bathroom feel more welcoming. My father had kept buying the same pattern for years after her death, unable to let go of these small choices she'd made that had shaped their life together.

I knelt down and opened the cabinet beneath the sink. More evidence of stalled time—extra rolls of toilet paper stacked the way my mother had always stacked them, cleaning supplies in the same arrangement, a box of tissues that had probably been there since before I "died." Everything frozen, preserved, waiting for a life that would never resume.

But what broke me completely was finding, tucked in the very back behind a bottle of bleach, a plastic bag containing my old toothbrush. Not thrown away, not displayed, just... kept. Saved for a son who would never need it again, by a father who couldn't bear to acknowledge the finality of its uselessness.

I sat back on my heels, the bathroom floor tiles cold against my knees, and let myself fully feel the weight of what I'd done to this house. It wasn't just the memorials in the living room or the untouched toiletries—it was this pervasive sense of time having stopped. My father lived in a museum of his own grief, surrounded by the physical evidence of loves lost, unable to move forward because moving forward meant accepting that his wife and son were truly gone.

The house was so quiet. That's what struck me most forcefully as I knelt there on the bathroom floor. Growing up, this house had been filled with noise—my mother's voice calling from the kitchen, my father's laughter at dinner, the television in the evening, visitors coming and going. A living home for a living family.

Now there was only silence. The heavy, thick silence of a man living alone in a space designed for three, keeping everything exactly as it had been because changing anything would feel like another death, another loss, another betrayal of the people he couldn't save.

I thought about the boy I'd been in this house. The Rafael Mercado who'd done homework at the kitchen table while his mother cooked dinner, who'd argued with his father about politics over breakfast, who'd sneaked friends in through the back door and stayed up too late reading by flashlight under his covers. That boy had been *sure*—sure of his identity, his future, his place in the world. He'd known exactly who he was supposed to become: a literature professor like his mother, maybe, or a doctor like his father. Someone who made his parents proud, who carried on family traditions, who added his own chapter to the story this house had been telling for generations.

That boy had been naive but genuine. Sheltered but kind. Intellectually ambitious but emotionally earnest. He'd believed in goodness, in the fundamental decency of people, in the idea that hard work and good intentions were enough to ensure a happy life. He'd trusted his professors, loved his best friend with hopeless devotion, and assumed the most dramatic thing that would ever happen to him was maybe publishing a well-received paper on medieval literature.

He'd been wrong about everything.

I stood slowly, gripping the edge of the sink for support. That boy was gone, drowned in Manila Bay along with his innocence and his certainty. What remained was this thing I'd become—not quite the monster I'd believed myself to be for so many years, but not quite human either. Something in between, learning slowly that maybe the categories weren't as fixed as I'd thought, that transformation could be survived even when survival seemed impossible.

But standing in this bathroom, surrounded by the untouched remnants of my mother's routines and my father's desperate preservation of everything we'd been, I felt the full weight of the cost. My survival had required their destruction. My new life had been built on the ashes of theirs. And no amount of rationalizing about protecting them from impossible truths could change the fundamental fact that I'd chosen my own peace over theirs.

I splashed cold water on my face, careful not to disturb the makeup too much, and took several deep breaths. In the mirror, I could see both versions of myself—the stranger Rafael Thompson that my father was getting to know, and underneath, the ghost of Rafael Mercado who had last stood in this bathroom thirteen years ago, still human, still innocent, still beloved by parents who were both alive and together and whole.

When I finally opened the door and stepped back into the hallway, I paused for a moment, listening to the voices from the living room. Erik was speaking to my father in his careful English, probably offering some comfort or asking questions to keep the conversation going while I was gone. My father's voice responded with a warmth I hadn't heard in years—not the sad, hollowed-out grief that had marked his words when he'd talked about his lost son, but something approaching genuine engagement with another person.

Perhaps that was the only gift I could give him now. Not the truth that would destroy what little peace he'd found, but this moment of connection with a stranger who felt somehow familiar, who made him feel less alone in this too-quiet house, who reminded him that life could still include unexpected moments of human warmth.

I wiped my eyes one final time, checked my reflection to make sure the tears hadn't ruined the makeup, and walked back toward the living room. Back toward my father, who would never know how close his son had been. Back toward Erik, who was bearing witness to this impossible grief. Back toward the lie that was the only kind love I had left to offer.

Erik Eriksson

When Rafael excused himself to use the comfort room, as referred to the toilet, Professor Mercado turned to me with an expression of quiet desperation.

"Forgive me," he said, his English becoming more formal with emotion. "But I must ask—your friend, Rafael. There is something about him... Do you think it possible that souls can return? That the dead can somehow make their presence known to those who mourn them?"

The question hit me like a physical blow. This grieving father was sensing his son's presence but interpreting it through the lens of spiritual comfort rather than recognizing the impossible reality sitting in his living room.

"I think," I said carefully, "that love is stronger than death; that sometimes, the people we've lost find ways to let us know they're still with us."

Professor Mercado nodded with the satisfaction of someone whose deepest hopes had been validated.

THE CONVERSATION

Rafael Mercado

When I returned from the comfort room—which still contained my mother's toiletries, untouched since her death—I found Erik and my father deep in conversation about family connections and the ways grief could be transformed into something bearable through unexpected encounters.

"Your friend has been telling me about his own family," my father said as I resumed my seat. "About losing grandparents, about the importance of honoring those who came before us."

I looked at Erik with gratitude for whatever comfort he'd provided during my absence.

"Professor Mercado," I said, maintaining my British accent and false identity, "I want you to know that your son... wherever he is now... he would be very proud of the man you are. The way you've preserved his memory, the dignity with which you've carried your grief, the kindness you've shown to strangers researching your family's history."

My father's eyes filled with tears that he didn't try to hide.

"You really think so?"

"I know so," I said, meaning it with every fiber of my being. "And I think... I think he would want you to know that he loved you completely. That whatever happened to him, whatever led to his death, it was never about not loving his family enough."

The words I couldn't say hung in the air between us—all the explanations and apologies and reassurances that would have to remain unspoken. But something in my father's expression suggested he was hearing more than my words conveyed, that some part of him understood the deeper communication taking place.

"Do you really believe," he asked quietly, "that he knows how much I still love him?"

"Yes," I whispered, my voice breaking despite my efforts to maintain composure. "I believe he knows. And I believe... I believe he loves you too. Still. Always."

My father reached across the space between us and took my hand in both of his—the same hands that had taught me to tie my shoes, that had applauded at my school plays, that had held me when childhood nightmares made sleep impossible.

"Thank you," he said simply. "For helping me feel connected to him again. For making me feel less alone."

Erik Eriksson

The goodbye was devastating to witness. Professor Mercado walked us to the door with obvious reluctance, clearly treasuring this unexpected human connection after years of isolation. He shook my hand formally, then turned to Rafael with an expression of profound gratitude.

"Will you come back?" he asked. "When your research brings you to Manila again?"

I watched Rafael's face as he struggled with how to answer a question that highlighted the impossibility of his situation.

"If I can," Rafael said finally. "If circumstances allow."

"I hope they do," his father replied. "You have given me a great gift today. You have helped me feel that Rafael is still present in the world somehow, still touching the lives of good people."

WALKING AWAY

Rafael Mercado

The walk back to the street corner felt endless. Each step took me further from the man I loved most in the world and could never acknowledge. Behind me, I could hear my father standing in the doorway, watching us leave with the same careful attention he'd given to my departures for school when I was a child.

I didn't look back. I couldn't. The temptation to run back, to throw myself into his arms and confess everything, was overwhelming. But the knowledge of what that revelation would cost him—the questions it would raise, the impossible choices it would force him to make—kept me moving forward.

"Are you alright?" Erik asked as we reached the corner where we'd have to call for transportation, though my tears were obvious answer enough.

"No," I managed. "But it was right. It was the right thing to do."

When Erik flagged down a taxi and we climbed into its air-conditioned interior, I finally allowed myself to look back through the rear window. My father was still standing in the doorway, one hand raised in farewell, his expression holding something approaching peace for the first time since we'd arrived.

Erik Eriksson

The drive back to our hotel passed in silence punctuated only by Rafael's quiet weeping. When we reached the lobby, Soren and Aleksander were waiting in comfortable chairs, books in their laps but obvious concern on their faces. They immediately understood that something profound had occurred without requiring detailed explanation.

"How was he?" Aleksander asked gently as we settled into the seating area.

"Alive," Rafael whispered. "Grieving. Lonely. But alive."

"And you?"

Rafael was quiet for a long moment, staring out the lobby windows at the familiar streets of his childhood.

"I'm ready to go home," he said finally. "Back to London. Back to our life. Back to the family that knows who I really am."

DEPARTURE

Rafael Mercado

The next day, as we sat in the departure lounge at Ninoy Aquino International Airport, I found myself reflecting on the strange journey that had brought us here. We'd come to Manila seeking documentary evidence of family connections, and we'd found that and so much more. But the greatest discovery had been understanding that some forms of love required sacrifice, that sometimes protecting someone meant accepting their version of the truth even when it caused you pain.

"Any regrets?" Soren asked as our boarding announcement echoed through the terminal.

I considered the question seriously. Did I regret not revealing myself to my father? Did I regret the years of grief I'd caused him and my mother? Did I regret the choice to let them believe I was dead rather than burden them with the reality of what I'd become?

"No," I said finally, surprising myself with the certainty in my voice. "I chose his peace over my own need for acknowledgment. That's what love is, isn't it? Putting someone else's wellbeing ahead of your own desires."

Erik Eriksson

As our plane lifted off from Manila, beginning its long journey back to London, I watched Rafael's face as he took what might be his last look at the Philippines. There was sadness there, certainly, but also something approaching resolution. He'd faced his past, made peace with his choices, and chosen to move forward rather than remain trapped by regret.

"What happens now?" I asked as the city grew smaller below us.

"Now we go home," Rafael replied, his hand finding mine in the dim cabin light. "We go home to the family that chose us, that knows all our truths and loves us anyway. And we build the life we want together."

As the plane leveled off above the clouds, carrying us away from the past and toward the future, I realized that Rafael was right. Home wasn't a place—it was the people who saw you completely and chose to stay. And we were flying toward ours.

43
MATERNAL SURPRISE

FLAT 7, 28 CADOGAN SQUARE, CHELSEA, LONDON SW1X 0JP

Soren Jensen

The returned package from my third attempt at purchasing the perfect gift sat accusingly on Aleksander's coffee table, its pristine wrapping paper mocking my latest failure. In the past month, I'd tried books on ancient Scandinavian history (too presumptuous), vintage wine from the 1800s (potentially insulting to suggest they might appreciate something from their youth), and handcrafted items from contemporary artisans (possibly offensive to beings who had witnessed the creation of actual masterpieces).

"You're overthinking this," Rafael observed from his corner of the sofa, looking up from the academic journal he'd been reading. Since our return from Manila, he'd thrown himself into scholarly pursuits with renewed energy, auditing courses at King's College and contributing to several research projects. "They're Aleksander's parents. They're probably delighted just to meet you."

"That's exactly the problem," I replied, running my hands through my hair in frustration. "They're not just anyone's parents. They're Elders who are literally older than recorded human civilization. What do you give people who have witnessed the rise and fall of empires?"

Erik looked up from where he was sprawled on the floor, textbooks scattered around him as he worked through assignments for his second year at King's College. At nineteen, he'd developed the confident bearing of someone who'd found his place in the world, though he still possessed the directness that had characterized him as a teenager.

"Maybe they don't want gifts," he suggested with characteristic practicality. "Maybe they just want to meet the human who made their son happy for the first time in centuries."

Aleksander Nordh

I emerged from the kitchen where I'd been preparing tea, noting the familiar sight of Soren in full academic spiral. Over the past three years of marriage, I'd learned to recognize the signs—the way he approached problems with increasing intensity until he either solved them completely or exhausted himself trying.

"Soren," I said gently, settling beside him and offering him a cup of tea, "you're making this far more complicated than it needs to be. My parents are remarkably unpretentious people."

"Unpretentious?" Soren turned to stare at me with disbelief. "Aleksander, your father has lived since before the Roman Empire. Your mother predates most world religions. How is that unpretentious?"

"Because they've also spent the last two millennia learning that wisdom comes from simplicity, not complexity," I replied. "They'll be more interested in understanding who you are than in evaluating your gift-giving abilities."

Soren Jensen

Aleksander's calm reassurance did nothing to settle my nerves. For months, I'd been building up this meeting in my mind—the formal introduction to Elder royalty, the careful navigation of ancient protocols, the pressure to prove myself worthy of their immortal son. The fact that Aleksander seemed completely unconcerned only heightened my anxiety.

"Have you told them anything specific about me?" I asked, my academic mind seeking data points that might help me prepare. "About my research, my family, my... ordinariness?"

"I've told them I love you," Aleksander said simply. "I've told them you make me happy in ways I didn't know were possible. I've told them you've helped me understand what it means to be part of a family. What else matters?"

Rafael and Erik exchanged a look that suggested they found my anxiety both understandable and slightly amusing. Easy for them to be relaxed—they weren't about to meet beings who could remember when their ancestors were learning to make fire.

"When exactly are they arriving?" I asked, glancing at the clock.

"That's actually somewhat flexible," Aleksander replied with a smile that suggested he found my precise scheduling endearing. "Elder travel doesn't follow conventional timelines. They'll arrive when they arrive."

The vagueness of this response made my eye twitch. How was I supposed to prepare mentally without a specific schedule?

THE UNEXPECTED ENCOUNTER

The next afternoon, my nerves had reached such a pitch that I'd decided to walk to the local bookshop for the third time in two days, hoping to find some obscure text that might serve as an appropriate gift. As I emerged from our building's entrance, I was so absorbed in my internal debate about the merits of first-edition versus annotated manuscripts that I nearly collided with a woman.

"Oh! I'm terribly sorry," I said, stepping back quickly to avoid the collision.

The woman I'd nearly crashed into was perhaps the most elegant person I'd ever encountered—petite, with silver-streaked dark hair pulled into a sophisticated chignon, wearing a perfectly tailored coat that probably cost more than my monthly salary. Her features held the kind of timeless beauty that suggested excellent genetics and careful maintenance, though she appeared to be in her mid-forties.

"No harm done," she replied with a slight accent that sounded vaguely Northern European. Her smile was warm and genuine, transforming her aristocratic features into something approachable. "Though you seem rather preoccupied. I hope nothing serious?"

Aleksander Nordh

From my flat's window, I watched the scene unfolding on the street below with a mixture of amusement and inevitability. Trust my mother to arrive early and immediately encounter the one person in London who was most nervous about meeting her. Trust Soren to be so lost in thought that he nearly bowled over a woman who could probably break him in half without disturbing her manicure.

I was already moving toward the door when I saw my mother's expression shift from polite interest to delighted recognition. Soren might not realize who he was talking to, but she had clearly identified her son's husband from my descriptions.

Soren Jensen

"Just meeting some family members for the first time," I found myself explaining to this elegant stranger, something about her presence inviting confidence.

"Rather important family members, actually. I'm a bit nervous about making a good impression."

"I'm sure you'll do wonderfully," she replied with the kind of assured warmth that suggested she was accustomed to putting people at ease. "Important family members are usually just people, after all. They want to be liked just as much as you want to like them."

There was something oddly specific about her phrasing that made me pause, but before I could analyze it further, I heard familiar footsteps on the pavement behind me.

"Mor," Aleksander's voice carried a note of amused exasperation. "I see you've met Soren."

The world stopped.

Mor. Mother. The elegant stranger I'd been pouring my heart out to about family anxiety was Aleksander's mother. The ancient Elder I'd been dreading to meet had just spent five minutes listening to me worry about impressing her while offering gentle encouragement.

"You're..." I began, then stopped, my vocabulary completely deserting me.

"Astrid Nordh," she said with obvious delight, extending her hand with formal politeness that couldn't hide her amusement. "And you, unless I'm very much mistaken, are the young man who's made my son happier than I've seen him in centuries."

Aleksander Nordh

Watching Soren's face cycle through shock, embarrassment, and dawning realization was worth every moment of anxiety he'd experienced over the past month. My mother, with her supernatural ability to put humans at ease, had managed to defuse his nervousness simply by being herself—warm, interested, completely lacking in the imperial formality he'd been dreading.

"Mor, you're early," I said, moving to embrace her with the easy affection that had characterized our relationship for over two millennia. "I thought you weren't arriving until evening."

"Your father got impatient," she replied, her eyes sparkling with mischief as she kept one hand on my arm while extending the other toward Soren. "He's been talking about meeting his new son-in-law for months. We decided to surprise you."

Soren Jensen

Aleksander's mother—one of the oldest beings on Earth—was treating me like a beloved family member she simply hadn't met yet rather than a human who needed to prove his worthiness. Her handshake was firm but gentle, her attention completely focused on me rather than assessing me, and her obvious affection for Aleksander made it clear that anyone who made him happy was automatically welcome in her life.

"I feel like I should apologize," I managed, finally finding my voice. "For nearly knocking you over, for complaining about family anxiety to the person I was anxious about meeting..."

"Please don't," Astrid said with genuine warmth. "It was delightful. It told me everything I needed to know about your character—that you care enough about family to worry about doing right by them, that you're honest enough to share your concerns with strangers, and that you're considerate enough to apologize when you think you've made a mistake."

Aleksander Nordh

My mother's immediate acceptance of Soren was exactly what I'd expected but hadn't dared promise him. She had this remarkable ability to see straight to the heart of people, to understand their essential nature within moments of meeting them. The fact that she was already treating him like family rather than a curiosity suggested she approved completely.

"Where's Far?" I asked, using the Norwegian term for father that I'd retained from childhood.

"Paying the taxi driver and collecting our luggage," she replied. "We weren't entirely certain you'd have room for guests, so we made hotel reservations. But if you're willing to put up with us..."

"You're staying here," I said firmly. "Both of you. We'll make it work."

Soren Jensen

The casual family dynamics—Aleksander's easy use of childhood terms, his mother's practical concern about imposing, the assumption that they would want to stay close rather than maintain formal distance—was so completely normal that I felt my carefully constructed anxiety dissolving into relief.

"Of course you're staying with us," I heard myself saying, my British politeness overriding my nervousness. "It's your family home, after all. I'm the newcomer here."

Astrid's smile in response was radiant. "Oh, I like him already," she said to Aleksander, though her eyes remained on me. "He has lovely manners and the good sense to understand that family trumps protocol."

Aleksander Nordh

The sound of measured footsteps announced my father's approach before he came into view around the corner, carrying two pieces of luggage with the same economical grace that characterized all his movements. At apparent fifty-five, he looked like an older version of myself—same height, same build, same careful attention to his surroundings that suggested supernatural awareness wrapped in human courtesy.

"Gunnar," I called out, watching as his face lit up at the sight of our small group clustered on the sidewalk.

"Aleksander," he replied, setting down the luggage to embrace me with the kind of careful affection that spoke of centuries of practice. "And this must be Soren."

Soren Jensen

Meeting Aleksander's father was like glimpsing my husband's future—if Aleksander aged normally for another thirty years, this was exactly what he would look like. The same intelligent eyes, the same thoughtful expression, the same air of quiet authority that suggested someone accustomed to being listened to when he chose to speak.

But what struck me most was his immediate warmth. No formal assessment, no testing period, no careful evaluation of my worthiness. Just the straightforward acceptance of someone meeting a family member for the first time.

"Sir," I said, extending my hand with probably unnecessary formality.

"Gunnar," he corrected gently, his handshake firm and welcoming. "We're family now, after all. No need for sir."

Aleksander Nordh

Watching my parents meet Soren, seeing their immediate acceptance and his gradual relaxation, I felt something settle in my chest that I hadn't realized was tense. For all my reassurances about their unpretentious nature, part of me had worried about this meeting—not because I doubted their acceptance, but because I understood how much it meant to all of us.

"Shall we go upstairs?" I suggested, noting that our sidewalk reunion was beginning to attract curious glances from neighbors. "I believe Erik and Rafael are eager to meet you as well."

"The boys," Astrid said with obvious delight. "We've heard so much about them from your letters. Is it true that Erik managed to convince Rafael to return to the Philippines for research?"

"Among other accomplishments," I replied, picking up one of their bags. "They're both remarkable young men. You'll love them."

Soren Jensen

As we climbed the stairs to Aleksander's flat, I found myself marveling at how completely my expectations had been overturned. Instead of ancient, intimidating figures who required careful navigation, Aleksander's parents were simply... people. Extraordinarily well-traveled, sophisticated people with supernatural abilities and millennial lifespans, certainly, but people nonetheless. People who seemed genuinely delighted to meet their son's chosen family.

"Thank you," I said quietly to Astrid as we reached the landing. "For being so kind about my anxiety earlier. I'd been working myself into quite a state about this meeting."

"Perfectly understandable," she replied with maternal warmth. "Meeting family is always significant, regardless of how long they've been alive. The heart doesn't distinguish between centuries and decades when it comes to love."

Her words, so simple and wise, made me understand something fundamental about Elder nature that all my research had missed. Time might change perspective, but it didn't eliminate the essential experiences that made someone a person. Love, family, the desire for connection—these remained constant across any lifespan.

As Aleksander opened the door to introduce his parents to our complete chosen family, I realized that my month of anxiety had been not just unnecessary, but completely beside the point. This wasn't about impressing ancient beings with gifts or protocol.

This was simply about family meeting family, and discovering that love really was the only credential that mattered.

44
THE WOODEN BOX

FLAT 7, 28 CADOGAN SQUARE, CHELSEA, LONDON SW1X 0JP

Erik Eriksson

The sound of voices in the hallway gave us just enough warning to close our textbooks and assume some semblance of respectability before Aleksander's key turned in the lock. Rafael and I had been sprawled across the sitting room in the comfortable disorder of serious studying—his advanced linguistics materials mixed with my second-year literature assignments, empty coffee cups balanced on every available surface.

"They're here," Rafael said unnecessarily, though I could hear the nervous excitement in his voice. After our experiences in Manila, meeting Elder parents felt less daunting than it might have otherwise, but it was still significant. These were beings who had lived for millennia, who had shaped Aleksander's understanding of the world, who were now becoming our family by extension.

When the door opened, I was struck immediately by how normal they appeared. Aleksander's mother—Astrid—was elegant in the way that suggested excellent breeding and careful attention to quality, but she moved with the easy grace of someone completely comfortable in her own skin. His father—Gunnar—looked like an older version of Aleksander, distinguished and authoritative but radiating warmth rather than intimidation.

"Erik! Rafael!" Astrid said with obvious delight, moving toward us with arms already extended. "We've heard so much about you both from Aleksander's letters."

Rafael Mercado

Being embraced by Aleksander's mother felt like receiving a blessing from someone who had witnessed the entirety of human civilization. But there was nothing overwhelming or otherworldly about her presence—just the genuine warmth of someone meeting family members for the first time and finding them exactly as wonderful as she'd hoped.

"Mrs. Nordh," I said carefully, unsure of proper protocol for addressing Elder royalty.

"Astrid, please," she corrected with a smile. "We're family now. And I understand congratulations are in order—Aleksander tells us you two have been together for over two years now?"

The casual acceptance, the immediate inclusion in family conversation, the complete lack of supernatural formality—it was exactly what I'd hoped for but hadn't dared expect. After the careful navigation required for my own family situation, this unconditional welcome felt like stepping into sunlight after years of shadow.

Gunnar Nordh

Looking at these two young men—one blonde and earnest with the kind of intellectual curiosity that reminded me powerfully of Aleksander at that age, the other dark and elegant with the careful composure that spoke of someone who'd learned to navigate complex social situations—I felt the deep satisfaction that came from seeing family connections form naturally.

Erik carried himself with the confident bearing of someone who'd found his place in the world, though I could see traces of the uncertainty that had characterized Aleksander's descriptions of their first meetings. Rafael had the subtle markers of someone who'd experienced trauma but had emerged stronger rather than broken—a resilience that spoke well of his character and the support system he'd found.

"Erik," I said, offering my hand with genuine warmth. "I understand you're studying literature at King's College?"

"Yes, sir. Gunnar," Erik corrected himself with a slight blush. "Second year. I'm particularly interested in comparative mythology and its influence on modern literature."

"Excellent field of study," I replied, meaning it completely. "I've always found that the oldest stories reveal the most essential truths about human nature."

Astrid Nordh

Rafael's handshake was firm but careful, suggesting someone who'd learned to modulate his strength—clearly a Regular then, though one who'd achieved remarkable integration into human society. The way Erik unconsciously positioned himself slightly closer to Rafael, the subtle protective gesture, spoke of a relationship built on genuine care rather than mere attraction.

"Rafael," I said, studying his face with the enhanced perception that came with millennia of experience. "Aleksander mentioned you've recently returned from research in the Philippines? That must have been emotionally significant."

The way his expression shifted—surprise followed by recognition that I understood more than casual interest might suggest—confirmed my assessment of his character. He was clearly intelligent enough to recognize subtext while being honest enough not to pretend otherwise.

"It was," he replied simply. "Difficult but necessary. And it helped establish some family connections we'd been researching for Soren's dissertation."

"The Jensen bloodline connections," I said with obvious interest. "Aleksander's letters have been fascinating reading. What an extraordinary discovery."

Soren Jensen

Watching Aleksander's parents meet Erik and Rafael, seeing the immediate ease with which they integrated our little family into the understanding of their son's life, I felt something profound settle in my chest. This was how family was supposed to work, I thought—not through careful evaluation or conditional acceptance, but through simple recognition that love created bonds worth celebrating.

"Shall I make fresh tea?" I offered, moving toward the kitchen with the automatic hospitality that came from years of managing these sorts of gatherings.

"Let me help," Astrid said immediately, following me into the kitchen. "I'd love to see how you and Aleksander have arranged things here. We've been so curious about your domestic life."

Aleksander Nordh

As conversation flowed naturally, I found myself marveling at how seamlessly everyone was connecting. In the kitchen, I could hear Soren and my mother discussing something that made them both laugh—already finding common ground. My father had managed to draw both Erik and Rafael into animated conversation about the intersection of ancient mythology and contemporary literature.

This was exactly what I'd hoped for but hadn't dared guarantee—a family that extended beyond blood or species lines to encompass anyone who chose to love and support each other.

"You've built something remarkable here," my father said quietly, appearing at my elbow while the others continued their conversations. "Not just with Soren, but with all of them. This is what we always hoped you'd find—a genuine family."

Erik Eriksson

Dinner preparation became a collaborative effort that revealed the underlying dynamics of our little family. Astrid and Soren moved around the kitchen with the easy cooperation of people who'd immediately recognized each other as natural organizers, while Gunnar somehow managed to make himself useful without getting in anyone's way—clearly someone with millennia of experience adapting to new domestic arrangements.

Rafael and I found ourselves responsible for setting the table and providing entertainment in the form of stories about our university experiences, our travels, and the various adventures that had characterized our relationship since leaving Sweden.

"Your grandparents," Astrid said to Erik as we gathered around the dining table. "Marta and Lars. Aleksander wrote to us about the wedding celebration. They sound like remarkable people."

"They are," I replied with obvious affection. "Mormor and Morfar have been the most stable part of my life since I was a boy. They're the ones who taught me everything. I... I love them very much."

"Dina morföräldrar är mycket lyckligt lottade att ha ett sådant kärleksfullt barnbarn," Astrid said warmly, the Swedish flowing from her so naturally, so perfectly, that it took me a moment to process what had just happened.

She'd switched languages mid-conversation without hesitation, meeting me in my mother tongue as if she'd been speaking Swedish her entire life. Which, I realized with a start, she probably had been—for millennia.

I felt everyone's eyes on us. Gunnar and Aleksander clearly understood what she'd said. Soren and Rafael seemed to grasp at least the sentiment, if not every word. Normally I'd translate for Rafael automatically, make sure he was included. But this... this felt different. Sacred, somehow.

The words she'd chosen—telling me my grandparents were fortunate to have such a loving grandchild—settled in my chest like warmth spreading through cold hands. I felt a tear threatening to spill and blinked it back, simply nodding instead.

Astrid's smile was gentle, knowing. She understood that this was a gift—a small, private moment of recognition in the language of my heart. Something for me to hold onto, to treasure.

I didn't translate. I didn't explain. I just held her gaze for a moment, hoping she could see the gratitude in my eyes, before the conversation moved naturally forward.

Rafael Mercado

The conversation that followed was unlike anything I'd experienced since my own family dinners in Manila before my transformation. Not the careful politeness of formal occasions or the surface-level chatting of acquaintances, but the kind of deep, meandering discussion that happened when intelligent people who cared about each other had time to explore ideas together.

Gunnar shared stories from their travels—centuries of observations about how human societies evolved and adapted, told with the kind of perspective that only came from literally watching civilizations rise and fall. Astrid contributed insights about language development that made my academic background feel suddenly relevant and valuable rather than simply interesting.

But what struck me most was how they listened. When Erik described his research into modern interpretations of ancient mythology, they gave him their complete attention, asking thoughtful questions that suggested genuine interest rather than polite courtesy. When I mentioned my work auditing linguistics courses, Astrid immediately began sharing resources and connections that could advance my studies.

Soren Jensen

As the evening progressed, I found myself relaxing completely for the first time since we'd begun planning this visit. Aleksander's parents weren't just accepting our unusual family structure—they were embracing it, contributing to it, making it richer through their presence and perspective.

"There is something we brought for you both," Gunnar said as we settled into the sitting room after dinner, his tone suggesting a transition to more formal business. "A wedding gift, though perhaps unconventional in timing."

Aleksander Nordh

My father's announcement caught my attention immediately. Elder gifts were never casual offerings—they carried weight, significance, often implications that extended far beyond simple generosity.

"You didn't need to bring us anything," I said automatically, though I was curious.

"Actually," my mother said with a slight smile, "this particular gift required considerable... procurement effort. It's not something one simply purchases."

She reached into her traveling bag and withdrew a wooden box that made my breath catch. The container itself was ancient—dark oak aged to near-black, worn smooth by countless hands but clearly crafted with extraordinary skill.

"Open it," my father encouraged gently.

When I lifted the lid with trembling hands, the interior revealed blackened organic material mixed with small crystalline structures that caught the light with inner luminescence. Six small vials, each sealed carefully.

"I don't understand," I said. "What is this?"

Astrid Nordh

I reached over and took Gunnar's hand, drawing strength from four thousand years of partnership.

"Aleksander, you know the story of how your father and I met—how I was ordinary Denisovan when he found me, with perhaps sixty years ahead of me." I paused, letting that sink in. "But you've never known the full truth of how I became what I am now."

I looked at Soren, then at Erik and Rafael, wanting them all to understand.

"We searched for twenty years, chasing myths about transformation compounds that could bridge the gap between our kinds. And we found them—found an ancient woman who possessed the last vials in existence."

Gunnar Nordh

"She gave one to Astrid," I said quietly. "And for forty-two days, I watched helplessly while her body fought to accept the change. Some days brought recovery. Others, renewed fever that made me certain I was losing her."

The memory was still sharp after all these years—the helplessness, the fear, the desperate hope that love might be enough.

"When she finally opened her eyes with clarity, I wept with relief I hadn't allowed myself in centuries."

Astrid Nordh

"The transformation nearly killed me," I said simply. "There's no guarantee, no way to know if a body will accept the change or reject it. But it worked. And because it worked, we had Aleksander. We had four thousand years together instead of forty."

I looked directly at Soren.

"That ancient woman gave us six vials. These six. The last ones in existence. We've kept them safe all these millennia, waiting for the right moment."

Soren Jensen

My heart was hammering. They were offering me what Astrid had received—the chance to stay with Aleksander not for decades, but for centuries.

"But it nearly killed you," I said quietly.

"Yes," Astrid replied. "And if you choose this path, it might kill you too. There's no test, no way to know. That's why we're telling you this—so you understand what you'd be choosing. Forty-two days of maybe dying. Gunnar watching helplessly. No certainty it will work."

She leaned forward.

"This isn't a decision to make tonight, or this week, or even this year. The vials will wait. We've kept them for four millennia—we can keep them longer. But when you're ready, if you're ready, the choice is yours."

Erik Eriksson

"Thank you," I said quietly, speaking for all of us. "For trusting us with this. For... for everything."

But even as the words came out, I found my hand reaching for Rafael's before I even realized I was moving. His fingers closed around mine, cool and solid, and I felt him squeeze gently in response.

I was nineteen. Nineteen, and sitting in this room being trusted with a secret that was older than civilizations. Being included in a conversation that most people would never even know was possible.

Part of me wanted to feel honored, special, chosen. And I did. But mostly I just felt young.

Astrid and Gunnar had lived for four thousand years. They spoke about decades like I spoke about weekends. And they were trusting me—*me,* who still got carded at pubs, who was barely into my second year of university—with knowledge that could change everything.

I squeezed Rafael's hand harder, suddenly, viscerally aware of what that meant. Rafael was thirty-two but would live for centuries. I was nineteen and would be lucky to see eighty.

I'd known that, intellectually. Had understood since the beginning that Rafael would outlive me. But it had always felt distant, theoretical—something for Future Erik to worry about when he was old.

But listening to Astrid describe forty-two days of maybe dying, of Gunnar watching helplessly, of the transformation that had given them millennia together—it made it real. Made me think about what it would be like when I was forty and Rafael still looked exactly like this. When I was sixty and he was still young. When I was dying and he was just... continuing.

"You alright?" Rafael whispered, so quietly only I could hear.

I nodded, not trusting my voice. But I wasn't alright. I was thinking about mortality for the first time in my life—really thinking about it, not as an abstract concept but as something that would happen to me while the person I loved watched.

And Astrid wasn't offering me the elixir. This was for Soren and Aleksander. Erik and Rafael had no magical solution, just love and time and the certainty that one was infinite and the other wasn't.

Astrid Nordh

"You're welcome," I said, smiling at Erik. "But understand—this isn't just about trust. It's about choice. About understanding that some questions don't have easy answers."

I looked at Soren, watching the four young people process what we'd told them. Rafael with that particular stillness that marked someone thinking deeply about family and connection. Erik gripping Rafael's hand like a lifeline, his youthful face showing the first real awareness of mortality I'd seen in him.

And Soren and Aleksander, looking at each other with the weight of an impossible choice settling between them.

"If you could extend your life to match Aleksander's, would you?" I asked. "Even knowing it might kill you? Even knowing the pain it would cause? Even knowing that nothing is guaranteed?"

I let the question hang in the air.

"That's what this gift is really asking. Not 'do you want to live forever,' but 'what are you willing to risk for love?'"

Soren Jensen

I couldn't look away from Astrid's eyes. She held my gaze with the kind of understanding that came from having made this exact choice—from having been where I was now, facing the same impossible question.

Would you risk dying to stay with him?

That's what she was really asking. Not in forty or sixty years when death was already approaching, but now. While I was young and healthy and had decades ahead of me naturally.

Would I gamble those decades for the chance at centuries?

Aleksander Nordh

I was looking at Astrid too, seeing my mother in an entirely new light. She'd done this. She'd survived forty-two days of agony for my father. Had risked everything for the possibility of time together.

And now she was offering Soren the same chance—and the same risk.

I wanted it. God, I wanted Soren to take it, wanted centuries instead of decades, wanted to never lose him the way I'd lost Mikael. But I also knew what it would cost. Knew that asking him to risk death for the possibility of extended life was asking for something enormous.

Gunnar Nordh

"We'll leave you to discuss it," I said, standing slowly. "This isn't a decision to make while we're watching. Take your time. Think about it. Talk to each other."

I paused at the doorway.

"And remember—having the choice doesn't mean you have to make it. Sometimes just knowing the possibility exists is enough."

Astrid Nordh

I let the silence stretch, let them all feel the weight of what we'd shared. Then I stood slowly, Gunnar rising with me.

"We'll leave you now," I said gently. "This conversation needs to happen without us watching."

I moved toward the door but paused, looking back at the four of them—these young people who'd become our family.

"Whatever you decide," I said, speaking to all of them, "you're loved. You're trusted. You're family. Nothing changes that."

Gunnar Nordh

"Take your time," I added. "This isn't a decision for tonight, or this week, or even this year. The vials will be here when—if—you're ready."

I put my arm around Astrid.

"And remember what the ancient woman told us: 'Be certain of what you're offering before you offer it.' That applies to accepting it too. Be certain, Soren. Be certain of what you're risking and why."

Astrid Nordh

As we walked toward the guest room, leaving them to their thoughts and their conversations and their impossible choices, I felt Gunnar's arm tighten around me.

"Do you think he'll take it?" he asked quietly.

"I don't know," I admitted. "But I think that's exactly right. This isn't something anyone should be certain about."

Rafael Mercado

After Gunnar and Astrid left, the four of us sat in silence for a long moment. The wooden box sat on the coffee table like a question that couldn't be unasked.

"That was..." Erik started, then stopped, clearly not knowing how to finish.

"Yeah," I agreed. "It was."

I was still thinking about my father. About impossible choices and the ways families could be rebuilt in new shapes. About trust and secrets and the privilege of being included in something sacred.

Erik Eriksson

"I never really thought about it," I said quietly, still holding Rafael's hand. "I mean, I knew you'd outlive me. Obviously. But I never really *thought* about it. About what that means. About watching me get old while you stay the same."

Rafael's fingers tightened around mine.

"I think about it," he admitted. "Late at night. When you're asleep and I'm lying there watching you breathe. I think about it a lot."

The weight of that admission settled over both of us. We sat there for a moment, just holding hands, the reality of our impossible situation finally acknowledged aloud.

I glanced at Soren and Aleksander, seeing the way they were looking at each other—that weighted silence that spoke of conversations that needed to happen in private. The wooden box sat between them, ancient and impossible, and suddenly I understood that Rafael and I were intruding on something deeply personal.

"We should probably head to bed," I said quietly, standing and reaching for Rafael's hand. "Let you two... talk."

Rafael Mercado

Erik was right. This wasn't our conversation to be part of—not this part, anyway. Soren and Aleksander needed space to process what had just been offered, to begin wrestling with an impossible choice that would shape their entire future.

"Good night," I said, squeezing Aleksander's shoulder as we passed. "Thank you for... for including us in that. For trusting us."

Aleksander Nordh

"You're family," I said simply. "This affects all of us, even if the choice is ours alone."

I watched them disappear into the guest room, leaving Soren and me alone with the wooden box and the weight of my parents' story.

Soren Jensen

For several minutes after Erik and Rafael left, neither of us spoke. I looked at Aleksander, and he looked at me, and in that moment we both understood exactly what Astrid and Gunnar had left us to ponder.

What would we do?

Risk everything for the possibility of forever? Or accept the natural span of a human life and make peace with the inevitable goodbye?

There was no right answer. There was only the question, sitting between us like the wooden box on the table—ancient, powerful, and impossibly heavy.

"We should talk about this," Aleksander said finally.

"Yes," I agreed. "We should."

But neither of us moved. Neither of us spoke. We just sat there, holding each other's gaze, feeling the weight of a choice that would echo through centuries—or cut them short entirely.

Aleksander Nordh

I was gobsmacked and frightened simultaneously. Having everything you'd ever wanted wasn't always good—I'd lived long enough to know that. I'd witnessed what power could do to people, how opportunity could corrupt, how the promise of immortality had driven humans to terrible acts across history.

But I reminded myself: I wasn't human. And more importantly, this wasn't just about me. This was about Soren. About his choice, his life, his risk.

I would help him think through it. But the decision would be his alone.

Soren Jensen

For several minutes, neither of us spoke. I was intrigued and skeptical in equal measure. A preparation that could extend life for centuries? This was the stuff of legends, not real biological science.

Except... it wasn't really immortality, was it? Astrid had explained it—this didn't bestow god-like powers or omnipotent knowledge. It was a biological mechanism that would fundamentally—possibly dangerously—alter my cellular structure. Change the means by which my body operated to maintain health, to literally stay alive.

And it carried enormous risks.

"There's no guarantee I'd survive it," I said finally, speaking the fear aloud.

Aleksander Nordh

"No," I agreed quietly. "No guarantee at all."

Soren Jensen

I stood and walked to the window, needing to move while I processed this. The chance to become something like an Elder—or at least closer to one. I'd never truly be what Aleksander was. I was homo sapiens, and he was descended from Denisovans, that minute speck of dust that remained of humanity's cousins. His family represented an evolutionary branch that had nearly disappeared from Earth entirely.

I could never be that. My blood would prove it.

But this mechanism, this catalyst toward fundamental change—if I survived the intense physiological alterations at a cellular level—would nudge me in their direction. Perhaps a first cousin instead of the distant one I was now.

If I survived.

Aleksander Nordh

That phrase hung in the air between us. The unspoken reality that dominated everything else.

I'd lived long enough to understand what it meant to watch loved ones age and die. I'd fought that battle repeatedly—allowing myself to become close to someone only to know we'd have perhaps forty, fifty, maybe sixty years together if we were lucky. Or hiding away by myself, forgoing relationships entirely to avoid the pain I knew would be inevitable.

But now this opportunity... this "chance" given to us... even knowing it might destroy the man I was so desperately in love with...

How did I temper my basest drive to hold onto the most precious thing I had with the realization that acting on it might crush the little time we'd been allowed to begin with?

Soren Jensen

"Your parents said it could take weeks or months," I said, still looking out the window. "Weeks or months of my body attacking itself. Of fever and sickness and delirium. Of essentially being bedridden while my cells wage war against each other."

I turned to face him.

"And at the end of all that, I might simply die anyway. My body might reject the changes completely, and we'd have spent my last months watching me suffer for nothing."

Aleksander Nordh

"Yes," I said, because there was no point in softening that truth.

Soren Jensen

But even as I voiced the fears, another part of my mind was calculating possibilities. Like any lottery, there was always the "what if" factor.

What if the process worked? What if my body was one that could accept the changes? What if I survived the weeks or months of sickness and misery? What if I emerged transformed, able to live like an Elder?

What if we were able to spend centuries together instead of decades?

"But if it worked," I said slowly, "we'd have time. Real time. Not just a few decades before you're alone again, but centuries. We could see Erik and Rafael's life unfold. We could watch the world change together. We could actually build something that lasted."

Aleksander Nordh

Hope and fear warred in my chest. "We could," I agreed. "But Soren, you have to understand—I've watched people die. I've held them while they slipped away. If you took this and it failed..."

I had to stop, the image too painful to complete.

"I'd be the one who gave you the opportunity that killed you. I'd carry that for the rest of my existence."

Soren Jensen

I crossed back to the sofa and sat beside him, taking his hand.

"Your parents were right," I said. "This isn't as simple as it seems. It's a great opportunity—perhaps the greatest. But it's equally a burden to carry."

I looked at the wooden box.

"No wonder the existence of this is kept secret. It's so easily done—the box looks ordinary, inconsequential even. We expect the greatest and most monumental things in our lives to be elaborate, spectacular, etched into our memories forever. But history has proven that the most foundational elements of change are often unseen, minuscule, so easily overlooked and underappreciated."

Aleksander Nordh

"So what do we do?" I asked.

Soren Jensen

"We don't decide tonight," I said firmly. "This isn't a decision to make in the heat of the moment, while I'm still processing what your parents told us. This is something that deserves time."

I squeezed his hand.

"We keep the box. We keep the possibility. But we live our lives first. We see what it feels like to be together without this hanging over us. And if there comes a time when we feel ready to face that risk—when the potential reward feels worth the very real danger—then we'll discuss it again."

Aleksander Nordh

Relief flooded through me. Not because the decision was made, but because it wasn't being rushed.

"You're right," I said. "This deserves careful thought. Not just about what we want, but about what we can handle. What we're willing to risk."

Soren Jensen

"Besides," I said with a slight smile, "your parents didn't give us any instructions on how to actually use it. We'd need to ask them about preparation, dosage, what to expect. That alone suggests this isn't meant to be decided immediately."

Aleksander Nordh

I found myself smiling back despite the weight of the evening. "Very practical of you."

"I'm a researcher. I don't make major decisions without data."

We sat in comfortable silence for a while, the box sitting between us—no longer threatening, but simply present. A possibility. An option. A question we didn't have to answer tonight.

Soren Jensen

"We should go to bed," I said finally. "This has been... a lot."

Aleksander Nordh

We moved to the bedroom together, and what followed was lovemaking of a different quality than usual. Tender, intertwined, passionate but deeply connected down to the very root of our being.

If either of us believed we had souls, we came as close to merging them that night as we ever could.

Afterward, lying in the darkness with Soren's warmth against me, I found myself staring at the ceiling and thinking about the possibilities. About the risks. About the strange gift my parents had given us—not an answer, but a question.

Soren Jensen

"I love you," I whispered into the darkness.

"I love you too," Aleksander replied.

For tonight, this was enough.

The wooden box sat on the dresser in the other room—ancient, powerful, waiting. A question that would remain unanswered for now. A possibility that might never become reality, or might transform everything.

But in this moment, wrapped in each other's arms, the question could wait.

Tomorrow would come soon enough.

45
GRIEF AND GROWTH

FLAT 6, 84 VYNER STREET, LONDON E2 9DG

Erik Eriksson

The call came at three in the morning London time, exactly one week after we'd returned from Stockholm celebrating Morfar's successful recovery. Rafael and I had been asleep in our warehouse flat, tangled together in the comfortable warmth of our oversized bed, when my phone's insistent buzzing cut through the peaceful silence.

I fumbled for the device in the darkness, my heart already racing with the kind of dread that came from middle-of-the-night international calls. The caller ID showed Mormor's number, and I knew with horrible certainty that something had gone terribly wrong.

"Mormor?" I answered, my voice rough with sleep and growing fear.

"Erik, älskling." Her voice was different—hollow, broken, carrying a weight I'd never heard before. "He's gone. Lars is gone."

Rafael Mercado

I was awake instantly, my enhanced hearing having caught the conversation from the moment Erik answered. I could hear the devastation in Marta's voice, could feel Erik's body go rigid beside me as the words registered. Lars—who had survived major surgery, who had been recovering so well, who had sent us cheerful messages just yesterday about returning home to the farm—was dead.

"What happened?" Erik managed, his voice cracking.

"Blood clot," Marta whispered. "The doctors said... they said sometimes it happens after surgery. His heart stopped during the night. They tried everything, but..."

Erik Eriksson

The world tilted on its axis. Morfar—the man who had been more of a father to me than my biological one, who had taught me about responsibility and love and what family truly meant—was gone. Just gone. A week ago we'd been celebrating his survival, his successful recovery, his return home to the farm. Now he was dead, and I was a thousand miles away hearing about it through a phone call in the middle of the night.

"I'm coming," I said automatically, though the words felt inadequate against the magnitude of the loss. "We're coming. Today."

"Erik, you don't need to—"

"Yes, I do," I interrupted, my voice stronger now as the initial shock gave way to fierce determination. "He was my morfar. My family. Of course I'm coming."

THE JOURNEY HOME

Rafael Mercado

The next twelve hours passed in a blur of activity that helped keep Erik's grief manageable through sheer necessity. Flight arrangements, university notifications, packing for what would likely be an extended stay—all the practical details that death demanded even when the heart was breaking.

Aleksander handled the logistics with supernatural efficiency, securing flights that would have been impossible to book on such short notice for ordinary travelers. By afternoon, we were aboard a private jet that would deliver us to Stockholm faster than any commercial airline could manage.

"He was supposed to have years left," Erik said as we climbed through the clouds above London. "The surgery was successful. He was getting stronger every day."

"I know," I replied, taking his hand. "Sometimes life doesn't follow the timeline we expect."

Erik Eriksson

The funeral would be held in three days, according to Swedish custom. Three days to say goodbye to the man who had shaped my understanding of what love looked like, who had welcomed me into his family when my biological parents had abandoned me to their own dysfunction.

I found myself cycling between numbness and rage as the plane carried us northward. Numbness at the impossibility of it—how could someone so vital, so necessary, simply stop existing? And rage at the unfairness—why now, when he'd fought so hard to survive, when we'd all believed the worst was behind us?

"I never told him," I said suddenly, the words escaping before I could stop them.

"Told him what?" Rafael asked gently.

"How much he meant to me. How he saved me. How he was more of a father than..." I couldn't finish the sentence.

THE GRADUAL ABANDONMENT

The plane hum was the only sound, and I kept staring out the window trying not to think about the funeral, about seeing my parents again, about the fact that Morfar was actually gone.

I couldn't stop thinking about how it happened. Not his death—the other thing. How I ended up living at the farm.

It wasn't dramatic. That's the thing people don't get. It was so gradual I didn't even realize what was happening until it was done.

First it was just a weekend. "Erik, you'll stay with Mormor and Morfar while we go to this conference in Brussels. It's only a few days."

Then it was most weekends because "the commute is exhausting, älskling, and we have so much work. You love the farm anyway."

Then it was holidays because "you're going back and forth so much, it would be better for you to just stay there for summer. More stable."

Then it was "you're starting sixth year and you need to focus on school, establish friendships. The country life will be good for you."

The country life my mother had spent her entire childhood desperate to escape.

By the time I was fourteen, I'd been living there full-time for eight years. And sometime in those eight years, weekend visits from my parents became monthly, then every few months, then just Christmas and maybe midsummer if they weren't "too swamped with work."

Rafael Mercado

I'd been quiet, just listening, but I had to ask. "Did they ever... did your grandparents try to get them to visit more?"

Erik Eriksson

"Mormor did," I said. "She'd call my mother every week. Sometimes twice a week. I could hear her in the kitchen—'Anna, he asked about you today.' 'He got an award at school, thought you'd want to know.' 'When are you coming to visit?'"

I rubbed my face.

"Morfar though... he knew from the start. Knew my mother had never wanted the farm life, never wanted to be tied down. Knew that having me wasn't part of their plan and they'd just... kept going anyway, trying to make it work until they couldn't anymore."

"He never tried to get them to come back?"

"Not really. He'd shake his head when Mormor hung up from another call where my mother promised to visit 'soon.' Just this sad headshake like he knew it was never going to happen."

Rafael Mercado

"That must have been hard. Watching your grandmother hope while your grandfather knew better."

Erik Eriksson

"Yeah, but..." I stopped, trying to find the words. "Morfar was never mean about it. Never told me they were bad parents or that they'd abandoned me or any of that. He just... reminded me who he was."

I could picture him so clearly—standing by the fence we were mending, or sitting in the tractor, or out on the lake fishing.

"He'd say, 'I'm your morfar, Erik. Not your far. Your grandfather. And you know what? That's even better, because grandfathers get to teach you the really good stuff.'"

My voice cracked a little.

"And he did. He taught me to fish, to row the boat, to ice skate on the pond in winter. How to ski. How to fix a fence. How to drive the tractor. All these things that made the farm feel like... like home instead of just the place I got dumped."

Rafael Mercado

The way Erik described it—this quiet man teaching him practical things, making abandonment feel less like rejection and more like opportunity—it hit me hard. That took so much love. So much restraint.

"He sounds like he was really special," I said.

Erik Eriksson

"He was the best," I said, and now I was definitely crying. "He barely talked, you know? Not a big words guy. But when I was upset about something—usually about my parents not showing up again—he'd always know. He'd just... find a project for us."

I laughed a little through the tears.

"'Erik, that fence needs mending. Come help me.' Or 'We should check on the tractor, might need oil.' And we'd go out there and work, and it was so easy to talk while we were doing something. I could tell him how much it hurt that they didn't come for my birthday again, or that my mother cancelled another visit, and he'd just listen. Actually listen. Not like adults usually do where you can tell they're just waiting for you to finish. He heard me."

Rafael Mercado

God. That image—this quiet farmer and his teenage grandson fixing fences and talking about pain while their hands were busy—it was beautiful and heartbreaking at the same time.

"What would he say? When you told him it hurt?"

Erik Eriksson

"Not much," I admitted. "Sometimes just 'I know, pojken. I know.' Sometimes he'd tell me a story about my mother when she was young—how she'd always wanted more than the farm could give her, how the city called to her even when she was little. Not making excuses, just... explaining."

I wiped my face with my sleeve.

"Once, when I was maybe sixteen and really angry about it, I said something like 'they don't want me' and he stopped what he was doing—we were stacking firewood—and he looked at me and said, 'They want their life more than they want to change it. That's about them, not about you.'"

Rafael Mercado

Fuck. That was exactly right. And exactly the thing a kid needed to hear.

"Did it help? Him saying that?"

"Yeah," Erik said. "Because he never pretended they'd change. Never gave me false hope like Mormor did. He just made it clear that whatever they were doing, it wasn't my fault. And he made sure I knew that being his grandson was something good. Something real. Not just a consolation prize."

Erik Eriksson

"The last time I saw him—the hospital visit after his surgery—he grabbed my hand and said, 'You turned out good, Erik. Better than good. I'm proud I got to be your morfar.'"

My voice broke completely.

"Not 'I'm sorry your parents weren't around.' Not 'I wish things were different.' Just... he was glad he got to be my grandfather. Like it was a privilege for him instead of a burden."

Rafael Mercado

I had to look away because I was crying too now. This kid—this nineteen-year-old kid sitting next to me—had been abandoned in the slowest, cruelest way possible. Not a clean break like my staged death, but a gradual withdrawal. A thousand small choices over eight years that all added up to: we don't want you enough to change our lives for you.

And his grandfather had taken that abandonment and somehow turned it into something bearable. Made Erik feel wanted and heard and valuable, all while never lying about what was happening or who was responsible.

"Your mother," I said carefully. "Your grandmother. They kept hoping she'd come back?"

Erik Eriksson

"Mormor did," I said. "Right up until the end. Every phone call, every visit that didn't happen, every cancelled trip—she'd make excuses. 'She's just so busy, älskling.' 'It's a hard time at work.' 'She loves you, she just has a lot going on.'"

I shook my head.

"Morfar would just look at her with this sad expression. Not angry. Just sad. Like he wished she didn't have to keep lying to herself about what was really happening."

Rafael Mercado

"Which was?"

Erik Eriksson

"That my mother chose the city. Chose her career. Chose freedom. And having a son didn't fit into any of that. So she let her parents raise me and convinced herself she was still a mother because she sent money and called on my birthday."

The bitterness in my voice was sharp enough to cut.

"She hated the farm growing up. Couldn't wait to leave. And now I'm there, living the life she ran away from, and she can't even pretend to care."

Rafael Mercado

"Daily choice," I said quietly. "That's what it is, right? Every morning they wake up and choose not to make room for you."

Erik Eriksson

"Yeah," I whispered. "Every single day for years. And Morfar knew it from the start. But he never made me feel like it was my fault. Never made me feel like I was a burden he got stuck with. He just... loved me. Quietly. In all the ways that mattered."

I turned to look at Rafael.

"And now he's gone, and my parents are going to show up at the funeral like they were part of his life. Like they didn't spend all those years letting him raise their son because they couldn't be bothered. And I don't know how I'm supposed to stand there and not scream at them."

Rafael Mercado

I reached over and took his hand. His fingers gripped mine hard.

"You're right," I said. "What you've been through—it's different than what I did. I made one impossible choice to protect my family. Your parents have been making that choice every day, and they're not protecting anyone. They're just... choosing themselves."

Erik Eriksson

"Daily… how did you say it? Abandonment?" I asked.

"In plain sight," Rafael finished.

Aleksander Nordh

I could hear every word from across the aisle, and I sat there thinking about Gunnar and Astrid. Four thousand years of existence and they'd never once made me feel unwanted. Never once chosen convenience over presence.

And Erik's parents couldn't manage a trifling of years.

The contrast was devastating.

But what struck me most was Lars—this quiet farmer who'd seen exactly what was happening, who'd never pretended otherwise, but who'd loved his grandson so completely that abandonment became something survivable. Who'd taught Erik that being chosen by grandparents was just as valuable as being wanted by parents.

That was a gift beyond measure.

THE FARM

Soren Jensen

We arrived at the farm as the sun was setting, painting the familiar red buildings in shades of gold and amber that made everything look like a postcard from memory. But the beauty of the evening light couldn't disguise the profound change that had settled over the place—an emptiness that went beyond Lars's physical absence to encompass the end of an era.

Marta met us at the door with the composed dignity that had carried her through eighty-three years of life's challenges, but I could see the fractures in her careful control. This wasn't just the loss of a husband—it was the severing of a partnership that had defined her adult life, the end of the shared story they'd been writing for over sixty years.

"Thank you for coming," she said, embracing each of us with the fierce gratitude of someone who needed family around her but wasn't sure how to ask for it.

Rafael Mercado

Walking through the farmhouse that had been the setting for so many joyful memories felt surreal. The kitchen where Marta had prepared countless family meals still held the lingering scent of cardamom and coffee, but the chair where Lars had held court during those celebrations sat empty now, transformed from a piece of furniture into a memorial.

"How are you managing?" I asked Marta as we settled in the sitting room, grateful for my years of navigating grief in Filipino culture where death was acknowledged directly rather than euphemistically.

"I'm not," she replied with characteristic honesty. "I'm simply... continuing. One moment at a time."

Erik Eriksson

That evening, as we sat around the kitchen table where I'd shared so many meals with my grandparents, I found myself staring at Morfar's empty chair and feeling something break inside my chest. This was where he'd taught me about responsibility, where he'd listened to my teenage problems with patient attention, where he'd celebrated my academic achievements with genuine pride.

"Tell me about the funeral arrangements," I said, needing practical details to anchor myself against the rising tide of grief.

"Traditional service at the village church," Mormor replied. "Then burial in the family plot. Nothing elaborate—Lars never wanted a fuss."

"Who's coming?"

"Family, neighbors, some friends from Stockholm." She paused, studying my face with the careful attention she'd always paid to my emotional state. "Your parents called. They said they would try to attend."

The words hit me like a slap. My parents—who had been absent from every significant moment of my life since forever—were planning to show up for Morfar's funeral.

Rafael Mercado

I watched Erik's expression shift from grief to anger as he processed the implications of his parents' sudden interest in family events. I'd learned to recognize the signs of his deeper emotional reactions—the way his jaw tightened, the careful stillness that meant he was fighting for control.

"After everything," he said quietly, his voice carrying a dangerous edge. "After years of letting Mormor and Morfar carry the burden of raising me, after missing every important moment of my life, they want to show up for his funeral?"

"Erik," Marta said gently, though I could see she shared his frustration. "They loved Lars too. In their way."

"Their way," Erik repeated, the words bitter with accumulated resentment." Their way has been to run away whenever things get hard—to let you and Morfar deal with all the shit while they—" *He caught himself, his face flushing.* "Förlåt, Mormor—medan de bara tänker på sig själva!" *He stopped abruptly, remembering I was there, and turned to translate for me.* "Sorry—I said, while they only think about themselves."

Erik Eriksson

The rage that had been building since the phone call found its target in the thought of my biological parents treating Morfar's funeral as a social obligation rather than the devastating loss it actually was. They would arrive with appropriate expressions of grief, speak meaningful words about family and legacy, then disappear again until the next crisis demanded their presence.

"They don't get to do this," I said, my voice rising despite my efforts to maintain control. "They don't get to show up now and act like they were part of his life, like they were part of this family."

"Älskling," Mormor said softly, using the endearment that always made me feel like her actual grandchild rather than the burden I'd sometimes feared I was. "Your anger is understandable. But the funeral isn't for them—it's for Lars. And he would have wanted all his family there, even the family that disappointed him."

THE WEIGHT OF RESPONSIBILITY

Soren Jensen

The next day brought a steady stream of visitors—neighbors offering casseroles and condolences, church ladies organizing flowers and funeral logistics, family friends sharing memories of Lars that painted a picture of a man who had touched many lives through simple kindness and steady presence.

But it was the conversation with the pastor that forced us all to confront the practical realities that death always demanded alongside the emotional ones.

"Mrs. Eriksson," Pastor Lindgren said gently, "we should discuss the service details. Will young Erik be speaking? As the... as the one who will be continuing the family legacy?"

The pause in his words carried weight that extended far beyond funeral planning. In traditional Swedish rural culture, Erik was indeed the logical inheritor of the family's social and cultural responsibilities—the one who would carry forward the Eriksson name and maintain the family's place in the community.

Erik Eriksson

The realization hit me like a physical blow. With Morfar's death, I wasn't just losing the man who'd been my father figure—I was inheriting his role as the family's anchor, the one responsible for maintaining connections and carrying forward traditions. At nineteen, I was suddenly the senior male in a family structure that had depended on Morfar's steady presence for over six decades.

"I..." I began, then stopped, overwhelmed by the magnitude of what was being suggested. "I'm still in university. I live in London. I don't know how to..."

"You don't have to know yet," Mormor said firmly, her voice carrying the authority of someone who had made difficult decisions throughout her life. "But yes, you will speak at the service. You will represent the family's future, because that's what Lars would have wanted."

Rafael Mercado

Watching Erik grapple with this unexpected inheritance of responsibility, I felt something profound shift in how I understood our relationship's trajectory. This wasn't just about supporting my boyfriend through grief—it was about helping him navigate his transformation from protected young adult to family leader, from someone who received care to someone who provided it.

"You're not alone in this," I said quietly when we had a moment of privacy. "Whatever this responsibility looks like, whatever it requires—we'll figure it out together."

"But what if I can't?" Erik asked, his voice carrying the vulnerability that he rarely let others see. "What if I'm not strong enough to be what this family needs?"

"Then you'll grow into it," I replied with certainty I hoped was convincing. "The same way Morfar grew into it when he was young, the same way every generation learns to carry the weight that comes with love."

. . .

ARRIVAL

Erik Eriksson

They arrived the morning of the funeral, driving a rental car that still had Stockholm dealer plates and looking exactly like the successful urban professionals they'd become. My mother wore a perfectly appropriate black dress that probably cost more than most people's monthly rent, while my father sported the kind of expensive suit that marked him as someone important in whatever business circles he now moved through.

Watching them emerge from their car in front of the farmhouse where I'd found safety and love despite their abandonment stirred a complex mixture of emotions I wasn't prepared to handle. They looked older, certainly, but also somehow more polished, as if the years since they'd dumped me on my grandparents had been kind to them in ways they'd never been kind to their son.

"Erik," my mother said, approaching with arms extended for an embrace I didn't want to give. "You look so grown up. So... sophisticated."

Rafael Mercado

I positioned myself slightly behind Erik, close enough to offer support but far enough away to avoid inserting myself into family dynamics that weren't mine to navigate. But I could feel the tension radiating from Erik's body as his parents approached, could see Marta's carefully neutral expression that suggested years of practice at managing her disappointment in her daughter and son-in-law.

"Anna. Björn," Marta said with polite formality, embracing them briefly before stepping back. "Thank you for coming."

"Of course we came," Erik's father replied, his tone suggesting surprise that anyone would think otherwise. "Lars was family. This is where we belong."

The casual appropriation of belonging—after years of absence, after leaving the emotional and financial burden of child-rearing to elderly relatives—made something cold settle in my chest. These were the people who had taught Erik that love was conditional, that family obligations could be abandoned when they became inconvenient.

Erik Eriksson

"We were so sorry to hear about his passing," my mother continued, her voice carrying the appropriate tone of sympathy. "He was such a wonderful man. So devoted to family."

The irony was devastating. Here was a woman who had essentially abandoned her teenage son praising the man who had stepped in to fill the void she'd created, speaking about devotion to family while standing in the home where she'd dumped her responsibilities.

"Yes," I said carefully, my voice steady despite the rage building in my chest. "He was devoted to family. All of it. Even the family that didn't deserve his devotion."

Soren Jensen

The tension in the room was thick enough to cut, and I found myself stepping into the kind of diplomatic role that my academic background had trained me for. Erik's parents seemed oblivious to the undercurrents of resentment their presence had created, talking about Lars with the casual familiarity of people who believed their absence hadn't diminished their right to claim family connection.

"The service begins at two," I said, offering neutral information that might redirect the conversation away from dangerous territory. "Pastor Lindgren expects quite a large turnout—Lars was well-loved in the community."

"Of course," Erik's mother replied. "He was always so social, so involved in everything. Unlike some of the family." Her eyes drifted meaningfully toward Marta, suggesting criticism of the elderly woman's more reserved nature.

Erik Eriksson

That was the moment my careful control finally snapped.

"Social?" I said, my voice rising despite my efforts to maintain composure. "He was social because he had to be. Because someone needed to maintain family relationships while you two were off pursuing your own interests. He was involved in everything because you left him to handle everything."

"Erik," my father said sharply, his voice carrying the authoritative tone he'd probably perfected in boardrooms. "That's enough."

"No," I replied, standing to face them both with all the fury that had been building for five years. "It's not enough. It's not nearly enough."

. . .

THE CONFRONTATION

The words that followed came from a place so deep and angry that I barely recognized my own voice. Five years of accumulated resentment, grief, and frustration poured out in a torrent that I couldn't have stopped if I'd wanted to.

"You don't get to come here and talk about family devotion," I said, my voice shaking with emotion. "You don't get to mourn the man you forced to raise your son because you couldn't be bothered. You don't get to act like you were part of this when you've been absent for everything that mattered."

"We did what we thought was best," my mother protested, her composure finally showing cracks. "We weren't equipped to handle a teenager with your... problems."

"My problems?" I repeated, incredulous. "My problems were that I was gay and lonely and needed parents who actually wanted to parent. Your problems were that you wanted to live like you didn't have a child."

Rafael Mercado

I could see Marta's distress at having this confrontation unfold in her home on the day of her husband's funeral, but I could also see her understanding of why Erik needed to finally voice years of accumulated pain. Aleksander had positioned himself near the kitchen doorway, ready to intervene if the situation escalated beyond words, while Soren watched with the careful attention of someone cataloging family dynamics for future reference.

Erik's parents looked genuinely shocked at his outburst, as if they'd never considered that their teenage son might carry lasting resentment about their abandonment.

"We sent money," his father said weakly. "We made sure you had everything you needed."

"Money," Erik repeated, his voice hollow with disbelief. "You think money replaces presence? You think financial support makes up for missing graduations, birthdays, every significant moment of my growing up?"

Erik Eriksson

"Morfar walked me to my first day of gymnasium because you were both too busy," I continued, my voice growing stronger as years of suppressed pain found expression. "He taught me to drive because you couldn't find time in your schedules. He was there when I came out because you'd made it clear that my sexuality was one of those 'problems' you didn't want to deal with."

I took a shaky breath, looking at these two people who had contributed genetic material to my existence but had failed at every other aspect of parenthood.

"He died knowing that he'd raised me better than you ever could have. He died proud of the man I'd become despite your neglect. And now you want to show up and claim some piece of that pride? Some credit for the family you abandoned?"

Marta Eriksson

Watching my grandson finally confront the pain his parents had caused him was both heartbreaking and necessary. For five years, I'd watched Erik struggle with feelings of abandonment that he'd never felt safe expressing, afraid that voicing his hurt might burden Lars and me with additional emotional weight.

"That's enough," I said firmly, my voice carrying the authority of someone who had managed family crises for eight decades. "Today is about Lars, not about old wounds or missed opportunities."

I stood slowly, my arthritis making the movement more difficult than it once had been, but my resolve absolute.

"Erik will speak at the service as the family's representative," I continued, looking directly at his parents. "Because he earned that honor through presence, not genetics. Because he was here when it mattered."

THE FUNERAL SERVICE

Erik Eriksson

Three hours later, I stood at the pulpit of the village church where Morfar had attended services for over sixty years, looking out at a congregation that represented the full scope of his impact on the community. Neighbors, friends, family members from across Sweden—all gathered to honor a man who had lived quietly but meaningfully, who had shaped lives through simple kindness rather than grand gestures.

My prepared remarks felt inadequate as I began to speak, formal words about loss and legacy that couldn't capture the magnitude of what Morfar had meant to me personally. But as I talked about his character, his devotion to family, his patient wisdom, I found myself speaking from the heart rather than from notes.

"Lars Eriksson taught me that family isn't about genetics or obligation," I said, my voice carrying clearly through the church. "It's about choice. It's about showing up consistently, especially when showing up is difficult. It's about love that doesn't waver based on convenience or circumstance."

Rafael Mercado

From my seat in the front pew, I could see Erik transforming as he spoke—from the grieving grandson struggling with loss to the family representative accepting responsibility for carrying forward Lars's legacy. His voice grew stronger as he shared specific memories, stories that painted a picture of a man who had devoted his life to making others feel valued and supported.

When he talked about Lars's influence on his understanding of love and commitment, his eyes found mine briefly across the congregation, and I felt the weight of promise in that gaze. This was who he was choosing to become—not just Lars's heir, but someone worthy of the example he'd been given.

Erik Eriksson

"The greatest gift Morfar gave me," *I started, feeling tears finally come after days of fighting them,* "was teaching me that I was worthy of—" *My voice cracked and the English left me.* "Att jag var värdig ovillkorlig kärlek. Att min sexualitet, mina intressen, mina drömmar—inget av det minskade mitt värde som person eller min plats i den här familjen."

I paused, swallowing hard. "Sorry, I—" *But then my eyes found Rafael's, and something in his expression told me I didn't need to apologize for honoring Morfar in my language, that of my family.* "I'm going to continue in Swedish, if that is okay."

I took a breath, seeing emotional eyes staring at me, nods of understanding encouraging me to continue. My gaze briefly found my biological parents in the congregation before returning to safer territory.

"Han lärde mig att verklig styrka kommer från att stödja andra, inte från att kräva stöd. Att ledarskap innebär att ta ansvar för familjens välfärd, inte bara familjens rykte. Att kärlek visas genom närvaro, inte proklameras genom ord."

I stopped, my chest tight, fighting to keep my breathing steady. My hands gripped the edges of the podium as I blinked back the tears threatening to spill over. After a moment, I looked up at Rafael—seeking something, approval maybe, or just confirmation that I'd done right by Morfar.

Then I remembered. The translation.

"For those who don't speak Swedish," *I said, my voice rougher now,* "I said that Morfar taught me I was worthy of unconditional love. That who I am, my interests, my dreams—none of it made me less. He taught me that real strength is about supporting others, not demanding support. That being a leader means taking care of your family's wellbeing, not just their reputation. And that love is something you show by being there, not just something you say."

Soren Jensen

As Erik concluded his eulogy with a traditional Swedish blessing that Lars had taught him, I felt something profound settle into place. This wasn't just grief being processed—it was a young man accepting inheritance of values and responsibilities that would shape the rest of his life.

The community's response was immediate and heartfelt—expressions of recognition, quiet amens, the kind of approval that marked acceptance of new leadership. Erik wasn't just Lars's grandson anymore; he was Lars's successor, the one who would carry forward the family's place in this network of relationships.

THE BURIAL

Rafael Mercado

The graveside service was smaller, limited to family and closest friends as Swedish custom dictated. The family plot held four generations of Erikssons, and now Lars would join the ancestors who had shaped this land for over a century. But it was the space beside his grave—clearly reserved for Marta when her time came—that drove home the full weight of what we were witnessing.

This wasn't just the end of one life, but the approaching end of an era. When Marta followed her husband, the farm would pass to Erik, and with it the responsibility for maintaining connections that stretched back generations.

Erik Eriksson

As the pastor spoke the final prayers and handfuls of earth were scattered on the coffin, I felt something fundamental shift inside my chest. Grief, certainly, but also something approaching peace. Morfar was gone, but the lessons he'd taught me, the love he'd shown me, the example he'd set—all of that remained.

When the service concluded and people began the quiet migration back to cars and transportation, my parents approached with the awkward hesitation of people who recognized they'd lost moral authority but weren't sure how to proceed.

"Erik," my mother said carefully, "perhaps we could talk privately? About... about things?"

I looked at her—this woman who had given birth to me but had never really learned to be my mother—and felt something settle into clarity.

"Perhaps," I said quietly. "But not today. Today is for Morfar, and for family that earns the title through presence."

As we walked back toward the cars that would carry us to the traditional post-funeral gathering, I felt Rafael's hand slip into mine—warm, solid, real. Beside us, Uncle Aleksander and Uncle Soren moved with the quiet authority of people who belonged, who had earned their place in this family through choice and commitment.

Behind us, Mormor walked with the measured pace of someone carrying enormous grief but also enormous dignity. And somewhere further back, my biological parents followed uncertainly, perhaps beginning to understand that genetics alone didn't guarantee family status.

"Are you alright?" Rafael asked quietly as we reached the car.

"No," I replied honestly. "But I will be. And more importantly—I know who I am now. I know what Morfar taught me about responsibility and love. I know what kind of man I want to become."

The funeral reception would continue for hours, filled with stories and memories and the gradual process of community healing. But driving away from the gravesite, I felt something like hope beginning to grow alongside the grief.

Morfar was gone, but his influence remained. And I was finally ready to carry it forward.

46
FULL CIRCLE

JENSEN FAMILY FARM (HISTORICAL) SILJANSNÄS 47, 795 91 RÄTTVIK, SWEDEN

Erik Eriksson

They arrived three days after the funeral, driving the same rental car with Stockholm plates, looking like urban professionals who'd taken time off from important business to handle an inconvenient family matter. My parents approached the farmhouse with the confident stride of people who believed their genetics granted them automatic rights to family property and decisions.

I watched them from the kitchen window as they parked beside the barn where Morfar had collapsed just two weeks ago, their expensive clothes and city mannerisms so at odds with the rural setting that had shaped my understanding of what family could be. Rafael stood beside me, his presence a steady anchor against the rising anger I felt at their presumption.

"They're here about inheritance," I said quietly, though we all understood why they'd returned so quickly after years of absence.

"Let them come," Mormor replied from her chair at the kitchen table, her voice carrying the steel that had helped her survive eight decades of life's challenges. "Some conversations need to happen eventually."

Marta Eriksson

I'd been expecting this visit since the moment I saw Anna and Björn at the funeral—the way they'd surveyed the farm buildings with calculating eyes, the careful questions they'd asked about property values and estate planning. After sixty years of marriage to Lars, I knew exactly what our assets were worth and exactly what legal protections we'd put in place.

The knock on the door came precisely at ten o'clock, suggesting they'd planned this conversation with the same professional efficiency they brought to their urban careers. When I opened the door, their expressions carried that careful blend of sympathy and expectation that marked people conducting unpleasant but necessary business.

"Anna. Björn," I said with neutral politeness. "I wondered when you'd return."

Erik Eriksson

We gathered in the sitting room where Morfar had held court during so many family celebrations, the empty chair where he used to sit serving as a silent witness to this uncomfortable discussion. My parents positioned themselves with the unconscious authority of people accustomed to controlling conversations, while Rafael, Aleksander, and Soren arranged themselves supportively around Mormor and me.

"We wanted to discuss the future," my father began without preamble, his businessman's directness cutting through any pretense of casual family visiting. "The farm, the property, the practical arrangements that need to be made."

"What arrangements?" I asked, though I suspected I already knew where this was heading.

Anna Eriksson

Looking around this sitting room where I'd spent childhood holidays but never truly belonged, I felt the familiar mixture of obligation and resentment that had characterized my relationship with this place for decades. The farm represented tradition, responsibility, the kind of rooted life that had always felt suffocating rather than nurturing.

"Well, obviously Marta can't manage this place alone," I said, gesturing at the scope of property visible through the windows. "She's eighty-three years old. The physical demands, the financial responsibilities—it's too much for someone her age."

"And Erik is just nineteen," Björn added, his tone suggesting he found our son's youth disqualifying rather than promising. "Still in university, no practical farming experience. Hardly prepared to take on this kind of responsibility."

Rafael Mercado

I watched Erik's expression shift from confusion to dawning understanding to barely controlled rage as his parents revealed their assumptions about his capabilities and Marta's needs. The casual dismissal of both generations—one as too old, one as too young—demonstrated exactly the kind of thinking that had led them to abandon their parental responsibilities years ago.

"What exactly are you suggesting?" Aleksander asked, his voice carrying the careful neutrality that I'd learned meant he was prepared for conflict.

Björn Eriksson

"We're suggesting the practical solution," I replied, appreciating that at least one person in the room seemed willing to discuss business rationally. "The property should be sold while the market is favorable. Marta can move to a comfortable retirement community in Stockholm where she'll have proper care and social opportunities. Erik can focus on his education without the burden of managing property he's not equipped to handle."

"And the proceeds?" Soren asked with the direct curiosity of someone accustomed to analyzing complex situations.

"Would be distributed appropriately among family members," Anna replied smoothly. "Marta's care would be provided for, Erik's education funded, and the remaining assets managed responsibly."

Erik Eriksson

The casual way they discussed dismantling the life Mormor and Morfar had built together, selling the land that had been in our family for generations, scattering everyone to urban convenience made something white-hot build in my chest. This wasn't concern for family welfare—this was opportunism dressed up as practical thinking.

"And you would handle this 'responsible management,' I assume?" I said, my voice deadly quiet.

"We have the experience," my father replied with the confidence of someone who'd never doubted his own competence. "The financial knowledge, the business connections, the practical skills that this kind of asset management requires."

"Unlike a teenager and an elderly widow," I added, letting the implications of their condescension hang in the air.

Marta Eriksson

I'd been listening to this discussion with the patience of someone who'd learned to let others reveal their true nature before responding. Now, as my daughter and son-in-law laid out their vision for dismantling everything Lars and I had built together, I felt something crystallize in my chest that had nothing to do with grief and everything to do with protective fury.

"How kind of you to be so concerned about my welfare," I said, my voice carrying the particular tone I'd perfected over decades of managing difficult people. "Though I'm curious about one thing."

"What's that?" Anna asked, perhaps sensing that the conversation was about to shift in an uncomfortable direction.

"Why now? Why this sudden interest in family property management after years of complete absence from family responsibility?"

THE REVELATION

The silence that followed my question stretched long enough for everyone to understand its implications. When I continued, my voice was steady but implacable.

"You see, there's something you don't understand about this property, about how Lars and I arranged our affairs." I gestured around the sitting room, encompassing generations of family history. "This farm has never belonged to Lars."

"What do you mean?" Björn asked, his business confidence beginning to show cracks.

"I mean that when we married in 1962, this property was part of my dowry. It belonged to my family, the Erikssons, for three generations before Lars ever set foot here. When we wed, it remained in my name, as Swedish law allowed even then."

Erik Eriksson

I watched my parents' expressions shift from confidence to confusion to something approaching alarm as Mormor's words sank in. They'd spent years assuming that Morfar's death would trigger inheritance procedures they could influence or control, never imagining that the property they'd been coveting had never been his to bequeath.

"But surely," my mother said, her voice showing strain, "surely there are inheritance laws, family rights—"

"There are," Mormor agreed pleasantly. "And I've consulted extensively with lawyers about how those laws apply to my situation. Shall I tell you what I learned?"

Marta Eriksson

I reached for the folder I'd prepared after consulting with the family solicitor, documents that laid out exactly what my legal position was and what options I possessed for determining the farm's future.

"As the sole owner of this property, I have complete discretion over its disposition," I continued, noting how both Anna and Björn had gone very still. "I can sell it, gift it, will it to anyone I choose, or retain it for as long as I live."

"And what have you decided?" Aleksander asked gently, though I suspected his enhanced hearing had already detected the answer from my cardiovascular responses.

"I've decided to offer it to Erik," I said simply, looking directly at my grandson. "With conditions."

THE OFFER

Erik Eriksson

The words hit me like a physical blow. The farm—this place where I'd found safety and love, where I'd learned what family truly meant—was being offered to me. Not as some distant inheritance to claim decades in the future, but as a living trust to accept now, with all the responsibilities and possibilities that entailed.

"Mormor," I began, overwhelmed by the magnitude of what she was suggesting.

"With conditions," she repeated firmly. "First, you finish your university education. Second, I remain here as long as I'm able, as the senior family member and keeper of traditions. Third, you don't take possession until you're twenty-one and married, demonstrating the stability necessary for such responsibility."

Rafael Mercado

The conditions were both generous and practical—acknowledging Erik's youth while providing a framework for growth, honoring Marta's continued importance while planning for future transitions. But it was the marriage requirement that made my chest tight with possibility. Marta wasn't just offering Erik inheritance; she was offering us a future together, a place to build the kind of life we'd only dared dream about.

"And if Erik chooses not to accept?" Soren asked, his academic mind working through all possible scenarios.

"Then I'll retain ownership and make other arrangements when I'm no longer able to manage alone," Marta replied. "But I won't sell to developers or distant relatives who see this land as commodity rather than heritage."

Anna Eriksson

The neat plans I'd constructed for liquidating family assets and securing our financial position were crumbling with each word from this elderly woman who'd always seemed so acquiescent, so manageable. The property I'd assumed would fall under our control as Erik's legal guardians was being offered directly to him, bypassing our influence entirely.

"You can't be serious," I said, my composure finally cracking. "He's nineteen years old. He has no experience managing property, no understanding of the financial implications—"

"He has something more valuable than experience," Marta interrupted, her voice carrying the authority of someone who'd made difficult decisions throughout her long life. "He has commitment. He has love for this place and understanding of what it represents."

Erik Eriksson

Looking around this room where I'd found family when my biological parents had failed me, where Morfar had taught me about responsibility and love, where I'd learned that home wasn't about genetics but about choice and commitment, I felt something settle into clarity.

"I accept," I said quietly, my voice steady despite the enormity of the decision. "All the conditions, all the responsibilities. I accept."

The smile that spread across Mormor's face was radiant, transforming her grief-aged features into something approaching joy.

"Then it's settled," she said with satisfaction. "The lawyers will prepare the necessary documentation."

THE AFTERMATH

Björn Eriksson

The drive back to Stockholm passed in tense silence as Anna and I processed the complete failure of what should have been a straightforward family negotiation. The inheritance we'd assumed, the property assets we'd planned to liquidate, the comfortable retirement financing we'd envisioned—all of it had evaporated in a single conversation with an elderly woman who'd proven far more legally sophisticated than we'd credited.

"We could contest it," Anna said finally as the Stockholm skyline came into view. "Challenge her mental competency, argue that she's being influenced—"

"By whom?" I replied, though the suggestion held appeal. "Her grandson who adores her? The family friends who've supported her for decades? We have no standing, no relationship that would give us legal leverage."

The bitter truth was that our years of absence had cost us more than just emotional connection—they'd cost us any practical claim to family decision-making.

Rafael Mercado

That evening, as we settled into the comfortable routine of farm life that had become familiar during our visits, I found myself marveling at how completely the day had transformed our understanding of the future. This morning, Erik had been a university student with vague plans for post-graduation life.

Tonight, he was the heir to family property and traditions stretching back generations.

"Are you scared?" I asked as we walked hand in hand around the property boundaries, Erik showing me the extent of what he'd just inherited.

"Terrified," he admitted with characteristic honesty. "But also... excited. This place shaped who I am. The idea that I get to be part of shaping what it becomes —that feels right."

Erik Eriksson

We paused at the edge of the hayfield where Morfar had taught me to drive the tractor, where I'd learned about the satisfaction that came from productive physical work. The evening light painted everything in shades of gold and amber, making the familiar landscape look like something from a fairy tale.

"What happens next?" I asked, the question that had become familiar in our relationship.

"Next, you finish university," Rafael replied with a smile. "Next, we get married when you're ready. Next, we figure out how to honor the past while building our own future."

"Our future?"

"Did you think I was going anywhere?" Rafael asked, his voice warm with affection and certainty. "This is home now. For both of us."

THE VISION

Soren Jensen

Three months later, I stood in the farmhouse kitchen watching Marta and Erik plan spring planting schedules with the comfortable collaboration of people who'd found their rhythm. The winter had been restorative for all of us—time to process grief, to adjust to new realities, to begin imagining what the future might hold.

Aleksander emerged from the barn where he'd been helping with equipment maintenance, his supernatural strength proving remarkably useful for farm work that would have challenged normal human capabilities. The sight of my ancient husband wrestling with entirely modern agricultural machinery never failed to amuse me.

"The soil preparation is nearly finished," he reported, settling at the kitchen table where planning sessions had become a daily occurrence. "Though I should mention that Gunnar and Astrid are curious about visiting this spring. They'd like to see where we're considering building."

Erik Eriksson

The building plans had been developing gradually over the winter—not just restoration of existing structures, but new construction that would accommodate our unusual family's specific needs. A guest house designed for Elder parents who might visit for extended periods. Workshop spaces for Rafael's expanding import business. Study areas where I could complete my final year of university coursework remotely.

"The southeastern corner would work well," I said, reviewing the site maps we'd been studying. "Close enough to the main house for family connection, far enough for privacy. And the natural windbreak from the pine grove would provide good cover."

"Cover for what?" Rafael asked with amusement, though he understood the implications.

"For family members who might need to avoid excessive sunlight," I replied diplomatically.

Aleksander Nordh

The practical integration of supernatural needs into traditional farm life had proven surprisingly manageable. The property's size provided natural privacy, while its rural isolation meant fewer questions about unusual schedules or dietary requirements. For the first time in decades, I could envision a life that didn't require constant performance of humanity.

"There's one more thing we should discuss," I said, producing the letter that had arrived that morning. "Erik, you've been accepted to Cambridge for graduate studies. Full funding, starting next autumn if you choose to accept."

Erik Eriksson

The acceptance letter represented possibilities I'd dreamed about but never quite believed attainable—advanced study with renowned professors, research opportunities that could shape academic careers, the kind of intellectual environment that challenged and inspired rather than simply credentialed.

But it also represented a choice between two futures: the cosmopolitan life of academic achievement or the rooted life of family responsibility.

"Cambridge," I said, testing the word. "It's an incredible opportunity."

"It is," Mormor agreed, though I could see the conflict in her expression. "Your morfar would have been so proud."

"But it would mean leaving here," I continued, looking around the kitchen where I'd found family, where I'd learned what love looked like when it was freely given rather than carefully earned.

Rafael Mercado

"Not necessarily," I said, an idea that had been developing for weeks finally finding voice. "What if we didn't have to choose between academic achievement and family responsibility?"

All eyes turned to me with curiosity.

"Cambridge is two hours by train from London. London is a few hours by plane from Stockholm. With modern communication technology, remote learning options, flexible research arrangements..." I paused, organizing thoughts that had been building gradually. "What if we created a life that honored both paths?"

Soren Jensen

"Split time," I said, understanding Rafael's suggestion immediately. "Academic terms at Cambridge, summers and holidays here. The best of both worlds, but requiring careful planning and significant travel."

"And significant trust," Marta added, looking directly at Erik. "Trust that you'll return, that the education will enhance rather than replace your commitment to family."

Erik Eriksson

The possibility that I might not have to choose between intellectual growth and family responsibility opened horizons I hadn't dared consider. But it also required a level of maturity and self-discipline that I wasn't entirely certain I possessed.

"What do you think?" I asked Rafael, whose opinion mattered more than any academic institution's.

"I think," he said with the careful consideration he brought to all significant decisions, "that the man Morfar helped raise would find a way to honor both his education and his heritage. I think Cambridge would be lucky to have you, and I think this farm will be here when you're ready to come home."

~

FULL CIRCLE

Aleksander Nordh

Six months later, I stood in the southeastern corner of the farm property watching construction crews lay the foundation for what would become our family's permanent home. The guest house was already complete—a structure designed to accommodate supernatural needs while maintaining the traditional aesthetic that characterized the rest of the property.

Erik was at Cambridge, thriving in the intellectual environment while maintaining regular contact with family through video calls and weekend visits. Rafael split his time between London business obligations and rural Swedish life with the easy adaptability that had characterized his integration into our family from the beginning.

"It's working," Soren said, appearing at my elbow with coffee and the satisfied expression of someone whose complex planning was proving successful. "All of it. The academic arrangement, the family structure, the practical logistics. It's actually working."

Rafael Mercado

The autumn evening carried the scent of woodsmoke from Marta's kitchen chimney, where she was preparing the kind of substantial dinner that had characterized every family gathering since I'd first experienced Swedish hospitality. Tomorrow, Erik would return from Cambridge for reading week, completing our family circle for the first time in two months.

"Kärlek," I called to Aleksander and Soren, using the Swedish endearment that had become natural in this environment. "Mormor says dinner in thirty minutes."

"Coming," Soren replied, though neither he nor Aleksander moved immediately from their observation of the construction progress.

Erik Eriksson

"The foundation looks perfect from here," I said, studying the construction site through my laptop camera as Rafael held his phone steady. "Exactly what we discussed in the architectural plans."

My Cambridge dorm room felt small and temporary compared to the sprawling Swedish landscape visible on my screen, but the contrast no longer felt like contradiction. Both places were home now—one nurturing intellectual growth, the other providing emotional anchor.

"How are your tutorials progressing?" Uncle Aleksander asked, leaning into the camera frame.

"Brilliantly," I replied with genuine enthusiasm. "Professor Morrison thinks my research proposal on Norse mythology in contemporary literature could become a proper thesis. Something about the integration of ancient wisdom into modern narratives."

Marta Eriksson

Watching my family connect across continental distances while building physical structures that would unite us permanently, I felt something profound settle in my chest. The grief over Lars's death would never fully heal, but it had transformed into something manageable—sadness that coexisted with gratitude for the love we'd shared and the legacy he'd left behind.

"Erik," I said, moving close enough to the phone's camera to be clearly visible, "your morfar would be so proud of what you're building. All of you. The education, the family, the way you're honoring the past while creating something new."

Soren Jensen

As the video call concluded and we prepared for the family dinner that had become our daily tradition during visits to the farm, I found myself reflecting on the extraordinary journey that had brought us all to this point. Three years ago, I'd been an academic researcher pursuing family history with no idea it would transform my entire existence.

Now I was part of a chosen family that spanned species and centuries, building a life that honored both ancient wisdom and contemporary possibilities. The bloodline helix had indeed come full circle, weaving together threads that had been separated by time and circumstance into something stronger and more beautiful than any of us could have imagined alone.

Aleksander Nordh

The evening light painted the Swedish countryside in shades of gold and amber as our unusual family gathered for dinner in the farmhouse kitchen where so many important conversations had taken place. Marta presided over the meal with the satisfaction of someone who'd successfully navigated the transition from grief to hope, while Rafael moved around the familiar space with the easy confidence of someone who'd found his place in the world.

Through the kitchen window, I could see the foundation of our future home —a structure that would accommodate everyone we loved while honoring the traditions that had shaped us all. Tomorrow, Erik would return from Cambridge, completing our circle. Next year, he would graduate and begin the careful balance between academic achievement and family responsibility that would define his adult life.

The bloodlines' continued spiral, carrying all of us forward into whatever extraordinary adventures awaited. But now we faced the future together, as family, with love that had proved stronger than time, distance, and every challenge the world had thrown at us.

"Shall we eat?" Marta asked, gesturing toward the table laid with her best china and laden with the kind of abundant feast that marked Swedish celebrations.

"Yes," I said, reaching for Soren's hand while Rafael claimed the chair that had become his usual spot. "Let's celebrate family."

As we settled around the table where generations of Erikssons had shared meals and dreams and the quiet satisfaction of lives well-lived, I realized that this was what I'd been searching for across two millennia without knowing it. Not just love—though we had that in abundance—but belonging. The knowledge that I was part of something larger than myself, something that would continue long after any individual life had ended.

EPILOGUE

Erik graduated from Cambridge with highest honors, his thesis on "Ancient Wisdom in Contemporary Narrative" becoming required reading in comparative literature programs across Europe. He married Rafael in a ceremony held at the Swedish farm, officiated by the village pastor who had baptized generations of Erikssons before them.

Rafael's import business expanded into a legitimate cultural exchange foundation, facilitating connections between Filipino artists and European markets while providing cover for supernatural community needs. His relationship with his father, maintained through occasional "research visits" to Manila, became a source of quiet healing for both of them.

Soren accepted a permanent position at Uppsala University, becoming the youngest professor ever tenured in the Scandinavian Studies department. His groundbreaking research on immigrant family connections transformed genealogical methodology across multiple academic disciplines.

Aleksander and Gunnar established a discrete consulting firm specializing in "historical preservation and cultural integration"—work that satisfied their need for meaningful occupation while advancing Elder community interests worldwide.

Astrid began writing what would become the definitive academic text on vampire sociology, a carefully disguised anthropological work that would influence human understanding of "theoretical supernatural communities" for decades to come.

Marta lived to see her great-grandchildren—Erik and Rafael's adopted twins, Maria and Nico. The brother and sister, both five years old, had been wandering Manila's streets during one of Rafael's educational research trips until he found them, and with Father Martinez's reluctant assistance and Dr. Mercado's endorsement of the 'kindly researcher from London,' they were able to complete the adoption. Rafael cherished watching them embrace his father goodbye at the airport, never knowing if the elderly Dr. Mercado understood he was becoming a grandfather in that moment, while Erik trusted Rafael's instincts despite his own doubts about young fatherhood, confident their family would help them raise children who understood they were loved.

The farm became a gathering place for their chosen family, hosting celebrations that combined Swedish traditions with Filipino customs, Elder observances with human holidays, creating something entirely new while honoring everything that had come before.

And through it all, the bloodlines continued their eternal helical spiral—carrying love across impossible distances, weaving connections that transcended every boundary, proving that family was always, ultimately, about choice rather than chance.

Yet some choices remained visible only to those who made them, held in silence between two hearts that had already chosen each other against impossible odds.

The wooden box from Gunnar and Astrid remained—though whether it remained complete or diminished by one vial, only Soren and Aleksander knew for certain.

There had been no announcement, no celebration, no dramatic transformation witnessed by family. If Soren had chosen to take the elixir, he had done so privately, enduring whatever trials came in the solitude of their home. If he had survived those forty-two days of cellular war, he had emerged looking exactly as he always had—which told them nothing, as the changes would be invisible, internal, only revealing themselves across decades or centuries.

Or perhaps the box still held all six vials, the question deferred year after year, the possibility preserved but not yet claimed.

Erik and Rafael often found themselves wondering, late at night when sleep evaded them and conversation drifted to futures and time. Wrapped in each other's arms in the farmhouse guest room during visits, or in their London flat during quiet hours, they would speak in whispers about their uncles.

"Do you think he took it?" Erik would ask, his voice soft against Rafael's chest.

"I don't know," Rafael would reply. "They've never said. And I can't tell—Soren looks the same as he did three years ago, but he would anyway. He's only thirty-two."

"But in ten years? Twenty? We'll know then, won't we?"

"Maybe. Or maybe we'll still be wondering."

The question hung between all of them—acknowledged but never directly asked. Because some choices were too private, too profound, to be shared even with family. Some decisions existed only between two people who loved each other enough to face impossible odds together.

Whether Soren and Aleksander were the custodians of six vials or five, whether they were counting down decades together or stretching toward centuries, they kept that knowledge to themselves. The wooden box remained on their dresser, a testament to its possibility—claimed or unclaimed, no one could say.

And perhaps that uncertainty was exactly right. Love didn't require guarantees. It only required the willingness to face whatever came next, together.

Some questions, it seemed, were meant to remain unanswered.

At least for now.

~

Mikael Johan
Jensen
1860–?
Born Sweden

Linnea Kristina
Jensen/ Svensson
1865–1940
Born Sweden

John Mikael
Jensen
1883–1950
Born Minnesota

Maria Esperanza
Mercado
1884–1905
Born Manila

Erik Anders
Jensen
1885–1965
Born Minnesota

Ingrid Maria
Jensen/ Lindstr m
1890–1968
Born Minnesota

Emilio Antonio
Mercado
1905–1978
Born Manila

Luisa Maria
Mercado/Domingo
1910–1985
Born Manila

Anders Mikael
Jensen
1912–1990
Born Minnesota

Elsa Margareta
Jensen/Johansson
1916–1995
Born Minnesota

Dr. Gabriel
Antonio Mercado
1935–
Born Manila

Dr. Sofia Elena
Santos-Mercado/
Santos
1948–2011
Born Manila

Lars Anders
Jensen Jensen
Born 1950
Born Minnesota

Brigitta Karin
Jensen/
Bergstr m
Born 1952
Born Minnesota

Rafael Gabriel
Mercado
1981–2002
Born Manila

Soren Mikael
Jensen
Born 1979
Born Minnesota

APPENDIX:

THE LANGUAGE OF ŠĒRAM-TAN

A Note on Transliteration and Pronunciation

The language spoken by Gunnar and Astrid Nordh in this novel has no modern name. For convenience, it is referred to by one of its possible self-designations: **Šēram-tan** (approximately: "words of the people"). This language predates all known language families and exists now only in the memories of a handful of Elder speakers.

For readability, **Šēram-tan** has been transliterated into Latin script, though several phonemes—particularly the glottal stops and pharyngeal fricatives—cannot be accurately represented in English orthography. Modern Homo sapiens vocal anatomy cannot comfortably produce all the sounds of this ancient language; what appears here is an approximation.

APPENDIX:

TRANSLITERATION GUIDE:

Symbol	Approximate Sound
'	Glottal stop (like the catch in "uh-oh")
š	"sh" as in "ship"
ħ	Pharyngeal fricative (similar to Arabic ح) - produced deep in the throat
q	Uvular stop (like Arabic ق) - produced further back than English "k"
x	Voiceless velar fricative (like German "ch" in "Bach")
ŋ	Velar nasal (like "ng" in "sing")
ā, ē, ī, ō, ū	Long vowels (held approximately twice as long as short vowels)

Consonants not listed above are pronounced approximately as in English, though with notable differences that cannot be captured in written form.

BASIC VOCABULARY

Pronouns & Person Markers

Šēram-tan	English
aš	I, me (independent form)
tu	you (singular)
ta	he, she, it
tam	we two, our (dual inclusive)
tan	we, our (plural)
tahēn	them, they
-ek	genitive marker (of, 's)
-ul	allative marker (to, toward)
-qa	benefactive marker (for)

Family & Kinship

Šēram-tan	English
naliq	son
k'ēran	chosen (one), adopted
naliq-qa k'ēran	son of choice (adopted son)
māt	mother
ām	father
qaħar	soul, essence, core self

Core Verbs

Šēram-tan	English
qašra	tell, speak, convey
weħ	hold, carry, bear
weħan	remain, continue, persist
k'weħan	end, die, cease
t'alaq	change, transform, shift
tĕnaq	remember, recall
qēr-weħ	love (literally: heart-hold)

Time & Aspect

Šēram-tan	English
xurā	time, duration
xurā-malak	forever, eternal (literally: time-beyond)
mit'	moment, instant
weq	before, prior to
weq-ām	before-memory (ancient past)
-āt	aspect marker (indicates ongoing/completed action)
-mēt	future tense marker

Emotional & Abstract Concepts

Šēram-tan	English
qēr	heart (both literal and figurative)
henaq	hope, expectation
naraḣ	excitement, anticipation
tehaq	belonging, being part of

Descriptive & Modifying Terms

Šēram-tan	English
šēram	words, speech, way of speaking
qešan	complexity, difficult things
xišbā	preparation-timeline (compound)
qē	old, ancient

Grammar Markers & Particles

Šēram-tan	English
-mek	obligation modal (must we, should we)
šēkum	emphatic particle (indeed, truly)
ehm	yes, affirmative
naršu	but, however
šāq-naḥul	for the purpose of, toward (purpose marker)

GRAMMATICAL NOTES

Word Order:

Šēram-tan typically follows a Subject-Object-Verb (SOV) pattern, though word order is somewhat flexible due to extensive case marking.

Example:
- **Qašra-mek tahēn-ul xišbā**
- tell-must.we them-to preparation.timeline
- *We must tell them about the preparation timeline*

Agglutination:
The language is highly agglutinative, with multiple suffixes attached to root words:
- **qašra** (tell) + **-mek** (must we) = **qašra-mek** (we must tell)
- **tahēn** (them) + **-ul** (to) = **tahēn-ul** (to them)
- **naliq** (son) + **-tam** (our dual) = **naliq-tam** (our son)

Possession:
Possession is marked by the genitive **-ek** or by possessive suffixes:
- **qēr-aš** (my heart) - heart + my
- **māt-ēna** (your mother) - mother + your

Kinship Classification:
Šēram-tan distinguishes between biological and chosen kinship:
- **naliq** = biological son
- **naliq-qa k'ēran** = son of choice (adopted/chosen son)

The suffix **k'ēran** (chosen) was considered a mark of higher honor in the original culture, as chosen bonds were viewed as more deliberate and therefore more sacred than biological ones.

APPENDIX:

ON THE DEATH OF LANGUAGES

As Astrid Nordh observes in the novel, "When the last native speakers of a language die, something irreplaceable vanishes." The creation of **Šēram-tan** for this work is an acknowledgment of the thousands of human languages that have disappeared throughout history, taking with them unique ways of understanding and describing the world.

This language represents not just the speech of the Elder community, but a meditation on linguistic loss, cultural preservation, and the question of what remains when ancient ways of thinking survive only in memory.

THE BLOODLINE HELIX:

Cultural Convergence and Identity Formation: A Study of Swedish-American Family Networks and Contemporary Chosen Family Structures

A Dissertation Presented to the Faculty of the
Graduate School
King's College London
In Partial Fulfillment of the Requirements
For the Degree of Doctor of Philosophy in Cultural History

By Soren Mikael Jensen
September 2015

ABSTRACT

This dissertation presents a comprehensive study of the Jensen family lineage, tracing Swedish migration patterns through five generations of American settlement while documenting previously unknown connections to Filipino family branches established during the Philippine-American War period (1899-1902). What began as a conventional study of Scandinavian-American cultural preservation evolved into a multi-continental investigation revealing complex patterns of family formation, cultural adaptation, and the contemporary emergence of chosen family structures that transcend traditional genealogical boundaries.

Through extensive archival research conducted in London, Manila, Stockholm, and Minneapolis, this study reconstructs the migration story of Mikael Johan Jensen (1860-1935), whose emigration from Sweden to America via Copenhagen represents a previously undocumented variation of typical Scandinavian migration patterns. The research reveals that Jensen's extended residence in Copenhagen (1878-1882) significantly influenced both his cultural development and subsequent family formation in Minnesota.

More significantly, this study documents the existence of a previously unknown Jensen family branch established in the Philippines through the relationship between John Mikael Jensen (1883-1950) and Maria Esperanza Mercado (1884-1905) during American colonial administration. Parish records confirm that this relationship produced descendants whose family line remained unknown to American relatives for over a century.

The dissertation employs innovative methodological approaches combining traditional genealogical research with contemporary ethnographic observation to document how separated family lines can reconverge through modern global connectivity. The research chronicles the extraordinary reunion of Jensen and Mercado descendants in contemporary London, facilitated by shared research interests and cultural preservation efforts.

Central to this study is the examination of how individuals from vastly different cultural backgrounds—Swedish-American academic communities, Filipino medical and intellectual families, and European research networks—can form lasting familial bonds that transcend biological relationships. The London-based chosen family documented in this research demonstrates innovative approaches to cultural integration, intergenerational mentorship, and the preservation of multiple heritage traditions within a single family unit.

This study contributes to scholarship in migration studies, colonial history, and family formation theory while demonstrating that genealogical investigation, when combined with ethnographic observation, can reveal patterns of human connection and adaptation that extend far beyond conventional family structures.

Keywords: genealogy, migration studies, Swedish-American immigration, Philippine-American War, chosen family, cultural integration, family formation, colonial relationships

This research would not have been possible without the extraordinary cooperation and trust of the individuals who shared their most personal family histories with me. To my research collaborators, identified in this study as A.H.N., R.G.M., and E.E., I owe a debt that extends far beyond academic gratitude. Their willingness to open their lives to scholarly examination, despite the deeply personal nature of the discoveries involved, demonstrates a commitment to historical understanding that exemplifies the highest traditions of collaborative research.

I extend my deepest appreciation to my dissertation chair, Dr. Eleanor Fletcher, whose expertise in migration studies provided the theoretical framework that guided this investigation from conventional genealogy toward its ultimate focus on contemporary family formation. Her willingness to support research that crossed traditional academic boundaries reflects the intellectual courage that distinguishes truly exceptional scholars.

Special recognition must be given to Dr. Isabella Santos of the National Historical Commission of the Philippines, whose extensive knowledge of Filipino-American colonial history enabled the breakthrough discoveries that transformed this project from a conventional family study into a complex investigation of cross-cultural relationships and their lasting implications. Her assistance in navigating Manila archives and her insights into the Mercado family history were absolutely essential to this research.

The remarkable individuals who became both my research subjects and my chosen family during this investigation have fundamentally changed my understanding of what constitutes kinship. A.H.N.'s encyclopedic knowledge of European historical archives proved invaluable throughout the research process, while his patient mentorship helped me navigate the emotional complexities of discovering that family extends far beyond genetic relationships. R.G.M.'s courage in sharing his family's story, despite the painful circumstances that had separated him from his heritage, provided crucial insights into the Filipino branch of the family lineage. E.E.'s youthful perspective and natural diplomatic skills facilitated connections that might otherwise have remained impossible.

I must acknowledge that this research fundamentally altered not only my academic trajectory but my personal understanding of family, identity, and belonging. What began as dissertation research evolved into the discovery of a chosen family whose bonds prove stronger than genetics, geography, or the conventional categories by which we organize human relationships.

Finally, I thank my biological family—particularly my parents, Lars and Brigitta Jensen, whose preservation of family traditions and stories provided the foundation for this work—and the remarkable individuals who became my family through the course of this research, demonstrating that the strongest bonds often transcend conventional definitions of kinship.

Introduction: Seeking Swedish Roots, Discovering Global Family

Family history research traditionally begins with simple questions about origins and migration patterns: Where did my ancestors come from? How did they adapt to new environments? What circumstances shaped their decisions to leave familiar communities and build new lives in foreign places? When I began this research in September 2012, I sought to answer precisely these questions about my Swedish-American family, expecting to document a familiar narrative of 19th-century Scandinavian migration to Minnesota's agricultural communities.

Instead, this investigation revealed a family story that spans continents, challenges conventional understanding of genealogical research methodology, and ultimately forced a fundamental reconsideration of how we define family, cultural preservation, and belonging itself. What began as my graduate thesis in Cultural History at King's College London became the most transformative research of my academic career—not only for its scholarly contributions, but for its profound personal implications.

The Initial Research Question

The Jensen family's American story begins, like thousands of others, with immigration from Sweden in the 1880s. My great-great-great-grandfather, Mikael Johan Jensen, left his homeland in 1882 at age 22, eventually settling in Minnesota where he established the farming community that would sustain four subsequent generations of Swedish-Americans. By all accounts, this represented a conventional success story of immigrant adaptation and cultural preservation.

Yet significant gaps existed in this narrative that had puzzled me throughout my childhood. Why had Mikael spent four years in Copenhagen before continuing to America? Why did family photographs show no images from that period? Why did his son John's military service in the Philippines remain unmentioned in family stories, despite the two-year deployment clearly documented in military records?

These questions guided my initial research proposal: to examine how Swedish cultural traditions persisted and evolved within immigrant communities in Minnesota, using the Jensen family as a case study for broader patterns of Scandinavian-American cultural preservation. I intended to spend my graduate years in comfortable archival research, tracing familiar patterns of migration, settlement, and assimilation within established academic frameworks.

The actual trajectory of this research proved far more complex and personally transformative than I could have anticipated.

Early Discoveries and Methodological Evolution

My first significant discovery emerged from examination of Copenhagen city records during the Christmas break of 2012. While seeking documentation of Mikael's residence in Denmark, I located registration records showing he had shared lodging with an individual identified as "H. Nordh" throughout his four-year residency. This seemed unremarkable initially—many Scandinavian immigrants shared accommodations during their transition periods.

However, this discovery led to my first encounter with A.H.N., a London-based researcher with extraordinary knowledge of Copenhagen's 19th-century Scandinavian community. A.H.N.'s familiarity with archival materials spanning multiple European institutions proved invaluable throughout my research, though his encyclopedic knowledge of historical details often seemed remarkably comprehensive for someone of his apparent age.

A.H.N.'s guidance led to the discovery that transformed this research entirely: documentation of the Philippine connection that had remained hidden in family history for over a century.

The Philippine Connection

The breakthrough that expanded this research beyond conventional genealogy occurred in April 2013, when examination of U.S. military records revealed that Mikael's eldest son, John Mikael Jensen, had served with the 13th Minnesota Regiment during the Philippine-American War. This deployment, lasting from 1902 to 1904, had never been mentioned in family histories despite being extensively documented in military archives.

Cross-referencing John's service records with Manila social registries revealed his regular attendance at events hosted by prominent Filipino families, particularly the Mercados—educators and cultural leaders who maintained complex relationships with American colonial authorities. Parish records and social documentation from early 1904 suggested that John had formed a significant relationship with Maria Esperanza Mercado, daughter of University of Santo Tomas professor Antonio Mercado.

Birth records from the Manila archives confirmed what military correspondence suggested: John Mikael Jensen and Maria Esperanza Mercado had maintained a relationship that produced descendants whose family line remained unknown to American relatives for over a century. Maria died in childbirth in 1905, and the child was raised by his Filipino grandparents. John appears never to have known of his son's existence.

This discovery fundamentally altered the scope of my research. The Jensen family lineage extended far beyond the Swedish-American community in Minnesota. Somewhere in the Philippines, descendants of my great-great-granduncle carried Jensen blood, representing a previously unknown branch of the family tree that had remained separated from the American relatives through four generations.

The London Convergence

The most extraordinary phase of this research began in January 2013, when A.H.N. arranged for me to meet R.G.M., a London-based researcher with extensive knowledge of the Mercado family history. R.G.M. possessed detailed understanding of the Philippine family line, including information that had never been publicly recorded and family photographs spanning three generations.

Physical characteristics, including distinctive facial features and genetic markers, confirmed R.G.M.'s connection to the Mercado lineage documented in my Manila research. More significantly, R.G.M.'s collaboration provided access to family documents and oral histories that revealed the full scope of the

Jensen-Mercado connection, including details about cultural traditions that had been preserved within the Filipino family line despite their separation from American relatives.

Simultaneously, my research expanded to include E.E., a young Swedish researcher whose family connections provided crucial insights into the contemporary preservation of Scandinavian cultural traditions. E.E.'s perspective bridged the gap between historical documentation and contemporary cultural practice, demonstrating how family traditions can evolve across generations while maintaining essential characteristics.

Contemporary Chosen Family Formation

What emerged from this research was not merely an interesting genealogical discovery, but a unique opportunity to observe the formation of chosen family bonds in real time. As A.H.N., R.G.M., E.E., and I collaborated on tracing these historical connections, we discovered that our shared research interests had evolved into something far more profound than academic collaboration.

The individuals who began as research contacts became family in ways that transcended biological relationship or cultural background. A.H.N.'s patient mentorship helped me navigate both the archival complexities of European research and the emotional challenges of discovering that my understanding of family had been fundamentally limited. R.G.M.'s courage in sharing painful family history, including circumstances that had separated him from his heritage, provided crucial insights into the resilience of cultural identity across generations. E.E.'s youthful energy and natural diplomatic skills facilitated connections between family members who might otherwise have remained strangers.

This contemporary family formation provided a unique case study for understanding how individuals from vastly different backgrounds—Swedish-American academic communities, Filipino medical and intellectual families, European research networks, and Scandinavian rural traditions—can create lasting familial bonds that honor multiple cultural heritages while building something entirely new.

Scope and Implications

This dissertation documents not merely an interesting family history, but evidence for family formation patterns that challenge conventional understanding of kinship, cultural preservation, and identity construction. The Jensen-Mercado-Nordh chosen family reveals innovative approaches to maintaining multiple cultural traditions within a single family unit, strategies for integrating individuals from dramatically different backgrounds, and methods for preserving historical knowledge while adapting to contemporary circumstances.

The research demonstrates that genealogical investigation, when combined with ethnographic observation of contemporary family formation, can reveal patterns of human connection and cultural adaptation that extend far beyond conventional academic categories. The chosen family documented in this study successfully navigates differences in age, cultural background, educational experience, and personal history that might otherwise prevent meaningful connection.

More broadly, this research contributes to scholarly understanding of how globalization and modern communication technologies can facilitate the reunion of family lines separated by historical circumstances, and how such reunions can evolve into chosen family structures that transcend their genealogical origins.

Personal Transformation and Academic Evolution

On a personal level, this research has challenged every assumption I held about family, identity, and belonging. I began seeking to understand my Swedish heritage and ended by discovering that family extends far beyond genetic relationships to encompass anyone willing to choose love and commitment over convenience and convention.

The individuals I encountered through this research have become not merely research subjects, but family in the deepest sense of the word. A.H.N. serves as both mentor and father figure, guiding my academic development while providing the kind of emotional support I had never experienced. R.G.M. and E.E. have become brothers in ways that transcend any biological relationship, creating bonds based on shared values and mutual commitment rather than genetic accident.

This chosen family has taught me that the categories by which we organize our understanding of relationships—biological versus chosen, traditional versus innovative, academic versus personal—prove far more fluid than conventional training suggests. The evidence presented in this dissertation requires acknowledgment that family formation encompasses variations and possibilities that exceed the boundaries of established social paradigms.

Structure of This Dissertation

This document presents findings as they emerged chronologically, reflecting the investigative process that led from conventional genealogical research to ethnographic observation of contemporary chosen family formation. Chapter 2 establishes theoretical frameworks for understanding migration, identity formation, and family structure evolution. Chapter 3 details the research methodology that evolved to accommodate both historical investigation and contemporary ethnographic observation.

Chapters 4 through 7 present the historical research that traced the Jensen family from Sweden through America to the Philippines, documenting the relationships and circumstances that created the separated family lines reunited in contemporary London. Chapters 8 and 9 examine the cultural preservation strategies employed by different family branches and the innovative approaches developed by the contemporary chosen family to honor multiple heritage traditions.

Chapter 10 documents the chosen family formation process and its implications for understanding contemporary kinship patterns. Chapter 11 addresses the broader questions raised by these discoveries regarding the nature of family, cultural preservation, and identity construction in globalized societies.

Ethical Considerations and Limitations

I present these findings with full recognition of the deeply personal nature of family history research and the ethical responsibilities that accompany academic investigation of living family structures. The individuals documented in this research have entrusted me with their most personal stories and family histories, requiring careful consideration of privacy and representation throughout the writing process.

To protect the privacy and safety of research participants, certain identifying details have been obscured throughout this document. The primary subjects are referred to by their initials (A.H.N., R.G.M., and E.E.) rather than full names, and specific location information has been generalized where necessary to prevent unwanted attention or intrusion.

More significantly, I acknowledge that my role evolved from objective researcher to family member during the course of this investigation. While this transformation provided unprecedented access to family dynamics and cultural preservation strategies, it also complicated the maintenance of scholarly objectivity. The findings presented here reflect both academic analysis and personal experience of chosen family formation, requiring readers to consider both the scholarly insights and the inherent limitations of such dual positioning.

Conclusion: The Helix Continues

The story that follows chronicles not merely the genealogy of a Swedish-American family, but the discovery of how family bonds can transcend time, geography, and conventional understanding of kinship itself. It documents the persistence of cultural traditions across centuries and continents, the resilience of human connection despite historical separation, and the innovative approaches contemporary individuals develop to honor their heritage while building something entirely new.

Most importantly, this research demonstrates that the boundaries between biological and chosen family, between academic investigation and personal transformation, between historical documentation and contemporary experience, prove far more permeable than conventional scholarly training suggests. The Jensen-Mercado-Nordh family helix continues to spiral forward, creating new connections while honoring ancient traditions, proving that the strongest family bonds often transcend every category by which we attempt to organize human relationships.

The bloodline helix, as we have come to call our family's complex pattern of connection and separation across time and space, represents something larger than genetic inheritance. It encompasses the full spectrum of human relationship—biological and chosen, historical and contemporary, academic and deeply personal. This dissertation documents not just where we came from, but who we choose to become when we commit to honoring both our heritage and our capacity for creating family bonds that transcend every limitation.

Alek - can you check with R. before I submit... other chapters attached. Need to hear back before Fri. If possible.

S

xo

ABOUT THE AUTHOR

Michael Manosca first pursued a career in the arts, studying in Chicago, but storytelling has always been at the heart of his creative expression. His travels across the world have shaped his perspective, infusing his writing with the depth and nuance of the people and cultures he has encountered.

Michael writes in a deeply personal format, inspired by the relationships and experiences that shaped his upbringing. He explores the intricacies of friendship, the search for identity, and the quiet moments that define us. Through vivid characters and emotional depth, he hopes to craft stories that linger in readers' minds long after the final page.

When not writing, he can be found wandering the northern woods, exploring new cities, or enjoying a lively conversation in a tucked-away café. He currently resides along the western coast of the United States and is already working on his next story.

ALSO BY MICHAEL MANOSCA

Beyond Ties that Bind

Treffen

Prism

Almost Always

Reflections at the Window

A Language of Water

Orbits

www.ingramcontent.com/pod-product-compliance
Lightning Source LLC
Chambersburg PA
CBHW071631260626
47170CB00001B/55
9798992766677